CRITICS RAVE
AND THE

S0-AJH-798

"Innovative and erotic!"
—*New York Times* bestselling author Christine Feehan

"An alternative universe that can match Laurell K. Hamilton's."
—Everything Romantic

"An excellent combination of fantasy and romance!"
—*Romantic Times*

"Sizzling romance and ghoulish thrills at a breathtaking clip!"
—*Publishers Weekly*

THE MASTER
"Readers who have come to expect wonderful things from Jackson will not be disappointed. Her ability to create a complicated world is astounding with this install-ment, which includes heartwarming moments, suspense and mystery sprinkled with humor. An excellent read."
—*RT BOOKclub*

DIVINE FIRE
"Jackson pens a sumptuous modern gothic... Fans of solid love stories...will enjoy Jackson's tale, which readers will devour in one sitting, then wait hungrily for the next installment."
—*Booklist*

"Once again, Jackson uses her truly awe-inspiring imagination to tell a story that's fascinating from beginning to end."
—*Romantic Times*

STILL LIFE
"The latest walk on the 'Wildside' is a wonderful romantic fantasy that adds new elements that brilliantly fit and enhance the existing Jackson mythos....action-packed."
—*The Midwest Book Review*

MORE PRAISE FOR MELANIE JACKSON!

THE COURIER
"The author's imagination and untouchable world-building continue to shine…. [An] outstanding and involved novel."

—*Romantic Times*

OUTSIDERS
"Melanie Jackson is a talent to watch. She deftly combines romance with fantasy and paranormal elements to create a spellbinding adventure."

—*WritersWrite.com*

TRAVELER
"Jackson often pushes the boundaries of paranormal romance, and this, the first of her Wildside series, is no exception."

—*Booklist*

THE SELKIE
"Part fantasy, part dream and wholly bewitching, *The Selkie*…[blends] whimsy and folklore into a sensual tale of love and magic."

—*Romantic Times*

DOMINION
"An unusual romance for those with a yen for something different."

—*Romantic Times*

NIGHT VISITOR
"I recommend this as a very strong romance, with time travel, history and magic."

—*All About Romance*

A PROMISE OF PASSION

Kris remembered now. There were many lifetimes tangled in his head. His friends Jack and Nyssa had done what they could, but his brain was still a mess of terrible visions he could not explain. He was old. So old. And nothing had changed. He'd told the humans how to love, but still they despaired and coveted. They hated and they envied and they killed. He didn't feel like going on anymore. Not alone. He was almost sorry that Jack had found him. If only the goblin hunter had gotten him, he would be dead and all this horror would be behind him.

"I know your weariness, child," a warm voice said suddenly. "But now I send glad tidings from the one who made you. For this last quest, you shall not be alone."

Shocked, Kris opened his eyes.

"What?" he asked aloud of the nearly forgotten voice. He hadn't heard it in centuries.

"I promise," the voice repeated. "You will not be alone. Look to the west, for it is from there that she will come."

Other books by Melanie Jackson:

THE MASTER
DIVINE FIRE
STILL LIFE
THE COURIER
OUTSIDERS
TRAVELER
THE SELKIE
DOMINION
BELLE
AMARANTHA
NIGHT VISITOR
MANON
IONA

THE SAINT

MELANIE JACKSON

LOVE SPELL NEW YORK CITY

To Chris and Jan and everyone at Blends.
Our conversations and coffee warmed more than my hands—
it also warmed my heart.

LOVE SPELL®

March 2006

Published by

Dorchester Publishing Co., Inc.
200 Madison Avenue
New York, NY 10016

If you purchased this book without a cover you should be aware that this book is stolen property. It was reported as "unsold and destroyed" to the publisher and neither the author nor the publisher has received any payment for this "stripped book."

Copyright © 2006 by Melanie Jackson

All rights reserved. No part of this book may be reproduced or transmitted in any form or by any electronic or mechanical means, including photocopying, recording or by any information storage and retrieval system, without the written permission of the publisher, except where permitted by law.

ISBN 0-505-52644-1

The name "Love Spell" and its logo are trademarks of Dorchester Publishing Co., Inc.

Printed in the United States of America.

Visit us on the web at www.dorchesterpub.com.

Important Dates in Fey History

8000 BC—The Goddess sends The Green Man to Earth to make peace among the tribes.

37 BC—Mabigon becomes Queen of the Unseelie Court after killing her mother.

39 BC—King Finvarra assumes throne of the Seelie Court after his father is assassinated.

212 AD—The fey retreat underground begins.

1367 AD—Gofimbel, Dragon Slayer, becomes the first goblin king of all European hives.

1692 AD—Qasim is created.

1778–1792 AD—At the death of Gofimbel, the Goblin Wars resume.

1793 AD—The human Expulsion of goblins from Europe begins.

1805 AD—Qasim, the hobgoblin leader and master, is imprisoned by Mabigon. Nyssa is born.

1973 AD—Humans Under Ground is formed.

1991 AD—The Great Drought kills off all pure-blooded fey, including Queen Mabigon and King Finvarra.

2001 AD—Jack and Io cripple Detroit hive and reopen fey stronghold of Cadalach. (As chronicled in *Traveler*.)

2002 AD—Thomas and Cyra destroy the Sin City hive. (As chronicled in *Outsiders*.)

2003 AD—Roman and Lyris kill the goblin and master vampire, King Quede of New Orleans. (As chronicled in *The Courier*.)

2004 AD—Lilith and Fornix are destroyed by Abrial and Nyssa, but Qasim escapes. (As chronicled in *Still Life*.)

2005 AD—Nicholas Anthony and Zee Finvarra join the fey resistance. (As chronicled in *The Master*.)

2006 AD—Kris Kringle is found.

PROLOGUE

King Quinox looked sharply at his chosen tool. This ambitious young goblin was his son, but the lutin made him very nervous. He would not trust Anaximander with anything as important as guarding his life. However, he did trust him enough to send him on this mission.

And if Anaximander died performing it, so much the better.

"You know what to do?" Quinox asked sharply. His tongue flicked out and licked his left eye. It was a nervous habit he hadn't been able to break.

"Yes. I will see that Niklas drinks the potion." Anaximander had no nervous habits. In fact, as far as Quinox could tell, he had no nerves at all. Perhaps he didn't understand what was at stake, that he was about to destroy the mind of The Goddess's favorite fey and put an end to the unification of the tribes of men under The Saint's latest, most popular incarnation—Santa Claus.

1

"See that he does, or the second dose goes down you." Quinox was not sentimental and he had many, many children, most of whom wouldn't dare to try to kill him.

CHAPTER ONE

"I found him," Abrial announced as he walked in late on dinner. It was the Cadalach Feys' Midsummer's Eve celebration. "Kris—I found him."

"Kris Kringle?" Thomas Marrowbone asked, putting down his fork and looking at Jack. "The one and only true Santa Claus? He's actually alive?" He looked back at Abrial, who nodded.

"Where is he?" Jack asked.

"Up north—where we expected. He's been wandering the wastelands, living with the polar bears and seals. He's suffering from total amnesia, and I'm betting it's either a goblin drug that did it or one of Mabigon's nastier hexes." Abrial's voice held distaste for the dead Unseelie queen. "I can't seem to reach him. There's a dense screen of voices in his head. Jack, you may have to try to contact him yourself."

"What are you going to say? What are you going to do?" Thomas asked Jack. He couldn't keep all awe from his voice. Kris Kringle was a legend, and not just in the human world. He was a death fey who had completely renounced his magical destiny and gone to do good works among humans. He had been—at the time of his disappearance and even after—the best ambassador of goodwill the fey ever had. Nowadays, everyone thought he was just a legend, a charming folk story. They no longer recalled that Kris Kringle, Santa Claus, the humans' beloved Saint Nicholas, was real.

But he *was* very real; Abrial remembered him well. The Seelie and Unseelie Courts had watched with interest and some dismay as he slowly, carefully introduced himself to the post-pagan humans in Turkey, and later in England and America. He had wandered Europe for centuries as Saint Nicholas, doing good works among the poor, and especially among women and children.

But times changed—violently, as times so often do—and in these lands of the Industrial Revolution, Kris saw a special need for his presence. Despair was being spawned in the slums of the New World, and spirit was dying. Religion alone couldn't hold back the inner desolation. If something wasn't done, the land would be poisoned for fey and humans alike. The earth itself would finally die, contaminated by the greed and endless pillage.

The Great Elf, as Kris became known, understood that he could not fight the battle for human souls alone, so he'd enlisted a few carefully chosen others in his cause—enlisted them through dreams and to a specific purpose. The first had been Washington Irving. The former ambassador to England and Spain had already proven himself an able writer and advocate for the underprivileged, and one part of his imagination was already in the faerie realm. But instead of writing another terrible and dark tale

4

like *The Legend of Sleepy Hollow*, or *Rip Van Winkle*, in Bracebridge Hall the essayist was moved to write about a feast, a place and time that fed the spirit as well as the body; and those of means had been enchanted and embraced the idea of a holiday where families gathered in love. Christmas was on its way to restoring the human spirit.

But one essay wasn't enough. What of those not born to affluence? Their souls needed joy, too. Even more than the rich, they needed to be fed something other than despair. So Kris had gone to that champion of the poor, Charles Dickens. He knew that the pen, in the hands of the right author, was indeed mightier than the sword. But this time he required something greater than rapier wit; he needed a hammer to strike the hardened hearts of the world and make them resonate like cathedral bells. And so Kris and Charles had given the world Ebenezer Scrooge.

A Christmas Carol was popular beyond his wildest imaginings, yet Kris still had not reached everyone. He had reached the rich and touched the poor, but his favorite humans—the ones upon whom he pinned his hope of a future where all races would live in peace—had not truly been affected. Christmas remained a time for adults.

Again, he turned to a human with a special gift. That sober cleric, Clement Moore, was an unusual choice to tell a magical tale about an elf who lived at the North Pole, but Kris knew he had done well when "A Visit From St. Nicholas" appeared in print and took the world by storm. Christmas was suddenly seen as a holiday for children, and through these children, the great magic he planned could finally happen. Unbelievably, he became the most revered figure of childhood. Saint Nicholas was reincarnated—this time in a fur-trimmed suit and with a team of flying reindeer. And though the image was nothing like the reality, in the name of the cause Kris enlisted the aid of Civil War artist Thomas Nast to spread the legend of the "jolly old elf."

Unfortunately, just when America had embraced the idea of a season of generosity and joyousness of spirit, the unthinkable happened. On his trip west to find the Nephalim, the giants whom many said were fallen angels, Kris Kringle disappeared without a trace. And without him, commercial interests— some human and some not—rushed to fill the void.

The kiddies couldn't be disappointed, could they? the retailers asked. Best dash out and buy something for them. And what about your spouse? Your parents? Your siblings and cousins, friends and neighbors? Genuine generosity quickly became an obligation, and then it became a burden—spiritual and financial. People stopped giving with a glad heart. Many stopped giving altogether. And worst of all, the message of *Peace on earth and goodwill toward all peoples* became *Peace on earth unless there's profit to be had by war*, and *Goodwill toward only certain human men*.

Humans had never recovered. For many, it was as if part of their souls froze, their hearts walled up tight against generosity and kindness, and nothing was able to unfreeze them. While they had not fallen from grace, men had fallen from joy.

Thus had passed Kris's legacy.

He had one other distinction that everyone in the room was aware of. The Great Elf, though "elf" was an incorrect classification for a death fey, was also the first and only pureblood fey discovered to have survived the Great Drought. Which meant that he, who was most beloved of the Goddess and the

Greater Power to whom She answered, was in fact far stronger than even the great fey kings and queens of old.

And he was a death fey—a very confused and possibly insane death fey, whose powers could either save or destroy civilizations . . . theirs included.

"What will I do? I'll go and get him, of course," Jack said at last. "I can't very well leave my uncle living with polar bears. Besides, what if the goblins find him?"

"The lutins would love to pick his brains," Abrial admitted.

"The goblins would like to pick his brains, all right—and not stop until they reached his teeth," Jack answered. "I don't know why they didn't kill him when they had the chance."

"Too afraid. Anyone *that* beloved of the Goddess . . ." Abrial suggested. "Who would risk it? Anyway, he always reincarnated. Why would this time be any different?"

"Well, damn," Thomas said, exhaling slowly. "Have you thought about what this means—what he'll do when he remembers who he is? Think, Jack. He's a death fey. And he's probably really, really pissed off."

"I know," Jack answered slowly. "It's a bit daunting, I must admit. But recall that he has never chosen Death. Never. Always Kris took the side of peace and love. And our way of holding back the tide of lutin hate can't work forever. My friends, we juggle well, but someday we will drop the ball and there will be war between the races—unless we can convince them they no longer need to fight." He smiled a little. "Anyway, don't you think it's time we took Christmas from the merchants and unbelievers and gave it back to the children of the world?"

Thomas shook his head slowly, then leaned down and looked under the table.

"What are you doing?" Jack asked.

"Just having a look at the biggest balls in the world," Thomas said, straightening.

Jack threw back his head and began to laugh. Thomas and Abrial just stared. They couldn't see anything even remotely amusing about what they were about to do.

A salty taste—familiar. Blood? Yes, blood. His own . . . ? Yes. He had fallen while rushing for the cave and hit his face, scraping his cheek on the rough ice. Stupid of him to step between the two male bears when they were fighting over food, but Sitka was a friend and getting too old to take on the younger bears.

Still, it had been stupid. Blame it on the voices. His head was full of them: endless prayers in the barely remembered human tongues of English, Latin and Turkish—pathetic petitions he didn't know how to answer. The babble made it so hard to think. His skull was so full that he wanted to drill a hole in it to let the sound out. The pressure on his bruised brain made him want to scream like the bears . . . but he had to be quiet. So, so quiet, else the beast with red eyes and foul breath would find him and eat him as well. It had been sent by . . . someone. Someone dangerous. An old, old enemy.

He could kill the beast—somewhere inside, he knew how. But that action would put him in more danger than he was in now.

Thou must not kill.

He touched his side. Blood was there, too, long streaks of hot red on the blue ice, marking his trail, which ended in a puddle. Sticky, warm. That was nice. He'd been so cold for so long. Cold since . . . But there was another blank wall in his mind. Perhaps he had always been cold. It seemed like he had. Cold, alone—except for the anguished voices in his skull.

The urge to sleep was strong. He climbed deeper into the cave, wriggling into a crevice where he hoped to be safe. Outside, he could hear the triumphant stranger tearing apart his prize. He didn't want the new bear-thing to see him. Monster—a terrible monster—but he was so tired. He could go no farther. He was leaving his entrails behind.

He dozed briefly.

Kris.

A voice. Clearer than the rest. The words at first meant nothing, but finally he listened and began to understand. Someone named Jack was coming.

Jack . . . The name was familiar, but he couldn't quite grab the memory any more than he could recall the name of the language this Jack used. But it didn't matter. The voice was comforting, and it drowned out all the other noise, bringing him peace.

He would sleep and wait for this Jack. Kris closed his eyes.

"Hello, Kris," a somewhat familiar voice said a short time later. Gentle hands pressed over the deep cut in his side. Kris searched his fractured brain and finally came up with a name to match the voice. He opened his eyes.

"Jack? I was waiting for you." His voice was weak, not like his voice at all.

"Yes. I came as fast as I could," the young man who looked so much like him answered with a smile. His face was very close in the narrow tunnel where Kris had hidden himself. "We thought you were forever lost. I had almost given up hope of finding you again."

"Lost . . . ? Yes." That sounded right. "I've been lost. I was . . . I've been here a long time. What happened to me, Jack?" he asked, weak and baffled.

"You . . . you were given a drug that affected your memory. Bad people drugged you and left you here. But that doesn't matter. I've found you now and I have some medicine that will make you better. The voices won't trouble you anymore, unless you want to hear them."

"Good, that's good. I'm so weak . . . Jack, how do I know you?" Kris asked finally. "Are you family? We look alike, I think—and I know your voice from a long time ago."

"I'm your nephew. My father, Phaneos, was your younger brother. Everyone says that he and I sound alike. Probably it is his voice that you remember."

"Phaneos." An image of a white-haired child rose up like a ghost from his memory. It made Kris happy, though he had no memory beyond the small face. "My little brother. Is he here, too?"

"No, Kris. I'm sorry. Phaneos is dead. A lot has happened while you were away. Many of the fey have gone." Gentle hands helped him sit up. They also helped him accept the sad tidings. "I was thinking that maybe you would like to come and live with me for a while. I'm married now and have a son. My family would like to meet you. You have other friends there too."

Feeling stronger than he had felt since . . . well, since he could remember, Kris forced himself to his feet. Dizziness tried to claim him, but he pushed it back.

"Jack, your father was a death fey, wasn't he? Are you one, too?"

Thou shall not kill.

"A death fey? Yes." The man named Jack went still, seemingly waiting for Kris's next words.

"And I am like you?" Kris asked. The idea disturbed him a little and he shivered. "Am I a bringer of death?"

"No, Kris. You were never like me." Jack's sudden smile was dazzling. Kris sensed the shadows inside the younger man but also felt the genuine love that this fey nephew, this son of Phaneos, had for him. "You were never like anyone else. It's why we loved you—why we need you."

He was loved. That made Kris feel even better. That was his purpose, wasn't it? To bring love? The babbling voices in his brain receded further as the fire of self-awareness grew.

"I would like to meet your wife and son. I'd like to have family again," Kris said. He added wistfully, "I would like to remember everything. My brain has been so broken that I only have pieces. How could I forget little Phaneos? Or you?"

"You will remember in time. Most of it." Jack wrapped a cloak around him and then offered his hand. It was warm. "Come on. Some old friends are waiting for you outside. We'll help you remember everything you need to know."

"There's a monster," Kris said, hesitating. "Perhaps I should go first."

"The monster is gone," Jack assured him.

"That's good. I don't think it was a real bear." Kris shuddered.

"No, it wasn't," Jack agreed. "But don't worry about that. My good friend Abrial is . . . talking with the monster now. We'll find out who made him, and things will be taken care of."

"I must not kill," Kris murmured.

"That's right." Jack nodded. "You must not ever kill. But *I* can—and I promise that whoever did this to you will pay, if they have not yet slipped beyond earthly vengeance."

"I don't want you to kill for me," Kris said sternly. He wasn't certain why, just that it was a fact. He could not kill, and others should not either. "That would be wrong—to kill for me."

"I kill for all of us. I must sometimes if we are to survive." Jack's eyes were suddenly bleak. "Let's pray that a day will come soon when I no longer have to."

During their childhood, when Men left the age of their innocence and first turned from Gaia, there came into the world a great shaman called Niklas, who was not of Mankind, but of the Sidhe. Men feared the Sidhe, but such was this shaman's kindness and love, he was able to live amongst them and to show the erring Sons of Man how to return by other paths to the Divinity that created all Life. Thus did order reign for a millennium. In return for this gift, every seven years a special sacrifice was made by the Sons of Man. The one most loved by Divinity was given back to Gaia in the Solstice fire. Many feared at these times of sacrifice, when the shaman returned to the Sidhe, but Niklas always returned at the dark of the Sun to again walk the Earth. And for a time there was peace and prosperity for both races.

—*Bioball Na Sidhe*, the Book of Niklas,
Chapter Two, Verse Four

CHAPTER TWO

Kris closed the book of illuminated fey scriptures and tried to focus on what he had learned. Little by little, his memory was getting better. It was difficult to get a complete picture, because all his past experiences had been laminated together, rendering them a monolithic, impenetrable block, and he was forced to rely on the perceptions of others to explain many things. Still, little by little, the edges of frozen memory were melting away so that he could examine them.

Jack had helped fill in the missing bits with family legends. And others were making astounding efforts, too. Access to the human Internet was a tremendous aid in learning modern culture, especially now that Kris had learned from Thomas how to control his body so that the varying magnetic waves didn't burn out the computer.

Of course, other than Abrial, there was no one old enough to recall Kris's past firsthand, no one who'd known him in his past incarnations. To everyone, he'd been this ridiculous fat creature, Santa Claus. Even Abrial could only recall back to when he still walked the Earth as Saint Nicholas. No one remembered him from the time of the fey scriptures, back when he was Niklas and one with Gaia. When he had understood his mission.

Kris could feel the death magic waiting to fill him up. It was always there, sometimes pressing close, sometimes hiding slyly, but always waiting for a chance to rush back into his mind. He recalled displacing it with a desire to promote peace. That had been why he'd decided sex was too dangerous to indulge in. No fey were left, and no human woman was the great love who would complete him—and to risk taking a life for anything less was cruel and immoral.

Now it was even worse, when his mind was not his own.

Kris sighed. More time was needed for him to recover, but that was not a luxury he had. The lutins drove his schedule. In light of the ever-increasing danger, plans had been made, and they had to move forward. He could only pray that he spiritually reconnected before things progressed too far. It was not enough to know Gaia in the abstract. He needed to again be one with Divinity if he was to carry on his work. How could he possibly convince the world of something as crucial as the need for World Peace and Brotherly Love if he no longer experienced such love himself?

"How is he today, Alphons? Manic or depressive?" Adora Navarra quietly asked the guardian of order whose job it was to repel chaos—unless chaos was a member of the Matthews Club, of course. She had met the diminutive attendant on only three occasions, but she had a facility for recalling names that produced wonderful results, especially among service people, whom it seemed liked nothing better than to be assured that they were not mere furniture. That would make it easier for her to get in and see her agent, Ben Hunter.

Alphons beamed and shifted onto his tiptoes, even as he delivered the bad news in a hushed voice. He always spoke softly to her, as if he knew that her sense of hearing was acute.

"Welcome back, Miss Navarra. To use a sporting metaphor, I'm afraid that it's the bottom of the ninth, miss. Two men are out and three are on—and it's starting to rain. He's yelled at everyone—even The Lord Almighty. Thank heavens his cell-phone battery died. Luther finally brought him an appetizer and some wine so he would quit taking God's—and the president's—name in vain." The stool Alphons bestrode behind the podium rocked, and he was forced to balance himself. Adora pretended not to notice.

Ben had been drinking before noon on a weekday? Terrific. Had he been doing this for long? Maybe she was here on a fool's errand after all.

"How many bottles?" she asked, shifting out of the sunbeam that shone through the transom over the club's French doors. She found direct sunlight hard to tolerate these days.

"Just two."

Two was at least one too many. Ben Hunter was not a drunk, exactly, but he was rarely completely sober after four o'clock. In the time she had known him, he had gone from recreational drinking on weekends to almost perpetual though well-managed inebriation. Divorce took some people that way, but he had seemed to level off at a manageable degree of alcohol abuse. Adora felt for him, because she had danced a few rounds of the drug-addiction tango not so long ago, but was dismayed at this sign. For many, there was no proper prescription for nihilism and despair. And it was a short step from wine to Demerol and Valium, and from there to lifelong drug dependence.

Not that this growing love of alcohol could affect Ben's ability to precisely pronounce obscenities in three languages, or move his attention from the bottom line. Ben was always all business. But on those occasions when he crossed the line from buzzed to actually drunk, he could get unpleasant and stubborn. More than stubborn. And his hard drunks could and often did last for days.

Still, this couldn't wait. A job had been offered—one that paid well—and Adora had to find some excuse to take it, because she was losing her mind as well as her house. But that meant extracting a few more details from Ben—ones that contradicted the incredible message he had left on her machine.

Squaring her shoulders, Adora said, "Thanks, Alphons. Shall I be informal and just show myself in?"

The attendant glanced at the table where Ben was brooding, sitting in an island of shadows, all of the club's other patrons having retreated to the edge of the room. Though an excellent employee and professional to the core, Alphons shuddered, and his smile slipped a notch. Adora didn't blame him. Ben had a thin mouth and an insulting conversational style with those he considered his inferiors. And while Ben never called him "the midget" to his face, his discomfort with Alphons's dwarfism was plain.

"Just as you like, miss. I'll send Luther over with your iced tea. You take it with lemon, yes?"

"Yes." Adora smiled. Apparently Alphons recalled people and their foibles too. She was touched. "It's kind of you to remember."

"Not at all. It's always a pleasure to see you."

She was glad that someone thought so.

Adora squared her shoulders and marched toward Fate.

"Hello, Ben. Please tell me that you're joking about this assignment. It's really mean to tease me about money," she said to her agent a moment later. She kept her sentences short because her breaths were necessarily shallow. She hated the odor that habitually clung to Ben even when he left his office: a mix of strong aftershave, cigarettes and burnt coffee laced with scotch, and now overlaid with a patina of wine. Many people would not have noticed, but Adora had developed a keen sense of smell since her illness. A single smoldering cigarette butt was enough to make her eyes water, and this more intense odor set her stomach to churning.

"Adora, my dear, you know that I never joke—especially not about money." This was sadly true. Ben had no discernible sense of humor these days. Perhaps that was what made him a good agent. It definitely wasn't his winning personality or clean living that got good contracts for what few writers he had left. "Sit down—I've been waiting forever. And stop frowning, this offer is on the level. This guy, this Mr. Bishop S. Nicholas, is a wealthy philanthropist, and he's willing to pay you a hundred grand to write his biography. Frankly, I don't see what your problem is. You said that you were better now, and that you're ready to get back in the game."

Adora pulled out a chair and sat down. Since Ben wasn't kidding about the job, the conversation might take a while. An unobtrusive Luther slipped a glass of tea in front of her, and she smiled in thanks while her agent glared and shook a nearly empty bottle of wine. She hoped that Ben tipped well. Perhaps bad manners were easier to take if one left thirty percent.

"So, are you ready or not?" Ben demanded.

"*You* don't tell jokes. *I* don't hurry my decisions," she answered. "This sounds very weird, and I have some questions."

"Hmph! So ask."

Right. But where to begin when it was all so weird?

Ben drummed his fingers on the table while he watched her, making Adora want to swat them. She also wanted to tear off his tie pin, which was probably very fashionable but was made of some bright plastic and looked like a tub toy. Ben chased fashion trends, and his tie was a reminder that he had never quite matured into an adult—meaning compassionate and responsible—human being. Instead of giving in to impulse, she sat calmly, saying nothing while he sulked and she thought the matter through.

There were many things to consider, but what interested her most was why she had been approached for this job. It probably wasn't because her prospective employer had actually read her work. After all, almost no one had. She supposed it might be a case of having tried everyone else and failed. Or maybe they had approached Ben and asked—discreetly—if he had any writers desperate enough to take this project on. Ben would have heard the word "desperation" and naturally thought of her. After all, she badly needed money. And she wasn't married—wasn't even currently involved with anyone—had no pets or other dependents to object if she took the job. Also, she didn't share normal people's interests. To her, ancient scandals were more interesting than current ones. She often found dead guys of more interest than live ones. To her, a deceased, crazed poet was more attractive than a live movie star, so perhaps Ben had a valid reason to believe that this project was one that would appeal to her.

On the other hand—Santa Claus? How big a kook did he think she was?

Even before she'd heard the outline of this job, Adora had had reservations about working for another supposed philanthropist. She hadn't known many people who worked full-time doing nothing but good deeds—only two, in fact—but two was plenty. "Old money" was peculiar—reserved, even hostile. She had always suspected that, had she made her request for their family historical documents—which might as well be called *Scandalous Family Secrets I'd Rather Die than Reveal*—in some lonesome library instead of a well-lit office with lots of witnesses, those so-called philanthropists would have ordered their loyal family retainers to bludgeon her to death with their sterling silver candlesticks, or to flatten her body with their Rolls-Royce limos.

They always questioned why she would want to hear the sordid details of past scandals. All she could think was, *were they kidding?* Any man on the street could tell them that the sordid details of past scandals were the mortar that held the dry bricks of a person's life together. And it was their foibles and flaws that made mythical beings back into humans, made them appealing to Joe Everyman.

Still, not everyone wanted to be descended from mere mortals, and many of the rich would do anything to see that their ancestors' legends remained just that. It was a free country, though, and so all they could do was refuse access to their archives—which they usually did. Not that such actions stopped Adora from getting at the truth—once focused, she was like a hungry wolf after its lunch. But it certainly slowed her down and caused her a lot of headaches.

Of course, not everyone was publicity shy. A couple of times she had been courted by the rich and famous who were finally feeling death's icy breath on their necks and were anxious to fix their place in the history books before their relatives did—even if it meant some liberal fact stretching. One had been a corrupt two-time governor, the other an empire builder doing his level best to rid his state of trees and clean water. She had declined both jobs.

She could afford to back then. Now? Well, she might just have to hold her nose and ignore what smelled. This client didn't simply want to be the son of immortals, he wanted to be immortal himself. That alone suggested an arrogance passing into true mania.

She was also worried because she liked to keep a low profile. Her privacy was like a religion. It wasn't that she had anything specific to hide—she wasn't wanted by the IRS, the FBI, or a sadistic ex-husband—she simply liked her solitude, and the thought of the possible celebrity to come with this project made her uneasy. She didn't mind writing about high-profile people, but becoming one was another matter.

And yet . . . the poverty thing loomed large. She had discovered that she really hated being poor—for all the usual reasons and then one more: boredom. Boredom was terrible enough on its own, but when she was idle too long, her brain—always hungry for information or new projects—began taking self-inventory, and it never liked what it found. This time it said that she was a weakling who couldn't stand being alone. And that was a little too close to the truth for any degree of comfort.

Adora knew from experience that, short of putting her inner voice in a chemical straitjacket, the only way to stop its carping catalogue of defects was to demonstrate to her inner critic that she was emotionally and materially self-sufficient.

But . . . *Santa Claus?*

"What's the problem?" she finally responded. "Well, gee, Ben, this guy thinks he's the real Santa Claus! Even you have to admit that that's crazy. And no one can write a biography about Santa—a *living* Santa at that—and not get laughed out of the field," she added reasonably. She always tried to be reasonable, she really did. It was just that some days it came harder than others. Especially when she felt like she was being teased for a paycheck.

"Look, Adora, most rich people are a little eccentric. It's their privilege. They earn it by paying higher taxes." Ben, as he had told her before, wasn't joking when he said this.

Many of them are also jerks, but she didn't say that out loud. Ben loved the rich. They were his hobby, his obsession. He was going to be one when he grew up. Sadly, he was running out of time to achieve his goal, and was becoming depressingly more aware of it.

"This isn't eccentric, it's insane—even for a rich man. It's the line between charmingly quirky and a wackjob—a slight but distinct difference, in my book."

Ben leaned forward and fixed her with his bloodshot gaze. "But it's a hundred grand, and to do a job

22

that should be fascinating. And no one else is rushing in with offers, are they? Look, Adora, just take the meeting. You don't like what you hear, *then* you walk away. In the meantime, you get to meet one of the great fruitcakes of our time, and you get to fly first-class in a private plane to Los Angeles and have lunch at the Beverly Wilshire. And think about this: People might eventually call you both nuts, but this book could easily be a bestseller. In fact, I'm betting this guy makes sure it's the *best* bestseller. You could be set for life!" And that would assure Ben some fresh and possibly famous clients when they decided that they, too, needed to be immortalized in print.

"Humph!" she said. But whatever her agent's motives, he was likely right. Santa Claus was a perennially popular subject. Chances were she wouldn't enjoy the interviews with the subject himself, but that was nothing new. Many of these chats with the famous were like catching a cold: You had to deal with a lot of snot and had a headache for a few days. Still, it was worth it in the end—if you got the story.

And she couldn't discount the fact that there was a distressingly large segment of the population that believed in weird things—like the idea that pro wrestling wasn't fixed, or that alien visitations happened all the time, or that Big Foot really lived just outside Seattle. Those kooks would probably all buy her book.

And she could write it under a nom de plume, she realized with a small burst of cheer.

"Do yourself a favor. Get noticed by the *Times*. Then you can go back to having scruples and writing about dead people no one cares about."

Ben's nose wrinkled as he said this. He was too smart an agent not to see the quality of her writing—particularly when critics kept pointing it out—but he had never understood what drove her to "live among the dead like a necrophiliac." Adora couldn't really explain it, herself. There were just certain people who fascinated her, and she felt compelled to get to know them—even when they were no longer among the living.

That aside, though Ben was a bit of a bastard and a control freak—with a now obviously severe drinking problem—he wasn't stupid. His advice, though often unpalatable and even insulting, was usually worthwhile. She also doubted that he would send her into any situation that looked truly dangerous. After all, he wouldn't get paid if she were dead and unable to write the book.

Adora took another sip of her iced tea and allowed herself to really ponder the idea of writing about the life of Santa Claus. What Ben said was true. Offers weren't rolling in these days, even from the magazines for which she usually freelanced. She'd been gone too long and lost her contacts. Her publisher was still around, but the biography of Ninon de Lenclos—though it had been received well by the critics—had not captured the popular imagination. Her book on Shelley had done only slightly better. And absolutely no one wanted to hear about her ideas for a book on Sir Walter Scott. In the real world, cream rose to the top. That didn't always happen in publishing. In fashion, taste in hemlines went up and down with every season. It was that way in the literary world too. And she was always a below-the-knee dress in a world of miniskirts. Put another way, her career as a biographer was currently at a standstill.

Except for this offer. Which was, as Ben pointed out, for a hundred thousand dollars. And there were all those medical bills to pay from when she'd spent time in her own chemical straitjacket, while the doctors tried to decide just what was wrong with her—an illness of the mind or of the body.

Santa Claus. Puh-leeze. It was The Voice, Adora's almost constant inner companion and master critiquer, who had survived even the strongest of medications. She called The Voice Joy—short for killjoy, which of course Joy knew and found amusing. The Voice, her childhood make-believe friend and sometimes bully coach, was disconcerting even after all this time. She had mysteriously appeared around age five, when Adora's family moved to Aptos in California, and still popped in to chat whenever Adora was in a stressful situation.

Like now. What have you gotten yourself into this time? Just do us both a favor and tell the man no.

I'm not into anything. Yet, Adora responded.

But you're thinking about it. I know you are.

So much for trying to sneak anything past Joy.

Okay, I'm thinking. Look, being noncorporeal, you may not need food and shelter, but I do. If you have something useful to say, please do. If not, pipe down. I'm weighing my options and you're distracting me.

Is that what you call it—weighing options? Better wipe the slobber off your chin. I guess we know what your price is. Ben mentions The New York Times *and you start drooling.*

Quiet.

"Adora? Are you listening to me?" Ben asked. "I swear, you get more spacey with each passing year."

"I'm listening."

But not to you.

No, not to him—and that was a little weird, wasn't it? Every once in a while, now that she'd given up pill-popping, Adora realized that talking to Joy was actually pretty strange. Other people didn't do this. Her former shrink had insisted Joy was a manifestation of her guilt over her anger at her parents' abandonment, but Adora didn't think so. There was guilt, sure; like Orestes of Greek mythology, she had been pursued by appalling Furies, ferocious hags with serpentine hair and fangs who chased her through dark dreams after her mother's death. But Joy had helped then, as much as she could. And what Joy couldn't kill, the Demerol and Valium had finally banished.

And Joy had been around long before Adora's parents died. If she was a manifestation of guilt, it was guilt over something far older.

Of course you don't listen to Ben, Joy answered. *He doesn't have your best interests at heart. Not the way I do.*

Which was probably true. Joy sometimes liked to shadowbox with Adora's emotions and much-needed rationalizations at inconvenient moments, but the two had more or less made peace. Joy was Joy. And it wasn't *really* that weird that Adora talked to herself, now was it? After all, her body kept all kinds of mysterious things going on all the time. Her lungs, stomach and heart performed their assigned tasks without specific permission or guidance; why believe she could or should control her brain? Some things were best left on autopilot. And Joy often had useful insights to share.

Of course, sometimes she just liked to nag.

Adora wasn't given to impulsive actions. But it was ridiculous to think that she could ruin her small store of hard-won literary credibility this way. Mightn't it be fun—just once—to be Alice and follow the rabbit down the hole? Just for a little ways? Like Ben said, she could go out and hear what the guy had to say. What would be the harm in that?

After all, Ben might have gotten it wrong—especially if he'd been drinking. Maybe the guy didn't think he was Santa. Maybe he thought he was a descendant of Saint Nicholas, or something like that, and he wanted a biography written about his illustrious ancestor, whose good works he was carrying on. Wouldn't she be dumb to refuse until she'd heard all the facts from the horse's—er, the philanthropist's—mouth?

Besides, hard as it was to imagine, she'd never been to a lutin city. Everyone said L.A. looked just like it had when the humans ran things, but there had to be some differences. And different could be exciting. A little cultural synergy might also spark new ideas for writing projects. A biography about some famous silent film stars, perhaps. She had recently heard a rumor that Buster Keaton was really a goblin.

"Have you gotten a cell phone yet?" Ben asked, interrupting her thoughts. Between him and Joy, it was hard to consider anything fully.

"No, Ben. Not yet." And not ever. She disliked phones. In fact, Adora had a passionate hatred of the favorite device of Satan. The device's spawn—the cell phone—was even more detestable. Just being near them made her head hurt. The radio waves seemed to bounce around her skull, beating on her brain until it wanted to burst free and explode.

Even without that, experience had taught her telephones usually brought ill tidings: cowardly lovers who didn't want to break up in person, bad news from your doctor about unheard-of and untreatable syndromes, even word of dead mothers favoring flamboyant suicides. Hearing a phone ring was for Adora like getting zinged with a stun gun. Or, from Ben's phone, like getting zapped with a cattle prod.

She had actual physical tingling in her hands and head anytime she touched the single phone in her house. It was surely psychosomatic, but the devices were still unpleasant and something she avoided.

Ben, who wouldn't dream of going anywhere without an electronic leash, still could not understand her attitude. He had let her coast until now, but this was different. After all, why wouldn't she want to supply him with hourly updates on the activities of this rich and famous—and clearly insane—client? And maybe he had a point regarding the wisdom of staying in touch with someone. There'd be no peace if she gave in, though. He'd call night and day. Joy was enough of a round-the-clock nag; she didn't need Ben riding her, too.

"Well, then, how will I reach you?" he asked, sounding peevish. "I don't think he plans to stay at the Wilshire for very long."

You won't *reach me.* The sudden thought was somewhat encouraging, a consolation prize for having to meet a loony and hire herself out to him— albeit for a very good price.

"Call Mr. Nicholas's assistant. You have his number, don't you?" she asked.

"Oh yeah," he said more cheerfully. The good mood wouldn't last. She had already braved contact with the instrument of Satan and tried the number last night. Ben had gotten it wrong. She had connected with some candy company whose employees didn't speak English. Maybe he had been drunk at the time he took the call. That was frequent after eight P.M. Or maybe Ben had tried to pump the man for gossip, and the assistant had purposely left a wrong number to punish him. The rich and arrogant often had equally arrogant employees.

Normally, Adora wouldn't try to duck her agent.

28

After all, she liked eating as much as the next person, and he was often the one who found her jobs between books. Still, it looked like she maybe had employment now, and she didn't feel like satisfying Ben's insatiable curiosity about her patron. Not even at a distance. Especially not until he sobered up.

"Do you have the ticket with you?" she asked.

"There's no ticket. It's a private plane," Ben said, shoving a printout her way. "It will be at the Alma Airfield tomorrow morning at ten. Pack an overnight bag."

Adora glanced at the paper. It had a map of an airport and a name scrawled on the bottom.

"Do you know what kind of plane it is?" she asked casually. She didn't like small planes. She didn't like large ones either, but they were slightly less scary than the flying coffins her mother had loved to fly.

"It's probably a private jet. The Bishop S. Nicholas Foundation has one."

A small jet? Well, that was okay. Unpleasant, but not impossible. She'd manage. And if she couldn't, she probably still had a few of those pills the doctor had given her. . . .

I thought you'd given those up.

I have. Really.

"Who and what is Robin Christkind?" she asked, squinting at Ben's spidery handwriting.

"He's the pilot. You're supposed to ask for him at the airfield."

Adora nodded and slipped the paper into her purse. "Okay. I'm going to L.A.—but I'm making no promises about taking this job. If this guy's a complete loony or a bastard, I'm gone."

Her agent nodded, looking marginally happier. He'd be getting fifteen percent, after all. That was a tidy paycheck for him.

"Good choice. Now let's have dessert," he suggested, forgetting that they hadn't had lunch. "I'll order champagne."

"No, thanks. I'm dieting." Ben didn't see anything odd in this answer, even though Adora was still gaunt and underweight from her prolonged battle with some Epstein-Barr–type virus—or insanity—which had killed her sense of taste and hence her appetite. In his world, everyone was always on a diet, whether they needed to be or not.

Feeling suddenly exhausted, as she did all too often these days, Adora got to her feet. "Thanks for the tea. I'll call if I decide to take the job, and you can get the contracts ready."

"They are ready. Mr. Nicholas sent them. All you need to do is sign." Ben was starting to sound peevish again. "Where is that stupid Luther? I ordered another bottle of wine hours ago."

"Well, then, I'll leave you to it." Adora began to back away, wanting to escape the sight of Ben's bleary, hopeless eyes. A small touch of guilt pinched her heart and she heard herself saying: "I'll talk to you soon."

Or not.

Or not. Experience told her it might be weeks before Ben sobered up again—weeks she'd rather not witness. Ben on a prolonged drunk wasn't something attractive. She could see a day coming when she'd have to find someone else to handle her work.

But that was just whistling in the dark. She wouldn't walk away from her agent, drunk or not, would she? He had, after all, been a friend of her father's and her last link to her childhood, the last person who shared her childhood memories and could testify that her father had ever lived. And she needed that, because she had very few memories of her youth. Pretty much everything before five was one big blank space in her brain. It was almost like she had come into the world as a kindergartener.

Stop worrying about it, Joy said sharply. *It's perfectly normal for people to not recall their childhoods.*

Is it?

Of course.

Nevertheless, Adora wouldn't be firing Ben. Not today. However, she would spend a little while hiding out in L.A. while he sobered up, and she would decide what to do with her life.

And so it came to pass that, one year at the time of the Solstice, a fierce cold seized the land and the Sons of Man were near death and greatly afeared of the dark that seemed to have no end. But Niklas came upon them and said: "Be not afraid. You shall not die in the Night, but instead the Sons of Man shall live." And he raised his flute to the sky and called down a bright fire. And the fire struck a sacred tree that burned with holy light for Twelve Days. And Death and cold were turned back from the Sons of Man, and the men rejoiced and blessed the shaman. But Niklas said: "Bless me not, for it is the Love of Gaia and not I that has saved you and brought you fire. If you wish to give thanks then worship thusly: Every year on the darkest of days you shall choose one sacred tree and hang offerings of thanks in its branches. And you shall set the tree alight and tend the fire for twelve days. Thus will the gift of your lives and thanks be returned to Gaia."

—*Niklas 3:1*

The Green Man dances, but not as lightly as before, because he is growing old just like the year. His hair is sil-

33

vering, increasingly rough. His body hurts, too, and every step is an ordeal. This is his burden, though, so he does not complain about the aches in his bones. Besides, there is the music and there is Gaia waiting, her loving hands at work on the spindle that reels his life back in and calls him home.

Around him people are crying, giving thanks for his offering. He appreciates this, but truly he does not dance for them. He does this for Gaia, for the love that, as a physical being, he has no better way of expressing.

The moon rises in the cold sky, white as cream, sweet as honey. He lifts his eye to it and weeps with joy because it is time.

CHAPTER THREE

The goblin Miffith hunched behind his computer and watched General Anaximander the way a cornered mouse would watch a cat offering cheese—except the cat would be far less scary. No sane person would take this job, unless they were in straits so dire that a fifty-fifty chance of being murdered by his boss were better odds than the thugs in his old life were offering. As it was, joining the L.A. rebels was a shade less dangerous than continuing to hang out with the goblin-fruit gangs. Gangs were no place for a goblin with no taste for rape and torture. His initiation had also been his final assignment. He'd raped the human fruit-junkie as ordered, but he hadn't been able to pinch and bite her the way he was supposed to. She was just too pathetic. And he'd kind of wanted to see her again.

So, now he was here. Truth be told, he would rather have signed on with Molybdenum. But L.A.'s hive master had a low tolerance for gang violence and would never let him on staff. And General

Anaximander had offered this job as his secretary—perhaps as an apology for strangling Miffith's father, who had also worked for him? No, more likely because Miffith spoke four human languages and also fey. Anyhow, it had seemed ideal at the time. But now . . .

Anaximander hissed something into his phone, and Miffith hunched down, trying to make himself invisible. Someone was in trouble. He just hoped it wasn't him.

Adora's small house already looked vacant, as though it could sense that she intended to be gone for a protracted period of time. It was strange and a little sad to think of it muddling along without her, its lights on timers, the plants watered by a sprinkler system. It would miss her, though; she could tell.

She stood in the yard and looked at the small garden she had coaxed out of the horrid clay soil that plagued their neighborhood. It had been a particularly hard winter by California standards, and the shy flowers were only just beginning to show off their fans and ruffled skirts, and she was leaving the glorious show just as it began. A part of her—a dark part whose existence she usually denied—wondered whenever she left if it would be for the last time. That happened sometimes: People went away one morning and never came back.

Like Mom. Like Dad.

"It's Ben's fault. I didn't want this assignment. . . . Look, I'll miss you too," Adora said quietly to the house. She sighed. "I can't lie. I love the idea of travel, and I really need the money, but you know I like you best. I'll be back as soon as I can."

The stunted lilac sighed back and forgave her. She turned to the house, laying a hand on the doorframe. Perhaps it was the cool breeze, but the wood seemed to shiver. This was her house—her *home*. It was the only place she had ever felt she truly belonged. However, the house loved her unconditionally and knew she had to go. It whispered a fond if sad farewell.

"Good-bye," Adora replied.

That done, she gave herself permission to run down her checklist one last time: She had her portable. She had an overnight bag. She had killer shoes—

And your voice of reason. Don't leave home without it, Joy added. *Not that you'll listen.*

As if I could ever be so lucky as to leave you behind, Adora replied.

She sighed again. Voice or no voice, she was ready—or as ready as she would ever be. There was no reason to delay. Shutting the door softly, she set off on her adventure.

The taxi driver, whose English was sketchy, assured her that she was in the right place before pulling away, but Adora still had doubts about her location. Where was the jet she had been promised? All she could see was a . . . what was that exactly on the runway in front of her?

Adora inched toward the contraption. Squatting in the middle of the runway where she stood was a giant wooden plane that head-on had the face of a beagle wearing aviator goggles. The canine head was mounted on the body of a somewhat skinny goose with splayed feet. She recognized it now from research she had done for an abandoned book on Mussolini. The plane was called a Fieseler Storch. The outlandish-looking high-winged plane had changed German history when it rocketed into the aeronautics scene after the First World War. It had an eight-cylinder, invert-V, air-cooled engine, a fifteen-thousand-foot ceiling, a stall speed of thirty-two miles per hour and a two-hundred-forty-mile flight range. And one machine gun, though it appeared that was missing.

It was also supposed to be a very safe airplane. Which was good, because though large by the standards of most modern, private planes, it was still smaller than the jet Adora had expected. Which meant it was too small for her liking. In fact, just standing near it made her nervous. And that—however irrational—made her mad.

On the other hand, this absurdity was a device of great historic value. She had always respected age. Anything that endured cruel, ravaging time deserved some deference.

Uh-huh, it's just old enough for the wings to be rotten—but don't listen to me, Joy said.

Fear of flying fought with Adora's love of history. Was this a sign, or was Joy right? Should she call off the trip?

High time you started believing in omens, Joy said nastily.

"Hey, there!" a cheerful voice greeted her.

"Robin Christkind?" Adora asked, turning to the young man who appeared around the back of the plane, hoping that he would tell her she had made a mistake and wanted the small Lear jet on the next runway.

"That's me. And you must be the writer, Adora Navarra. I hear you're an historian and come from a family of pilots." He stepped forward and offered a hand. It was encased in a fine kid glove. She was also amused to see that he was wearing a leather helmet with aviator goggles and a long white scarf.

He looked like a young Charles Lindbergh. She liked a man who knew how to dress for a role.

Still, the clothes were a little odd under the circumstances, so she consulted her inner weirdometer and was relieved when nothing stirred on the psychic dials. This guy was eccentric but probably safe.

Probably—but you can't really be sure, Joy inserted.

"Adora Navarra. The one and only," she agreed.

"Do you have any other bags?" Robin asked.

"No, this is it. I travel light. But—"

"Then let me tuck it away and we'll be off. Can you manage on your own?" he asked, eyeing her skirt and heels. "The seats are a bit high."

"Of course, but—"

"Good. We're running a little late, and I hate to keep Kris waiting. His schedule is so tight these days."

"I'm so sorry if I delayed you," Adora said immediately. "We had some bad traffic—"

"It's fine. But maybe I better help you in." Robin reached out, but Adora stepped back quickly.

"No. I can manage." She barely stopped herself from smacking away his outstretched hands. She thought she liked Robin Christkind, but that didn't mean she was ready for him to touch her. She didn't like strangers getting too close. She'd manage the climb somehow.

"Okay. Holler if you get stuck." His tone was good-natured as he turned away.

"I will." *Not.*

It helped that the second seat was in the back of the plane and somewhat closer to the ground. Still, it took a bit of maneuvering to get in without snagging her stockings or showing off far more than was polite on two minutes' acquaintance. True to his word, it took Robin only a moment to stow her bag, and then he joined her in the cockpit, looking back as she was arranging her somewhat twisted skirt. Adora frowned at him and he turned to face forward.

The plane interior was larger than expected, not much like a coffin at all. Still, she could feel her heart skittering nervously. A part of her feared planes for reasons that were not entirely logical. Though it made no sense, something inside her was convinced that if she ever went up again, she might jump out.

"Don't be such a coward," she muttered to herself. Adora braced herself and then leaned out to close the door.

"Ready?" Robin asked, looking over his shoulder one last time. His gaze stayed on her face.

"As I'll ever be," she muttered, then gave him a thumbs-up.

He smiled once and leaned forward to touch the starter. The plane hesitated for a moment before clearing its throat. There was a pause, then it coughed loudly. Finally, a bronchial wheezing began that lasted for almost a minute.

Adora raised her voice. "Uh, Robin? Is that normal?"

"Don't worry. The old girl's not an early riser and has spent too many years smoking. But she's as reliable as the sunrise, and Jack Frost serviced her himself. Give her a minute and we'll be off."

"Sure." Adora folded her hands in her lap and bit her lower lip; she wouldn't ask to be let out of the plane. But the cockpit was shrinking inch by inch as she waited for the engine to stop wheezing, and she wished desperately that she could open a window—or a door, though the bright sun scorched her eyes and warned that she would be sick if she tried to exit.

"Okay, we're ready now." The words were hardly out of his mouth when Robin released the brake and advanced the throttle a few degrees. Adora felt her muscles tighten as the plane moved, but nothing alarming happened. The vehicle rattled out onto the runway, acting very much like a harmless old lady out for a stroll. Adora reminded herself to breathe.

"See? Nothing to it. She's a lamb, and I can get this old girl in the air in just under a hundred and sixty feet," Robin announced proudly. "First time, I needed two hundred, but I'm getting better."

"Amazing, but let's not try to set any records today, okay? I'm actually not real fond of small planes. They make me a little nervous," Adora confessed.

"This isn't a plane. It's *history*," Robin said earnestly. "There are only a handful of people alive who've had the pleasure of piloting one of these babies!"

Adora was touched by his enthusiasm. She didn't meet too many people who shared her affinity for the past.

She said, "I know. I've read about the Storches. They're amazing planes. Who would have guessed that an airplane could actually land on the roof of an alpine fortress and get away again? I wish I had seen it."

Robin laughed. "Mussolini's rescue? Well, if you know about that, then you know what an honor this is. I still can't believe that Kris lets me fly this thing."

"Kris?"

"Oh—Bishop Nicholas. We call him Kris."

"I see," she said, though she didn't see at all. There was no way that she knew of to get *Kris* from either *Bishop* or *Nicholas*. The engine was louder now, and she had to raise her voice. "He must be an interesting man. Is he interested in all antiques, or just planes?"

"Kris is pretty much interested in everything," was Robin's diplomatic reply.

The Storch waited politely for the pilot to finish his sentence before ceasing its dainty gait and demonstrating that it could actually run like a cheetah. With no warning beyond the flick of Robin's hand, it leaned into the hazy sky and leapt for the horizon. It ran flat-out, screaming mechanically as it raced along the runway. Adora was pretty sure that she heard Robin shouting "*Woohoo!*" right along with it.

Adora shrieked too, though not with enthusiasm, and she said some really bad words. Her hands, still clasped together, did their best to strangle one another. She wanted to close her eyes to the horror but couldn't.

The plane gave one last playful skip and then jumped for the sky with an ecstatic scream. It nearly pulled a loop-the-loop before Robin brought her back under control.

"What a rush!" the pilot exclaimed. "God! I feel so alive!"

"Enjoy it now. I'm going to kill you as soon as we land," Adora said loudly to the back of his head. "And I may punish you first by vomiting on you."

He glanced back at her, contrite.

"Hey, I'm sorry. Here." He reached under his seat and offered her a thermos. "Have some mint tea. It'll soothe your stomach."

"Thank you," Adora said. "But I think it might be best if I did nothing right now."

"Okay—I really am sorry. I heard your mom was a pilot, and I thought you were kidding about being scared, since you got on the plane and knew all about Mussolini." His boyish smile was appealing.

"Hmph! Just don't do it again. *Please*."

Adora had calmed by the time they reached the L.A. basin, but she could still measure her heartbeats in the throbbing of her joints and spine. She told herself to relax, but it wasn't really an option. Though she hadn't felt any urge to do a swan dive herself, her mind was still half-convinced that they were going to fall out of the air, collide with a mountain or have a smashup with one of the many jets that filled the busy southern sky arcing over the immense sprawl of overlapping cities below.

"Why is the plane shaking?" she asked, proud that her voice didn't quaver any more than it should, given the vibration of the plane.

"Currents off the San Gabriels," Robin said. "Just hang on another second or two. We're almost there."

"What airport are we going to—not LAX?"

"No, today we're flying into Santa Monica. Morrison will meet you there."

"Morrison?"

"The limo driver. I think he has the little girl today. You're in for another treat."

Another treat—and a little girl at that. Adora wondered if she could stand it.

"Look out your left window," Robin commanded as they started to descend toward the vast sea of buildings that had finally turned into miniature tract homes rather than what looked like the rough leather of an alligator purse. "Isn't that the second prettiest thing you've ever seen?"

Adora complied, but gingerly. She didn't fancy seeing the ground rushing up at her.

"Holy cow! What is that?" she asked, staring down at what was clearly an automobile and yet something so much more.

"That is a nineteen thirty-seven Packard Town Car, with an independent front suspension and an eight-cylinder engine that runs smooth as fine whipping cream. It used to belong to Mae West. What a gal!" There was some question about whether he was referring to the vehicle or the actress. "She's one of Jack's restorations. He's great with cars."

Adora stared, mesmerized. The engine wasn't the only thing creamy about the vehicle. The entire automobile was a long vanilla undulation that gleamed seductively in the noonday sun. Adora had never suffered from automobile lust, but she felt the pangs now. It even made the flight in the small plane worthwhile, since she got to see the car from the air.

The Storch returned to earth with more decorum than it had used at takeoff. The engine died, and the only sounds were the last lazy *whup-whup*s of the slowing propeller and Robin's sigh of repletion.

In spite of his claim of urgency, the pilot moved languorously, maybe looking for a cigarette in the briefcase on his lap. But the limo driver had the airplane door open in short order, and Adora exited just as enthusiastically. Morrison had her body and bag tucked inside the Town Car in under a minute and they were on their way before Adora could even say thank you and good-bye to Robin.

"Ma'am, there's some champagne if you're in the mood," he suggested.

Adora took a deep breath of expensive leather and groaned appreciatively. "Not just now, thanks. I want to take this in without distraction."

"I know," Morrison said. There was a smile in his voice as he started the car. "I wish it was legal to marry an automobile. I'd be on my knee with ring in hand in a heartbeat. It's a good thing Kris doesn't mind me lusting after his girl."

"He's a good employer?" Adora asked, reluctantly starting the process of interviewing. "An open-minded one?"

"The best. He even lets me drive the Jag." His tone was reverent.

Adora laughed, then decided that perhaps this visit to Mr. Bishop S. Nicholas might not entirely be a hardship. He seemed kind to his employees. It was possible that she would even like him.

At the last moment, Adora remembered to wave farewell to Robin. She had to lower the window and dangle the upper half of her body outside to get his attention. It wasn't the most graceful posture in her skirt, but she was glad that she did it. Robin's wan expression stretched into a wide smile, and he waved back.

But some of Mankind were not content with their gift of light, and they asked why they could not be the masters of all the Earth and all her seasons. The shaman pointed at the burning tree and spoke thusly: "Recall, O Sons of Man, that you are like this sacred tree. Your Light is not so great as the Sun and cannot cover the earth. And Man's Light burns but for a short time. Yet it is in this Light that refuge from the darkness may be had by others of your kind. Rejoice in it, and be not envious of the Sun that loves you."

—*Niklas 3:2*

Kris closed his eyes against the pale March sun and, eavesdropping on Cadalach, he listened to the children— though, sadly, not his own children—playing.

I'm tired, *he thought.* And with cause, damn it. My brain is still half-scrambled, but I already remember too much. How can I bear this alone?

And he did remember now. There were so many life-times tangled in his head. His friends Jack and Nyssa had done what they could, but his brain was still a mess of terrible visions he could not explain. He had seen "eter-

nal" monuments and religions rise and fall. He'd even been around long enough to see them exhumed by archaeologists and lost again. Of all the places of his youth, only the stone tower of Jericho remained, and it was more than half buried.

He was old. So old. And nothing had changed. He told the humans how to love, but still they despaired and coveted. They hated and they envied and they killed. He didn't feel like going on anymore. Not alone. He was almost sorry that Jack had found him. If only the goblin hunter had gotten him, he would be dead, and all this horror would be behind him.

"I know your weariness, child," a warm voice said suddenly. "But now I send glad tidings from the one who made you. For this last quest, you shall not be alone."

Shocked, Kris opened his eyes.

"What?" he asked aloud of the nearly forgotten voice. He hadn't heard it in centuries.

"I promise," the voice repeated. "You will not be alone. Look to the west, for it is from there that she will come."

CHAPTER FOUR

Though she had never been to L.A., Adora knew by sight the Regent Beverly Wilshire, which was said to be the crowning jewel in the golden diadem that was Rodeo Drive. Adora had an old postcard of the hotel from her paternal grandmother, who had been an actress in silent films. She had never met the old woman, but her father had left Adora with the impression of her being a woman with an awareness of what was due her, and who was every inch the grande dame.

Adora shied away from that line of thought. Family wasn't something upon which she liked to ruminate.

Dashiell Hammet had written *The Thin Man* at the Beverly Wilshire. Many writers had stayed there over the years. Inspiration probably saturated the walls.

Not sure what to expect architecturally in a city run by goblins, Adora found herself relieved that the building had not been altered. The classic European facade was fronted by a row of sculptured trees that spread lacy limbs over the distinctive round awnings covering the first floor windows. There were few enough buildings like this in the New World—in California especially, where the twenty-year-teardown was almost mandatory and where earthquakes got the rest. A structure this grand was a true rarity, being constructed in an era when artists weren't afraid of being decorative.

They drove past an ornate verdigris gate whose plaque announced in formal script that she had entered the hallowed precincts of the Regent Beverly Wilshire, and stopped under the broad portico. A uniformed valet had her door open in a trice—probably because he wanted to touch the splendid car—and helped her alight. A bellman rushed over to take her bag. Both men looked normal, but something about them made her think that they were goblins.

"This is Miss Navarra," Morrison said.

"Of course. This way, ma'am. I'll show you up to the presidential suite. You are expected."

Adora nodded, keeping her smile to herself. The presidential suite? It had to be nice to be rich.

"Thank you, Morrison," she said, smiling at him and taking a last look at the Packard. Parting was such sweet sorrow.

"My pleasure, ma'am. I'll see you later, I'm sure."

Adora sincerely hoped so.

The presidential suite overlooked Rodeo Drive. She had little time to appreciate the view, though, because she was shown immediately into a library, which had heavy drapes drawn over the massive windows. She took a quick look at the shelves, half-expecting to see a complete oeuvre of modern mystics and crackpots represented, but neither Edgar Caycen or Nostradamus were anywhere in sight.

Oddly, many of the books appeared written in foreign languages she couldn't identify.

Hearing soft footsteps, she turned to find the man she assumed was her new employer.

"Mr. Bishop Nicholas?" she asked as the door to the hallway shut softly behind her. The bellman, who had grown increasingly nervous as they approached the suite, hadn't waited for a tip; he had dropped her off and then fled.

A man with silver hair and wearing a dark Armani suit paused for a moment in a shaft of sunlight that had sneaked through the velvet drapes, and then walked toward her. His long legs ate up the distance. With every step, his stunning features grew clearer, and Adora's first thought was that he was the most radiantly beautiful creature she had ever seen.

"Only in my public life," he replied. "Please, call me Kris. Kris Kringle. It's a bit of a joke." He offered his hand and a long, unblinking gaze with a half-smile. Up close, his eyes were a shade of silver-blue that Adora had never seen. They invited her to step into them and drown.

"That would be Kris with a *K*?" she asked, accepting his hand and allowing his fingers to briefly touch hers. She felt a bit stunned, as though the earth had spun off its axis. She didn't gasp or swoon, but Adora felt the sudden flush of color that flowed into her cheeks. If her employer was paying attention, even in the dim light he would also notice that her pulse was gratifyingly unsteady—presuming he was hoping she'd be disconcerted by her sudden attraction to him.

"Naturally with a *K*. It makes for excellent visual alliteration."

Adora reluctantly dropped his hand and took

51

a half-step back. She forced herself to form a complete—and hopefully more realistic—impression.

On second glance, her would-be employer's face was rugged and experienced rather than beautiful. And it wasn't so much youthful as ageless and mobile. His voice was as flexible as his face—though at the moment better controlled and directed at her with some as yet unrevealed purpose.

His hair was silvered and long enough to touch his shoulders, but rather than the texture of gray hair it had the gossamer quality of a baby's tresses. Adora was willing to bet that this was the same shade of hair with which he had been born. It was impossible to guess his age.

The brows above his startling silver-blue eyes were dark, a sharp contrast to the locks that framed his face, and they swooped backward, giving him a permanent quizzical expression. The body beneath the face was lean, and it moved quickly and efficiently, reminding Adora of a cat—one of the dangerous, hunting types.

His voice wasn't feline, though, she thought as he spoke again. It was pure magic—sugarplums and dark chocolate and every type of delicious sin. Combined with his unblinking stare, it made her feel like she was slipping into a hot spring on a snowy February night. She didn't know how it could be, when she was usually immune to male charms, but Adora admitted—at least to herself— that this man was exerting some sort of psychic gravitational pull on her. *Charisma.* She had met people who had it before, but never to this degree.

Her second thought was that he was the most unlikely-looking Santa she could imagine. There had to be some mistake.

If she was guilty of staring a bit too hard, then so was he. She would like to think that it was because he was equally stunned and attracted by her person but doubted that was the case. She had been ill for several months—perhaps a final present from Derek, the lying rat bastard—and though she had put a lot of the lost weight back on, Adora knew that the only thing really striking about her was her golden pallor. Unfortunately, illness hadn't made her fragile and cuddly; the hollows under her cheeks could almost qualify as caves, and her limbs were bony and angular. Instead of a waif, she looked more like an anorexic Valkyrie.

"I don't mean to be rude or abrupt," Adora forced herself to say in a businesslike voice, "but I wish to be plain right from the start. You do understand that your assertion that you are Kris Kringle—Santa Claus—is more than a bit farfetched, and that I will require some proof—actually a great deal of proof—of this claim as the project progresses? I am not willing to lie to the public about such a thing."

You aren't, huh? Joy had stirred. *Anyway, are you sure you really want proof?*

"But of course you aren't. And I'm not fond of lying myself." Kris smiled fully, making himself twice as charming. He added gently, "I don't mean to be rude either, but you're staring awfully hard. Have I got something caught in my teeth?"

"I'm looking for wings or a halo," she said defensively, embarrassed by her lapse in manners. She hoped he wouldn't notice her tripping pulse. "Is it a great effort to hide them from the world? Or do you just have a good tailor?"

He laughed. "Wrong legend. I never claimed to be an angel, only a saint. If you recall your childhood

literature, you will note that my appearance supposedly ran more to red suits and reindeer." Briefly, a
dark look crossed his face.

"So you're sticking to that story? You are Santa
Claus?"

"Oh yes, absolutely. Santa Claus. That's the one I
want you to tell. Didn't your agent explain? I asked
Pennywyse to be explicit about the project." His
smile was hard to resist. It made even the unreason-
able seem possible—even probable. Perhaps this
project would work as a book on tape. If he nar-
rated, he could hypnotize the audience into believing him.

"Pennywyse?" Adora asked, unable to focus on
anything except his voice.

"My assistant. He called your agent and arranged
for you to come here."

"Ah." Pennywyse was the one who had given Ben
the wrong phone number, so she supposed she
owed him. She sighed and heard herself saying out
loud: "They'll throw me in the nuthouse, you know.
If I do this."

Kris shook his head and smiled again. "No,
they'll want to throw *me* in the nuthouse. You'll just
be branded as an exploitative, publicity-hungry
kook who took advantage of a mentally ill person."

"Which is much better," Adora retorted dryly,
though she was both gladdened and surprised that
he understood and admitted to the likely consequences of their actions. He might be crazy, but he
wasn't stupid. So, score one point for Kris with a *K*.

He seemed to take her words as a question. "Oh,
yes. At least I think so. Far better to be thought an
opportunist than an idiot, or so it seems to me," he
said, echoing her thoughts.

"That doesn't sound like a very Santalike thing to say," Adora pointed out. "I thought you were always jolly and looking on the bright side of things."

He shook his head and asked reasonably, "Now, how can you know what I would or would not say? Everything you've heard about me is at best garbled legend and, at worst, downright lies. You're here so we can set the record straight."

"They'll make us publish this as fiction," she warned in a final attempt to break free of the deal. But it was less than wholehearted. In spite of herself, she was drawn to this man and wanted to hear his story.

And maybe feel him up, Joy inserted.

"No, they won't," Kris said confidently, squashing her last feeble hope of rescue from Wonderland. "I've already spoken with the publisher, and he's a believer. The fact that he is also something of a distant relative is a help too. Sadly, the old saw is right in publishing: It isn't what you know, but who you know. Now, won't you have a seat? May I get you something to drink before we start?"

Adora was suddenly aware that her feet hurt. Against all common sense, she had chosen to wear her highest heels to this interview. Her usual pumps would have been okay, but these strappy sandals were problematic. They were fine for about three hours—if one stayed seated—but standing in them was unpleasant and walking well-nigh impossible once her feet began to swell and the straps got tight as Tupperware. Why she had worn them, Adora didn't know; she'd just had some vague sense that this multimillionaire deserved her most frivolous footwear. And somehow being tall had seemed advisable.

Adora looked up from her feet. Kris was closer, and she had to tip her head backward a bit to make eye contact. If her object in wearing high heels had been to appear taller than her client, she would have been disappointed. Kris, with a *K,* was built along impressive, nonelfin lines.

She took a breath and agreed to his terms. "Fine. It's your commitment proceedings. If the contracts don't have a clause indemnifying me from future lawsuits, we'll add one." Adora sat down on a plush chair and pushed up the sleeves of her dress. It was a soft gray cashmere, very pretty but also reasonably businesslike. She opened her small briefcase on the glass-topped table and pushed a vase of flowers aside. "Let's get started. Do you mind if I take notes while we talk?"

"Not at all."

Kris seated himself across from her. As soon as her feet were out of sight, she slipped off her sandals. The relief was immediate.

"I'm afraid that we'll only have about half an hour to talk this morning," he said apologetically. "Perhaps we should discuss your schedule first."

"My schedule?"

"Yes. I'll be moving around quite a bit and will need you to travel with me. In fact, we'll be leaving for New York the day after tomorrow."

Adora blinked.

"We're going to be traveling? To New York?" She frowned. Ben hadn't said anything about traveling. She didn't mind—was thrilled, in fact—but it did complicate things. She had packed for the more casual environs of L.A. It would mean a fast trip home—*please, God, not in the Storch.* She said aloud, "Where else would we go? Assuming I take the job, will I need my passport?"

"Oh, no. We won't be going anywhere that requires a passport. Yet. To begin with, I plan New York and San Francisco. And perhaps Palm Springs. These days I'm also doing a bit of a Robin Hood gig and need to stick close to home while arrangements are made to rob Prince John. He goes by the name of General Anaximander these days. His Sheriff of Nottingham is a creature called Raxin."

She'd heard the name Raxin but couldn't recall in what context. Adora wanted to ask what he meant, but she was interrupted by the entrance of a small, nervous man in a dark green suit.

Kris said, "Miss Navarra, let me introduce my publicist, Maxwell Brand. He handles many of L.A.'s up-and-coming stars and will see to it that your book is made known to the world. Max, this is Adora Navarra, the biographer."

The biographer. She liked the sound of that.

"A pleasure," Max said, and somehow managed to sound like he meant it. Perhaps she was looking like a sane ally in the land of sugarplums and legends. Even for L.A. publicists, Santa Claus had to be an *out-there* kind of client. "I'm sorry to disturb you, Kris, but Mugshottz has been looking for you. He's had a cable from . . . from your nephew. Things sound . . . on course. But Jack would like a consult as soon as you're able to get away."

"Excellent. I think of Mugshottz as my Little John," Kris added as an aside to Adora. "He's certainly tall enough." He turned back to his publicist. "Max, tell him I'm—never mind. Here he is. Mugshottz, come and meet Miss Navarra. She's going to be writing about me."

Adora looked at the creature lumbering down the hall toward them and swallowed hard. She had understood that she was in a goblin city and that it was possible she would see some lutins, but her online research had led her to believe that goblins were diminutive creatures that had surgery to appear human. This person was the size of a smallish grizzly bear, and if he'd had any surgery to help him look human it had been done by a mad scientist who spent too much time watching B horror movies.

"Call the Fab Five. We have a fashion emergency," she muttered, again speaking aloud without meaning to. And when she got a better look, she whispered, "He's got a head-piercing—right through the temple!" Adora found herself staring at the bolts projecting in a Frankensteinish manner from Mugshottz's head. She didn't like to make snap judgments about people, but she thought it unlikely that she and this creature would be best friends. Certainly she would have to be nuts to take style advice from him.

"Yes, Mugshottz is a troll-goblin mix," Kris answered, assuming she was speaking to him. He added loudly, "He claims to have some gargoyle blood too. I'm not exactly sure where he keeps his brain, but I have long suspected that it isn't in his head." His voice returned to normal. "He's a good bodyguard, though, and would die to protect me, which is all I can ask." Then he again lowered his tone to add one more thing: "By the way, he's from the Bronx. Pretend not to notice the accent. He's self-conscious about it."

Adora pulled her eyes away from the monster long enough to see if her new employer was kidding. He didn't seem to be. He looked genuinely concerned about hurting this creature's feelings— and why shouldn't he? Kris was apparently kind to all his people. She could feel herself being drawn in to his vision of the world, despite her reservations.

Trolls and gargoyles as bodyguards? Why not? At the moment, it seemed believable.

You are such a sucker, Joy complained.

And maybe she was. This Kris had an irresistible sense of purpose that swept everything before it. Adora had expected a certain operatic greatness to surround him—most wealthy men had a touch, and this one thought he was a living legend—but whatever else her employer was, he wasn't a lamebrain pretender. He might be delusional or psychotic, but he was sincere and energetic, and seemed to have a mind as sharp as a headsman's ax.

A thought occurred to her. Maybe Kris thought he was the *reincarnated* Saint Nicholas. That was a little less weird. Lots of people believed stuff like that, especially in Hollywood. Heck, she hadn't entirely ruled it out of her own philosophy. Reincarnation was something she could get behind, since she believed in second chances.

"Your bodyguard—is he likely to be called upon to die anytime soon?" she asked, pretending concern. She joked: "Should I ask for combat pay?"

Kris shook his head. "Of course not. Having a bodyguard is just a precaution I've taken to please my nephew and other backers. Jack worries a lot."

Adora nodded. "I guess you have to keep the insurance company happy."

Kris blinked, and she had a feeling that something she had just said surprised him, though she couldn't imagine what.

"Insurance company. Just so. Tell me, Miss Navarra—"

"Adora, please. We're in California. Last names sound ridiculous—unless you like them, of course," she added politely. "I want you to be comfortable with me."

"Adora, then." The words were an unintentional caress. Or maybe not. Maybe he knew exactly what he was doing. The thought made her frown.

"Given your obvious reservations about the project—and the added, though limited, danger—are you willing to take on this job?" Kris asked. "I hate to rush you, but time is short. I think you've met most of my staff now—at least the ones you'll see daily. Can you stand to live with us while you do this work?"

Adora forced herself to take a last long think. The man's pilot, limo driver, publicist and secretary were all reassuringly normal. She had half feared that they would resemble the cast from *Santa Claus is Coming to Town*. But they all—except the bodyguard—eschewed any semblance to elves or pixies or fairy-tale monsters of any stripe, and Mugshottz . . . Well, he wasn't that scary now that she saw him up close. Just large and silent and looming. And she wasn't a species bigot, was she?

"We won't be taking the Storch to New York, will we?" she asked suspiciously. "Because I have to tell you that I don't do well in small planes."

"No. There isn't enough room for all of us. And I prefer speed as a rule. I only sent the Storch as a treat for you. I figured that as an historian you would appreciate it more than an efficient but characterless means of travel. I myself am quite fond of antiques."

"Hm. Well, thank you. I certainly loved the car. What a gorgeous automobile." The words were absentminded but sincere. She was still thinking, still weighing. Kris nodded and waited while she finished. Unlike her agent, he seemed to feel no need to rush her into conversation or decision.

"Okay, I'm in," she said. "And God have mercy on us all."

"Wonderful. Max, would you ask Pennywyse to

fetch the contracts? Adora, I have put together some biographical material for you to read in your spare time. It will fill you in on some of the more colorful details."

Colorful? Joy laughed. *I bet they're blinding.*

"Fine. But please hurry, before I change my mind," Adora muttered. At Kris's concerned look, she added: "I just know that this is a mistake for both of us."

He chuckled at her complaint and she smiled, but it wasn't really a joke. Adora had the clearest feeling that she was making a decision with huge future consequences, all of which were presently unknown. Still, what did she have to lose—except her house and professional credibility and credit rating?

Kris leaned toward her. "Now, how about something to drink? Iced tea perhaps? Or coffee?"

"I'm fine, really. I . . ." Adora stopped speaking and stared into Kris's eyes, lost for a time and rescued only when another man appeared and laid a set of contracts and a thick file folder in front of her. The spell broken, she looked down and tried to make sense of the documents before her.

It was difficult, because what she really wanted to do was open the file beneath and find out some details about Mr. Bishop S. Nicholas, aka Kris Kringle of the stunning eyes.

"I'll leave you to read over the contracts," her employer said, rising. "Please feel free to request anything you need or want from Pennywyse. There's a fax machine on the desk, and a computer."

Adora forced herself to look up and focus on the dark, slender man who stood in the shadows of the room and looked quite content there. He smiled slightly.

"I'll be back this afternoon," Kris said, drawing

her attention. "We can have dinner and talk about the material in the folder then. I'm certain you'll have questions."

"Without a doubt," Adora agreed. Briskly, she began searching under the desk for her sandals, her sore toes questing after the runaway shoes. She looked slightly to the left of Kris, not wanting to get lost in his gaze again.

"That's all right—don't get up," he said, as though guessing what she was doing. "Please be comfortable. I want you to be happy here. That's very important to me."

And Adora was certain that he meant it.

Santa Claus, she thought as he left the room, taking the warmth with him. . . . Well, she'd researched more obscure beings. And since he claimed to be Saint Nicholas himself, she wouldn't have to worry about him calling in psychics to raise ghosts. That was a relief. She didn't like psychics and didn't need them to tell her about the dead. She had books should Kris's memory—or imagination—fail them when it came to period details.

Books. She was glad he had a library here. Looking at titles was her favorite way to know the minds of others.

Then Adora had a minor revelation. Those odd books she had seen—they must be written in lutin. Of course! But they probably belonged to the hotel instead of Kris. It would have occurred to her sooner, but she'd never been inside a hotel with an actual library before. Still, the books could likely tell her about goblins. Which would be a less scary way to find things out. She loved books. They were how she would talk to future generations, since having children now seemed unlikely.

Some Men traveled to foreign lands and, seeing many treasures there, opened their hearts to envy. They knew discontent and wandered even farther from their homes, and soon they became truly separated from Gaia. Thus the Sons of Man became two tribes and were divided on Earth, some as Celebrants who were with Gaia; and some as Worshippers, who gathered in groups and made images of other gods who looked like Man and bore weapons. The Worshippers feared and were jealous of the Celebrants, who could see Gaia's love everywhere and carried it with them in their hearts. And though the shaman was with them still, bearing Light in the dark of every year, the Worshippers turned from him and his teachings. The shaman did not the same, for he loved them still and would not forsake the Worshippers. Instead, he walked among them doing good deeds, and in time the Worshippers forgot that he was a Celebrant shaman and fey, and they called him Saint Niklas and sometimes Christkind. And the daughters of Man came especially to ask for his aid in finding husbands—and to fill their barren wombs.

—*Niklas 4:6*

Petyr stared at the dice and then, in anger, beat all four fists on the table.

"The Goddessss alwaysss did love you bessst," he hissed.

"True. I don't know why you insist upon gambling with me," Niklas agreed, grinning.

The goblin, though angered at losing, found himself smiling back. One couldn't stay angry at this fey. "What do you demand of me thisss time?" he asked.

Niklas's smile grew wider, and Petyr knew a moment of alarm. "You know that I sometimes go out on Saint Nicholas's Day to bring gifts to human children?" the fey asked.

"Yesss," the goblin answered warily.

"Well, there are more children than ever, and this year I need an assistant. You'll enjoy it—truly."

Petyr's mouth fell open. "You want me to go among the humansss?"

"Yes. There is one town in particular I need to visit. They have been struck with plague, and many of the children have been orphaned. They need food and clothing as well as toys, and the other humans are too afraid to go there."

"But I can't—I daren't." Petyr tugged nervously on his ears and nose. They stretched comically.

"Don't worry. Neither of us can catch this disease. It only affects humans."

"It'sss not that. You know it isss forbidden for lutinsss to go among humansss. Gofimbel hasss outlawed it."

"We shan't let on that you're a goblin," Niklas said. "We'll dress you in a black cloak that will hide your arms, and we'll rub ash on your face and say it is from the chimneys you and I have been down. We'll call you Black Peter, the gnome."

Petyr snorted, but he was resigned.

"They'll think me a demon," he warned. "Or their Satan-devil."

"Just so long as they don't think you are a goblin," Niklas answered.

Petyr sighed and picked up his dice. He hesitated before dropping them back into his pouch. Normally he was very lucky, but he could never win against Niklas.

"I'm getting new dice before we play again," he warned.

"Certainly," Niklas answered. "It won't make any difference, though. The Goddess always wins."

CHAPTER FIVE

"Did Hell freeze over while I was sleeping?" Adora asked the Satanic instrument in her hand, knowing it would relay her question to Ben. Glancing over at Kris, she lowered her voice. "I haven't a clue. And even if I did, that is confidential material beyond the scope of the book and I won't discuss it. Ever. So don't ask again. . . . Did the contracts arrive?"

The phone squawked, and she held it away from her ear. She grimaced when Kris looked up from his ledger. Ben's favorite tool of information procurement was a shaming tongue that he used to cut people to the quick. But saws and knives, useful as they were, didn't work when a lockpick was needed. Adora figured that he would eventually figure that out and leave her alone.

Ha! You've heard about old dogs and new tricks? He'll never change. What an asshole, Joy commented.

Now, now. Don't insult the rectum. At least it *does something for me,* Adora thought back. She focused on getting off the phone with her agent. Kris was sitting here patiently in the hotel suite, waiting for her to begin her interview.

"Soooo that's everything. I have to go now. I'll call if anything comes up. Good-bye." She put the phone down, cutting off shrieks and stutters. Adora reached for the ringer, planning to shut it off, then realized that it was Kris's phone and that he might want to use it.

"Your agent?" Kris asked politely, sipping his after-dinner coffee. Outside, on the deck, bees droned lazily, happy in their early evening bacchanalia, drunk on foxglove and columbine nectar.

"How did you guess?" Adora asked, forcing her scowl to disappear. She'd have to get plastic surgery for the frown lines if she didn't stop letting Ben get to her.

"Pennywyse mentioned that he is . . . forceful. And very concerned about you. He has been calling hourly since seven A.M."

It figured that Ben had somehow found the right number. Where there was a will and all that.

"Concerned? Not exactly. Ben has barbed wire where his heart should be, and a two-inch thick skull. He also has a conversational style a bit like death by a thousand paper cuts." Adora sighed and then admitted: "That isn't true. Well, not all the time. Just when he's been drinking. But he's very nosy even when he's sober. Once in a while you have to post giant No Trespassing signs. And sometimes—when he's being selectively illiterate about the signs—you have to pepper him with buckshot to get him to pay attention. Still, I want you to know that nothing private will be passed along. I can be discreet."

Hearing what she had just said, Adora frowned. What was she doing, mentioning something so personal about her agent to a client? How unlike her! But there was something about Kris that made her spill her guts even when she knew better.

Pennywyse stuck his head in the door. He didn't say anything but somehow still managed to convey a message to Kris. He walked with catlike stealth to the French doors, closed them and twitched the drapes into place. He didn't seem to like light or fresh air.

"Your luggage has arrived. It's in the second bedroom," Kris said suddenly. He had sent someone to retrieve her clothes, sparing her the necessity of another trip in the plane. Ah—to be so wealthy! The idea that someone else might go to her home and pack for her had been a little shocking, but Adora had looked deep into Kris's eyes and then surrendered her house keys without protest—or even any real worry.

There isn't anything there worth stealing anyway, she'd explained to a sputtering Joy, who was less happy with her acquiescence.

"Thank you. I appreciate everyone's kindness," Adora said to Kris. She wasn't sure if she felt guilty for being the recipient of so much effort from his staff, but she was definitely delighted that she hadn't had to fly home again. Instead, she had stayed at the hotel, skimming the rather amazing and impossible file Kris supplied, and had enjoyed a fabulous late lunch of roasted eggplant soup and *steak au poivre* with her new employer, who'd managed to squeeze in a meal with her between meetings.

Over the repast, Adora finally decided she had an angle on what Kris was doing. He was constructing a new identity. For some reason, he wanted the world to believe that he was Santa Claus, *but not the commercial Santa they all thought they knew*. It was a crazy thing to do, beyond all normal eccentricity. And it would be expensive too. She cringed just thinking of the cost of free toys for the world. But philanthropists were notoriously eccentric.

Joy had argued with her assumptions, naturally.

Even now, Adora admitted that there were some problems with her theory—angles she hadn't entirely worked out—but she liked it better than believing this man really was . . .

A fruitcake with a double helping of nuts? her inner voice asked.

No—but confused. Maybe on medication.

Why don't you ask him, and find out what he thinks about your theory? Joy suggested. *I bet he'll tell you the truth. As he knows it.*

Fine. I will. Right now, Adora vowed. *It's time for the interviews to begin.*

But first she had to decide where to sit. The sofa looked inviting, but she already knew it was too soft. She couldn't stay perched on the edge, and that was the only place she liked. It was silly, her requirement, but she always felt smothered and vulnerable on sofas because there was a chance that someone might join her. She liked chairs. Chairs were solitary. And while they weren't always comfortable, they were usually solid and you could get up from them quickly.

So sit in a chair already. Or walk around. Just get on with it.

"Okay, enough shilly-shallying. Let's get to it," she said aloud. "What about the whole going-down-chimneys thing?" she asked. Kris blinked slowly as she demanded: "Can you really do that? Or was it just another exaggeration?"

Kris set his coffee aside and answered readily enough. "In Saint Nicholas's day, many homes didn't have chimneys per se. There were simply smoke holes in the roof. But where there's smoke—"

"There's fire?" she guessed.

He smiled. "Yes. But there is also a path. I learned the trick of traveling on smoke from my days with Freya. I can be very, very quiet."

"Uh-huh. That would be the Norwegian goddess Freya?" Adora asked. She congratulated herself on getting very good at keeping her tone even. In her notebook she wrote *Freya*, and underlined it. She wasn't sure why. There was no way she was bringing this subject up in her book.

"Yes. Though 'goddess' is not really the word for her. She was an aspect of divinity, a being who carried an usually large slice of Gaia's power." Kris studied Adora. He was smiling slightly, as though aware of and amused by her skepticism.

"And Gaia is *The Goddess?*" Adora asked, unearthing her limited store of pagan mythology.

"Gaia is everything—God, Goddess, Allfather, Allmother. Everything that is life and light and love."

New Age religion. Swell. For half the U.S. population that meant devil worship. There went all the royalties from sales in the Bible Belt. She probably wouldn't be talking about this part, either.

"Oooookay," she said. "Maybe we can go over this part later. Though I am curious about whether you're a Christian or not. Being a saint would rather suggest leanings in that direction."

She tried to smile, but Kris made a *tsk*ing noise and wagged a finger at her. "You're jumping to conclusions again. I followed Christ, but I am not a Christian in the modern sense of the word—and the whole saint thing was never my idea."

"Hm." Adora made a note and followed it up

with three question marks. They'd have to do something about that. There was no way that anyone was going to want to hear that Saint Nicholas wasn't a Christian and hadn't wanted the job. That dog just wouldn't hunt, even among New-Agers. She could help Kris construct a fantasy, but it had to be consistent and logical and not offend potential readers.

"You know, the legend I can't believe people fell for was that I moved my operations north because I loved the snow. Sheesh! If I loved the cold so much, why were my first American headquarters outside of New Orleans?" Kris added: "The only reason I was ever at the North Pole was because the goblins drugged me and left me there to feed the polar bears. Santa's toy factory at the Pole—ha! That'll be the day."

"You had headquarters near New Orleans?" Adora asked, somehow finding it more diverting than Kris's comment about being drugged by the goblins. The file had several references to goblin leaders that Adora had never heard of. She was probably going to need a crash course in goblin history if she was going to fit this stuff into the book. Of course, the question of whether she *would* fit it in was another matter. The equation might look too much like demons + Saint Nick = goblins. Santa Claus couldn't be associated with demons.

"You didn't know that? It isn't common knowledge among humans?" Kris asked. He suddenly looked more cheerful. "Well, well. I'll have to get Thomas to look into it for me. I mean, if the property outside the city is still undeveloped, there's a chance some of my belongings are still there. . . ."

She wondered if she should mention the devastating hurricane that had happened last year and decided against it. "You'd never be able to stand that

71

velvet and fur suit down south," she warned. "And what about the reindeer? They'd croak in the heat. Also, I'm betting that the elves would have to unionize. It would drive the cost of toy construction right through the roof—not good if you're planning on keeping up the philanthropic work. You *are* planning on carrying on, aren't you?" she asked as she ran out of breath. "I mean, that *is* the plan, isn't it?"

Kris smiled again and shook his head. His pale hair shimmered as it moved, reminding her of moonlight on water. It was distracting.

"I never wore that red suit but twice—one *would* be the one time I was seen and reported in the newspapers. And frankly, I don't want to use reindeer anymore. Most are mule stubborn and none-too-bright. Horses are much better. Besides, I need to update my image. Just so you know, I don't actually use animals to pull my sleigh—no point in being accused of equine cruelty, is there? It's all public relations these days, I see. And I have other ways to travel when I make my rounds. . . . Maybe manatees would be a good replacement, mascot-wise. Or condors. Or a dragon! Kids would love a dragon, don't you think?" He sounded enthused.

A dragon. He said a dragon. Are you listening? This guy is nuts. Joy was sniggering.

He might mean a dragon from the Muppet people. You know, a puppet.

Adora said, "If not a sleigh and reindeer, what will you use to get around on Christmas Eve—a jet? A train? The Space Shuttle?" The conversation had entered the realms of silliness, but she persisted valiantly. All this could be possible without making sense right away—like super-string theory.

Kris shook his head. "Now, now. That sounded very facetious—and we were making such progress.

Perhaps, if you're a good girl, I will take you to see my favorite means of travel. It is rather unusual, and has to be experienced to be believed."

He steepled his fingers and studied her from the depths of his chair, and Adora fought an urge to squirm as her employer's gaze probed her. It never failed; her nose began to itch anytime someone stared at her intently. Eyes watering and maddened by the unreachable itch, she almost didn't hear him when he added, "Of course, this tour will depend upon your heritage being what I think it is. I can't take the wrong sorts to this place."

"What? Are you . . . are you talking about my ethnicity?" she asked, feeling a sudden crushing disappointment. Was this man a bigot? Did he worry that she was a Jew or Hispanic, and he wouldn't be able to show her off to his WASP friends?

"No, I'm talking about whether you are descended from a human clan that is part fey."

"W-what? Fey?"

"Yes, fey—elves, faeries, pixies. Don't look so shocked. Surely you read through the folder."

"Yes, and most of it was written in a language I don't know."

"Oh." He looked surprised, then nodded, as if he should have realized. "Well, fey crossbreeds are quite common these days. And you have to know that many of the Scots and Irish have one foot in the land of the still folk. Personally, I suspect you're a MacLeod descendant—you have the look of the Viking raiders about you."

Adora felt her mouth tighten. Every time she thought she had him more or less safely stowed in the sane column, Kris said something crazy like this. She could feel a pressure headache building in her skull. But . . .

"My grandmother was a MacLeod. How did you—? Did you have me investigated?" she demanded. The idea was offensive, though she supposed it made sense, given that he was opening himself up to her, paying her a lot of money and trusting her with his secrets. He had a right to know if she was trustworthy.

"No, there was no need," he said. He leaned forward. "I read your books about Ninon and Byron, and that was recommendation enough. The rest is just a guess. But an informed guess. As I said, you have the look of the ancient MacLeods about you."

"You've read my books?" she asked, diverted. Very few people had.

"Of course. Did you think that I selected your name out of a hat? The books were excellent," he said enthusiastically. "You captured your subjects well. The portraits were uncanny. It was like seeing them alive again. Your empathy and ability to look into their souls, and to see the truth of them, is what convinced me you were right for this job."

"You . . . you *knew* them? Ninon de Lenclos and Byron?" He couldn't possibly have known them—that was just part of his fantasy construction—but she found herself awaiting his answer anyway.

"Of course." Kris got up and began to prowl. "But then, I know everyone. And they apparently think that they know me!" he complained. "At least, by sight. Who would have thought that those Coca-Cola Santa illustrations would be so popular? Do you know why they decided to use my image in the first place?" He was conversation-leaping again. Adora began to wonder if he might have Attention Deficit Disorder.

Among other problems, Joy suggested.

"Uh . . . no, actually. Why did they choose you?"

Adora wanted to ask why being a MacLeod made her a candidate for knowing his Christmas Eve travel secrets but knew Kris couldn't be pinned down when he didn't want. He was as slippery as an eel—a charming slippery eel, of course, but one that could still shock anyone foolish enough to get close.

"Back in the nineteen thirties, Coca-Cola was made to a different formulation," Kris explained.

"I heard about that," Adora interrupted, diverted as he had no doubt intended. "There was a rumor that Coke was made from coca leaves. You were supposed to add aspirin, and it would make you high."

"So I gather. Mind you, I've had to learn all this from research, since I was drugged out of my gourd and wandering the wastelands when it happened. Anyhow, advertising Coke to children was not allowed. So the company hired an artist called Haddon Sundblom—a smart man. Wish he was still alive, because I'd hire him myself. They had him come up with a campaign to make the drink more family friendly. I was his answer. Kids couldn't be shown drinking Coke, but they could be painted bringing soda to me. It was a brilliant bit of iconography. Later the laws changed, but the advertising campaign was such a success that they went on using me—*and that blasted red suit*—until the nineteen sixties."

"Are you angry about that?"

He sighed. "I wasn't thrilled at first. I hadn't tried Coke and was suspicious of its ingredients. Besides, they made me fat in those paintings! But I've lately found it an enjoyable beverage, so I won't kick too much—especially since I do drink it, and they were using an image that was mostly a construct and will shortly be replaced."

Adora raised her eyebrows. "You sound surprisingly cheerful and complacent about this identity hijacking. I mean, if nothing else, the whole red-suit-and-reindeer thing could be seen as your intellectual property. I would think that such merchandising would have you frothing at the mouth. Aren't they profaners of the holiday?" She herself had always thought so. Not that her family had celebrated Christmas with any regularity, but the rampant commercialism had always bothered her.

"Minor sin. It's all water under the bridge." He waved a careless hand. "And why not be cheerful? After all, *you're* beginning to believe in me—just a bit here and there," he pointed out happily. "Pretty soon you'll stop thinking of me as a schizophrenic and see me as a man."

His words made her blink. Had she been too obvious about distrusting his mental state?

Maybe he's reading your mind, Joy suggested.

Are you kidding?

I don't know.

"I may stop seeing you as schizophrenic, but I doubt you'll ever be *just a man*," Adora said, getting up and going to the window. Kris was making her restless. She couldn't get a handle on him. It was like herding a pack of cats; she wanted to tie him up and inject him with sodium pentothal so he'd sit still and answer any questions she asked.

At least you aren't swallowing his bullshit hook, line and sinker, Joy said.

"I gather from your agent's comments to Pennywyse that you greatly prize your privacy. He seems surprised you agreed to stay on. I'm pleased, of course," Kris announced to her back. Once again, he seemed more interested in hearing her story than telling his own. Normally Adora would enjoy such a novelty, but this situation was far, far from normal.

"'Good fences make good neighbors,'" she quoted glibly. "Not everyone likes the limelight."

"In some cases, you may be right," Kris answered quietly. "About the fences. Some races have never gotten the knack of playing together and should be separated until they have some spiritual growth spurts." Then he brightened, adding, "Fortunately for us, I play well with everyone. I truly think you'll be happy here when you stop fighting reason and accept who we are and what we're doing."

That was the second time he had said that—*we*. She didn't know how to answer him.

"Um, speaking of other races," she said, glancing out the crack in the curtains and looking down in astonishment at the suddenly thronging Rodeo Drive. The day was beginning to change colors with the sunset, and everything was colored by soft rose light. That was unusual enough, but the creatures so backlit were truly unique. "Kris? Did you know that there are a number of naked greenish people running through the street—and that many of them have more arms than they should?"

"Those would be goblins going through species reassignment," he replied calmly.

"Species reassignment? Are you kidding?" She turned to look at him.

"In L.A., it's popular to look human—you get more work in film and television. Many other hives do it as well, at least the ones that want human tourism. Goblins in those hives have to make a choice: If they want to live aboveground and interact with humans, they have to have surgery. It's understandable, but what a shame. I mean, what an awful message to send to your people. Bad enough that humans are convinced the height of beauty is an anorexic fourteen-year-old girl, or a barely pubescent boy who is nearly androgynous and likely hooked on heroin. Now they've got the lutins striving for the look too!" He sighed. "Anyhow, this is their last swarm as unmutilated goblins."

"I see." Adora stared, both fascinated and repelled. Their four arms made the goblins look a bit insectlike. "But . . . why are they naked?"

"Well, you've heard of the running of the bulls in Spain, which is used as a rite to prove your courage?"

"Yes, but that's in Pamplona. And last I heard, the runners are clothed in that event."

Kris laughed. "Well, this is southern California. And it's the running of the trolls, who are also naked. You may notice some humans down there as well. It's a popular cross-species event, beloved by modern Los Angelinos. It isn't my cup of tea, but I can't completely condemn anything promoting interspecies bonding."

"Looks like a sport for drunks, fools and suicides. Good heavens! What's that? A troll? But it's *huge*. How can anything be that big and walk on two legs?"

"It takes all kinds," Kris said, finally moving to the window and twitching the drapes aside. Adora could smell his scent, the damp green of an ancient forest with a touch of bonfire. It was the kind of smell that made her want to bury her face in his neck and breathe deeply. "Yes, that is a troll—a young one. They don't let the adults out in public anymore. There's a limit to how much aboveground mayhem the city government will tolerate—and be-

lieve me, a troll frenzy is as much mayhem as anyone can handle."

"I see." Adora took herself away from the temptation of her employer's cologne and went back to the
table. But once there, she found herself disinclined
to sit down. She had definitely picked up some of
his nervous energy. She began to pace. "Where were
we?" She glanced at her notebook. "Oh, right. You
are rumored to have a naughty-and-nice list. What
exactly do you have to do to get on the naughty list?
Does it have to be a capital crime? Or was Grandma
right—will a messy bedroom and dirt behind the
ears get you there?"

"Sin," Kris answered, startling her. She turned to
look at him. His craggy face was as serious as she
had seen it. "*Sin* gets you on the naughty list."

"You believe in sin? Even if you aren't a saint or a
Christian?" she asked, trying to hide her surprise.
And annoyance. She just couldn't get this guy
pegged, and it was making her crazy. Well, something was.

"Yes. However, unlike many religious types, I believe that there is no sin except one—or perhaps
that all sins are the same one."

"Explain, please. You can't mean original sin.
That would be too unoriginal."

Kris smiled a little at her joke. "Each of us has
something special within us—let's call it Divinity.
We are born touched by this Grace—by *Gaia*, which
is the old name for this Divine Love. It tells us what
is right and what is wrong. It is what feels compassion and lets us love other people. To deny this grace,
this voice, which is in all living things, *that* is sin.

"You have asked who is on the naughty list. At
the very top are the hollow men: they who dress up

in the Season's holy robes but spread emptiness instead of cheer. They who do not believe in love, but only in money and power and fear. I know that some act in ignorance, and because they have never known the true light. But whether done out of ignorance or malice, they must be stopped before they ruin other souls with their bleak vision. There will never be peace on earth as long as our leaders have fear and greed in their hearts."

Kris's voice was firm, almost grim. Adora swallowed.

"These hollow men—don't you mean the merchandisers as well as the politicians? The ones who have taken your image and used it to sell things? While you are fairly tolerant, you can't actually approve of the modern idea that you have to buy Christmas at a store."

Kris sighed. "It is the brains behind the merchandisers—as well as behind other things—that I despise. *They* are the puppet masters. Many have profaned the holiday, or tried to kill it altogether. The vendors themselves are simply parasites come to feast on a sickening body. But we ailed long before this. In fact, it all started once Constantine entered the picture. It was then that the old religions fell hard, and they are slow getting back up."

"So Constantine along with—oh, let's say that puritan Cromwell—would be on the naughty list?"

"Oh, definitely—when they were alive. Especially Cromwell. Christmas has rarely had a greater enemy." Kris shook his head, looking thoughtful. "I think he grew up mean because he was so very ugly in an unforgiving society. There is a saying about that."

" 'Beauty is only skin deep, but ugly is to the bone?' " Adora suggested.

"Something like that—except in Latin, and it referenced the soul and not the skeleton."

Adora nodded. "What happens to those on the naughty list?" she asked, morbid curiosity getting the better of her. "Do they get coal in their stockings?"

"That depends. Often I am especially kind to the errant person's spouse and children." Kris grinned. "Winning their kids' love and devotion usually pisses them off."

"Hm. Devious, but I like it." Adora scribbled down notes. She could use this. It made Kris seem clever and clearly nonviolent. That was good in a kook. "So, going back the capitalistic beat of Christmas in modern America. You said in your notes that you encouraged Washington Irving and Dickens to write about the giving of earthly things—of commerce, really. Isn't some of this your fault?"

Kris gave her a piercing look. "I will assume you are playing devil's advocate and aren't really blind to the difference between charitable giving and conspicuous consumption that does nothing but fatten the body and deplete one's coffers. Speaking of the Devil, have I told you how I won the services of Black Peter in Holland?" His conversation, which reminded Adora of a hard-thrown Superball, bounced on to the next topic. He needed Ritalin. "No? Well, another day. But as for the misguided people trying to find Christmas at the mall—don't blame that on me. At no point did I tell the masses to go and worship at the House of Nike or the Gap—though I like their clothes well enough. Damn, I don't want to sound like I'm condemning them."

Adora leaned over and wrote down both names and then: *possible endorsements?*

"And I have never said: Have a merry Christmas,

and now go forth and buy presents you can't afford for people you secretly despise—though giving to our enemies can be a valuable lesson." Kris shook his head. "And Goddess be my witness—I never told anyone to make fruitcake, let alone inflict it on their family and friends annually."

Adora bit back a smile. Kris saw—he always saw—and his face relaxed. His eerie blue eyes began to twinkle. Adora sat down again. She turned the page in her notebook.

"I'll tell you something that sounds funny after that speech," Kris confided. "You actually *can* find Christmas at the mall. You can find it anywhere if you look with the heart. It's just that you can't *buy* it. Some things, like love, are not for sale."

"Any other dark confessions or trade secrets?" Adora asked, leaning forward. She looked intently at his shadowed face. The sun was nearly gone, but Kris hadn't turned on any lights. Perhaps it was easier to share secrets—and believe them—if the room wasn't too brightly lit.

"Just one." He also leaned forward. There came the spark of electricity that only happened when two people recognized the potential attraction between them. Kris blinked once, then said in a hushed voice, "Please don't tell a soul, but I like some fruitcake. Missus Etta Dixon used to bake one for me when I came through Savannah. It was stupendous. But I can't encourage consumption by the masses. Like fireworks, fruitcakes should be left in the hands of those who are trained to make them."

Adora became aware that she was watching Kris smile with a little too much fascination, and she forced herself to lean back, providing a professional distance.

"I'll never tell a soul—cross my heart and hope to

die. What happened to the reindeer, anyway?" she asked, changing the subject, half-hoping to trip him up or find a hole in his story. But she was only half-hoping; she didn't really want to find out that he was a con man looking for some way to make a buck or influence the more gullible segments of the population. Of course, that left insanity as his motivator, didn't it? Which wasn't a great option either. Adora sighed. She had to hope for some acceptable undiscovered motivation to surface. "There *were* flying reindeer, weren't there? That wasn't all made up?"

"Yes. I had to give up the horses when I moved to Finland. That was after my gig in Asia Minor. Sadly, some of these reindeer became venison steaks."

Adora was shocked at his words, and also annoyed with herself for feeling shock. After all, none of this was real.

"You ate Vixen?" she couldn't help asking.

"Don't be ridiculous," Kris replied. "The *goblins* ate them, after they fed me their filthy drug and left me to die. They didn't get Vixen, though. Clever girl, she got away."

Adora hurriedly changed the subject. She still wasn't ready to hear about bad goblins. The good ones running naked through the street were weird enough.

"Was the now-lamented red suit your idea?" she asked.

Kris shook his head.

"Not entirely. Clement Moore advised it. It was a nice blend of the red of Saint Nicholas and the fur robe of the pagan shaman. A bit flashy for my tastes, but even then I understood the power of the right icon when it came to capturing human imagination. And we needed a powerful icon." Kris shook his head. "Since Cromwell and his Puritans had done such an excellent job of wiping out the few Celebrants who survived the Inquisition—he killed some thirty thousand 'witches' and drove the rest into deep hiding—it was necessary to revive the old symbols here in the New World. Thankfully, ancestral memory supplied a spiritual understanding for those who were descended of the Celebrants. I could sense the reawakening in the land, and it encouraged me when the task of reinventing Christmas looked too daunting."

"Celebrants? You've used that word twice. What does it mean? The Puritans weren't Celebrants?"

"No, poor creatures. They couldn't celebrate. They didn't know it, but they were terribly impoverished, spiritually speaking. As for understanding what a Celebrant is, I'll give you some of the fey holy texts—the Fey Bioball Na Sidhe—to read. Basically, Celebrants were those humans—mainly what you would call pagans, though some Christians were also of this ilk—who saw Divinity in the natural world all around them, who knew joy every day, with or without prayer. Celebrants don't have a coherent religion really. For them, God is everything. This tends to annoy more organized religions."

"God is everywhere," she said, recalling her brief Sunday school teachings.

"Precisely. Now, Worshippers are men and women who strayed from the old relationship with Nature, and who now require enforced worship—what we might term the magical ceremony of a church, and the prayers of a middleman, a priest, to get outside of themselves long enough to connect with their Creator. It's sad that it happened, but not unexpected. Worshippers have always been organized souls, and it was natural that they should evolve their religion indoors and make it tidy and clean." Kris spread his hands. "The trouble really began when they locked their idea of God into a house of prayer, as though fearing that thieves might steal their Deity when their backs were turned. But out of sight, out of mind—and they often forgot him anytime they weren't inside their portals. I say *Him* because the Worshippers also forgot that Divinity is both male and female. They created idols too, and some arrogantly gave Divinity human shape—male human shape. Frankly, I found the Worshippers' insistence on a human-looking male god annoying, because it is so exclusionary of other races. I nearly gave up on them more than once. But that estrangement ended with the coming of the Son."

"The Son? You mean Jesus?" Adora gulped. "You personally knew the Christ? The Messiah—the Lamb of God?" This was much, much worse than saying he wasn't Christian. This was out and out blasphemy. You weren't supposed to lie about Jesus, even if you were nuts.

Kris's face softened and his eyes lost their intense inner focus.

"Yes. The Son changed my mind. I learned from Him that pure Divinity *can* be made human. It's a pity that humans have managed to muck His message up in the intervening years." Kris leaned forward, his eyes focusing again. His gaze could be felt as clearly as a touch. "But, again, the story of our meeting is a tale for another day. There's no point in telling you about it when you don't yet accept my story as truth."

Adora tried to regroup, but she was shaken by his sincerity. A part of her was even beginning to believe Kris's yarn, in spite of her inner warnings that it couldn't in any way, shape or form be true. It just couldn't.

But what if it was?

"Talk of religion makes you uncomfortable, doesn't it? And magic as well?"

"Yes," she admitted. "Both seem like a lot of hocus pocus: Let's fool the people while we rob them blind."

He nodded, but in understanding, not agreement.

"How old are you?" she asked suddenly.

Kris tilted his head, considering. "I'm not certain. In the beginning, we did not reckon time as we do now. I think, in human years, I first came into the world about ten thousand winters ago."

"T-ten thousand winters?" Her brain stuttered too. This was too much of a fantasy, even for a craz—eccentric—man. She flopped back hard in her chair and scrubbed her face. Kris wanted her to believe, and she wanted to believe. But she couldn't. And now her headache was getting worse. Her thoughts were too large and crammed into too small a space.

"Yes, that would be about right. Of course, my presence in human affairs was not documented until the Christians decided that I should be made a saint. Then I started turning up regularly in religious art. It was rather nice. In those paintings—unlike the ones in the caves—I always had clothes on. They occasionally even painted me with women. It was a pleasant change to have a feminine presence for company."

Adora shook her head. This was impossible. Just . . . impossible. She could never put this stuff in a book. What the hell was she going to do?

"Are you all right?" Kris asked. "You look very tense. Would you like to try a Goblintini? Pennywyse says they're very good. They're made with vodka and strawberry juice."

"No, thank you. Vodka and I don't get along. I'm not much of a drinker, really. No one in my family was. None of us could hold our liquor." There she went again—telling Kris things he didn't need to know. What was wrong with her? She was such a mess! What had made her think that she could do this job?

Kris stared, as though her statement were somehow significant. Another time she might have asked what he was thinking, but she was determined in that moment to follow at least one thread of Kris's story all the way to the end. It was annoying that she was getting tired and her brain had all but locked up.

"Uh, where were we? Feminine presence ... Okay, let's talk about women. In all your wandering, through all these years, you never met Miss Right?" Adora was trying for something light and normal to talk about, since the subject of his nudity was almost as disturbing as his proclaimed age, or his assertion that he had known Jesus. "I mean, I always heard there was a Mrs. Claus in the background, baking cookies."

Kris shook his head. "Actually, I met a few candidates, but it would have been wrong to ask any woman—human or fey—to share my vagabond existence. It was a form of exile, you see. And I never stayed in one place for very long; there was always some new fire that needed putting out, some new outbreak of despair, or an attempt to crush the human spirit. And then there was the whole sacrifice thing." Kris's silvered eyes focused on her, first her lips and then her eyes. Adora's pulse began to hammer. The scrutiny was both thrilling and scary. "Sacrifice thing?" she managed to say. "How much sacrifice?"

"As much as anyone can give," he said. "But things are different now. That era is done. The fey are at the very edge of extinction. We must all do what we can to ensure survival. When the spirit next lists in a lady's direction, I shall follow—if I am able."

"So . . . you see marriage in your future?" Adora asked. Her voice nearly squeaked, and she noticed her heart was beating heavily.

Kris smiled, his eyes dancing merrily in the gloom. She could almost swear they glowed.

"How very alarmed you look at the idea, my dear. I assure you, I am not all that frightening. Indeed, many people have no fear of me at all. In fact, in the under-six crowd, I am still very much beloved and known for benevolence."

"More fools, they. You're about as harmless as a heart attack," Adora muttered, ducking her head to escape his scrutiny. Scribbling nonsense in her notebook, she said, "This would be a big change for you, becoming a family man."

"Yes, but change is good. Stubbornly continuing in your daily rut is like digging your own grave. I mean that metaphorically, of course," Kris added in what should have been a soothing voice but that stroked her nerves and made them tingle. And: "Don't let that death fey stuff you've read about bother you. I turned from that path long ago. Anyway, the whole wife matter is one for the future. I don't propose to worry about it now. Worry is negative meditation, you see. Concentrate on the bad long enough, and you can make every dark concern come true."

Death fey stuff? She must have missed that. She couldn't be certain, but she was willing to bet that anything that had the word "death" in it wasn't something she—or readers—wanted to know about Santa. He was clearly a kook. And that was a damn shame, because this was the best-looking man she had ever seen. She was really attracted to him.

What?

Where the hell were these thoughts coming from? Adora rubbed her forehead. She was definitely getting one of her bad headaches, and it served her right. She could not—*could not*—be attracted to Kris Kringle. Because that would lead nowhere. And even if she was attracted, she could never let him know that. No way, no how.

Maybe she had jet lag.

"Kris? You call yourself 'fey.' But you mean that in the sense of being an elf or a pixie, not in being precognizant or psychic." Abandoning subtlety, she added desperately, "No bullshit now. Tell the truth. You really and truly believe that you are . . . ?"

"An elf? No. Humans got that wrong." Adora had no time to sigh with relief, for he added, "But I am a bit what you would call psychic, and of the magical persuasion. It's just that I come from the other side of magic. It's understandable that they got it mixed up—death feys and elves look a lot alike. Both races are always very attractive. For death feys, perhaps it's a sort of consolation prize." Kris looked at her pale face, then did some subject changing of his own. He asked lightly, "Have you been a good girl this year? I'm obliged to ask, you know. I'm making my Christmas list."

"Can't you look into your magic ball and tell?" Adora asked grumpily. She began hunting in her bag for aspirin. Sometimes, if she took them early enough, she didn't have to resort to the other prescription her doctor had given her. She probably had a few tablets left, if she really needed them.

"No. Don't do that." Kris shook his head. He reached out suddenly and pressed his finger against her forehead. Adora froze as a gentle warmth traveled through her skull and down her neck, unknotting muscles and sluicing away the pain in small, undulating strokes. Her head seemed to expand and suddenly there was room for all her thoughts and feelings.

She sighed with pleasure, letting her arms go limp. The pen dropped from her fingers and her purse slid to the floor. "How did you do that? What did you do?" she asked slowly.

He ran a finger along her brow, down her temple and across her cheekbones. His finger paused on the bridge of her nose. And, "I'm a healer," he said simply. Then: "Do you believe that, Adora? That in spite of being a death fey, I can heal with touch?"

"I . . . yes. I guess I have to." And, at that moment at least, she did. It was a compulsion she couldn't resist. And her senses did not lie; the pain in her head was gone, wiped out with a stroke of his fingers.

"It's odd the fairy tales you choose to accept as true," he said matter-of-factly, dropping his hand. He got up and went to the wall to flip a switch. The room assumed a normal brightness. "To answer your comment about the crystal ball, I don't 'see you when you're sleeping'—not unless I'm there with you. But I can listen in on dreams and prayers. If you want me to. Though a millennium and a half has passed, I still remember how to hear prayers. They're usually in Turkish these days. A person has to ask, though. It got a bit unnerving, having all those voices in my skull, let me tell you, so I don't keep the ears open unless asked. . . ." He looked into her eyes. "Do you want to ask me to do this for you? I can. And it might put a lot of your doubts to rest if you knew I could see into your mind."

Don't let him! Joy's voice was fearful.

Adora shook her head: partly refusal, and partly to clear the confusing thoughts he wanted her to jettison. She closed her notebook, which appeared to list her growing acceptance of his wild assertions, as if that action would somehow contain the craziness of her thoughts. And it was crazy to be writing this story at all, assuming she ever found a place to begin. No one else who was sane was going to believe a word. She would be thought a prankster or—worse yet—a fraud. They'd say she was a kook.

"No thanks, Kris. I've never been into the Big Brother thing. I'd prefer to do it the old-fashioned way—you know, drink too much one night and then spill my guts before I pass out. Anyway, there's no need for you to see all my flaws at once," she said. Then she realized that she meant what she was saying, that at some point she'd been ferried across the river of utter disbelief and deposited on the foreign shore of partial acceptance. She wasn't convinced of everything yet—that would require a lot of mental island hopping—but she had suspended her complete disbelief. For a while anyway. After all, at the very least, Kris was some kind of a healer, and he seemed to believe what he was saying. He wasn't a complete charlatan. And there were more things in heaven and earth and all that. Maybe he *was* psychic. Maybe he *had* been Saint Nicholas in another life.

"So, have you been good?" Kris asked again. "Should I leave something nice in your stocking?"

"This year?" Adora's brow wrinkled. She impulsively decided to be truthful. Maybe her honesty and linear storytelling would set an example. "Well, mostly, I think. I had a bad moment last February," she admitted, though the memory was still humiliating. "I was dating this guy and he turned out to be a cheater. I'm afraid I didn't take the news well."

"A cheater? Do you mean that he did not play fair in games of sport?" Kris asked.

Adora tried to think of an explanation of Derek that wouldn't be too vulgar. Mentally she discarded the words *rat bastard* and *slut*. It had taken her an embarrassingly long while to realize the truth about him: Derek's soul didn't match the angelic packaging. His conscience—assuming he ever had one—had atrophied, and he had turned into one of those men who believed in the survival of the fittest, and who were not encumbered by any antiquated notions of chivalry or fidelity. It had taken her too long to realize that he was always on the lookout for number one, and that she had never been anything more than a distant third.

It had been stupid to fall for him so quickly. The relationship had started—when? It was when she had gotten desperate and refinanced her home—and it had been over before the loan was approved. She was an idiot sometimes. She got in a relationship and her IQ dropped to the level of the speed limit in a hospital parking lot. That's what love did to some people.

Adora felt something move through her head, a gentle breeze that cooled her sudden anger. Grateful, she sighed.

"You might say that Derek didn't play fair. I certainly think he sees relationships as sport. But he didn't cheat at chess or volleyball, he—ah—betrayed me with another woman and an S-and-M porn site. I wouldn't have minded the latter so much, but he used my computer and let it catch a nasty virus. I have spam filters and a firewall, but really—there is just no such thing as safe sex these days." Her tone was joking, but her mood was not. The affair had left her . . . diminished. And she'd had to replace her hard drive, which had been expensive.

"I see." Kris nodded once. "It's sad, but some men are simply Janus-faced. It's a common human failing. They can kiss two women at once, loving neither."

"Well, Derek was two-faced *and* fork-tongued. What a liar. He denied the affair even after I confronted him with witnesses. . . . Not that I needed them. It got so that I could smell her on him."

"You have a keen sense of smell?" Kris asked.

"I guess, but her perfume was like a force field. I think she was deliberately marking territory with it."

"Ah—perhaps. Indirection can be popular in these matters," he said obscurely.

Adora retrieved her pen, giving herself a moment to put her poker face back on.

"I think what offends me most is that he thought I'd be stupid enough to believe him because he was so handsome and wealthy. Of course, I should have seen trouble coming long before that. He'd begun using the same tone of voice with me that he used on his dog." Adora knew she sounded outraged, but she couldn't help it.

Kris coughed into his fist, and she knew he was laughing.

"He spoke to you like a dog?" he asked.

"Yes. You wouldn't think it, in this day and age, but some foolish people actually believe that old saw about blondes being dumb and of easy virtue. There are some people who even think that women should be grateful for male guidance to keep them from straining their brains. But I am not anyone's pet. And since I don't actually have four legs, or bark at cars—*or men*—I really felt it would be best if I went on thinking for myself." She exhaled, releasing her anger. "He didn't react well to the it's-her-or-me ultimatum."

"Your views came as a surprise to this man?" Kris guessed.

"Oddly enough, yes."

"How did you ultimately prove his betrayal?" her employer asked curiously. "You did, didn't you? I can't see you walking away without some vindication."

"You're right. I set out to catch him," Adora admitted. "It wasn't hard. I started with an intuition that he'd lied about what he was doing for Valentine's Day. Once I caught the bad vibes, I went looking. Proof wasn't hard to find. He was as faithful to his schedule—if I can use the word *faithful* in conjunction with this man—as an atomic clock. And he had no sense of discretion. The bimbo got lunches at the same restaurants where we ate dinner on Monday and Thursday nights." Adora cocked her head as she added, "You know, I understand why he was attracted to her. She *is* better arm candy than I am. I think Derek only kept me around because of his work. He needed a female companion with an IQ greater than her bust size to show off to the boss."

"Bimbo? This word is not familiar," Kris said.

"It means to have a low IQ and lower necklines. I have a theory about them. I think maybe it happens when women diet too much. They kill their brains with protein deprivation. Or maybe they get the wrong things lipo'ed. Think about it: You go to have fat sucked out of your neck, and oops—there goes the brain! And if it was itty-bitty to start with. . . "

"Hm. What did you see in him?" Kris asked, plainly curious. "There must have been something besides an attractive face."

Adora found herself answering with a degree of truthfulness she hadn't realized she possessed.

"I was attracted intellectually. And he was polite, knew how to wear a tux. He also associated with the kinds of people who could help me with my research. Old money cherishes its secrets, you know. The only way into their vaults is with an escort of their class." Adora exhaled and admitted, "I was also needy enough that I wanted to believe he cared about me. I . . . I had just lost someone important to me the year before, and I was feeling very alone. That's not a good excuse for being stupid, though, and I knew it at the time. I just couldn't stop myself."

Yet another reason why she had given up those damn pills. They affected her judgment. They made her stupid.

"You're not stupid. And your indignation and hurt is understandable," Kris said gently. "No one likes to lose, and certain failures are more difficult than others. Lost loves—even the lost chance of love—can cast long shadows over our hearts." His words, though kind, touched a sore spot. So Adora was grateful when his tone turned brisk. "You still look very angry even after all this time. Did this incident lead to bloodshed? Am I harboring a violent fugitive?"

His words were playful, and Adora found herself beginning to smile. Somehow, Kris made her feel absolved for her stupidity and weakness. Maybe Catholics had something there, about confession being good for the soul.

"No blood was spilt, but I'm betting he would have preferred that to what happened. Derek hated being made ridiculous. I mean, publicly."

"What did you do?"

"Well . . . this guy was big on cleanliness, and he kept a cabinet full of those blue toilet bowl–cleaner tablets. I'm afraid that they somehow all ended up in his hot tub—which worked out rather better than expected," she added cheerfully, refusing to feel repentant for her vengeance. "All I'd hoped for was making a mess of his favorite seduction spot, but it turned out he had his floozy over and they decided to go for a midnight dip. They were both drunk—or so the neighbors tell me—and didn't bother turning on the outdoor lights. They boiled out there for a while before noticing things smelled funny. He finally turned on the lights, and all was revealed—to everyone on the block! She started screaming when she saw her hair—she was also a blonde—and that brought everyone running. The two of them ended up a lovely shade of blue that lasted for almost a week. It put an end to the jerk's denials that he never knew the blue floozy!"

Kris's lips twitched. "But you regret doing this now?"

"Not really," Adora answered. "Though I suppose it was a waste of perfectly good toilet cleaner."

Kris shook his head, but his eyes twinkled.

"You know, I think maybe we should go to Reno," Adora said suddenly.

"Why?" Kris looked startled.

"Well, anyone with my love life would have to be lucky at cards."

Kris laughed aloud, and Adora found herself tingling with pleasure.

"You could be my backer," Adora elaborated. "We'd split the profits fifty-fifty and make a killing."

"I am backing you," Kris pointed out. "Just not at the card tables."

"Hmph. Okay—enough about me and my stupidity and horrible love life," she said firmly. "It's your turn again. Tell me something fun about being Santa Claus. Everything we've talked about so far has been grim. Wasn't anything enjoyable or nice? Tell me something good about being you."

Kris considered.

"Hm . . . let's see. Ironically, considering the image, I have a wonderful metabolism and can eat as much as I want without getting fat. By the way, would you like some brandy?" he asked. "Or chocolate mousse?"

"If you're having some," Adora agreed, surprisingly herself again. "Brandy, I mean. And just a small one. Like I said, I'm not much of a drinker."

"Please, let me pour you a glass. I very rarely drink either, because I have very little tolerance for alcohol. It's a family trait too." Not waiting for her to comment, he went to the sideboard and poured her a small glass. "Pennywyse tells me that this is exquisite. Being part goblin, he can drink. In fact, he can drink *a lot*. He metabolizes very well, too."

Pennywyse was part goblin. That seemed strange to Adora. Why would Kris hire a goblin if goblins had tried to kill him? In fact, what was he doing in this goblin city? None of it made any sense to her.

So what's new? Joy asked, piping up for the first time in several minutes.

"Thank you," Adora said, taking a sip. The brandy was delicious, smooth and warm. She relaxed in her chair. "So, tell me something else about yourself—

something about your time in early America." Something fairly recent and slightly more believable, was what she meant.

"I love America, as you must know. I chose it as my home. And as you read, my first organized PR campaign was headed up by the literary trinity of Washington Irving, Charles Dickens and Clement Moore. Things were going great—for the literate masses. But I knew we needed something for those who couldn't read. That's when I contacted Thomas Nast. Unfortunately, we never had the chance to speak in person before I was shanghaied, and his earliest illustrations showed me as a doll-sized elf."

"So, how was all this playing out with your home-boys?" Adora asked. At his blank look, she rephrased. "Did the rest of the fey—your family and friends—understand what you were doing, and did they approve? It seems to me that most of them were keeping a low profile. Here in America, we never heard anything about faery mounds and the like—all that stuff in that folder. Even in Scotland and Ireland, people don't seem to talk about such legends anymore."

"Most fey understood to different degrees. Fortunately, things moved more slowly in those days, before mass communication. Finvarra thought of me and my campaign as great public relations for the Seelie. I think he might have been persuaded to eventually go public himself—"

"Finvarra?" Adora asked.

"King of the Seelie Court—the good faeries, you might say. But Mabigon—queen of the Unseelie—simply couldn't stand what I was doing. She saw it as degrading of a superior race to pander to human stereotypes and to do things to please them. She really was a bigot where humans were concerned. Angry with my growing popularity, she went to the goblins and made a deal. Too bad she didn't live to enjoy it, poor hate-filled creature. . . . Anyhow, the goblins did their part and I got 'disappeared,' as they say. And goblins and human merchandisers have been running Christmas ever since."

"And you aren't angry about this?" she asked again. "I'd think you'd be ready to crack some skulls." Adora added, "I would."

Kris shook his head.

"Anger is a waste of time, and I have never turned to violence to solve my problems. However, that doesn't mean I'll turn a blind eye to what has happened. I have every intention of balancing the scales of this gross injustice. I will not let all my work to bring peace to the divided tribes of Man and lutins go to waste because millennium-old prejudices have again reared their ugly heads." Adora didn't know how it could be that a man who supposedly disavowed violence could still look so ruthless and just a little scary, but he did. "It's a tricky business, though. It can be a bit of a hydra—chop off one head and two grow in its place. We can't strike at the mind, for prejudice has none. This is all about the heart." This last was said to himself.

"So, this Mabigon—she was a faerie queen? She's dead too? Was she ever in the United States?" Adora asked.

"Sometimes. She . . . traveled. We all like to travel."

Adora swallowed more brandy. "We? You mean the fey?" She kept coming back to this.

"Yes."

"So, you are fey," she repeated. "All fey. Not part

99

goblin, not part human, a hundred percent, grade-A, USDA fey."

He chuckled. "The United States government has not given me a stamp of authenticity, but essentially you are correct. I am all fey."

Adora sighed. He certainly looked human to her—except for his unusual beauty. That, she had to admit, was almost supernatural.

Oh, please. Didn't you learn anything from Derek? Joy asked.

Yes, and she didn't want to go there. Especially not when she'd been drinking.

"I've been doing some research online. Did you know that there are more churches along the coast of England dedicated to Saint Nicholas than to Saint George—the patron saint of England?" she asked when she realized that she had been staring again. She hoped he would think she'd been thinking deep thoughts and not ogling.

"It was the sailors," Kris said. "And the traveling merchants. They had great faith that Nicholas would protect them. It was a holdover from an earlier religious cult." He poured her a second glass of brandy.

"And did you?" Adora posed the question both because as a responsible, thorough biographer she had to, but also because she was curious about what he would say. Something wild, probably—something she couldn't use in her book or even believe, but that she still wanted to hear.

There were disadvantages to being a rationalist in the world of the . . . not insane—he was her employer now, so she couldn't use that word. It was gone, exiled from her vocabulary for the duration. She could use the word "contradictory" though. And "imaginative." And "illogical."

You had it right the first time. He's insane, Joy

carped, feeling chatty under the influence of the brandy. *There are no such thing as faeries. You need to believe this.*

Oh, go back to sleep, she replied. *He isn't insane. He's . . . colorful. And he's paying the bills. Show some respect. Anyway, who says there aren't faeries? Those old legends often have some basis in reality.*

Her inner voice actually snorted. *Then why hasn't anyone ever seen one?*

"I protected them as best I could," Kris spoke up finally. It was almost as though he knew she was engaged in inner debate and had chosen to wait politely for her to finish before interrupting.

Adora said, "You must have led an adventure-packed life. I think maybe I envy you a little. I have always been a bit . . . cautious." Cautious in mind, body and spirit. As the child of neglectful daredevils, she'd had too many close-calls in her youth. Also, it was probably because her childhood crises and triumphs had been left for her alone to explore that she hadn't learned how to take on the wider world with any degree of confidence.

"Hmph. Don't bother being envious," Kris said. "You know, adventuring often means going short on sleep—and lunches. You meet dangerous people and have your life threatened daily. I have decided that adventures are more fun in theory than in practice. It's time to settle down."

Adora couldn't have agreed more, and she looked on Kris with fresh benevolence.

He asked suddenly, "So, how will you begin my tale?"

"Um . . . '*Long ago and far, far away in a foreign land . . . ?*'" Adora suggested.

Kris shook his head.

"This isn't a child's story."

"But it is a fairy tale," Adora pointed out with a smile. "If you are fey."

He shook his head, ignoring her joke. "Not really. It's a human tale. My species doesn't matter—I'm just an agent of change. This is the story of a journey through humanity's ages, and the lessons that were lost."

Species. That took care of her smile. She was beginning to really hate that word. Her alcoholic glow began to fade. Her headache would likely return.

"Well, if you want to be serious . . . This is a tough one, Kris. Readers have expectations. You see, you— as Saint Nicholas, Santa Claus, Kris Kringle, or whoever—are going to be identified with Christmas as we know it. You are Christmas and Christmas is you. And that's assuming anyone reads this book— which is far from a given. Your publisher may take one look and deep-six the whole project." A wide audience was, in fact, damn near an impossibility given her recent sales. She wasn't quite relaxed enough to say that, though. "The trouble is that Christmas in many other people's minds is about Christ, and I'd really hate to go there first thing in the story. If we make it a religious issue, your beliefs are going to upset a lot of people."

"Why not begin at the beginning?" Kris suggested. "We'll have a nice long time to work up to the birth of Christ, and maybe people will be ready by then."

Write about life ten thousand years ago? Adora shook her head slowly. Talk about a saga. This epic tale would be so long that it disappeared over the horizon. She couldn't think about it just then; the task was too daunting.

"I can't begin at the beginning because I don't know where that is. So far, our interview is all over the map," she pointed out. "I don't have anything to grab hold of. You know that story about the three blind men who are sent to examine the elephant?"

Kris nodded and said, "And you don't believe me yet, so you can't write anything with conviction. I understand. I am also patient."

"I'm trying to believe. I *want* to believe," she added, and found it was true.

"Fair enough. That's all I can ask." Kris nodded. "Very well, it seems we need to make a clear distinction between me and the holiday as people know it. Perhaps the book should include some photographs of me in a Hawaiian shirt. I could play tennis or something."

"It couldn't hurt," Adora admitted. Regardless of other considerations, he really was spectacular to look at. The camera would love him.

"I think the second thing we need to convey is that many elements making up the Christmas celebration of today are thousands of years older," Kris went on. "The Nativity is Christ's, but His birth did not begin the holiday, as such. Perhaps we should give our holiday, the older holiday, the other spelling—x-m-a-s. That might avoid confusion about which event we are speaking of."

"You make it sound like He was . . ." Adora hesitated. "The halftime show. How can you say that if you were a follower?"

"Because, in a sense, He was. At least, in terms of this winter holiday. He was just one more element of the broader celebration. Christmas then and today is an amalgamation of many ideas and beliefs, and 'Santa Claus' is himself a polyglot of characters and legends from many human cultures. He's a jumble of emotional truths, hopes and aspirations. Santa isn't . . . The Santa people think they know isn't real. He never existed. It was probably a mistake to build the image so thoroughly. I should have found another way to make humans understand the importance of generosity and charity."

"But *you're* Santa," Adora said. She was slightly confused. "You were there with the reindeer and the red suit delivering presents. How can you say that wasn't real?"

"Yes, I am Santa" he admitted. "But again, I stress the fact that Santa as you know him is an advertiser's invention, created when I was missing. What I am is . . . different." He sighed. "Yes, I was that third-century bishop in Asia Minor. But I've had other incarnations. I was known to the German peoples as Wodin, and to the Celts and Picts as the Green Man. I had even older names." He picked up a lighter and began lighting the candles on the table, though the room didn't need any more illumination. "Through the millennia before Christ, I was a chanticleer and healer and wise man. And just as I have been many people, so too has this winter celebration been many holidays and been known by many names—a holiday beloved of Mesopotamians, Babylonians, Greeks, Romans, Norse and Celts. I want the world to see that Xmas and I are living things, not just historic events that are too old to have meaning. Nor does the joy belong to one religion. It continues to charge and adapt. Xmas is *alive.*"

Kris went to the wall and turned off the lights, leaving only glows from the fireplace and candles. Then he made another of his abrupt conversational shifts. "Did you know that there was actually a fourth Magi who never got mentioned in the Bible? He came not from the East but from the ice-covered North—a bit later than the others—and instead of frankincense, gold or myrrh, he brought with him a sacred tree, a blessing and an invitation to a foreign land. What a pity that it was a perverted form of the Son's word that finally traveled north. I should have carried the message, myself, but I was . . . delayed by Herod."

"*You* were the fourth Magi?" She heard no skepticism in her voice, which surprised her. Was that good or bad? Did she believe him just a little?

It's the brandy. You know you shouldn't drink, Joy said.

Adora nodded. She very rarely drank for a reason. She should put off any decisions or deep thoughts until tomorrow.

"Yes," Kris went on, though by now Adora had mostly lost the thread of the conversation. "And what I saw so amazed me that for a time I tried working with the organization He left behind. Sadly, without its head the body ran amok, pulled one way by Peter and another by Paul. The Church divided, became a many-headed hydra biting at itself. I could soon see that, like all other nations and kings, it was turning into a power that pursued wealth and influence instead of enlightenment and happiness. And like all political princes, the Worshippers who ruled came to believe that the ends justified the means. Of course, this has failed in the wider world. It always fails. I don't know why Men never learn."

" 'Babylon the Great has fallen, has fallen, and become the habitation of devils,' " Adora murmured, quoting from Revelations. It seemed appropriate in that moment, with the candles flickering between them, somehow brighter than the electric lights had been overhead. The firelight seemed to set Kris's hair ablaze, along with his eyes. "This all keeps coming back to religion, doesn't it?" she asked tiredly.

Kris shot her an odd look, and for a moment it seemed like he might actually be looking around inside her head. She was transfixed.

Could he truly be psychic?

You better hope not. Joy sounded uneasy.

"In a sense," Kris said, finally dropping his gaze and freeing her. "Bishop Nicholas tried to disappear then, so he could work anonymously in other parts of the world, but it was too late. Generosity was rare in those days, and people remembered his kindness. The legend was firmly established and grew with every telling. Soon, he was known as a saint supposedly performing miracles. That was never what I wanted, you know—fame. All I have ever tried to do was to show people how to love: God and themselves, and one another."

He shook his head and changed the subject. "I have begun translating some of the fey gospels. Pennywyse is typing them up. I think you will find them interesting, and perhaps they will give you the starting place you need for your story. But, in the morning. There is no need to think about this any more tonight." He gave a glance at the clock on the wall. It was late.

"Well, thank God—I mean Gaia—for small miracles, because I think my hamster has had a heart attack and her corpse has jammed the wheel," Adora mumbled as she realized that she had spent the last several seconds staring at the serpents of candlelight writhing through Kris's hair instead of taking any notes.

Kris raised a brow in enquiry, and she explained: "My brain has stopped. The gears aren't turning. The dynamo is dead. I need sleep."

"Then sleep you shall have. Let me show you to your room—" Her employer rose politely.

"It's all right," Adora said, forcing herself to her feet. She swayed slightly. The brandy had definitely been a mistake. She walked carefully to the library door and then turned back. "Kris?" she said.

"Yes?"

"I really am trying to believe you. I . . . I want this project to go well, since it clearly means so much to you. But I'm having some problems. Your story is really . . . *improbable*," she finally chose.

Kris smiled. "I appreciate that you are willing to try. Please don't worry. In time, everything will make sense to you. And it isn't such a stretch, is it? Why is it any harder to believe my story now than it was to believe in flying reindeer when you were young?"

"I don't know. It just is. Maybe because you look like a man and not Nast's elf." Adora turned away. "Good night," she said.

"Good night," he replied.

She paused once more as an idea struck her. "Kris, I think I have the title for this book."

"Yes?"

"Santa Claus: The Second Greatest Story Ever Told."

Kris chuckled. Adora found herself smiling too as she headed for her quarters.

"Sweet imaginings," Kris called after her. "Dream of me."

"Like there was ever any doubt," she muttered softly. Kris likely heard, for he chuckled.

And so it came to pass that the Sons of Man divided themselves again, this time the Rich from the Poor. And the Rich climbed into the mountains and built fortresses around their treasures and around their hearts, and became ever more removed from the Source of Love. And in fear of the Celebrants and the Worshipper Poor, whose numbers increased yearly, they made more weapons for their armies and began to hide the sacred rituals and words. Soon the Poor could only talk to Divinity with payment to the Rich, which payment they were made to offer inside special houses of worship open only on certain days.

Saddened by their cruelty and ignorance, still Niklas did go among the Sons of Man, rich and poor alike, and he did more good works amongst them.

—*Niklas 4:7*

There was a low fire in the hearth, and a few patches of cobwebbed light thrown out by the odd lantern. Planks had been laid over the hard-packed earth of the tavern's ancient floor, but other than that, the building was the same as in the year it was rebuilt after the Great Fire, right down to the ale and bitter cider stored in the blackened barrels that had been old even when Charles II brought Christmas back to England.

Few of the hard-faced laborers that patronized the establishment could read or write, but they would still recognize the name Charles Dickens, so the two men kept their voices low.

"Charlie, the pen is mightier than the sword, as we both know. But I need something mightier still this time. I need a hammer to strike at the new world—and you're going to craft it for me."

CHAPTER SIX

The bedroom was more than generous, and elegant, decked out in its silk and brocade. The bed was raised and had to be approached with a *prie-dieu* that was carved out of cheery warm wood.

Stepping into the bathroom, Adora sighed ecstatically. It was all marble, every last bit. There was a gigantic shower, but also a large tub deep enough to officially qualify as decadent. Reaching out, she plucked one of the bath towels off the rack and brought it to her face. She rubbed the cottony velvet, allowing herself to feel spoiled for the first in a very long while.

Turning, she walked unsteadily into the small alcove on the right. Two works of porcelain perched on marble steps seemed too pretty to be called anything as mundane as *toilet* or *bidet*, yet that was clearly their intended function. And she was going to get to leave her toothbrush and comb on the counter of this art-deco palace? They'd never been so honored. The rest of her ablutions would have to wait for morning; she was just too tired to cope with the little jars and bottles that were supposed to preserve her youth and protect her from sunburn and wrinkles.

Exhausted, weary to the bones, Adora treated herself to a hot shower and then sought out the comfort of her bed. Her last thoughts were about Kris—if that was even his name.

Who was he really? she wondered sleepily. Mr. Bishop S. Nicholas? Kris Kringle? Niklas? Until she had a name—a real one—she could hardly do any research on her own.

Should she ask for a birth certificate? No, that wouldn't work. He'd just say they didn't have them ten thousand years ago. So what about a driver's license? He must have one of those. Or at least some form of ID. Who did the IRS think he was? Surely he didn't pay taxes under the name of Santa Claus! She'd seen one of his old cards in the file folder. The yellowed card stock actually said:

S. CLAUS
PURVEYOR OF TOYS

Like he couldn't get ID to be the Easter Bunny if he bribed the right people, Joy sneered. *Hell, he could have had his name legally changed to anything.*

Damn it. Adora sighed. She just wanted to know his real name. There was a certain power in that. And how could she ever get a handle on him if she didn't know who or what he was?

Just as she was drifting off, lines from an old poem, "The Glory Hand," came into her head:

And the North Wind howled,
And the shadow prowled,

And the Lightning did claw and bite;
And they huddled together
As they hid from the weather,
On that terrible Beltane night.

Yeah, it's almost May Day, Joy said. She didn't sound happy, but Adora couldn't imagine why.

Kris stood in the doorway, watching Adora sleep. He felt guilt for having gotten her drunk and using his truth-magic on her while they were talking, but he sensed that there were many hidden layers to this woman, and that it was important to know the facts about her. Was she the one the Goddess had predicted would come into his life? Certainly she'd come from the west.

Adora Navarra. She had an inexpressible delicacy that hinted she was at least part fey. But how to tell her this? She identified herself so completely as human. She could barely allow for the possibility that he was fey; would she ever be able to accept that she herself was of mixed blood? Even if she eventually accepted, the cultural collision could be messy, and she really didn't need any further pain.

Adora's description of her last brief affair had at first made Kris suspect that she'd been fey-struck by another oblivious half-breed. But the longer she spoke, the more he'd come to understand that all the compulsions moving her were strictly internal and uninfluenced by magic.

Which was something of a relief. The fey-struck rarely recovered from the experience.

He felt for her, though. A child of mixed fey parents who didn't realize what they were and who had therefore given in completely to the attraction of a magical mating would be very lonely indeed.

Unchecked, the attraction between fey mates—especially between certain kinds of feys—would slowly exclude everything and everyone, even a child of that union. Not necessarily selfish people, like Narcissus they would become obsessed, so taken by the object of their affection that there would be no room for anything else. A few feys, away from their *shians*—their underground homes, their magical centers—had starved to death. They had made love incessantly, going without food or water until they finally died.

That wouldn't happen to Adora, though. He had found her. He could protect her from such a needless waste, eventually inform her and warn her of the truth.

Kris knew it was a bit voyeuristic, but he enjoyed watching her sleep. Adora lay like a child, or maybe a pill bug, rolled up in a ball, hands pressed together in prayer position and tucked under one cheek. She looked innocent—angelic, even. How very misleading. He was an excellent judge of character, and though he could see great kindness in her, there was mischief in equal measure. Which was to be expected in one of Seelie blood.

Kris doubted that Adora was aware of it, but something—probably her parents' steady application of indifference to her existence—had given her a little-girl-lost air that remained with her even in the rare moments when she smiled and laughed. Combined with her startling thinness and the soft murmurs of her emerging fey nature that rose from her like perfume, it made her almost irresistible to him. He wanted to protect her, to slay dragons for her—at least, metaphorical ones; he had nothing against the flesh-and-blood creatures.

He wanted to do a few less noble things as well.

Which was a very bad idea. It was, as his English friends were wont to say, a bit of a sticky wicket, because he was not—*really* not—cut out for the role of a lover.

Despite his unsuitability to the role, he wasn't blind to her reaction to him. He hadn't forgotten what often happened between death feys and certain other magical beings—sirens, especially—and he could see that she felt the same attraction that pulled at him. She was resisting it with all her unconscious might, which helped, but it was hard for both of them, and getting more difficult with every passing hour. He was almost certain that it was Gaia, again at work in the form of the Goddess, gathering up her lost lambs before the storm and mating them like the creatures on Noah's ark so that Her fey would survive.

He wished he knew for certain if this was Her will. She wasn't talking right now, though. Perhaps he was too far from the shian. Still, there was a way to test his theory if he really wanted to know. One kiss would do.

But . . . no. It was probably too soon in their relationship to suggest such an intimacy to Adora, and he didn't dare risk a permanent bond forming between them before she understood and believed what they both were; there was too much danger that such a relationship could entail. He had turned away from romantic love and hope of a mate when he had turned away from his magic and his people. For death fey, the two were often bound together. He'd had to let his magic go if he was to live among the warring tribes of Men and not be seduced into killing. But magic didn't die simply because he denied it. Left alone, its need grew ever stronger. It was reasonable to assume that his need for love—

for a permanent bond with another of his kind—had grown too.

But to love one such as he was to willingly embrace death, and Kris could see that there was something in Adora terrified of her mortality and unwilling to trust anyone. No, it would be a long time before he heard the words that Adora needed to speak to make their union possible: *Eat my heart. Drink my soul. Love me to death.*

Kris closed his eyes as yearning washed over him. It had been so long since he'd heard anyone say those words. His dusty memory of love was buried under a sort of cataclysmic ash hangover at least as thick as what covered poor Pompeii. But his memory wasn't dead like that city, wasn't yet petrified. He'd thought he'd given up on the idea of a wife long ago, that he'd put all thought of romance from his mind. But something about Adora Navarra made the old longings struggle against the suffocating darkness and try to dig their way out of his partially voluntary amnesia.

Making a small sound that might have been a sigh, he turned from temptation. The Goddess would have to wait. He had a previous commitment, one that was ten thousand years in the making.

The seas he traveled were never calm, but this was likely to prove the most turbulent yet. He would have to be careful from here on out. His dark dreams of unanswered love could call storms, and the part of Adora that was magical would answer with lures of her own. They *both* had to be careful.

Unless . . .

Kris decided spontaneously—which was the way he decided almost everything—that it would be wise to take Adora to Cadalach. The mound would know if she was fey, and it could help her adapt if she was disturbed by the news.

At the end of next week, after they visited San Francisco.

A ferocious downpour began at midnight, alarming because it was out of season and because she shouldn't have been able to hear it so clearly through the thick walls that guarded her. Pushing aside the covers and going to the chattering window, Adora was puzzled and then alarmed to see that the rain fell only on their building. The streets beyond looked dry in the glow of the streetlights, and the line of demarcation was clear even through the blurred glass.

Her ghostly reflection in the window frowned back at Adora. This was impossible. Was she dreaming? There had been movement in the darkness. Something sly. She peered out sharply, but now there was nothing. Just rain, just wind—black and cold, beating at the French doors, they demanded she let them in so that they could ravage her with chilly fingers.

Unable to explain why, Adora was suddenly filled head to toe with mortal dread. It was not concern of an unexplained weather phenomenon; she had seen enough strange natural disasters and meteorological anomalies to no longer be amazed by Mother Nature's seeming schizophrenia. No, this was an atavistic fear of something out there in the night, a fear that told the hare to flee before the hound, to run for its life because danger was coming swiftly.

"Don't open the door!" a voice behind her said urgently. It sounded like Kris.

Adora looked down, surprised and appalled to find her hand resting on the door latch. Unable to help herself, she ignored Kris's words and watched her fingers depress the handle.

Wind tore the French doors from her grasp, then reached for her with vicious fingers.

Adora cried out, terrified that she would be carried onto the balcony and flung off, then swept to the coast and out to sea. But in an instant Kris was there, wrapping her in his arms and pulling her back from the killing wind. He murmured words in a strange language, soothing her.

He closed the door, and Adora willingly fainted.

When she woke again, it was seven in the morning and the sun was shining. Shade dappled her wall and urged her to leave the comfort of her bed. Like the old TV ad used to say: It was just another perfect day in Paradise. There wasn't the slightest trace of the storm—except perhaps inside her body. She felt . . . waterlogged. Like she had nearly drowned. And her thoughts were confused, as if a cyclone had blown through them.

What might have happened if Kris had not pulled her back in time?

He *had* pulled her back in time, hadn't he? It seemed that she remembered this, but her recollection was hazy. Could it have been a dream?

She stumbled to the doors and threw them wide. Stepping out onto the balcony, she looked over the edge. The hotel swimming pool was below. Hundreds of ragged mimosa blossoms littered its surface. Others were captured in the pool boy's net, which he dragged to and fro.

So, it had rained. There were also bruises on her arms in the shape of a man's hands.

Too tired to care, Adora got back into bed and pulled the covers over her head. She fell into an uneasy sleep and her brain, with Joy's help, soon forgot most of her nightmare.

* * *

Somewhat heavy-eyed because she had been woken by exuberant birds on her balcony, Adora wandered into the hotel library a little after eight. Kris, looking bright-eyed and cheerful, was at work writing a letter longhand. He didn't seem to care for computers, leaving cyber-business to Pennywyse. Adora understood this. The damn things were always breaking down on her and losing files. She herself preferred to take notes in longhand. Luddites of the world unite!

"Good morning. How did you sleep?" Kris asked, and he smiled warmly before going back to his letter.

"Good morning." It wasn't yet all that good, but Adora lived in hope. Coffee sometimes improved her outlook.

She stared hard at Kris's bent head, not wanting anything to do with the thoughts in her mind but unable to escape them. Scrutiny didn't help. The more she looked, the more she liked. Kris was wonderful—absolutely gorgeous. Almost . . .

Inhumanly beautiful? her inner voice suggested.

Adora swallowed but didn't correct Joy. She had learned from numerous bloody battles with her inner voice that if you couldn't win an engagement, it was wisest to back off and look for a battle you could.

Fine. So she might be a little attracted Kris. But that wasn't so bad, was it? It was just magnetism. It wasn't like she had wandered into quicksand.

No?

Well, maybe it was a little like that. But she could still breathe and think . . . and escape, if she wanted. It wasn't as if she had fallen in a snake pit and needed to be rescued from a giant pit viper.

Isn't it?

Of course not! Hell, she *wanted* to be in love—or at

least lust—didn't she? As long as the guy wasn't an asshole.

Or insa—

Shut up! What a Johnny-One-Note, she hissed at Joy. *And he isn't insane. He just has different ways of seeing things. And I'm not in love—just attracted,* she clarified.

Uh-huh.

Still, this attraction was hardly ideal. How could she be objective about a book, dig for the truth, when she was so sympathetic—okay, *fascinated*—with its subject? Even if they never slept together, she could never be unbiased, and therefore might get led astray by his wilder imaginings. The critics would crucify her. Assuming there was anything left after an editor tried to "fix" things.

Worse, what *was* she going to do about Kris in the flesh? Her fingers actually itched to touch him. Could she flirt gently to see if he responded? Sneak up on him when he wasn't paying attention and move in for a fast kiss?

Why be subtle? Go right for a direct fondling with an indecent proposition.

Adora snorted. Yeah, like she'd ever walk up and fondle anyone, let alone Kris. It wasn't the kind of thing she would do. For God's sake—he was her employer. And she had rules.

And he's Santa Claus. Let's not forget that, Joy laughed.

Okay, that too.

And he's a few sandwiches short of a picnic.

I'm not listening, Joy. If you don't have anything new to say, go away.

Fine, but you know I'm right. Get involved at your own peril.

Peril? Adora almost snorted. Still . . .

Her brows knit as she watched Kris study the report on his desk, apparently oblivious to her.

How could he ignore the tension in the room? He liked her, didn't he? She'd read the signs. He was definitely attracted, and old-fashioned enough to probably want to do the chasing himself.

So, why was he waiting for her to say something, for her to start the dance? Didn't he want to relieve some of the pressure building between them?

Maybe he felt like she did: that this was something important. That it was something that shouldn't be rushed or treated cavalierly. And maybe he was as concerned about the book being compromised as she was.

Or maybe he's too busy being Santa Claus to notice you. You know, making his lists and checking them twice?

Shut up! Shut up! Shut up!

Fine, but don't say I didn't warn you.

Adora exhaled again, counting slowly to ten. *Joy, I mean it. Go away. I have to work now.*

"This must be a tough dilemma you're contemplating," Kris said, glancing up and smiling in ready sympathy. "I've seen men marching off to war who haven't looked half so grim."

"You have no idea," Adora muttered, returning her gaze to the bulging file Pennywyse had supplied. The diverse and unorganized information wasn't helping her get to know Kris, and there was so much of it to read, much of it in stilted English. She couldn't quite repress another sigh. "Beginnings are always hard."

"Well, let's not rush into work this morning," Kris said suddenly, and he reached for the phone. "I'll have Morrison bring the Silver Cloud around—you'll love that—and we'll go out to the farmers' market. There's nothing quite like starting your morning with fresh croissants and raspberries."

Adora didn't need her arm twisted. She happily put the file aside, keeping only a small notebook.

"Give me just a minute. I need to get my purse," she said. And a hat, and to put on some sunscreen. The late morning sunlight would be harsh. At that moment she desperately wanted to go out with Kris in the light of day. Perhaps the sunlight would reveal something new to her.

"Don't rush. I need to send for Mugshottz. He fusses if I go out without him. Poor fellow, he sees goblin assassins under every bush."

"Then by all means, let's have him along," Adora said agreeably—but she was less than pleased. Her fantasy of a day out with Kris didn't include a bodyguard.

"Look!" she said a little while later; pointing out the car window at the small billboard on the side of the city bus. The ad was for a new documentary about Saint Nicholas. She murmured: " 'Funding for this program is supplied by the Bishop S. Nicholas Foundation, and from contributors like you. . . .' This is part of your PR campaign?"

"Yes. It will air Thanksgiving weekend. It doesn't tell my whole story—just the parts about Bishop Nicholas."

"I'd like to see it, if I may," she said. Maybe the director had managed to put some order to the chaos of Kris's life—even if only for the last several hundred years. If she could borrow his files . . .

"Of course. I'll arrange it as soon as the final cuts are made," Kris agreed.

The car rolled to a stop at the end of the parking lot, and Mugshottz leaped out to get the door. He could move quickly when the impulse was on him, and Adora found it a bit unnerving to see him hovering like a dark angel. But it wasn't for long; Kris was there immediately, offering his hand, helping her out of the car and guiding her toward the largest market she'd ever seen.

"Will the car be okay?" she asked. She loved old cars, and Kris's were particularly wonderful. She had supposedly inherited the fixation from her paternal grandfather, whose car collection had been added to Harrah's Car Museum in Reno. While she was too practical and poor to keep an automobile that needed constant care and whose replacement parts were scarcer than human donor organs, that didn't prevent her from enjoying Kris's.

"Morrison will watch it," he assured her. "Come on. You have to see things before they get picked over."

"Wow. What a sight!" Adora stared gleefully at the carnival of colors under the acres of gay-striped awnings. There were pyramids of citrus, tomatoes and grapes. Other tables held crates of cherries and berries of blue and purple, scarlet and pink. It would be at least another month before they had this kind of produce on the coast.

Flowers abounded, sweetening the air with soft scents of flox and hyacinth and lilac. Everything glistened, washed clean by the rain, and the hues were so vivid and shiny that everything might have been covered with fresh paint.

Most seductive of all were the loaves of bread and pastries stacked like cord wood, and the smell of roasting coffee beans that slyly wrapped about her. Buoying up the scents that floated toward them— come hither, they called. Come hither and eat! Adora's stomach rumbled loudly.

"Where would you like to begin?" Kris asked.

"Coffee, strawberries—and cinnamon rolls," she answered promptly.

"That sounds perfect. Can you manage the coffee if I get the rest?"

"Definitely," Adora agreed. "There are still some vacant tables under those umbrellas. Let's meet there."

Kris nodded and started for the bakers' tables. Mugshottz followed at a distance, his face hidden under a hat and his body enveloped in a large coat. A few people stared at the troll-cross, and all gave him wide berth, but no one seemed particularly alarmed.

They all met up a few minutes later at one of the small picnic tables. Though she was still uncomfortable with the crossbreed, Adora forced herself to smile at Mugshottz as she handed him a coffee. "I didn't know how you took it," she said, "so I brought some sugars and a packet of creamer."

"Thanks, but I take it black," Mugshottz answered.

The tall cup completely disappeared in his massive and scarred hands. His forearms had also been to the wars, and they were a tapestry of interlaced marks that looked for all the world like they had come from a chisel. Adora thought about asking what had caused them, but she held her tongue. It was beyond the scope of her book, and anyway, she wouldn't care to discuss her own less visible scars. There was no reason to suppose that Mugshottz would be any more enthused than she.

The bodyguard regarded her for a moment out of his flat stony eyes; then, perhaps sensing her discomfort at the attention, retreated about five feet and started scanning the crowd.

Kris spoke up. "Sit on this side. There's more

shade. Forgive my speaking plainly, but you've clearly been ill, and I don't think the sun agrees with you." He pushed a basket of strawberries her way. "Eat up. They're good for you. Lots of vitamins."

Adora blinked at his commanding tone but answered without heat.

"I look like reheated tuna casserole, don't I? It's some exotic virus, they think, though they've never been sure what kind. The sun makes it worse," she added, for some reason unoffended by the personal observation. Maybe it was because she had been doing a lot of prying into Kris's life, and this exchange of information seemed fair. And maybe she just liked the attention. Still, her next words were harder. "It's worrying, because my dad died of some undiagnosed viral disease. Only, he was more affected than I am. He got weaker and weaker and . . . well, his immune system just failed. He died very quickly. From first episode to last, it was only three months."

"When was this? What precisely happened?" Maybe it was the sun, but a nimbus surrounded Kris's hair, reminding her of Renaissance paintings of saints and angels. She wanted desperately to touch him. Or maybe she wanted desperately to not answer his questions about her father, and was building a normal phenomenon into something unworldly to avoid that.

"What an expression!" Kris's tone was teasing, but his eyes were serious. "I'm not suggesting that you drop peyote and then go to a bullfight—just tell me a little about yourself."

"I'd probably like peyote and bullfights better," Adora replied. "That might be more fun too. This isn't . . . It isn't a nice story."

"I want to hear it anyway. Please."

"It happened about three years ago," she answered at last. "It was a horrible summer. Every-thing was so dry. The drought went on and on out west. Mom and I were sick too—but not like Dad."

"Are you getting worse?" Kris asked. There was no overt sympathy in his voice, but his eyes were warm and compassionate. Again, though she had never willingly discussed the matter with anyone, Adora felt compelled to tell him the truth.

"No. I seem to have plateaued. As long as I stay out of the noon sun, I'm fine. I live at the coast now, and we have a lot of fog in the summer. It's just that I'm not getting any better, either."

"And your mother? Is she still alive?"

Adora looked away. This was tougher. She had been lonely before, but her mother's death had made that aloneness so final. There was no hope now of ever winning the woman's love, and nearly everyone who recalled her childhood was dead. If Adora died tomorrow, other than a few scholars who had read her work, no one would know she had ever existed. It made her feel very small and lonely. And that was pathetic: not the way she wanted Kris to see her.

Adora made an effort to pull herself together. "No, Mom is . . . Mom was a pilot—usually a care-ful one. But after Dad was gone, she . . ." She swal-lowed and blinked hard, upset to find she had tears in her eyes. "She was broken inside. I've often thought that their relationship wasn't so much a love affair as a love addiction. She hung on for a cou-ple of years, waiting for me to finish graduate school and get settled in a career, but it was like watching a ghost haunt the house." Adora took a drink of her coffee. It was hot enough to burn her tongue, but she welcomed the distraction of physical pain. "Offi-cially, the crash was listed as an accident, but those who saw her said that the engine was fine and that she just dove that Piper Cub into the ground."

Kris made a noise of sympathy. Adora flinched, but once started, the horrible words continued to bubble out.

"I dropped her off at the airport that day, and went into town to choose a dress to wear to a friend's wedding. I was going to Hawaii at the end of the week and was feeling as carefree as a little lamb going off to nibble spring pastures. Hawaii in the spring—what could be better? I think of it now and cringe at how stupid I was. I should have had some premonition; she was too quiet. . . . But I didn't. Not one little bit of worry clouded my horizon. Lambs aren't real bright, you know. They can gambol right by the slaughterhouse and not even notice." Her voice was full of self-contempt.

"I'm sorry." Kris's hand covered hers fleetingly. Too fleetingly, she thought. "You've had more than your fair share of losses. I do hope you know that neither of your parents' deaths were your fault."

The hand had been nice—so warm—but his eyes! She wanted to crawl into his eyes and roll around in the kindness she saw there. The thought disturbed her. She had made the mistake—far too often of late—of seeking relief from her grief in relationships with men. They always ended disastrously.

And she didn't really want Kris's pity.

Adora let out a long breath and tried to smile reassuringly. "Yes, I know. And there's no need to worry about me, okay? I've never been that in love, and I don't suffer from suicidal tendencies. You'll never find me wearing a rope cravat, or doing home surgery on my wrists in the bathtub."

"I know. I can sense that isn't your way." Kris

nodded slowly, then said abruptly, "I have a friend who specializes in. . . immune disorders. I think he can help you. Would you consider seeing him?"

Adora thought about it.

"He isn't the Tooth Fairy, is he?" she asked with a half smile, attempting a joke to see how he reacted. " 'Cause I think I've reached my weird quotient for the week."

Kris smiled. "No, just one of my many helper elves. His name is Zayn, and he lives in a place called Cadalach."

Mugshottz twitched once, but then went back to doing a fine impersonation of a statue.

"Ka du lac?" she asked. The name sounded vaguely familiar.

"That's close enough. It's named after a . . . a town in Ireland. We may be going there later. Not to Ireland—my Cadalach isn't too far from Palm Springs. I have family there."

Adora tried not to gape.

"You have family?"

What? You thought he grew on a tree or was cloned in a lab? Joy asked, but Adora could tell she was surprised too.

"Yes. I didn't mention my nephew? He's the one who restores the wonderful cars I use. He's a bit of a car buff."

"I'm speechless," Adora said, wondering if her prayers to the gods of research had been answered. Surely Kris's family could tell her more about him. "I don't know why—"

Yes, you do, Joy inserted.

"—but I somehow pictured you as coming into the world like Athena, sprung whole from the brow of Zeus."

127

"Wrong legend again," Kris said. "Jack is the son of my younger brother, Phaneos. He's a lot younger than I am."

"Isn't everyone?" Adora asked. Kris just nodded.

At the next table, Adora heard the click of a camera shutter, and even without Mugshottz's hard glance, she knew who was being photographed: Though he had done nothing but sip his coffee, Kris had still managed to attract the attention of every female in a three-table radius. Even in the land of beautifully engineered people, he attracted attention.

It's probably super-pheromones.

"Eat your breakfast," Kris cajoled. "You don't want to miss the street musicians—the lutin mariachis are fabulous. You won't believe what they can do with a twelve-string guitar. They close up shop before the sun gets too warm, though. Goblins don't do well in bright sunlight. They dehydrate. The condition is called hydrophilia."

"Why do they go out in it then?" Adora asked.

"You don't know much about goblin hives, do you?" Kris said. The question might have been condescending but wasn't.

"Nothing," she admitted. "I feel very ignorant and am afraid I'll say something foolish before I finish doing my research and offend someone. It would be easier if goblins looked like goblins," she added.

"No, we couldn't have that," Kris said mildly, though he looked a bit serious. Then he went on to explain, "The situation is complicated, and every hive is different. Molybdenum is the new leader—king—of the L.A. hive. He's only been in power a few months. Being fey, I would normally be considered an enemy of the state, but we've reached a sort of agreement about my staying here in town. I have dispensation because of an old debt. This is . . .

restitution from this hive for an ancient wrong they did me."

"I see. What happened to the last king?" Adora asked.

"*Queen.* Sharyantha. The story is that she tragically cut her throat while shaving."

"Goblins shave?" Adora said. She wasn't certain if Kris was kidding.

"The females do."

"You'd think she'd prefer facial wax. Much safer," Adora remarked.

"Indeed. Especially since such shaving accidents kill off a lot of goblin kings and queens. Coup d'etats are very common in lutin hives. In fact, I don't think any goblin ruler ever has died of old age. Don't get the wrong idea: The average lutin is quiet and law-abiding, but the leaders—many of them— are monsters. And monsters don't have many friends, and way too many relatives who want their job. It compounds their already raging paranoia, and they tend to be tyrannical. Molybdenum is better than most, but still . . ."

"Kings everywhere have this problem," Adora pointed out. " '*Uneasy lies the head*' and all that. It has to be a hard life. Still, there's an up side to assassination—for the general populace at least," she suggested.

"Yes?" Kris cocked his head, waiting for her to go on. A slight smile hovered about his mouth.

"Well, at least with a revolution you don't have to go through two primaries and a general election. Our last presidential election almost put me in a psychiatric hospital."

Joy didn't speak up, though Adora half-expected her to.

Kris shook his head. "How very cynical you are. I

take it that you don't approve of politics. I was going to introduce you to someone today, but perhaps it would be best if you didn't spend time with him. You and my political adviser might not get along."

Nodding, Adora bit into her cinnamon roll—and almost moaned aloud at the pleasure. Nothing was as good as cinnamon and too much butter.

"It's that good?" Kris asked, taking a smaller bite of his own. He closed his eyes for a moment. "I am so glad that cholesterol isn't a problem in my life," he remarked.

"Your political adviser. Alistair Hyatt?" Adora said a minute later in a somewhat sticky voice. "We've already met. He went hurrying by this morning with a file even bigger than mine. He seems surprisingly nice—too nice for his job. I'll just have to see about getting him some vocational counseling. It's never too late to change careers," she joked.

"Bite your tongue. I need him," Kris replied. "I share your distaste for politics, but I have learned— at huge cost—that you cannot completely ignore that realm and the people who dabble in it."

"No? I certainly try. I have no use for politicians— scoundrels and liars, one and all."

Kris shook his head, looking surprisingly serious. "True. But you're in a goblin town now. Ignore politics at your peril."

"Explain," Adora demanded. As she took another bite of her roll, she noticed Mugshottz look Kris's way. He did that fairly frequently, and it was hard to read his expression, but now it seemed more curious than nervous. That was probably a sign that she should take notes. Adora wiped her hands on her napkin and reached for her notebook.

"It's complicated," Kris said.

"I have all day."

"Very well. In the human world, consider how politics influence fashion and art, from deciding what clothes we wear to what musicians and artists will be favored in our society," he proposed. "There are unholy alliances built by greed, all around us, influencing us daily. And this is in the *human* world, where there are some checks and balances, and a supposedly free media to inform the masses of abuses of power. Now, there is no United Nations or free press for lutin hives."

Kris got up from the table and began to pace. Mugshottz watched him worriedly. Adora had the feeling that the troll-cross would start pacing also if his boss got more than a shadow's length away.

Kris went on: "And politics do much more than influence the aesthetics of our lives. Humans think that because there is no body count on the nightly news that there is no war between the goblins and the humans—but they couldn't be more wrong." He shook his head, and Adora knew that he was searching for a way to explain how large the problem was, and how it was growing into something nearly impossible to control. He finally said, "The odds of confrontation have grown astronomically. I have watched through the ages as human political agendas have left thrones and oval offices and climbed into pulpits, both in the old churches and now in the secular church of the media. There it puts words into the mouths of priests and newsmen. Thus are rich men's political ambitions implanted in the hearts of society. The resulting abuses are often small, petty bigotries, and go unnoticed. The more spectacular ones make headlines. Often there is an element of evil. Think of all those zealous reformers who kill to *save lives*."

Adora nodded, recalling all the hypocrisy she'd witnessed. There were the many forms of religious terrorism that plagued the world. There were always people killing for Christ, or for Muhammad, or for someone. . . .

"The goblins have watched and learned," Kris continued. "And the effect is more than double in the lutin world, where goblin masses have never been allowed to think for themselves and where no dissenting view is offered. You don't see it, but lutin leaders—especially in the United States, though there are new movements in Japan and Europe too—are taking advantage of the common lutin anger over at what has happened to them. They have been ghettoized and believe they have never been offered a seat at the American political table. If goblins have shared in the capitalist bounty, it is because they have taken their prosperity by trickery or force. None was offered willingly. And like their greediest human counterparts, the goblin leaders believe completely that the end justifies the means, and they will lie and lie and lie—and worse—if that's what it takes to get what they deserve. They will no longer tolerate being second-class—" Kris stopped abruptly. "I was going to say second-class citizens. But they aren't citizens. Lutins have been born in this country for hundreds of years, yet none has the right to vote. And humans are stone blind to this injustice and the anger it has caused." Kris's gaze was hot. "Think about it, Adora: The goblins are here in the hundreds of thousands, yet they are nearly invisible in daily human life. Even you, an educated woman, never saw a goblin until two days ago."

There was a scattering of applause from nearby tables, causing Kris to blink and then sit down abruptly. The applauders all looked human, Adora thought, but they might not be. They could be species-reassigned goblins. The thought made her squirm.

Yet, Kris had a point. She had always shied away from stories about faeries and goblins. It had been easy, because there was no mention of the fey in the news and hardly ever anything about goblins.

It goes deeper than that. There's stuff on the Internet, but you never ever look up anything about it.

Joy was right. Adora's avoidance had bordered on the pathological; she saw that now. She wondered how many other humans reacted the same way. The thought made her frown.

" *'Therefore submit thy ways unto his will,'* " she murmured, earning a surprised glance from Kris and Mugshotz. "It's Spencer's *The Faerie Queene*," she explained.

Kris nodded but said nothing. Apparently he was actually expecting her to think about this and to answer his questions.

Adora exhaled slowly, doing as he asked and considering the situation for the first time—and then wondering why she had never thought of it before. Was she so influenced by the media? Was she so blind? The notion chilled her. She had always believed that she could rise above cultural conditioning, that she was a seeker of truth and understanding and a champion of downtrodden people and animals. Yet here was this massive blind spot in her view of the world—an entire species ignored. She had fought to save timber wolves and mountain lions and panda bears in other states but had done nothing—*thought* nothing—about the goblins next door.

And what of the fey? If they were still here, where did they fit in this political landscape? If Kris was right and they really existed, were they angry too? Because they would have cause. No one had been suggesting that what the U.S. needed was a faery president. There weren't any voter drives to register elves. She'd seen no suggestion that they needed a few good pixies on Capitol Hill.

"Kris . . . I don't know what to say," she finally admitted. "It's weird. Scary."

Kris nodded. "I'm not saying that we should discount everything we hear in the media and from politicians," he went on after a moment, his voice softer. "Their information—and *mis*information—can help guide us. And I'm not railing against human politics and politicians per se. They can be tools for change. But they need supervision from the people, and they cannot be *ignored.* Not if you are a person of conscience. As goes the leader, so goes the country. It's about survival."

"Kris?" Adora said, her voice troubled.

"Too much lecture?" he asked, smiling quickly. His eyes warmed, and even began to dance. "My apologies. The situation troubles me, and has for centuries. But there is no need for me to thrust all this on you on your second day in the city."

"No. It isn't that," Adora said. "I want to know. But I was just wondering . . ."

"What?" His head cocked. "Ask me anything. Wait—you want to know if I'm running for political office here in L.A."

"No. Uh—you aren't, are you?" she asked. The thought dismayed her.

"Not at the moment—though it is one of the few places where a fey might participate legally. So, if it isn't that, what's troubling you?"

Adora hesitated. Asking her next question would

be taking the next step to acknowledging that Kris might be what he claimed. Part of her was afraid to follow where the line of inquiry led. Still, she heard herself ask, "What do the fey think of all this—the humans and goblins and stuff? Are they mad at humans too? We talk about them even less frequently than we do goblins. I mean, at least people know goblins are real. Fey are just . . . stories. Fairy tales."

"The fey . . ." Kris sighed. "No, the fey aren't angry. The fey barely *are*. We are hovering near the edge of extinction, and are doing what we can to avert disaster for all races. When our leaders were still alive they had their political agendas—the Seelie and Unseelie Courts barely got along. Things are different these days, thanks largely to my nephew Jack."

"Seelie? Unseelie? Oh—that's right. The good faeries and the bad ones."

"Sort of. It's more a case of light and darkness." He smiled a little. "It's also more political history, I'm afraid. You see, the Seelie Court was ruled by the clan Finvarra. They are the 'creatures of light' that you read about in happy faerie stories, though those are gross simplifications and distortions of reality—old Finvarra could be as perverse as anyone. The Unseelie are creatures of night."

"And you're Seelie?" she asked.

"No." Kris shook his head. He looked at his clasped hands and then back up. "As I said before, I am a death fey. Had I a political allegiance, I would have belonged to Queen Mabigon and the army of darkness. But I ignored her and the goblin kings, not paying attention to their machinations because I was pursuing other goals—good goals, I thought. It was a mistake, though. I thought that if I did not participate in their power struggles that I would be left alone, a noncombatant who could go out and do good deeds unmolested. After all, why should they care about my efforts to bring peace to humans? It was a laudable objective that would benefit all races." His tone was full of self-mockery that was clearly new. Adora didn't like it. And it was clear that Mugshottz didn't either.

Adora swallowed and steeled herself to ask her next question. "Okay—let's talk about this now. What happened to you? Were you really at the North Pole while the goblins and merchandisers were hijacking Christmas and putting your face on soda pop?"

"Yes, I really was. I was drugged out of my head, my insanity caused by a clever curse, courtesy of my dark queen, who hated humans, and was jealous of what she saw as the Goddess's favoritism." He paused. "I wish that I could tell you more, Adora, explain everything logically and linearly. But though the memories of that time are there, they are badly disarranged. I rummage around in the cupboard for the bits and pieces, but it takes time to reassemble the story, and there are gaps. And I have many other irons in the fire these days. It is, after all, only one hundred and ninety-eight days until Christmas." The last was said as a joke.

Adora took this all in, not believing but not disbelieving either. She suspected that there was more— much more—to the explanation. A part of her sympathized with Kris and believed him. Looking at her own childhood was difficult. Her memories were just outlines, like the bones of structures mostly burned away in some mental fire. She could see the foundations where memories should be but could not reconstruct them. Something had been there, of course—she *had* been a child once—but whatever it was, it was gone now.

Drug use could explain a lot. And the rich are not immune to addiction, Joy pointed out, trying to explain Kris's lack.

This isn't about pill-popping turning into hallucinations. Something else happened to him. Maybe the goblins really did drug him.

And that made him eccentric? Joy scoffed.

"Why didn't she just kill you? Wouldn't it have been easier?" Adora asked, managing to sound cool and collected.

Is this for the book? Joy teased.

Yes, and maybe for herself.

"Ah. Well, I have been killed many times," Kris answered. "And I always come back. Admittedly, my deaths are always sacrificial, and plain old murder without ritual might have prevented my resurrection. But she couldn't risk it. She needed me gone, out of the game. So she set out to destroy my mind and hide my body where no one would find it. It accomplished the same thing as murder, yet didn't risk provoking the Goddess's wrath."

Goosebumps arose on Adora's arms—arms that had Kris's prints on them.

"So, you're saying that you're the shaman in those texts you gave me to read. You're the one who was sacrificed every seven years?" she asked, tearing her eyes away from the strange bruises.

"Yes." Kris for once looked serious and a little sad. "I am—or was—that Niklas."

"Kris?" Adora closed her little notebook—she hadn't been writing in it anyway.

"Yes?"

"Are you *sure* you're Niklas?"

For some reason, her question made the lines of tension in his face ease, and Kris began to smile. "Quite sure. Why?"

"Because I don't think I can be friends with a sacrifice," she said plaintively. "The whole Green Man thing is creepy. Surely you see that. It's like cooperative suicide."

Her employer began to laugh, and the sound dispelled the gloom that had been building around them.

"My dear! I haven't been a sacrifice for many years. Drug-abused and insane, yes. Not a burnt offering. Those days are over. I have found a better way to help the world."

Why didn't that news make her happier?

Because zealots are scary and make bad partners, was Joy's reply.

"You have?" she asked Kris, trying to sound upbeat and encouraging.

"Man doesn't realize it, but he is very fragile— one ice age, one comet strike, one nuclear winter away from extinction. The goblins are just as fragile in their own way, but they don't realize it either. The fey—sadly—*do* know how precarious life can be, but the others haven't learned from our experiences. We must find a way to bring peace to all races before it's too late. One can't learn a lesson if one is dead." He added, "At least, not as a rule. Abrial and Nyssa have sometimes seen it, of course. They talk to ghosts."

"I think I'm getting a headache again," Adora warned. "My limit is one arcane lecture per day. Education of the dead is a little too out-there."

Kris stood again and offered his hand. "Okay, no more lessons, lectures or political plots. Maybe I can write some of this out for you. Or get Thomas or

Abrial to supply a chronology with human parallels. Perhaps seeing things in context to your history would help you."

"Okay," Adora said, leveling a pen at Kris before she stuffed it and her notebook back in her purse. "But let's get something else straight here. I'm the interviewer. You are the interviewee. Your job is to be the straight man and supply facts to my questions. My job is to write the homey witticisms and make you epic. You're the engine, but I'm the driver."

"Is that how it works?" Kris asked, amused. "You're the new king maker?"

"Certainly. Don't you know Oscar Wilde? 'Any man can make history—only a great one can write it.' Best leave this to the professionals."

"You clearly haven't heard that 'A foolish consistency is the hobgoblin of little minds.'"

"Don't start with Emerson. I don't like to get mean before noon, but I'll drag out the Shakespeare if I have to," Adora warned him.

"Oddly enough, I was reading some essays of a contemporary of good old Bill this morning."

"Really?" Adora asked. "Did you know this guy too?"

"No, actually. It was by a Michel de Montaigne. He was a rationalist in an era of religious hysteria and intolerance. My favorite quotation I read was, 'After all, it is setting a high value on our opinions to roast people alive on account of them.' It seems apropos now. In his day, saying something like that could indeed get you roasted alive. He was a courageous man. There have been many of them, the reasonable men, the peacemakers . . . just not enough—"

He was cut off as Adora reached up and stuffed

the last of her cinnamon roll into his mouth. She couldn't swear to it, but she thought maybe Mugshottz smiled.

"No more. Not another word about Shakespeare or politics. Honest to God, Kris, you need to relax or you'll get an ulcer. And no one will want to date you, even if you are Santa Claus and richer than God." She wasn't sure why she said the last.

He seemed unaffected. "Ha! It has been my experience that a man can be a cannibal with tentacles and still get a date—if he has enough money." His voice was sticky.

"Hmph. Not with me."

Kris's eyes twinkled. He looked wonderful. Worth just about anything she could think of.

But, what was his angle? He definitely had politics on the brain, it seemed. Could this whole book thing be a con—a way of setting up a campaign to appeal to goblins? Or to humans? The mood the world was in, people might just vote for Santa Claus. They'd elected stranger.

Or did he truly believe all that he was saying? And if he did believe it, was it because he was . . . because there was something in his psyche that *needed* him to believe it?

You just can't say the word 'crazy,' can you?

But can it be real? Can everything he's told me be absolutely true? Can he be a fey who has reincarnated many times?

Get thee to a therapist! her inner voice advised. *It's called a Messiah complex, and you don't want anything to do with it.*

But Adora did want something to do with it. Damn it, she did. And Kris's—not delusions, but rather beliefs—were swallowing her whole. She was truly in danger of slipping into the bowels of the fantastic beast that was the Bishop S. Nicholas machine.

Ugh. Bowels? Joy said.

Okay, that was gross. No bowels. And Adora hadn't been swallowed. But she was being rapidly enveloped in the story of feys and goblins. And she was definitely part of Kris's group. Everyone had accepted her. Even Mugshottz.

Adora glanced up at Kris and felt her heart stutter. There was no one like him—no one at all. And she had never been so attracted to anyone in her life. In that moment, she wanted him almost as much as she wanted her next breath.

But what to do? He'd made no overtures—or, for that matter, no effort to push her away. And she was not the kind to march up to a strange man and offer to be his mattress, even when she wanted. But he was fascinating and she certainly was tempted to offer. Those, black, black lashes and the silver striations in those eerie blue eyes that could be so kind! They made her shiver.

Adora groaned softly. She had a thing for Santa Claus. How warped was that? Even her salivary glands were worked up. Damn! She was all but drooling. Worse, whenever she was with him, she actually felt inclined to believe everything he said without question.

Kris broke their gaze. He looked back at Mugshottz and said something in a language Adora didn't know but wished passionately that she did. Whatever the words meant, they were filled with warmth and joy, and she wanted him to whisper them in her ear—preferably right before kissing her.

Eat my heart. Drink my soul. Love me to death.

The words were not loud enough to be a whisper, just a shadow that slipped through her mind.

That wasn't me! Joy said. She sounded a little scared. *Adora? That wasn't me.*

If it wasn't Joy, where had that come from—and what did it mean? And what the hell was she going to do about this growing attraction?

Then it came to pass that the Rich Worshippers grew wroth with the Saint, who was more beloved by the others than their human king. Thus hunters were sent out to find the shaman, and to put him to death for the glory of the new god made in that king's image.

—Niklas 4:8

"Mommy?" Cyra's daughter Meriel asked in a grumpy voice as she rubbed her eyes.

"Yes, sweetie?" Cyra put her parchment aside and reached for the child.

"When is Uncle Kris coming home?" The girl snuggled into her mother's lap. There was less of it than there used to be, because Cyra and Thomas were expecting their second child. They were fairly certain that it was a boy, because Thomas's jinn had taken to making spontaneous appearances whenever Cyra slept. Jinn were drawn to male children.

"I'm not sure. Why do you ask?" Cyra smoothed back her daughter's silken hair.

"I dreamed of the lady again. She's supposed to come here with Uncle Kris."

"Is she?" Cyra asked, but knew it was true. It just surprised her that Meriel knew. She shouldn't be shocked—not really. Thomas had warned her that the ability to communicate with the faerie mound was an inherited trait.

"Uh-huh. And guess what, Mommy?" Meriel looked up. She sounded more cheerful.

"What?"

"She's sort of like . . ." Meriel paused, clamping down on what she was about to say.

"She's like the dragon?" Cyra guessed. She and Thomas were certain that their reptilian friend had shared his secret name with their daughter on her birthday, and that the child was doing her best not to betray his confidence.

"Yeah. She got mad at a bad man once and lit his shoes on fire." Meriel giggled. Cyra and Thomas had tried explaining to their daughter that lighting things—and especially people—on fire was not amusing, but they hadn't yet convinced her of it. All the dragon's pyrotechnic tricks were harmless and amusing—and allowed—because the canny beast was still being very careful not to expose the children to his true nature.

"Hm. Well, I am looking forward to meeting her," Cyra said diplomatically. "But in the meantime, I think we would both do well to get some rest. I don't think we'll be getting much sleep after Uncle Kris comes home."

CHAPTER SEVEN

You're like a fish in a pond. You're so busy staring at the juicy worm, you don't see the hook underneath.

You know, Joy, I've looked it up. Talking back to the voice in my head is one of the symptoms of paranoid schizophrenia, Adora snapped.

And your point is?

My point is, I'm not sure the whole split-personality thing is healthy. I mean, this usually indicates that something dreadful happened to a child before the age of five. But nothing happened to me, so I shouldn't need you to cope with everyday life.

There came sudden silence from Joy that was unexpected and a bit unnerving.

Joy—nothing did happen, did it? Adora asked.

Joy still didn't answer. One of the most annoying things about her: she would often up and disappear just at the point when Adora wanted to talk. It seemed that was the case now.

The sunlight and the crowd began to weigh on Adora as she and Kris walked, and she sought the shade provided by the pepper trees at the edge of the paved lot. There were fewer people there, and Adora felt like she could breathe again.

They weren't alone, though. Adora glanced warningly at the cooing birds above. They were half-hidden in the pink pepper berries, but she was aware of their mood and of their guerilla-bombing techniques used to chase everyone away from their feasts.

"You don't like pigeons?" Kris asked, seeing her scowl.

"Sure I do—roasted with a side of risotto and asparagus," she muttered.

Mugshottz made a strangled barking sound that Adora realized was a chuckle. When the troll laughed, his cheeks creased into deep folds like fissures. She half-expected to see bits of stone crumbling from his face.

Kris smiled too. "Mugshottz has been known to eat pigeons Tartare. It's revenge for all his cathedral-dwelling relatives, condemned to live under mounds of their poop."

Adora blinked, then recalled that Mugshottz was supposedly part gargoyle. She glanced over her shoulder and smiled at him. It was getting easier to read the man, even if he wore less expression than the standard English butler.

"Please help yourself to squab," she said. "I mean, don't hold back on my account."

Mugshottz smiled but shook his head. He was now walking almost abreast of Kris, more of a peer and less a servant or bodyguard.

"Have you ever heard the song 'Poisoning Pigeons in the Park'?" she asked. Mugshottz shook his head but looked intrigued—at least, Adora thought so. "Look for it the next time you're in a music store. I think you'll enjoy it."

"Title like that, I'd have to." His voice was like gravel, and Adora winced in sympathy. Maybe Mugshottz didn't say much because it hurt to talk.

Kris found an alley of deeper shade between the cement-bound trees and guided her under it, switching sides so that he walked in the partial sun and shielded Adora from the odd passers-by.

"I've just recalled something about Saint Nicholas's church," he said, smiling with sudden pleasure. Adora felt the familiar empathic swerve in his direction. His stories, however odd and improbable, resonated with her, stirring in her brain chords of some half-forgotten song. He went on: "The temple overlooked an older home—one they built for me when I was Poseidon. We had some real wild festivals there," he said.

The song met a note of discord.

"Poseidon . . . ?" Adora stumbled over a small crack in the uneven pavement, and as Kris caught her she thought: *Here we go again.* She half-expected Joy to say something snotty, but apparently Joy had given her up as a lost cause. Left on her own, the best Adora could manage was a weak: "You were Wodin *and* Poseidon? So, you were the one responsible for making the Queen of Crete fall in love with that sacrificial bull."

Kris didn't blush. He even grinned.

"That was all her idea. She was one of the dark fey, you know. I had nothing to do with the conception of the Minotaur. She did that to get even with her husband, who liked that poor bull more than her."

"I see."

At her flat tone, Kris became wary. "But it was all

a long, long time ago. I can barely remember those times. My brain is so scrambled that I can barely recall this life. Maybe I'm not remembering properly. That happens sometimes."

Adora made a *tsk*ing sound. "Kris, you're not supposed to lie—even to comfort me."

"My brain *is* scrambled," Kris insisted. "I could have it wrong. I'll have to ask Thomas."

"Maybe the details of architecture or the geography are hazy, but you do recall being Poseidon, don't you? I mean, it's not just everyone who is worshipped as a sea god. One would tend to remember that," she groused.

He hesitated a second. "Yes. I recall it."

"So, though it may have been a long time ago, the underlying message of what you're saying is that you've been worshipped as a god at least twice, and that this Santa gig—though the latest and greatest for us modern-day humans—is just not that big a deal. I mean, what are flying reindeer and a sainthood when you can command oceans?"

Kris shook his head, clearly dismayed by her reaction.

"I didn't 'command oceans.' That isn't my main . . . gift. It was more mistaken identity. They were looking for a sea god when I arrived in town."

Adora snorted.

"And Santa *is* a 'big deal,'" he insisted. "We are talking about faith, so of course that incarnation is important. In these days of mass communication, branding's more important than ever." Kris exhaled in a rare show of frustration. "I would let it go, you know. I'm not an egomaniac. But Santa isn't being interpreted in the right way, and the concept has been corrupted. It's doing more harm than good. I don't know why this happens. I never wanted to be worshipped. I don't need adoration. All I ever wanted was for there to be peace among races, to unite in a common goal and to love all things in this world. But the message always gets lost. Goblins always get brainwashed, and humans . . ."

"Humans?" she prodded.

He looked at her, perhaps weighing what he should say. He looked unhappy as he answered. "Humanity needs gods, I guess. And most of them can't seem to embrace a formless deity. For some reason, God can't simply be love. God has to be something smaller—something tangible and flawed that allows loopholes for men to war and do hateful things in that name."

For the first time ever, Kris looked sad and discouraged, and Adora found herself equally disturbed. She was used to empathizing with her subjects, but this was something else—something she didn't entirely like. She needed to keep her emotions separate. She couldn't afford to head into another emotional spiral.

"Even after all this time, there are some things I still don't understand. Man is so frail," Kris said more softly. "Knowing he can be broken, I don't understand why he does what he does. Like aggressive hedgehogs, men do terrible things to one another. Then, when vengeance comes, they curl about their pain, almost treasuring it even as they put out their quills. Those quills keep everyone away, even those they love, so they never receive comfort. And the cycle goes on." He sighed.

"Strangest and most illogical of all, the entire time they are posturing and threatening, they're also hoping no one will notice their vulnerability and hurt them more." Kris shook his head. "The most frustrating part is that they never learn. Millennium after millennium, it's the same damn mistakes, the same damn denials that anything is wrong with the way they organize their lives, and the same refusal to admit that anything can change. They're fatalists." Kris shot Adora a look that she could not decipher.

Adora swallowed and looked away. It actually hurt to see Kris's frustration. His pain was suddenly her own, a dark stain blossoming in her heart that made her want to pull away from him. Maybe it was because she understood this "curling about one's pain." At her core, there was already a vast hurt. And fear. Fear that she might never be well and whole again. And fear that if she loved—true, deep, forgetful love—she might very well end up like her mother. And that terrified her, because she knew such love could be shattered—was almost always broken, in fact—and then what would become of her?

The question left her feeling bereft, and more alone than she had ever felt in her life. And that was saying something. A part of her had always been lonely. Her parents' intense—

Admit it, that was a gloriously *selfish relationship,* Joy interjected at last. *In fact, you could say it was hermetically sealed with you on the outside.*

Their love had left Adora feeling displaced, not a part of a family. She often wondered if she'd been an accident, or conceived on a whim then conveniently forgotten, an unwanted houseguest or a pest that lived in the attic. She was like a mouse, often sneaking into the kitchen for food when no one was there to see because she hadn't wanted to spend another moment at a dinner table where she was unwanted. Though it had never been expressed to her in so many words, she had always had the feeling that she was allowed to stay in her home only because she didn't make any trouble.

It was a harsh thought. But all too frequently, when her parents would awake from their dreamy enchantment with one another, they'd stare at her as though her presence in their home—or at the dinner table, or in the back seat of the car—came as a complete and not entirely welcome surprise.

Even when her mother decided that life without her husband was no life at all, she hadn't remembered her daughter long enough to think of leaving a note of good-bye and absolution. Adora had needed that desperately; to hear that it wasn't her own fault that they weren't close, that her mother's sorrow and loneliness hadn't been caused by her daughter's inadequacy.

But there came no release, no absolution from such suspected guilt. The dark, hurt place from childhood remained inside, and Adora wrapped herself around it; yes, she did. And though sometimes she wanted to scream with frustration and pain, she couldn't because fear gagged her, made her mute. She wanted to lash out but was bound tighter to this pain than any mummy in a tomb.

Adora, Joy whispered sadly. *Don't.*

Weird to think, but when she had buried her dead she had somehow buried part of herself with them—maybe because it felt safer than leaving herself open to the world that had hurt her.

But that was no way to live life, encysted by her loss, by fear, by anger. She understood that now. But how to escape?

After her mom's death, Adora's life had slowly stalled. First her career and then her health, and she'd been left treading water while the tide of change rose around her, taking her further from her goals. She was haunted by the almost chronic fear that she was physically vulnerable like her father, or emotionally weak like her mother, or—heaven forbid—she was both, down deep inside where the pain lived, eating away at her self-confidence.

She was also revolted to discover that she had an endless wellspring of tears inside that flowed at any provocation. The tears were endless because loss seemed endless, renewed daily as she saw other families who were open and generous and loving and felt the sharp pangs of envy in her heart. Her tears fell at movies, in parks, when she saw stray dogs or hurt birds.

But finally, since the weeping fixed nothing and made people around her—even total strangers—act crazy, she had given it up. Who needed a casual lover's hysterical sympathy? The pain was internal and would have to remain that way until she figured out how to deal with it. There were better ways to express sorrow, she'd decided—when you couldn't avoid it altogether.

And then your cocoon of pain washed up on Kris's shore and every day is filled with sunshine and roses. Joy was sarcastic, bracing as a whiff of ammonia.

And what of it? Adora demanded. Wasn't it a good thing that recently things had been better? She hadn't felt either the familiar pain or fear since meeting Kris. Something about him had coaxed her to uncurl her clenched heart, and to consider letting the old hurt go. She had caught her first breaths of fresh air. She felt ready—or nearly ready—to cut her ties and open herself to new experiences.

Are you sure? 'Cause I think you have issues, girl— stuff you aren't even aware of.

Suddenly Adora was again aware of her body. Her restless blood was pounding. And though she wasn't the least bit cold, she felt herself shiver. Lust—she had all but forgotten what that was.

Oh, yeah. I'm sure. Issues or not.

She was aware that Kris's eyes rested on her while she ruminated, his gaze intent. He reached out now for her cheek, his fingers finding a tear that she hadn't been conscious of spilling. He stared at it, mesmerized. Then he looked into her eyes and she wondered, not for the first time, if he could somehow see into her mind. He'd said he was psychic—and he'd fixed her headache last night. . . .

He sees you when you're sleeping. He knows when you're awake.

Is that supposed to be scary, Joy? 'Cause it's not.

If you're not scared, you're an idiot. How can you be so trusting?

I don't know.

Though she complained about the intrusion, a part of Adora was glad to have Joy back because the snotty comments helped balance her—not that she would say so.

Like I don't already know what you're thinking. When will you wise up? You have no secrets from me.

I'll never wise up—or give up. Not 'til I'm old—too old to feel or care about anything. I am not my mother. Adora felt defiant.

"I'm so glad that this tear does not belong to me," Kris said, his voice slightly dazed and his eyes unfocused. "I wonder, though, for whom you shed it."

"Not who—just what," she whispered. "It's history."

"Ah."

For a moment, Adora thought that perhaps Kris would touch the tear to his lips, but instead he rubbed the moisture between his fingers and dazedly shook his head. She thought to herself: I am so glad I didn't run into you when I was a teen and my hormones were raging.

Kris's eyes snapped back to hers.

"I've found that getting older is not a problem. Getting wiser is another matter," he said suddenly. Could he be eavesdropping on her thoughts at this very minute? she wondered. No. Didn't psychics have to go into a trance or something? But then he added, "I wouldn't worry too much about having mental crutches. You break something, you need some support for a while until you heal."

Adora inhaled sharply. Kris's conversation could be a lot like Chinese mustard—an assault on the senses if you got too big a bite or weren't expecting it. However, it left one's nasal passages clear and ready to breathe fresh air. And she liked the image he suggested. She *had* broken something, and needed a crutch until she mended.

Therapy wouldn't hurt, either. Why not see another shrink if you want someone rummaging around in your head? Joy suggested.

Was he rummaging? Adora didn't like that idea.

"What do you mean, I need a crutch? Look, I'm a few beans short of a burrito today, but that's no reason to be impolite," Adora said aloud with a deliberate scowl. Kris only laughed. The sound shifted the last of her sadness aside.

"I am never impolite," he assured her. "And I am certain that all your beans are there and fully cooked."

Adora's stomach rumbled loudly, and her mouth flooded with saliva. She changed the subject. "Speaking of food—that roll was good, but keep an eye out for something with protein in it." She swallowed. "Besides pigeon. All these wonderful smells are making me feel piggish. I suddenly have *such* an appetite."

Kris went along. "Good. You could use a couple of trips to the trough," he said. "Let's find something tasty, and I'll stand you an early lunch."

Glancing up at him, again struck by his impossible beauty and kindness, Adora said, "You're on. I have to warn you, though, today I feel very greedy. This may cost you some big bucks."

"Excellent. Greed isn't always bad, you know. Not if you're greedy for the right things: love, faith, family, education—*Polish dogs*." Kris sniffed the air. "Has anything ever smelled so wonderful? I only just learned about hot dogs. They're great."

Adora caught the clear scent of sausages, and it made her mouth water. She hadn't been this hungry in months. It suddenly seemed that she was a starving person awakening from a coma, and she couldn't wait to taste everything.

She glanced over at Mugshottz. He looked dubious at Kris's choice of comestibles, but perhaps a gargoyle would consider barbecuing to be an abuse of perfectly good meat. Or maybe he was one of those people who had actually read about what was in hot dogs, and was therefore unable to think about them with enthusiasm.

"Of course, there is the added stipulation that you shouldn't hurt anyone to achieve your goals—yourself included. In fact, yourself especially," Kris went on, returning to his earlier point. He tucked a strand of hair behind Adora's ear. The touch could have been impersonal, but it wasn't, and for a moment Adora had the insane impulse to lean into him and kiss that perfect mouth.

What was he lecturing about? Oh, yeah—greed. Perhaps it would be more accurate to discuss gluttony. She had never been so hungry, ever! It was like she had suddenly acquired the appetite of a beast—

maybe two beasts. She wanted to rip and shred and chew and swallow. . . .

"So, I can't knock off nasty Aunt Gertrude to get extra hot dog money? Not even if I'm really, really hungry?" Adora asked, trying to divert her rising lust for Kris with humor. She took a physical step back as well. It was about the most difficult thing she had ever done. She felt like she was in orbit around him. Even backing off, inevitably she would come back around—and each time she got a little bit closer, found it a bit harder to pull away. One of these days, they were going to actually collide and then—

"No. No offing Aunt Gertrude," he agreed. His eyes were bright, and she lost herself in them.

"That was a quick no. After all, you don't know my aunt. I mean, her name's *Gertrude*. Think about how that's warped her. Getting rid of her could be a public service." Adora was speaking, but she wasn't really thinking about what she was saying. She was simply basking in Kris's presence.

He laughed. "I've known many Gertrudes, and I couldn't advocate killing any of them. That isn't what you really want to do anyway." Kris's eyes were dancing, and his knowing smile took her breath. He had to guess what she was feeling! It wouldn't be hard. She could feel the stain of desire in her cheeks, and when she looked down, she could almost see the pounding of her heart in her chest.

She stumbled, and Kris caught her arm. His touch was warm and made her skin tingle. The contact called to something in Adora that was pushing its way to the surface. Something hot. Sexy. Hungry. Perhaps a bit dangerous. It was as though all her appetites were awakened, which were muscling all her usual caution aside. If only she were slightly less inhibited, she would make a pass at him right in the middle of the market. She wanted to tear off his shirt and rub herself all over him.

Damn it, Kris! she thought at him directly. *Help me.*

He stopped abruptly, turning toward her with a lifted brow. "Just tell me what you need," he began.

Loud voices interrupted him. They were ugly and foreign, speaking a language of sibilants but with low guttural sounds that made Adora think of vicious hogs fighting over scraps. The noise raised the hair on her nape. She saw Kris stiffen as she herself had.

In an instant, Mugshottz spun about and placed his body between Kris and the speakers. She couldn't see around the troll's huge form, which had somehow swollen up. She wondered if maybe he had wings beneath his clothing.

"What are those men saying?" she asked, trying to see their assailants. The thing inside of her that moments before had been sensual and curious had turned dark and angry. It still wanted to rip and tear, though—that hadn't changed.

"They are casting racial slurs at us." Kris frowned and moved closer to her. "They really should know better. Come on. It's time to leave. These are Raxin's creatures. Things are going to get messy."

The angry thing inside Adora didn't want to leave, though. It wanted to see bones broken, skulls split open.

"Shouldn't we wait for Mugshottz?" she asked.

Before Kris could answer, a rock flew through the air and struck the bodyguard's chest. He didn't flinch, though the sound was terrible. The beast inside Adora was outraged at this insult.

"Now they've gone and done it," Kris said, taking her arm and urging her back. Her skin tingled violently, the warmth of their contact now a burning.

Kris's voice was strained. "Goddess take them! Why throw rocks? They've made Mugshottz really angry. You need to step back—*now*."

"How can you tell?" Adora asked, not moving. Mugshottz's stony posture hadn't altered at all.

"His feet." Kris's voice was rough. "They've turned black. You know a troll is angry when his feet get dark."

For the first time, Adora noticed that Mugshottz wasn't wearing any shoes. The sight of his naked, horny feet appalled her and filled her with intense pity, which she knew was probably misplaced but which was there all the same. She understood him: not troll, not goblin, not gargoyle—he didn't fit in anywhere. And once again, the misfit was being picked on, brutalized. Abandoned. Shame flooded her.

"Don't worry about Mugshottz. The rocks are just a childish insult," Kris said sharply, again guessing her thoughts. "It would take a double-barreled shotgun fired at point-blank range to do him any lasting harm. You aren't so impervious. Come away."

Adora couldn't explain that it wasn't the actual rocks she was concerned with, it was the *words*. There was such ugly emotion behind them, such sick anger, and they caused a burning pain in her soul. The vicious pigs squealed again, their words a tusk in Adora's gut that she could feel even without understanding their exact meaning.

She wanted to hurt them. Mugshottz hated these creatures and wanted to hurt them too, but he didn't react—couldn't react—because for some reason it would hurt Kris if he did.

Kris. Even as she thought of him, she could feel something shift in her employer's brain—in her own—and she realized that she'd been right: They were somehow psychically connected. He could read her thoughts and she his. At least, some of them.

A part of her began to panic.

Another rock was hurled with another insult, and anger roared through her without any warning. She was only partly aware of Kris's sudden indrawn breath, and didn't see the weird fire that leapt into his eyes as her rage arched into him, mingling with his own and dancing over his skin in a small ripple of lightning. A giant corona of red light encompassed them both, scorching the trees around them.

A part of Adora resisted the rage, wrestling for control of her mind and body—"hoc est corpus neum;" *this is my body*, something whispered in her head—but the fury was stronger and wanted to punish the people who had hurt Mugshottz. Or Kris. She wasn't sure now who was being hurt—and it didn't matter.

"Leave him alone, you stupid bigots!" she shouted, pulling away from Kris and trying to jump in front of Mugshottz. She saw their assailants. She was suddenly filled with a strange power, and was certain that if she wanted to, she could blast the offending goblins with a kind of psychic ray-gun that would crisp them before her eyes. "Back off or I'll show you what pain is, you cowards!"

The creatures spat, green slime arcing through the air. It spattered near her feet and began to sizzle.

Mugshottz snarled, and his shirt tore open. Clawed wings spread out, their taloned tops flexing as they ripped through his coat. In the distance someone screamed, and Adora saw people begin to run.

"Mugshottz! Don't do it! Stop—please!" Kris's voice was strange, almost a bestial growl. From the corner of her eye, Adora saw that he had dropped to his knees, his fingers digging into the hard-packed soil beneath the trees, leaving deep ruts. Thick roots tore lose with a nasty popping sound. Part of Adora wanted to turn and look at him because clearly something was wrong—no human had that kind of strength—but more of her wanted to attack the small gang of rock-throwers, to scorch them, wound them. To kill them. She wanted to reach inside and barbecue their hearts. She could do that. She could snuff them—kill every last one!

Adora! Kris was suddenly in her head, clamping down hard, trying to shut off her rage, to drain her anger. The experience hurt enough to make her moan.

Then Mugshottz threw off his paralysis. The bodyguard's arms wrapped around Adora, pulling her back and enveloping her in smothering curtains of stony flesh. Another rock flew at them, but it didn't connect: Adora pushed back with her remaining anger, a pressure wave that expanded out of her skull, rearranging the molecules in the air. It met up with the flying stone, which exploded into stinging dust. Then, as the three goblins began to flee, she sent a last blast of anger after them, setting their shoes and pants on fire.

The goblins howled, dropping to the ground to roll and beat out the flames, and Adora liked the sound. That was exactly how bad people should sound.

You've lost it, girl. How many times did your parents tell you not to play with fire? Joy asked sadly. *Don't you ever learn?*

Fire? Her parents? What . . . ?

Suddenly, Adora was back in control, and the realization of what she'd done stunned her. She went limp in Mugshottz's arms.

"Adora!" Kris's harsh voice cut through the haze of her anger. Or perhaps it was lack of oxygen. It was hard to be active when you couldn't breathe, and Mugshottz was squeezing awfully tight as he hurried her away from the scene.

"Put me down," she gasped. "I'm . . . I'm going to be sick."

"No, you're not." Kris's voice was firm.

"I am!"

"Go ahead," Mugshottz said. "I'm washable."

But then Kris was there with her, pale but upright. His smudged hands touched her face, closing her eyes against the searing light. Before her lids closed, she was shocked to see that the pupils of Kris's eyes had contracted into nonexistence, and that the silver-blue of his irises had spilled over into the whites and was filled with what looked like lightning.

I'm hallucinating, she thought.

No. Sorry, but this is all real. And you can't say I didn't warn you, Joy added. *You were never, never to use this power again. And now he knows about you. How can I keep you safe?*

What? What power . . . ?

Just go to sleep. And forget.

"Boss, are you all right?" Adora heard Mugshottz ask. "Jack'll skin me if I let you get hurt."

"I'm fine, but I need to get away from the crowds." Kris exhaled. "Her anger—*your* anger—caught me by surprise. It was that tear, I think. I could feel it running through my body, making me crazy. . . . I thought I'd controlled it, but then I felt her rage thrown out at those lutins and nearly lost it myself." Kris's voice was calmer, but he still sounded shaken. "Give her to me. I'm all right now."

"You're sure? Your eyes are still kind of funky." Their pace slowed but stayed rough. Mugshottz's body was hard as Adora bounced against it.

Kris said, "No, I'm fine. She isn't angry anymore. And I need to hold her. I was rough with her—too abrupt. I hurt her." His voice was filled with remorse.

Adora was handed over, and suddenly the world was softer, warmer. She sighed, relaxing. Everything would be all right now. Kris would keep her safe.

"Whoa! That was the strangest thing I ever felt," Mugshottz said. "Suddenly she was in my head and I could feel her anger like a blast of hot air. Look, it burned my shirt!" he pointed out.

Adora realized they were talking about something important, but she didn't understand. She was confused, and the voices were fading. Sleep rushed down on her, too heavy to fight, though she wanted to comprehend what was being said.

"This isn't good, I know, 'cause word about this will spread fast and piss off the goblin rebels trying to bring down Molybdenum. But . . . she's a plucky one, isn't she?" Mugshottz's rough tone was mitigated by clear admiration. "Imagine, her trying to protect me! Nobody except you has ever cared before."

"She's plucky all right—and more. Much, much more. I have to talk to Io and Jack. I thought I knew what she was, but I think we may have a fire-starter on our hands."

"That wasn't you?" Mugshottz sounded surprised.

"I've never used fire to hurt anyone. That was something in Adora—something not siren."

Something in me? A fire-starter? Not siren? Joy, what is he saying . . . ? Adora asked.

Go to sleep. It's just a bad dream. Forget, now—just forget.

"Will she remember anything when she wakes up?" Mugshottz asked.

"Not if we're lucky. I'll wipe her mind as best I

can—and I think I'll have some help from the Other in her. This isn't something she's ready to face. I don't think she has any inkling of what she really is."

"How can that be? I mean, if she's a fire-starter, wouldn't she have had trouble as a kid?" Mugshottz asked.

"I don't know how she can be what she is. The longer I'm with her, the more questions I have." Kris sounded worried.

"Weird. Well, I sure hope Morrison has an extra shirt in the car. I kind of wrecked this one. And it was the last non-Hawaiian shirt they had at the big and tall store," the troll bodyguard added.

"True. But you were damn impressive," Kris said kindly. "One of those goblins wet himself, and I saw a lady faint."

"Really? She *fainted*?" Mugshottz sounded proud. "I haven't done that in centuries."

Adora let herself faint.

There came a time when the shaman saw that he could do no more, and he left the world of Man. He no longer walked among them every day, but came instead only one day a year. The day he chose was in the dark of winter, when the Sons of Man most needed comfort and reassurance that Light would again return.

—Niklas 4:9

It was Beltane Eve, Walpurgis Night, and in the northern lands the shamans were gathering their people in pastures, in forests, on mountains for the holy celebration. He, too, was gathering his flock, calling them to the Goddess that they would worship with their bodies in the holy fire's light.

The one who had been many lifted his flute to his lips and began to play, a haunting paean that called his people to this feast of the heart, to the fires of spring, to physical love.

A man of silver, he stood naked, save for the mantle of moon and the leaping pyre's light. His hair rode back from his face, a silvery banner carried by the mountain wind. His eyes shone bright in the semidarkness, bits of shattered stars that gleamed with the Goddess's fire.

Around him, the people swayed, some moaned, and others danced ecstatically, tearing at their clothes until they were also naked. The one who had been many smiled, because he saw that this was good.

CHAPTER EIGHT

Miffith listened in consternation as an informant relayed the information that Kris Kringle—the ancient fey known as Niklas—had been involved in some battle at the human farmers' market, and that he'd had some woman with him who was able to light goblins on fire. He didn't know what to make of this. Niklas had been missing for a long time, and had never believed in violence. He had actually been very kind to many poor goblins, Miffith's family included.

Miffith finished writing up the informant's tale, then sat with fingers poised over the delete button. His first impulse was to lose the memo and never tell General Anaximander what had happened.

But that wouldn't work. This was too amazing a story. And if the general discovered that he had withheld it . . . Miffith shuddered.

No, he'd have to tell the General. Besides, maybe it was a good thing, he thought, cheering up. Maybe Niklas would help the rebel cause.

* * *

Voices. Words.

"It's ancestral consciousness coming awake."

Adora understood the individual words, but the sentence didn't mean anything to her. Still, she knew she was with Kris in body and mind, and was therefore not alarmed. There was no logical reason for her feeling; she simply knew it was true because . . . well, because something inside told her so.

A hand not her own brushed back her hair, pulling the curtain of darkness aside. Slowly Adora took stock of her body, pushing herself back into the space she seemed to have temporarily abandoned. Yes, this was her body, but . . . something was different. She couldn't say precisely how it differed, because she couldn't quite recall how she had been before. She tried to look back, but her memory stalled. Her brain was like a turnstile, allowing thoughts to travel one way but never back again. It seemed to her that Kris had stripped the cogs and was forcing her to use some other part of her mind to think another way. Maybe to forget something.

Was that bad—forgetting?

Can you hear me? a voice asked.

What?

Adora's eyes cracked open again. She was looking out a narrow gap in a curtained window. The blue sky of morning had been reupholstered in gray smog and stitched with white contrails. Closer to the ground, the scenery rushed by in a gray blur.

She was in a car. A big car. On a highway.

Good. Getting far away was good. But where were they, exactly? She tried to sit up straight, but it was no use. Kris's arm was around her and it was heavy.

A thought popped into her head. Kris and his

band of merry men were about to retreat into Sher-wood Forest—all the better to lie in wait for the nasty Sheriff of Nottingham. But that made no sense at all. She must still be dreaming. Or something.

You . . . fainted. The voice was very faraway, muf-fled. She knew the voice but for the moment couldn't put a name to it. She pushed harder, trying to remember. Joy?

"Adora?" Kris asked, and then his arm was help-ing her sit up. "Feeling better now? If you're awake, we'll get you some lunch. You're probably still hun-gry and I think you need to eat."

"Okay," she said, but the word was mushy like her brain. Her hand rested a moment on Kris's leg, and she was grateful for his heat and solidity. It had been quite a while since the world had gotten away from her like that. If Kris hadn't been there, making her feel safe, she might have reached for her purse and started pawing around in hopes of finding one or two of those little happy pills that were probably still hiding at the bottom her bag.

The thought jabbed at her. She hadn't thought se-riously about those pills for a while. At one time, she had been dependent on them and they had known it. They would whisper to her every time things got rough: *Take me! Take me, and I'll ease your pain.* Later, when she had been completely lost and despairing, they had spoken to her more seductively: *Take me! Take all of me, and I'll ease your pain forever.*

It had been a tempting offer, too, on those very long dark nights when it was impossible to escape the knowledge that she was alone. She had already felt as if she'd died and passed on to some other horrible afterlife where she'd been left in an aban-doned limbo. They had almost gotten her.

But there had been a book to finish, a story that

needed to be told, and so she had reluctantly said *No, not now* to the pills. And that had eventually become a *No, not ever*. Finally she had found the strength to throw the bottle in the bathroom away. She had decided on life.

It wasn't that she really believed there would be a day of judgment where she'd be called up from the dead to answer for throwing her life away, but a part of her had faith that there was *something*, and to take her life would be to profane the soul that had been gifted her by Another.

The impulse to end it all hadn't gone away at once, of course. It would still creep over her sometimes when she was driving her car along a cliff road, or standing somewhere very high without a railing. In fact, she feared that a part of her might still have this destructive impulse buried deep down inside, with a lot of other emotions she preferred not to examine. She also sometimes wondered if this was what had made her sick—a subconscious rationalization from this powerful, suicidal fragment of personality that had said it wouldn't really be suicide if illness took her.

Adora made a soft noise of denial and thought again—for one tiny moment—about the pills that might be in her purse. They could take all this fear and pain away....

Kris's hand smoothed her hair. "Don't worry," he said gently. "You're safe now."

And suddenly she was.

Thinking of her purse, Adora looked about blearily until she spotted it on the floor. The sight was reassuring. Things couldn't be all that wrong if she still had her bag.

"There's Caveman Joe's." Those were the first words from someone other than Kris that made complete sense, and Mugshottz actually sounded excited.

Mugshottz. Adora turned her head. The bodyguard looked perfectly normal—or as normal as he ever looked. Hadn't his shirt changed, though? She'd thought he was wearing white and not blue.

"I've heard of it," Adora said thickly, then swallowed. Her mouth was dry and she still felt a little dizzy. She must have fallen asleep for a while. Napping always made her sluggish and stupid. And it was embarrassing that she'd done it in front of Kris—she hoped she hadn't snored. She made an effort to open her eyes wide and tried to speak more clearly. "They specialize in what is being called nouvelle carnivore cuisine, which means they do lots of exotic meat carved into artistic shapes. And small portions."

Mugshottz sniffed at this last bit of news.

"They also do a chocolate mousse torte that makes people see God," Morrison piped up from the driver's seat. He popped something into his mouth and began crunching noisily. "That isn't in small portions, though. And I hear that if you're human and can actually finish your dessert, you get a second one free."

Kris grinned. Adora felt him smile against her hair, and she turned her head to watch his face. His features could stretch like rubber bands. He was fascinating to stare at. Even dizzy, she thought so.

"Then by all means, let's do Caveman Joe's. I haven't seen God in centuries," Kris said. He glanced at Mugshottz and added, "We'll just keep our visit short and sweet."

Everyone except Adora laughed. She still didn't have the hang of Kris's humor. In fact, she often didn't know when he was kidding. If he ever was.

"Here, have a sip of this, Adora," Morrison said, handing back a small silver flask. A gust of coffee-scented breath wafted her way.

"What is it? Not brandy?" she asked.

"No, just . . . just water. It's from a . . . a health food store. It's great for restoring electrolytes."

Feeling suddenly very thirsty, Adora unscrewed the cap and took a small sip. She was aware that Kris and Mugshottz were both watching her carefully but couldn't think why. She frowned at their attention but had to admit that maybe it was justified. Sometimes she got weird when she was dehydrated—forgetful and confused.

Of course, that did beg the question of how she had gotten dehydrated. What had they been doing? The farmers' market—that's where they'd been.

She glanced at her wrist: 11:04. Thank heavens, it wasn't late. She hadn't lost that much time.

"Did I faint or something?" she asked Kris, trying to recall how she had gotten back to the car but drawing a complete blank. Her final memory was of talking about Polish dogs for lunch—which was odd, because she didn't actually like Polish dogs.

"You were a bit overcome," Kris said. "We'll have to be more careful to keep you away from . . . the sun."

Adora nodded slowly. The sun—that made sense. It could make her very sick, especially inland, where there was no protective fog to screen the rays. But a part of her didn't believe this explanation and inside she asked, *Joy? Did I really faint out there?*

Later. Kris is right. You need to eat, and I need to think. The voice was coming in clearer now, wasn't so muffled, but if she didn't know better, Adora would think that Joy sounded slightly shaken, too.

Reviving as she sipped the water in the flask, yet still tired and floating mentally, Adora decided not to pursue the topic. If Joy wasn't squawking about what happened, she herself wouldn't bother to expend the energy either. At least, not right then.

The car stopped. Morrison had parked at the far edge of the parking lot, in the limited shade of a high cement wall covered in dusty, sunburned ivy. The sound of constant traffic suffused them, amplified by the ten-foot barrier.

"I'll stay here and listen to the . . . radio," the driver said, turning in his seat as he popped a square of gum out of its foil packet. The brand name startled her. Adora watched as he began to chew the nicotine gum with loud crunching noises.

"I didn't know you smoked," she said.

"I don't. I just like riding the nicotine rush, you know?" He grinned at her. "It's better than speed!"

Looking from Morrison to the dashboard, she noticed that there was a small bowl of roasted coffee beans balanced there. That was probably what he had been munching earlier. The thought of the constant buzz caused by a combination of nicotine and caffeine was enough to make her teeth ache.

"Guys, have a heart and send something out to me. I can smell the ribs from here," Morrison said.

Adora shuddered. Ribs. Yeah, those would go great with nicotine gum and coffee beans.

She got out of the car in the shade. Noon was coming—that horrible beast of heat and light that would feed on her like a vampire, sucking her dry no matter how much water she drank. Noon wasn't so bad on the coast, but in the city, with all its reflective concrete . . . Well, she would just have to be out of the sun before the worst of it hit.

Guessing at her distress, Kris reached under his seat and pulled out a parasol. It was antique, a silly thing made of yellowed cutwork linen, but it would do a fair job of getting the sun off her.

"Let's go."

The first thing Adora noticed about Caveman Joe's was that the restaurant didn't observe the statewide ban on cigarette smoking. Of course, the owners probably figured there wasn't any point, what with all the greasy meat smoke roiling into the air from the open pits. The employees had embraced the caveman theme and were running about in animal pelts that were, she was almost positive, made of real fur, though she would have been hard-pressed to say just what kind.

The second inescapable thing about the restaurant was the acoustics. The place had an authentic echoing-cave feel. The rumbling babble of dozens of voices in the chamber was deafening.

The final unusual aspect of the decor did not become apparent until her eyes had adjusted to the dark, and that was the bones scattered all over the floor. Adora had a bad moment where she thought that the giant rib cages might be real, but a second glance—and sniff—assured her they were only plaster replicas. She was still careful to step around them—especially the Tyrannosaurus Rex head, which was stuffed full of ivory fangs that were realistically sharp.

Usually the combined assault on her senses here would be enough to drive Adora away, but just as Kris had predicted, her appetite was once again being stimulated and she wanted nothing quite so much as to sink her teeth into a giant hamburger. Normally she wasn't big on beef, but perhaps being with Kris had influenced her tastes. There were certainly moments when the focus of her thinking shifted in his direction and she felt as though she could almost see things through his eyes.

Or his rose-colored glasses.

A hostess—if that was the correct term—with a short fuzzy skirt that looked very old, and large breasts that looked very new, came bustling over. She paused for an instant, taking them in, and then with a pat of her blue-streaked hair and a small shimmy, she leaned into Kris and asked what she could do for him.

The breathy voice, the overpowering perfume, the proximity and mostly the silicone breasts combined to annoy Adora. Before she had time to think about her actions, her hands were reaching for the woman's red-taloned fingers, which were inching up Kris's arm. She swatted them away as she would a spider.

Startled, the hostess backed up. Her mouth actually trembled, and disappointment filled her face. She looked like a little kid who'd had candy stolen. But the doe eyes only made Adora want to smack her with the parasol.

Adora could feel Kris's amusement at her actions, as well as Mugshottz's concern, and she was suddenly embarrassed by both. It wasn't like her to make a scene, but she absolutely could not stand to see this woman rubbing up against Kris.

"We'd like to get an order to go," Kris said, his voice smooth and somehow seductive. Charm wafted off him like a wave of warm air, and it displaced some of the noise and smoke, enclosing them in an intimate bubble. "Can you do that for us?"

The hostess's pouting mouth quickly smoothed and she nodded obediently, her eyes aglow.

"We need beef ribs, zucchini slaw and chocolate

mousse for three," Kris began, without consulting a menu.

"And a hamburger—medium-well done," Adora put in. Catching a stray whiff from the deep fryer, she added, "And an order of onion rings. And a root beer float."

Kris repeated the order to the hostess, who nodded, then he turned to Mugshottz, who ordered a venison steak, raw, and an orange soda. The girl never blinked, not at his request or at Mugshottz's hard, inhuman voice. She seemed unaware of anyone but Kris.

"Better throw in two ginger ales. Do you need to write this down?" Kris asked gently, and the woman nodded again, reaching for a pad of paper at the podium constructed of stegosaurus tails. She scribbled quickly and then backed away, smiling all the while at Kris, her eyes slightly glazed.

"Goblin-fruit addict," Mugshottz muttered.

"She's been fey-struck," Kris contradicted.

Once the hostess had backed around a tunnel corner, Adora allowed herself to stop glaring and to take in some of the restaurant patrons. They all looked human enough, but she had a strong feeling that many of the diners had been born with a second pair of arms.

There was one table of young toughs who seemed particularly interested in Mugshottz. They scowled a lot, and their eyes blinked independently under tattooed lids. One of then pulled out a cell phone and laid it on the table. His black-nailed finger tapped it repeatedly. It somehow seemed like a warning.

"You see them?" Kris asked quietly. He had melted back into the shadows.

"Yes," Adora answered, before she realized that he was probably talking to Mugshottz. "What's wrong with them, anyway?"

"I suspect they are part of the rebel force massing at the outskirts of the city."

"Are they dangerous?"

"Most of them are like ants at a picnic—annoying but not lethal. But some of those groups are well-trained, well-organized and well-funded. In sufficient numbers, they can be a threat."

"Rebels against what?" Adora asked, keeping her voice down. She glanced up at Mugshottz and found his eyes riveted on the goblins. His expression was unusually forbidding. She noticed above his head a sign that read:

BURNT OFFERINGS
TUESDAY NIGHTS
12 A.M.
BYOS

BYOS?

Bring Your Own Sacrifice, Joy suggested, making Adora shudder.

She saw Joy's point, though. This was a hostile place. The tables near the dance floor and bar were large, but the to-go area where they waited had a grudging look; it was small and almost shabby, and there were no chairs. She understood the psychology they were employing. If you took your order out, they could only soak you once. They wanted people to come in and stay, to have dinner and then dance wildly, after which you would need snacks and something to drink at twenty bucks a pop. They probably had other offerings too. What had

Mugshottz said about that stupid slut waiting on them? She was a goblin-fruit addict?

"For one thing, this rebel sect is against the current laws mandating all goblins who live aboveground have surgery to look human," Kris said, interrupting her unkind thoughts. "Their eyes are the giveaway. The first surgery hive-goblin children have is on their eyes. Surveys have shown that humans are more disturbed by lutin independent blinking than they are by extra arms, so it is corrected almost at birth."

"They look nasty," Adora admitted. "But I guess I can sympathize. I mean, I can't imagine living in a place where they ordered bodily mutilation of infants. I should really interview some goblins. I can't believe how ignorant I am."

"No," Kris said.

Adora blinked at the flat reply.

"Why not? It would help with the book."

"No."

"Look, with nonfiction you have to be accurate and balanced. Research and input from many sources is important. You can't just hum a few bars and then fake the rest."

"I'm sorry, but it isn't safe. The bodily mutilation is the least of what goes on," Kris said. "And don't be misled by sympathy into attempting to socialize with them. These rebels are also against the laws that forbid the hunting and eating of humans."

"You must be joking."

"I only wish I were. It used to be a common farming practice, using humans as fertilizer in the goblin-fruit fields. And most goblin rebel leaders have one thing in common—a certain innovative sadism that appeals to their followers. They practice what you might term a tombstone philosophy."

"What's that? A tombstone philosophy?" she asked.

He seemed not to hear her. "It's very interesting that they are here and sitting openly in this public space. I think we've stumbled into a wretched hive of scum and villainy." Kris did a wonderful Alec Guinness impersonation. He added in his usual voice: "In fact, I bet if we went into one of the back rooms we'd find a stash of goblin fruit—the real stuff, fed on blood and bones."

Mugshottz grunted. Adora, having a sudden nauseating visualization of heavily laden tomato plants whose roots were twined through a human skull, decided that maybe she would take all produce off her hamburger—just to be safe.

"That might be wise," Kris agreed.

Their hostess reappeared bearing two large bags covered in the restaurant logo. She hadn't been gone long, and Adora was willing to bet that their order had been filled with food that belonged to some other patrons.

"I've included utensils and extra barbecue sauce. If you're sure that's all—," the hostess began.

"Yes, thank you." Kris's voice was again deep and smoky. He smiled. "What do I owe you?"

The woman looked disappointed that there was nothing more she could get him: salt and pepper, extra napkins, a blow job . . .

Meow. We are *in a bad mood today, aren't we? Why do you care what she does?*

Stupid bimbo—she's all but drooling. It's disgusting.

He's not drooling back, so just cool it.

"The total is two hundred and eight dollars," the hostess said.

Adora almost squawked in protest.

Yeah, even with a blow job that would be kind of high, Joy agreed.

But Kris reached in his pocket and handed over the bills without protest, including a generous tip. "Thank you very much. You've been very helpful," he assured her, and the hostess shivered with pleasure.

"Our number is on the receipt. If you want anything, just call."

"Come on," Adora muttered as she stalked for the door. It was hot and bright outside, but it still felt cleaner. She'd had more than enough of bimbos, bug-eyed rebels and burnt offerings.

Kris and Mugshottz apparently felt the same, since they followed immediately, though the troll took the time to open his bag and fish out his raw venison. Adora watched in fascination as his jaw unhinged and he swallowed the steak whole, just like a python would.

"This has been the weirdest day of my life," Adora muttered.

"And it's still young," Kris said cheerfully, re-opening the parasol.

And then they killed the burnt offering and took it to the king, who was pleased. But though praised for their gift by the king's priests, still famine and darkness came to the land and many died that winter.

—Niklas 8:9

"You cannot possibly hope to pass me off as a Bishop," Niklas objected.

"My son, new religions are like infants taking their first steps. They must be assisted. You are already revered far and wide for your many kindnesses, and I strongly suspect . . ."

"Yes?" Niklas asked gently. "What do you suspect, Father?"

"I think that it is not so new, this veneration by the masses. You have known it before."

The two men looked at one another, both old but only one of them wrinkled.

"If you believe this to be true . . . then, I am a blasphemy," Niklas pointed out. " 'I am the Lord thy God and thou shall have no other god before me,' " he quoted. "You could hardly want me associated with this church."

"New religions also tend to be somewhat simplistic," the old human said diplomatically. *"But they evolve. And I believe—in time—that we can grow to accommodate other points of view. My task—and yours—is to see that this faith has the time to develop, to be cultivated."*

"You wish to make me a farmer of men?" This amused Niklas.

"Of men's souls. Yes."

181

CHAPTER NINE

It was seven o'clock. The last few despairing rays of sun slid off the buildings, and the deep blue of night eased itself into the air. The sky turned a velvet indigo that showed no stars: It would get no darker above the city and those would remain hidden by lights no matter the hour.

Standing at a stoplight, Adora sighed with relief. With the sun gone she could enjoy herself a bit. Things had been frantic since they returned to the hotel, people rushing about and phones ringing endlessly.

Adora admired the cars piled up at the light, all thoroughbreds, engines snorting and their riders ready to go the moment the signal turned green. It made no sense to take the Packard out when they were wandering from store to store, but she wished they had anyway. That was an automobile with a pedigree, even among these finest of the fine. It made Mercedeses and Jaguars look like stable nags.

She hadn't planned on doing any sightseeing, but

there was no avoiding it or the tourists. Rodeo Drive, like its well-heeled visitors, had kept itself in good shape and demanded attention, was beautifully dressed and accessorized. There had been a facelift or two on the older buildings, some dermabrasion for the younger facades and chemicals all around so things were smooth and glossy. Exhausted as she was, Adora wasn't sure if she loved or hated its artificial beauty.

There were strange women too, dressed exotically in embroidered togas and golden veils sitting behind large plate-glass windows. Mugshottz explained that they were lutin women whose virtue could be negotiated—though the sliding scale apparently stopped far short of bargain-basement prices. This was Rodeo Drive, after all. Adora wasn't certain how she felt about that, either.

Mugshottz was distracted, constantly scenting the area and scanning their surroundings with hard eyes that didn't give any clue about his feelings. Still, he followed without protest as she went from boutique to boutique, searching for the things Kris had instructed her to buy: hat, coat, gloves, an amber pendant. And they ended up in several unlikely stores because this wasn't coat season except for furs, which though perennially popular she wouldn't wear. She had never been able to tolerate fur on her body. It was the curse of a too vivid imagination, but it had always seemed to her that she could hear the pelts whimpering and feel their blood on her skin.

"I'm sorry," she said softly to Mugshottz, "but I just can't wear any of these coats. They're . . . awful."

"It's okay," he assured her, finally showing some animation. "It's important that you find something that doesn't bother you. . . . What about that one?"

he asked, pointing at a coat displayed in front of an old movie poster of *Casablanca*. Awe entered his voice. "Isn't that great?"

"Do you think it's me?" Adora asked dubiously.

"Oh, yeah! Don't you love Humphrey Bogart?" Mugshottz sounded wistful. "Anyway, it isn't fur."

Adora had some misgivings, but she said, "Okay. I'll try it on."

"Here—I'll help you."

This is a mistake, Joy warned.

I know.

But unwilling to quash Mugshottz's new enthusiasm, Adora trailed after him, trying to smile when he proffered the coat.

Kris eyed her over the rim of his cup, and Adora scowled as his eyes began to twinkle. Annoyed as she was, she couldn't help but notice that he still looked gorgeous—like the best man at a wedding, or perhaps the officiate, a well-heeled judge who favored Italian designers. He had on an exquisite coal-colored suit with a white silk shirt and tie, and his long hair was pulled back tight. From well-shod feet to silvery locks, she was attracted to every inch of him.

Can't you just see him in sexy red bishop's robes? Joy asked—but softly, as though afraid of being overheard. She had been behaving oddly since Adora's fainting spell.

Actually—no. She couldn't. Or wouldn't. The thought of the clergy made her feel uncomfortable, and desiring a priest was just—well—icky.

"Um . . . admittedly I am not up to the very latest in women's fashion, but what are you wearing, a parachute?" Kris asked, leaning back in his chair, long legs stretched before him, elegant hands put-

GET UP TO
4 FREE BOOKS!

You can have the best romance delivered to your door for less than what you'd pay in a bookstore or online. Sign up for one of our book clubs today, and we'll send you **FREE* BOOKS** just for trying it out...**with no obligation to buy, ever!**

HISTORICAL ROMANCE BOOK CLUB

Travel from the Scottish Highlands to the American West, the decadent ballrooms of Regency England to Viking ships. Your shipments will include authors such as CONNIE MASON, SANDRA HILL, CASSIE EDWARDS, JENNIFER ASHLEY, LEIGH GREENWOOD, and many, many more.

LOVE SPELL BOOK CLUB

Bring a little magic into your life with the romances of Love Spell—fun contemporaries, paranormals, time-travels, futuristics, and more. Your shipments will include authors such as LYNSAY SANDS, CJ BARRY, COLLEEN THOMPSON, NINA BANGS, MARJORIE LIU and more.

As a book club member you also receive the following special benefits:

- **30% OFF all orders through our website & telecenter!**
- **Exclusive access to special discounts!**
- **Convenient home delivery and 10 day examination period to return any books you don't want to keep.**

There is no minimum number of books to buy, and you may cancel membership at any time. See back to sign up!

*Please include $2.00 for shipping and handling.

YES! ☐

Sign me up for the **Historical Romance Book Club** and send my TWO FREE BOOKS! If I choose to stay in the club, I will pay only $8.50* each month, a savings of $5.48!

YES! ☐

Sign me up for the **Love Spell Book Club** and send my TWO FREE BOOKS! If I choose to stay in the club, I will pay only $8.50* each month, a savings of $5.48!

NAME: _____

ADDRESS: _____

_____

TELEPHONE: _____

E-MAIL: _____

☐ **I WANT TO PAY BY CREDIT CARD.**

☐ VISA ☐ MasterCard. ☐ DISCOVER

ACCOUNT #: _____

EXPIRATION DATE: _____

SIGNATURE: _____

Send this card along with $2.00 shipping & handling for each club you wish to join, to:

Romance Book Clubs
20 Academy Street
Norwalk, CT 06850-4032

Or fax (must include credit card information!) to: 610.995.9274.
You can also sign up online at www.dorchesterpub.com.

*Plus $2.00 for shipping. Offer open to residents of the U.S. and Canada only.
Canadian residents please call 1.800.481.9191 for pricing information.
If under 18, a parent or guardian must sign. Terms, prices and conditions subject to change. Subscription subject
to acceptance. Dorchester Publishing reserves the right to reject any order or cancel any subscription.

JOIN NOW!

ting his porcelain cup aside. The act should have looked effeminate but didn't.

"You said to be discreet and get something full-length. This covers everything." Adora peered at him over the top of her giant sunglasses.

"My dear!" He positively grinned. "This is your idea of discreet? Anyway, that looks like it would fit Mugshottz. Didn't they have anything in your size?"

Frowning, Adora turned and checked herself in the full-length mirror and gave a start. Not having seen the outfit in its accessorized entirety, she hadn't quite comprehended the extent of the fashion disaster she had perpetrated on her hurried shopping trip the night before.

"Damn." That's what came of shopping when one was exhausted.

And from taking advice from a gargoyle.

Joy was right. The expensive coat truly looked ridiculous in the bright light of morning. The sleeves were a hand's breadth too long, and it was absolutely the wrong shade for a blonde. It made her skin look muddy green. She had on a fedora as well that was a shade too large and compounded the sins of the coat—also purchased yesterday for an outrageous price at a vintage clothing store under advisement from an enthusiastic Mugshottz, who said it completed her outfit. Which it did, in a horrible way.

Maybe it was the way she was wearing the hat, she thought, adjusting it. The brim was pulled down until it almost met the upper rim of her oversized sunglasses, which were so dark that she could barely see her hand in front of her face, and which forced her to wear them down on her nose so she could walk without falling. That made her nose look awfully long.

If that wasn't bad enough, she had the collar of her trench coat—which sported entirely too many pockets and shoulder flaps for her taste, but what could you do on short notice in the spring when the stores had no selection?—turned up so it reached past her cheekbones. She had thought herself dashing, but really she was a walking cliché. All that was missing was a walkie-talkie wristwatch and a handgun. So, fine. She had to admit—to herself, anyway—that perhaps she had overdone it with her accessories too.

Also bony as she was, the effect of all that flapping fabric was a bit scarecrow-like. She should have known better. She *did* know better. This wasn't her style. She'd been a steady 29-29-29 until her sophomore year of high school. She'd filled out a little then in the traditional places, and gotten a lot taller, but though her statistics had improved, she was still far from curvaceous.

And it was annoying, because what she had really wanted was the white marabou coat with the coral satin lining paired with those silly beaded sandals. But those had been hideously expensive, and no one except perhaps Liberace's ghost would have thought it "discreet." Still, she wished now that she had bought those instead. It was deflating to have Kris look better than she did.

Adora pulled off her sunglasses and tossed them aside.

"Well . . . I thought people would see me and think: There goes a spy," she invented glibly, trying not to sound despondent. "Or maybe a private eye. They probably have lots of those here, what with the movie stars and all."

"And the addition of a spy to my entourage helps

how?" Kris asked politely, though she sensed hidden laughter.

"Well . . . if they think I'm a spy, they won't think I'm your biographer. Hell, they probably won't even notice you. Anyway, don't you like the hat? It's classic." She offered her profile, changing the subject. "Do you think a cigar would help? Or a flask of whiskey? A gun?"

"Hmm. You do know that I don't like to lie unless there is absolutely no other choice?" he said.

Adora dropped her chin and made a face, which only amused him more.

She said, "This might be a good moment to say nothing, then. This damned hat and coat were expensive. And Mugshottz really liked them." Adora flipped down her collar and pulled off the fedora. "This is all a bit new to me, you know. Usually my jobs are much less exciting or dangerous. My biggest danger is paper cuts—and absolutely no one has ever cared that I'm a biographer."

Which wasn't strictly true, but she was willing to stretch the point.

"Of course," Kris said soothingly. "And I am very sorry about all this haste and skullduggery. Just to satisfy my own curiosity, how many pockets does that coat have?"

Adora grinned. "Seven visible, three hidden and a place for a small holster. I got it in the Spies-R-Us department at Kingman's, if you're interested."

"Oh, I'm fascinated, believe me. You see, I think the coat was designed for an unmodified goblin. That's against city ordinances."

"Oh." The idea hadn't occurred to her. The coat did seem to have double pockets in the right places and plenty of space for an extra set of arms.

"But, please—let me atone for causing this distress. I shouldn't have sent you out when you were so tired. Or with Mugshottz. I'll arrange for someone to take it back for you. I am certain that we can do much . . ."

"Yes?" she prompted as he paused.

"We can find something that suits you better. The coat is simply not doing justice to your intelligence or beauty."

"Good save," Adora remarked with a half-smile.

Kris grinned fully. "Thank you. If you live long enough, you finally learn what to say to women. In certain circumstances." He called out: "Pennywyse!" Then, to Adora: "So, what would you really like? You know, all it need do is keep the sun off and offer a small degree of warmth at night."

"Well . . ."

Tell him about the pink coat.

I can't. You know I can't. It's a bimbo coat. He'll think I'm a frivolous ditz—and an expensive one at that.

"Um, something in a tasteful camel-hair would be nice," she said, but without enthusiasm, as she peeled off the olive monstrosity. Yes, it definitely looked like it was made for someone with more appendages. Maybe Mugshottz could use it. . . . But no, big as it was, it was still too small for him.

Pennywyse materialized.

"Do you have the receipt?" Kris asked Adora.

"Yes."

"I'm sorry to add to your work, Pennywyse, but this coat must be returned, and since Mugshottz is out—"

"I feared this would happen," Pennywyse said.

Adora protested, "I can go myself. I don't need a bodyguard—it's broad daylight on Rodeo Drive, for heaven sakes." But both Kris and Pennywyse shook their heads.

"But . . ." Adora faltered. She had no way of knowing Kris's regular travel routine, but she was certain that it didn't usually involve so many furtive phone calls in foreign languages or hurried packing assisted by a bodyguard and political adviser. There was, though she hated the stray thought that wedged in her brain, a sense of soldiers preparing for battle and evacuating the noncombatants from the war zone. What they didn't need to worry about was her shopping.

And yet that was exactly what was worrying them.

"Trust me. You don't want to wander a goblin city alone. Not today," Pennywyse said. "Not right now, when there is so much unrest. And anyway, it isn't my burden. The hotel will take care of this. Believe me, it's what the concierge lives for."

This made Adora feel somewhat better.

"I have also decided that discretion is not called for in this instance due to a change in plans, so please choose a replacement that's"—Kris tilted his head and squinted at her—"pink. With feathers or fur, or something frivolous."

Adora stared at him. "Are you reading my mind?" she demanded. "Damn it, Kris! Are you some super-psychic? If you are, it's really impolite to peep in my brain without telling."

"I am Santa Claus," Kris pointed out. "But I also simply know about the other coat. Mugshotz said that you stopped dead in your tracks and forgot to breathe when you saw it."

"It's too expensive," Adora began, regret strong in her voice. "And I'd probably drop fifty I.Q. points if I wore it."

"Please!" he scoffed. "And it's entirely my fault that you need a coat. This is a business expense, and my responsibility to bear. Anyway, I know the young goblin designer who made that coat; I've taken an interest in her career. You would be doing her a favor by wearing it."

Pennywyse had gathered up her discarded trench coat and was waiting for her decision. He didn't fidget, but she felt his impatience. She had temporarily forgotten—probably because no one had explained why—that they needed to make haste from the city. Their trip to the farmers' market and Caveman Joe's still seemed like a strange dream.

"You know, the Puritans got it all wrong: Not everything that is fun and beautiful is sinful," Kris remarked softly, studying her face. "You aren't afraid to have fun, are you?"

That sounds like a challenge, Joy pointed out.

Was she afraid?

You're sure out of practice at the fun thing.

"Adora, if you could just accept that you are different!" Kris stood and came toward her. She had to tilt her head back to look into his eyes. "For some people it is enough to grow up in the dirt of civilization, to bloom briefly, to reseed their bit of ground and then die. They draw in their horizons, root in one place and keep their world small so it seems less frightening. They live brief, tiny lives. And though the world is full of magnificent things that feed the mind and spirit, these people have sad, starved souls that never know joy or wonder.

"But that isn't the destiny of all people. Writers, artists, musicians, poets—these are touched by the finger of Gaia, and though they may try not to see how vast the world is, still the wide world comes to them and forces them—and then to share their vision with others. The gift sometimes destroys them, forces their talents into early, painful flowerings that leave them too spent to go on. But these are the chosen messengers of Divinity, and they are so beautiful, so filled with light."

Kris looked at her—*into* her—and Adora felt suddenly beautiful, luminous. He said, "You were not born to live an ordinary life. Even had you been planted in the barest soil, your vision would still grow to light the world. And when the time is right, the ground will tremble and your destiny will burst forth and bring beauty to all you touch."

And maybe this was the time when it would happen, she thought, caught up in his words even though she was aware they were a bit over the top. Perhaps this time, her book would reach the masses and move them.

"Bloom," he commanded.

Easily conjuring to mind a field where dreams and magnificent stories looked a lot like wild blue coastal lupine that sprang up in the barren rocks every April, Adora had to admit that Kris was something of a poet himself.

Or a very good psychiatrist, Joy suggested. Adora's field began to fade.

But Kris went on: "Though scythes of disbelief and fear may cut dreamers down, it does not matter, because others will remember and the ideas will live on, feeding still more. *That* is immortality."

The whole scythe thing was probably meant metaphorically, but Adora didn't care for this part of Kris's speech as much. Possibly because her deplorable taste in movies had shown her too many masked maniacs wielding farm equipment to grisly and effective purpose.

She sighed. The earlier vision was gone. Something told her that this matter was important to Kris, though. And he had more energy than she had, and would be relentless. This was too much argument over a small thing, anyway.

"Okay, I give up. Get the pink coat—but not the shoes!" Mugshottz had likely mentioned her drooling over them, too. Then, unable to help herself, Adora dumped all her lingering feelings of guilt—after all, she couldn't end world hunger by denying herself—and let a broad smile come to her face. "And thank you. I will enjoy wearing it. Even if it makes me stupid."

Kris and Pennywyse both beamed.

"Wonderful." Kris looked for a moment like he wanted to embrace her, but instead he backed away. He was being very careful about touching her today.

Which is probably for the best, Joy said.

Adora turned and picked up her sunglasses. *Joy, was I just bribed?*

I'm not sure. But the die is cast. You may as well enjoy it.

You just want that coat, Adora grumbled.

Are you nuts? Of course I do. It's gorgeous. And I hope he gets the shoes, too. This was said loudly, and Adora wasn't entirely surprised when Kris nodded his head.

He hears you, Joy, Adora hissed.

Not if I whisper.

Kris smiled a little.

Adora answered: *I'm not so sure about that.*

The shaman came again in secret on the holiest night, the Eve of Baal's Fire, when Sol's path crossed between the Equinox and the Solstice. A great famine was upon the land, so need-fires were set ablaze atop the highest mounts so that the Sun's light might be called down to Earth, where all the beasts of the field and grains did falter and die. In defiance of the Worshippers, the Celebrants who remembered the story of an ancient savior danced around the fires calling on the Goddess and their lost saint, Niklas Rhédon, to reappear and help them in their time of great hunger. Their prayers were answered. At midnight Niklas Rhédon did come, stepping out from the *eadar dà theine Bhealltuinn,* where he shone brighter than the purifying fire that birthed him. Many wept with joy as he caused all other fires to be extinguished in the land, and even the moon darkened. Only flames from the holy need-fire remained, and those were used to rekindle the Celebrants' hearths, again bringing the saint's blessings and good fortune into their households and fields.

—*Niklas 26:5*

The one who had been Niklas looked into the starry sky where the lights of a billion souls blazed. Nothing had ever seemed so beautiful to him. Nothing except . . .

But as beautiful as this place and time was, tomorrow, at dawn, he would give up this body, this life, this world. His work was done and it was time to go home.

CHAPTER TEN

Adora and her new pink coat walked into the small hangar behind Kris. The only occupant was a pudgy single-engine aircraft painted the same bright red as her childhood wagon. In spite of Kris's oft-repeated need for haste, she approached it slowly and unenthusiastically.

"What is that?" she demanded—meaning, *Where's the jet?*

"That's an Aeronca Chief—quite an anachronism in this digital age. Just look at the control panel!" Kris threw open the door. Adora peered in and had to admit that her old Volkswagen Bug had had more dials. In fact, so had her fourth-grade soapbox-derby entry. The plane was also equipped with a bench seat that reminded her of her father's '57 Chevy. Very cute.

But she still didn't like it.

"Very nice. But, Kris, I think I mentioned before that I don't like small planes."

"I know, but we have little choice. Roadblocks are

up, and I had to send the others off in the jet as a decoy. Understand, the rebels are trying to topple Molybdenum. If they succeed there will be a bloodbath. There are parties—short-sighted and stupid—who would see this as an excellent time for something to happen to us. Anyway, you've nothing to worry about. She's easy to handle, safe as can be. It only took me a couple of hours to learn to fly her." Kris took Adora's arm and vigorously assisted her into the plane when she failed to move on her own. "And this little lady is a complete wolf in sheep's clothing. My nephew, Jack, has tweaked the engine so she's a real screamer."

"So am I," Adora muttered, but she let Kris help her inside. As he climbed in after her and reached for the ignition key, she said, "Can you wait a sec? I need to meditate a bit."

"Sorry, no time." Kris glanced out the hangar doors. "We have company, and I can't know of what persuasion."

He reached for the keys and Adora tensed. A part of her began to whimper. He didn't understand: She needed time to get ready! This plane was much smaller than the Storch. It was stupid to get so freaked out, she knew, but hell, for a while after her mother's death she had even been afraid of her car. Sometimes she would look down at her hands clenched on the wheel of her Honda and wonder if there wasn't some part of her that was like her mother. Certainly there were days when she felt as lost and wanted an easy way out.

But you never did it. And you aren't driving, anyway, so quit panicking before you pee your pants. Joy's voice was sharp, a kind of mental slap in the face. It slowed Adora's hysteria.

No. You're right.

And those days were less frequent now. She didn't need the little white pills anymore, those tablets of indifference the doctor had given her when she was unable to eat or sleep or work. In fact, they made her quite sick these days—even the sight of them.

Sick? They made you despise yourself for being weak.

Yes, that too. Being weak wasn't acceptable.

And you're all better now. Joy's voice might be slightly mocking. Adora accepted the goad because anger could make her strong. And she needed to be strong now.

She said, *Damn straight, I'm all better. So shut up. I need to do some alternate nostril breathing before I throw up on my new coat.*

Fine, so breathe already.

Feeling Kris's eyes on her, Adora turned her head and offered up her best smile. It probably fell somewhat short of the genuine article, but it was all that she could manage at the moment.

"This was one of the first planes that didn't need anyone on the outside to turn over the prop. Bit of a safety hazard that," Kris said informatively. He might have been reciting "The Jabberwocky" for all the sense it made to Adora. She grabbed her nose and started breathing.

The plane answered his observation with a soft knocking sound.

"Why is it making that noise?" Adora asked between exhalations. *Inhale, one-two-three-four-five, pinch off right nostril for a slow five count, then a long exhale—one-two-three-four-five.*

"That's its normal sound. They call them air-knockers. Isn't it melodic?" Kris asked. He didn't comment on her nose-pinching.

"I guess.

"Kris?" she asked, as they rolled out of the hangar and onto the taxiway. The plane gathered speed quickly as it headed for the line of headlights coming in their direction. He wasn't giving her time to back out. Or maybe he was worried about the police cars speeding toward them from left field. Were those police cars? *One-two-three-four-five.* "Aren't we supposed to go down some kind of pre-flight checklist or something?"

"No time for that," he answered.

"But   " *Exhale, one-two-three-four. Uh-oh,* she was out of air! She had to slow it down, take bigger breaths. *Inahale, one-two-three*—

"Hang on a second," Kris said. The plane began to growl and go much faster than Adora liked, and she forgot to keep breathing.

"Shouldn't you talk to the control tower—see if we're cleared for takeoff?" she asked with the last of her air.

"No radio," Kris answered. "But don't worry. No one's around here. It's a private airstrip."

"What?" she shrieked as the plane jumped into the air. "No radio! Kris? Is this thing even legal?"

"I'm not really sure," he answered, banking to the left and gaining altitude. There came a few popping noises that Adora sincerely hoped were not bullets hitting their plane. "I suppose the answer would depend on which countries' laws one was looking at."

"Kris, do you have a pilot's license?" she demanded, slapping hands over her eyes and gasping as she was forced back into the seat. The *knock-knock-knock*ing now sounded like Doom banging on the door. The plane was definitely a screamer.

"Not yet. I'll get one eventually," he shouted cheerfully. The plane leveled out. She thought she heard him add, "I'm really sorry about this, Adora. I hadn't planned on taking the plane, but the goblins have forced my hand. I need to get back to Cadalach quickly, and there's no faerie road from L.A. or I'd take it. I'll get you on the ground as soon as I can." Kris raised his voice. "Buck up, girl. Open your eyes and look out there. The city absolutely sparkles at night."

Adora moaned. The bubble she had kept around herself had finally shattered. Panic was gnawing at her intestines.

"What's wrong? Kris asked. "You've gone whiter than my hair. Do you feel sick?"

"N-nothing's wrong. It isn't the plane. I . . . I just suddenly realized that it's all true. It's really happening. There really are goblins having a revolution . . . and you're probably really Santa Claus. That is insane. I didn't really believe it until now, you know, because really you seem very normal most of the time."

Kris didn't smile.

"You thought I was—what?—kidding about everything?"

"No. I thought—I don't know—that you were crazy. Or maybe that you had some ancestral memory because your great-great whoever had been Saint Nicholas. Or maybe that you were a reincarnation. I could buy into those things."

"So, you can believe in reincarnation, but not Santa?"

"Sorry, my madness couldn't accommodate that."

"Poor child. But yes, Adora, there *is* a Santa Claus." His tone was wry. He asked curiously, "Why did you stay if you thought I was insane? Was it the money?"

"No." Adora forced herself to meet Kris's eyes.

"Then why?"

"Because . . . because after a while it didn't matter anymore what you were. I didn't care if you were stark, raving mad. I just needed to . . . to stick it out."

"Because . . . ?" He prompted.

"I don't know! Because I felt alive again. Intrigued. And because I care about you for some reason," she snapped. "But let's just leave it at that, okay? I believe in the don't-ask, don't-tell policy where you're concerned. I don't want to know what's going on in my subconscious."

She thought she heard Kris say, "We can leave it at that for now, but I imagine Fate has other plans."

"Great. We have goblins and Fate. And you said this wasn't dangerous—that I'd be safe!"

"You are safe," he replied.

Kris glanced at her as she resumed her five-count breathing. She had to admit that the sound was a little ragged. All she was doing was hyperventilating.

"So, how about getting on with your interview? Surely you have more questions for me, especially since you've finally decided that I'm real."

Interview? Right—the biography. The reason she was here. Of course, writing it all down was the first step to commitment. It was admitting to the world—and to herself—that there was still some story here that she wanted to tell. And once she gave it to Kris, or Ben, or a publisher, there would be no turning back. Did she really want to travel that path?

We've been over this. You're going to do it, so stop stalling.

"Now?" she asked, clutching her nose. "You want to be interviewed now?"

"Why not?"

"Why not?" she echoed mostly to herself. "Fine, then. So how *do* you manage to travel the world in one night? Not in a single-engine plane, one trusts," she said, trying to get her mind on other things.

"I manage by obeying the laws of eternity but not the laws of time."

Adora sighed. "As always, I don't understand. Can't you ever just say 'reindeer'?"

"I know. Sorry, you picked a hard question. Let's put it this way: Some things are eternal and therefore timeless."

"These are just words—"

"Look, time is a human-made thing. Man has a passion for dividing the days, first by hours, then by minutes, then in degrees too small to matter to anyone except a scientist. Time is the boundary that predicts and restricts most human activity. Man's reality is nanoseconds and cells and molecules—transient things all. And sadly, most men have only the truth of the moment—their minds can't grasp bigger things. But we, the fey, can. You'll see. I promise that in time you will understand."

Adora chewed on this for a while, but she still didn't comprehend his meaning. She decided to come at the question from another angle.

"The fey worship the Goddess, right? And she supplies their magic?"

"The fey come from the part of Divinity they call the Goddess," Kris agreed. "The fey are more aware than most humans of the Divinity—the *magic*, as some call it—within them. They are closer to the source, and can commune with it. But all living things are touched by this Divinity. It is within all of us—human, goblin or fey."

"Yes, but being fey, you have greater access to this

magic than your average Joe Blow human on the street."

Kris started to answer, then paused. Finally he shrugged somewhat helplessly. "Yes."

"So what you do, traveling the world, is a—"

"Magic trick?" he asked politely. Too politely. Adora knew that he was disappointed and perhaps even offended by her persistence.

"No. I was going to say '*miracle*'—something divine. It's just that . . . the word has certain religious connotations I don't like." She tried to explain. "I mean, I think of miracles as burning bushes that talk, or raising the dead, or angels announcing virgin births."

Kris's brow relaxed as he pondered the notion. "I understand what you mean," he said finally. "Culturally, it's difficult for you to approach this because it sounds so mystical. This isn't your mental orientation. But perhaps 'miracle' is a good word for the situation. Personally, I have always seen miracles as what happens between people in moments of compassion and love and understanding."

"But not burning bushes?" she clarified.

"Fire often comes with Divine revelation. Miracles are more . . . mundane. They can happen person to person, no Divine intervention needed."

"Have you read much about quantum physics?" she asked suddenly.

"Yes. And they almost have it right. It gives me hope." Kris looked back at her, then out of his window. He said to himself, "No sign of pursuit yet, but they'll have us on radar. The sooner we set down the better."

Pursuit? They'd follow us out of the city? Why? What are we to them? And who?

Don't think about it, Joy said. *You'll just hyperventilate again*. She didn't sound happy, though.

Right. Adora definitely didn't want to think about this because it would make her stomach worse. "So, back to my questions. Describe your average day to me. What were you doing every day for the last ten thousand years?" she asked.

"That is another difficult question," Kris answered seriously as he banked the plane to the left. "Century to century, my activities varied. And I wasn't on earth every day for the last ten thousand years. Much of the time, I was at home."

"I don't understand. Again. What home? Where? With whom?" she asked in frustration. "Are you talking about Heaven?"

He glanced at her. "It will all become clear eventually. Maybe you should breathe some more—just more slowly."

"It would be nice if could become clear *now*. I need to get a handle on this before I start writing—and everything you say just confuses me more. You're heaping enigmas upon conundrums."

I'd like an explanation before we get shot down by goblin rebels, Joy piped up. Adora tried to stay calm.

Now is not a good time to panic, Joy. No one is getting shot down.

Once again, Kris answered her real concern and not the one she had spoken aloud. "Stop worrying. You'll get an ulcer. No one is going to catch us; I guarantee it." Apparently he was permanently tuned into her brain waves.

Adora sighed again and gave up trying to hide her thoughts. She would like to insert herself in the lovely rosy bubble where Kris lived but feared that even if she managed to find a way inside, the weight of the real world was bound to shatter it. The thought depressed her. She didn't really want Kris ousted into her reality; it was lonely and despairing.

You'd rather share his world—and be what to him? Mrs. Claus?

No, not really.

Good. Red just isn't your color, and I don't think you'll ever be fat enough for the part.

Don't be frivolous.

That's funny coming from you.

You know, you're a real bitch when you're worried.

But I'm still right, Joy crowed.

Adora looked over at Kris. Maybe part of the reason she couldn't see him as Santa, or herself as Mrs. Claus, was because he just didn't look like she'd pictured Saint Nick. The only part that was right were his laughing eyes, and she sincerely doubted those were dancing with thoughts of sugarplums and gumdrops.

But that was Kris's point, wasn't it? He wasn't Santa, per se. Santa Claus was a fabrication, a public relations ploy. And he had never been an honest-to-goodness saint. He was a . . . a pagan demi-god. One who liked music and dancing.

And sex, I bet. All the old gods were into ravishing virgins and so on, Joy suggested.

Yes, Adora admitted. From what she'd read, there had apparently been quite a bit of that going on at ye olde solstice festivals.

Yet not with you. Do you think that maybe he only has sex on holidays—equinoxes and solstices? Joy asked.

Kris interrupted her thoughts. "My dear, what are you thinking? I haven't seen a look like that since Victoria was on the throne!"

Adora sighed. "If you must know, I'm thinking

about fertility rites and wondering how many you've participated in while being a Green Man. The stories are rather lurid." She sounded crabby and knew it. She wanted to ask him why he hadn't made any moves on her, but she couldn't quite bring herself to be so blatant.

He grinned widely, unrepentant. "Freedom of religion is an inalienable right. Even the president says so," he added. "I was only doing my part to uphold the standards of the day."

"Uh-huh, I bet. And Laffite-Rothschild is just a red wine."

"It *is* just a wine. Though a particularly fine one." Kris added, "I knew Baron James Rothschild."

"Of course you did." Adora shook her head. "And I'd love to hear about it—but after we discuss your *freedom of religion.*"

Kris sobered. "That was many lifetimes ago, Adora. I haven't indulged in . . . well, the pleasures of the flesh—not since coming to the New World. By then it was simply too dangerous."

This answer startled Adora, enough to make her forget her fear of planes and goblins alike.

No sex for centuries? Joy asked.

I'm more concerned about the "dangerous" part, Adora thought. She asked, "Really? Why? Do you mean because of AIDS or other diseases?"

"No. That affliction wouldn't affect me."

AIDS doesn't affect him. I told you he was delusional! If you have sex you will make him wear a condom, won't you? Joy was having a conniption.

Joy, please, please, shut up.

"Why wouldn't it affect you? Are you like Superman?" Adora asked aloud.

"Superman? Oh, yes! The comic book character. Well, I guess I am a bit like him. I know that's a startling idea for you to grasp, but it's nonetheless true," Kris said, frowning. "Zayn explains the differences between humans and feys—corporeal feys—this way: We both come with the standard equipment—lungs, stomach, heart, eyes, ears and so forth—and they all work the same about eighty percent of the time. But feys have slightly different brains. I guess some brain scans have been done, and the differences are obvious. In feys, it's as though we don't need actual light to stimulate the optic nerve. We can see without external illumination. We can hear beyond the standard range of hearing. We're faster and stronger, because we can sense in advance how to react to unseen danger, and we know intuitively how to heal ourselves. We have inherent balance, and subconsciously try to maintain it. That's why we avoid alcohol—it shuts down our inner perceptions. It blinds and deafens us, shuts down our 'magic.' It makes us almost human." Kris cleared his throat, giving her a chance to speak. But when Adora didn't know what to say, he added, "Because we have all these extra senses, faith is easier for us. We rarely need any external proof of Divinity. We can feel . . ."

"God?"

"Gaia. Yes. We can merge with part of it. Use it." Kris paused again, then went on with some reluctance. "It uses us too. Sometimes. We are its anchor to this world. We are its love, the last line of defense against loneliness. The Goddess, the part of Gaia we are hooked into, has an agenda, and that is to do whatever makes for the greatest good for our species—at whatever cost. Usually that means our individual good as well. But it doesn't always feel that way—not when she hijacks our will and forces us into certain courses of action."

"Does that happen often?" Adora asked, sensing Kris's unease.

"No. Not often. But believe me, once is enough." He straightened and peered ahead. "Okay, time to put this baby down. Jack's left a car for us out here."

"Are we just going to leave the airplane?" Adora asked.

"Yes, it'll be retrieved later. If the goblins don't destroy it. They can be so petty and destructive."

It sounded extremely wasteful, but since she really didn't want to remain any longer in the contraption than was absolutely necessary, Adora silenced the responsible part of her that protested leaving a valuable piece of machinery unattended in the desert. She peered out the window, not really expecting to see landing lights and therefore not surprised when all that greeted her was darkness. She was a lot calmer now—not happy, exactly—but Kris seemed to know what he was doing. Maybe they wouldn't die after all.

"Look at those weird lights!" she exclaimed suddenly. "Over there, near the horizon. I've never seen anything like them."

"I've seen them before." Kris's voice went flat as he looked where she pointed. "The last and most powerful of the solar flares that took the lives of the pureblood feys were actually rather beautiful. We had the aurora borealis all the way to Mexico. There were nightly magnetic rainbows all over the northern hemisphere. Scientists talked later about the shifts in the magnetosphere, which we are having now, but the poetic part of me wants to believe that the heavenly lights were caused by the thousands of fleeing souls leaving their earthly bodies."

Adora turned stricken eyes on him. "Souls can become disturbances in the magnetic field? How?"

"Fey souls do. Lutins too—in large enough numbers. I think there was a huge goblin slaughter to-night in L.A. In fact, I know there was. It would take thousands of deaths to light up the sky that way. We'll have to wait and see who's won. For the sake of all the races, I pray Molybdenum came out on top."

His words numbed her brain. There had been a slaughter. Real death. Many real deaths. And it had happened while she whined about flying to safety in an airplane. In spite of everything Kris had said during the day, she hadn't really thought this would happen.

"I . . . Kris, this is awful. How could it happen? Here? This is America. *California.* We don't have revolutions and slaughters." She felt suddenly weak, and slumped in her seat.

"Of course we do—though humans don't see what we do. They'll never know what happened. They'll see the lights and blame it on UFOs or magnetic atmospheric fluctuations. A few psychics may feel the mass lutin death, but they'll dismiss it as an aberration, perhaps even as perseverations from some other war."

"But you feel it?" Adora's voice was small. "You know it's real?"

"Of course. As do you—though it affects us differently since I am Unseelie."

"I . . . Shit. This is terrible. I don't want to feel this."

"No. I don't imagine you do. In so many ways, we fey are the canaries down in the coal mine. Changes of climate affect us first—as you've seen, photosensitivity has run amok. We're hardy in so many ways. Viruses, bacteria, extremes of temperature—these we can fight off without effort. But the constant solar flares? I don't know. Those bursts of radiation are deadly and they make us—and to a lesser degree, the goblins—temporarily insane. When they don't kill us outright. And our condition grows worse as more of us die. It's odd, because day to day we aren't as affected by sunlight as the lutins, and we aren't hydrophilic either, so we can live in dry climates without getting heatstroke. But I greatly fear the loss of our ozone layer will eventually be the undoing of any fey not living underground. And we are hypersensitive to the deaths of others who are like us. Others with magic. And as it continues, our magic will dwindle until one day as a group we simply won't want to live."

We simply won't want to live. Adora thought about this.

"That's what you think is wrong with me?" Adora asked. "What's been wrong with me? I have some sort of sunstroke that makes me half-suicidal . . . ?"

Kris was slow to answer. "Yes. I believe that you have solar poisoning. Can't you feel the influence of those lights, the energy in flux around us? It affects many mixed-bloods like yourself. Fortunately, your case isn't that advanced. There's treatment."

"You're saying that I'm fey too? You really believe this?" She was truly taken aback.

You shouldn't believe it, Joy said urgently. *Really, you don't want to go here. Just say no.*

But why not think about it, Joy? It's just an idea. Why are you so frightened? Adora was intrigued.

Look, I can't help you if you won't take my advice. You don't want to start down this path. You don't want to know about being fey.

Why, Joy? Why? If he can make me well . . .

"You're part fey. Yes, I believe that you have fey blood running around in you and it . . . it hasn't been cared for." Kris smiled encouragingly and then focused on the ground before them, which was coming up quickly. "The good news is that—if I'm right—there is medicine that can make you well very quickly."

Adora thought about this. A part of her believed him. Until this weird sickness came on her and her father, she had never been ill—no colds, no flu, no chicken pox. And no one in her family had ever been sick, either.

She truly hated being ill, but she wasn't certain what she should hope for. She wanted to be well, but a cure would mean she was inhuman.

You're not inhuman! Joy insisted.

"I don't know about taking drugs," she began, then closed her eyes so that she wouldn't see the plane land. Her conviction that blindness was bliss didn't last long—not looking was worse, so her lids popped back open. Shadows rushed at her through the window.

"It isn't a drug, exactly. You wouldn't be popping pills for the rest of your life," Kris assured her. "It's just something that can give a boost to your immune system. It's a combination of vitamins and antihistamines that exist in fey living places. It's in the water and air."

"And I'll be . . . exposed to this when we go to—where are we going?" she asked.

"Yes. And we're going to Cadalach."

"So, if I don't get better, will that mean that I'm not fey?"

Kris frowned. He answered slowly. "I'm not sure. Maybe."

Adora nodded. "Then I guess we'll find out soon enough which of us is right about what I am."

"I have a question for you—if you don't mind me being personal," Kris said, turning the plane sharply. "Who is this Joy you keep talking to?"

Joy gasped. *I told you he heard you, Big Mouth.*

"My evil twin," Adora admitted without thinking. The plane's wheels touched the ground and it began losing speed. She was finally able to relax.

Hey! Who's the evil one? I didn't start this, you know, Joy snapped.

"Or maybe I mean she's my imaginary friend." When Kris glanced at her, Adora found herself explaining: "She's the voice in my head that I talk things out with. Like my subconscious. Or a muse. Lots of writers have those."

Boy; that was an understatement, but at least it wasn't a lie. Lying to Kris would be very hard. Adora wasn't actually sure that she could do it.

"I see. Does it make you nervous to have this voice?" he asked. Then, he added with a second quick glance, "It probably shouldn't. Many feys . . . well, we have the normal five senses and some others besides—a sort of ancestral memory, I guess you could call it. Quite often that manifests itself as a voice. I know two people who can talk to mountains and caves—or rather, the caves talk to them. They are quite normal otherwise. Even I hear voices— prayers, mostly. As I've said, it's nothing to be upset about. It's the magic protecting us, giving our brains information in a way they can understand."

Kris's speech, though ridiculous when she listened with practical human ears, was still somehow reassuring. Possibly it was his matter-of-factness. He was the first person she had ever told about Joy, and he didn't think she was a freak.

Yeah, well, he hears voices too—just like the Son of Sam, Joy commented. *That's real reassuring. And I want you to know that I'm not buying the whole souls-as-magnets thing, either. It could just be weather phenom-*

ena. Her words were tart, but she seemed more relaxed. Maybe Kris had reassured her too.

No? But I do believe it, Joy. Heaven help me! I do.

You poor fool. You always were gullible.

The plane stopped and Kris switched off the engine. "We get out here. Do you see the car?" he asked.

Adora peered into the night. "Yes! It's a Jaguar!"

"Good. I know it isn't the usual choice for desert
travel, but it's been modified. We'll make great time."

Adora pushed open the plane door and stepped
out eagerly into the night. If she never saw another
aircraft again, it would still be too soon.

Kris drove like there was a hanging posse on their
trail—and maybe there was. Adora couldn't see anything through their back trail of dust. They weren't
traveling on any sort of regularly paved surface, and
the markers out there were few and far between.
They had passed only one town and it was deserted, a
cemetery of crowded old shacks abandoned long ago.

"Travel is an education, but this is more education
than I signed up for this semester," Adora complained through clenched teeth. The Jaguar had excellent suspension but the ride was still very rough.
She was beginning to miss the airplane.

Kris glanced her way, but only for a second. The
road, if one could call it that, was uneven and required his full attention. "No desire for an advanced
degree?" he laughed.

"Not if it's on this road. Didn't you promise me
San Francisco and New York? I swear that's where
you said we would be heading next."

"Just a bit farther now," Kris assured her. "And
we'll get to the big cities, never fear. When we do, I'll
show you sides of them you've never imagined."

Kris, when he wanted to be, was something of a Scheherazade, but only a woman who was completely besotted would believe him. Cities of any sort were far, far away, and there was nothing but stunted manzanita as far as the eye could see. The desert was beautiful though, now that the moon was up. The land shone like a snowscape, and no sky had ever been as bright with stars.

"How about some music?" Kris asked.

"Sure." Adora was curious about what he liked. She was betting on Mozart.

Kris pushed a disc into the CD player and out poured Ian Hunter's *Rant*. Adora gave him a shocked look.

"Brother Ian is pissed about things too," Kris said. "Jack knew I'd want some cruising tunes. He's a very thoughtful boy."

"Sorry, I just . . . When did you have time to acquire a taste for Ian Hunter? I would think there would be more important things to catch up on in the last century and a half."

"Music is important—good for the soul. My nephew likes Ian, and I do too. Actually, a lot of today's music is invigorating. And I appreciate the directness, the questioning of authority." Kris's brow furrowed. "I wonder if Ian would like to do an Xmas album for me. I think it's time for some new kinds of carols."

Adora could only shake her head. Kris laughed, his spirits apparently restored by their journey so far.

"I don't think that someone born into this age can understand how miraculous it is—how *possible* everything feels," he explained. "When I was last in the world of Men, there were still places—in fact, most places—where people were born and lived out

212

their entire lives in one small town, without ever reading a foreign newspaper or seeing a stranger's face. They were like oxen yoked to a plow, tied to the land or a village that they couldn't—and didn't wish to—escape. I would return every century or so, and the same closed faces would look back at me from the same village windows and the same tilled fields. The baker's son became a baker, the farmer's son a farmer. Innovation was something to be suspicious of—if not greeted with actual fear. . . . But it's different today. People are still people, of course, but their minds have been wedged open by television and radio. They've seen other races, seen wars, watched men walk on the moon. Our communities are larger—even global. . . . I think that perhaps, this time, they will be ready and able to hear and do the right thing."

Adora wasn't sure exactly what he was talking about, but she hoped he was correct. The global community had her rather worried.

"Damn," Kris said suddenly, and put on the brakes. The car spun sideways, kicking up a cloud of dust. Adora's seat belt bit into her shoulder.

"What's wrong?" she asked, but could already see why he was stopping. The car's headlights had picked out a pile of rags. On top of it was the body of a large white animal, lying half-hidden by dead scrub, sucked dry as a spider's dinner.

Kris jumped out of the car and knelt by the dessicated remains. He took the body's face in his hand and turned it toward the moon. It was human, Adora saw with a shock.

She was slower to approach now that she knew what it was. The smell of the poor creature's wretched carcass was a barrier she had to force herself to cross. Behind her, Ian sang on about Purgatory.

Staring at the broken body in the dirt, Adora was prepared for blood and perhaps some broken bones. But what waited there was more horrible, more terrible than she had imagined. The woman—Adora thought it was a woman because the body had no visible external genitalia—looked shriveled, like her tissues and organs had been sucked dry. Her features were dilapidated, something that belonged on a mummy. Her red hair was filled with oil and dirt, though there wasn't much left on her scalp; most had been pulled away in bloody clumps.

The emaciated creature convulsed suddenly, the muscles under the skin contorting in a constant stream of ripples. Adora watched, horrified, morbidly afraid that the body might rip itself open.

Kris held the body through its spasm. As the violent contractions ceased, the woman turned her head away and vomited up something pink and lumpy that looked like a mix of red fruit and liver. She rolled onto her back and gave a choked, staccato cry that barely escaped her constricting throat. Adora saw tattoos on her chest and belly. The poor creature had been into boy bands.

Understanding hit her, made her dizzy and sick.

"She's not very old, is she?" Adora asked in a cracked voice. "This . . . this woman is just a teenager."

Kris leaned over and inhaled, his face pained. "No. She is not old chronologically. But she has squandered all her physical and spiritual resources as goblin-fruit addicts always do."

"My God. Why?" Adora whispered, seeking comfort in his gaze but finding none. "Why would anyone do this to themselves?"

"They have no notion of what the consequences will be. Damn it! We tell the children about heroin and cocaine and cigarettes—but not about goblin fruit. The FDA doesn't even list it as an addictive substance."

Kris turned back to the shuddering husk. Clouds sprang up out of nowhere and a light rain began to fall around them. This reminded Adora of something, but it took her a minute to place the memory—it had rained in just this way her first night at the Beverly Wilshire.

It's Kris. He's causing the rain, she thought stupidly, staring at her wilting cuffs, the marabou matting under the rain's increasingly harsh lash. He was making the heavens weep.

"Let go, sister," Kris said softly to the girl, pulling her gaze up to him.

His voice was the gentlest thing Adora had ever heard. It was like the tone he used on the hostess at Caveman Joe's, yet different. Adora understood that he was coaxing a soul someplace much darker and, for the dying woman, more frightening. The battered face stared up at him. Only one eye seemed able to focus. The chest heaved as she tried to draw in more air. He said again, "Let go, my sister."

"My . . . baby?" the girl gasped, gulping air that seemed to do her no good. She was strangling like a hanged man at the end of an amateur noose. The rain slowly covered her face with tears.

Adora touched her own cheeks. Some of the moisture there was hot. She wanted to plead with Kris to do something—anything—to end this woman's suffering, but something held her back. She couldn't really ask him to kill, could she?

In answer, the wind swirled around them. It gusted so hard that it blew back her eyelashes and eyebrows, and seemed to force any words back inside of her. Almost, she thought she heard, *Thou shalt not kill.*

Joy?

It's not me. And it's not Kris, she answered, and the small hairs on Adora's nape stood on end. Adora turned around quickly, looking for a physical enemy, though she knew none was there.

Kris ignored the storm. "All will be well, sister." He leaned closer and whispered something in a language Adora didn't know, but the words raised the hair on the rest of her body. She was fascinated by the long liquid string of vowels that sounded like . . . Gaelic music? That wasn't quite right, but it was the closest description she could think of.

"I hurt," the goblin-fruit addict whispered, but her body eased even as she spoke and sank in on itself.

"Let go, sister," Kris said a third time. "Hurt no more."

The woman gave a last, long, pain-filled sigh and then stilled. Adora didn't see anything, but she thought she could feel the woman's soul rush by as it fled the ravaged body that had been its prison.

Adora's knees gave out and she sank down in the dirt. Her hand found a tired, exposed root of a manzanita plant that clutched the ground with arthritic fingers. She didn't pull hard, because she feared breaking the plant's tenuous grip, and the thought of any more death tonight was unbearable.

Kris closed the woman's sagging eyelids, then picked a small, unnoticed bundle up off the ground. It let out a thin, exhausted wail that was raw with fear and outrage. He turned to face Adora, the baby in his arms. His expression was bleaker than she could ever have imagined.

"That's what goblin fruit does to humans. And, believe it or not, this woman was lucky. She died before she started eating herself, before she turned to murder. Before she sold her baby to the goblin gangs."

Unable to bear his expression, Adora looked down at the infant in Kris's hands. Its sleeper was wet and filthy. There was also something wrong with the child. The head was shaped like a cinderblock, and its jaw was too jutting. She could see tiny teeth that looked like they belonged on a miniature xylophone. Its scruffy hair was so matted with filth that she could only guess at the color. It also looked malformed in the rib cage.

"Will we take the baby to the mother's family?" she asked, looking about for some sign of habitation and forcing herself to stop her useless crying. She wasn't the one who had died. She was alive and relatively healthy.

"No, they rejected that poor woman and her child. There will be no shelter for the baby there."

"And the father?" Adora asked, but she already knew the answer.

"You don't understand about the addiction process, do you?" Kris asked. Then he added, "Well, thank the Goddess you don't. Their bodies are the first things some of these poor creatures sell to the goblins—they're usually runaways and have nothing else. The transaction usually turns into a sort of gang rape, since the goblin-fruit pushers travel in packs. She probably didn't know who the father was—and wouldn't have wanted the baby with him anyway."

Adora shivered. Unable to bear the increasing cold and the proximity to the dead woman any

217

longer, she reached for the baby, saying, "Give the child to me. You can't drive and also hold the baby."

Kris hesitated, staring hard at her. "You want to hold this child?"

"Want to? I don't know. It just seems reasonable and right, given our circumstances." Adora forced herself to meet Kris's eyes. She knew that he could see into her and would sense her reservations. She didn't know how to explain that her hesitation was half that the baby was so odd-looking, and half that the sight of any unprotected child disturbed her, made her anxious. "Look, I wouldn't reject a baby just because it has birth defects and its mother was a junkie. What kind of heartless bitch do you think I am?"

"The baby doesn't have birth defects. It has its father's arms and teeth," Kris said.

"Those aren't its ribs?" Adora asked, looking again at the filthy bundle. She wasn't sure if this was good news or not.

"No. The mother tried to bind its second set of arms so that it would look more human. If you're going to beg on the streets where normal people live, you need a human baby, not a cross-breed monster."

"Don't say that—she'll hear you!" Adora pleaded, though she knew the child couldn't possibly understand their conversation.

"I only speak the truth," Kris replied. He glanced down briefly. "And it's another sad truth that no one wants this baby. As far as the world is concerned, it's inhuman garbage. They would see it as a kindness to leave it here to die."

Adora put a hand on Kris's chin and coaxed his head up. She looked into his eyes. The sorrow and anger there was unbearable, a knife in her gut until he sensed what he was doing to her and pulled away mentally. She could feel a barrier slide up between them.

"Except you," she reminded him. *"You* want this child."

Kris nodded, his lips compressed. In the moonlight, his eyes seemed filled with an angry blue fire. His skin took on a silver glow.

"But I want them all. Every last lost and broken body that has been thrown away like last week's rubbish." He shook his head. "The truly tragic part is that the cycle never ends. The junkies' kids grow up unloved, outsiders, some little more than animals. Hungry and scared, they turn to their parents' addictions, looking for some relief from their miseries. It's an endless wheel. And there are always more unwanted babies." His usually lovely voice was harsh and deep, and made her heart constrict.

"Kris, you can't save the world." When he scowled, she added hastily, "Not all at once. But we can save this bit of it. Give her to me. It's starting to rain hard now. We don't want her to catch a cold."

Kris tilted his head to the sky as though only just becoming aware of the water that fell on them, and only on them. The line of demarcation was clear in the car's headlights.

"You can tell that she's a girl?" he said, almost to himself. "That's a good sign. I wasn't sure you could see past her arms. You've been so resistant to the idea of having mixed blood yourself—and I can tell this child makes you nervous."

Adora didn't mention that the sleeper was pink and she'd just been guessing about the baby's gender. Nor did she protest that the situation was abnormal enough for anyone to resist accepting it. He was right. She was very resistant to the idea that she wasn't completely normal or human.

"Of course she's a girl," she said instead. This time, Adora reached out and took the child. She wrapped her frivolous pink coat around it and staggered to her feet. The baby smelled of the same sour fruit that covered her mother's body. Adora added in alarm, "And her lips are turning blue. We have to get her someplace warm."

Kris nodded, shaking off the melancholy and anger that had gripped him. "I know a place. I hadn't planned on taking you there just yet, since it's a bit scarier than where my nephew lives, but I think Fate has just intervened. We need a refuge now. The baby is sick and will die without help."

"Where are we going then?" Adora asked. She pulled the child close, trying to shelter it. Her protective instinct, though unwanted, was exerting itself.

"It's part of what we call the tomhnafurach, but it's an area long abandoned—a fey ghost town. I mentioned it before. It's . . . it's part of my nephew's property, Cadalach, but an outskirt used by the Nephalim."

"Nephalim? Fallen angels?"

"Giants, not angels—well, not exactly angels. Zayn and Chloe go there sometimes. They'll take this child in. You can stay at the tomhnafurach while I see to the mother's body. I'm not going to leave her on the road where the goblins can get at her."

Adora shuddered. Seeing, Kris quickly removed his coat. She couldn't tell what it was made of, but it was softer than cashmere.

"She's dead. Why would they want her now?" she asked.

"You have a lot to learn about goblin drug lords. Most humans only become really useful after they're dead," Kris answered, wrapping his coat around her, then wiping the rain—and her tears— from her cheeks. Again, he stared at his hands as though he could somehow feel her tears.

"Kris, don't put that on me!" she protested. "You'll wreck your coat too. The baby and I are both wet and dirty."

"That is a tragedy, of course," Kris said, finally smiling a little. His eyes had returned to normal and the rain had almost stopped. "And yet I am sure that with time I can come to accept a ruined coat."

Adora let out a slow breath, relieved that he was himself again. "Kris, if . . . if there's any chance of the goblins getting at that body, let's take it now. Put it in the trunk." It took an effort to say that, and she couldn't repress a shudder at the thought of riding with a corpse, but the thought didn't bother Kris.

He said he was a death fey, Joy reminded her. *Why would a corpse bother him?*

"Okay. That might be best, if you truly don't mind."

Adora did mind, but she realized that Kris wasn't eavesdropping on her thoughts at the moment.

"It's fine," she lied.

He carefully eased Adora and the baby back into the front seat of the car, then reached over her to shut off the CD player. The time for music was over.

Adora let the door close on their conversation. Pushing away the horrible thoughts of worldwide addiction his words about goblin drug lords had provoked, she tried to comfort the freezing baby. She hoped the child didn't sense her ambivalence at being a nursemaid. Kris was wrong: It wasn't that she hated the baby's mixed blood, it was that she had never thought to be near any child at all. Children were not supposed to be—not ever—part of her life, because . . . because . . .

You can't protect them? Joy asked, her voice subdued.

Adora flinched. Yes. Joy was right. Somehow she had always known that she wouldn't be a good mother. She didn't know how to protect anyone, not even herself.

And a voice called to him in the darkness saying: Awake, awake, put on strength again, my son. For are you not the one who makes the road that shall lead the Redeemed? Arise and build a way of hope for your people who are lost and weary. And hearing the voice, Niklas pulled himself out of dust of the earth and was again made whole.

—*Niklas 5:19*

Maxentius ground his teeth and snarled at the "angel" that had appeared and smashed the two giant wheels upon which he had been set to break the body of the troublesome human, Catherine. He wanted to shout to the crowd that the angel was no angel at all, but the fey called Niklas. But he could not risk that in turn Niklas would reveal to the humans that their emperor was actually a goblin.

"Thisss isssn't over," Maxentius hissed at the fey as he gathered up Catherine's body.

"It's over for today," Niklas said, and carried the woman away.

CHAPTER ELEVEN

A storm closed in, battering the car and howling like a beast in pain. The wipers couldn't cope, but that didn't seem to bother Kris, who was preoccupied and failed to notice—or at least be concerned—that they were riding around in the world's biggest dishwasher.

"Don't worry," he said. "It's just Thomas's jinn setting up a howl. The bad weather discourages people from messing around this back door, and will confuse anyone following us. It'll pass off soon, and we're not in a flood plain. Yet."

"You aren't reassuring me. Can't we stop until it passes? Or tell the jinn to go away?" Adora stared at the fussing baby, wondering if she should take it out of its sleeper. It had to be cold and clammy. Probably it should have a bottle too—though a bottle of what, she did not know.

"Sorry about dragging you out in this weather and . . . well, everything," Kris said, again pulling the car out of a slide and back onto what passed for a road. "This wasn't a part of the plan." Then he muttered, "Not part of *my* plan."

"Ha! Bet you aren't sorry enough to take a room at that motel," Adora answered as a small, illuminated sign flashed past.

"It's miles out of the way—almost a hundred. Kids put the sign out here as a joke," Kris explained. "And it isn't a proper motel anyway, just a couple of broken-down motor homes with rotting floors and colonies of biting insects."

"Maybe so, but you're missing my point. I can tell that you're upset about something and you wouldn't halt now if there was a five-star hotel and the Angel Gabriel himself appeared carrying a sign that said: STOP HERE." That wasn't fair. She knew he was worried about the baby and what had happened in L.A. Still, a part of her was certain that he was keeping something else from her.

"If the Angel Gabriel appears—sign or no sign— we will stop," Kris assured her with a smile. "I wouldn't leave a friend out on the road on a night like this."

The words were hardly spoken when the storm ended abruptly. Kris smiled wider but didn't say *I told you so.* Instead, he swerved off what was left of the road and started toward a cliff face that towered in the distance.

"This entrance is almost never used—too close to the L.A. hive. But it's the closest, and I want to get the baby inside. It's safer for all of us." But for the first time, Kris didn't sound completely certain.

"This is the back road into Cadalach?" Adora asked. She used the term *road* very loosely. There actually wasn't one that she could see.

"Well . . . it's *a* back road to Cadalach now."

Adora nodded, her eyes widening with alarm. A

wall of stone had appeared in the desert. The cliff rushed at them, and Kris only slowed when there was danger of actually striking it. The car skidded to a stop, dust floating around it.

"What now?" Adora asked. "It looks like your road is closed. Permanently."

"Now we wait. We missed the moonrise, but there will be another chance at the lunar setting."

"Okay." Adora cradled the child to her chest, as much seeking comfort as offering it, but eased the little girl away again almost immediately for biting her collar bone. Deprived of her shoulder, the child gave a small grunt and began chewing on its own fist.

Adora looked around as the dust settled. This was an eerie place, a haunted one. Cracked rocks were scattered about—immense geological wreckage from when the earth was made. A dead cedar had wound its branches into the cliff face as though fearing it might be torn from the soil. For some reason, this idea put Adora on edge. She was already keyed up, and her nerves began to jitter as she looked about quickly, half-expecting an attack.

North, south, east, west—nothing there. Just rocks and manzanita beaten down by the heat. Yet, there was something—something hovering just beyond the realm of her limited five senses. And it was growing, coming closer.

"Kris, do you feel—," she started to ask.

"There it goes," Kris said softly. "Watch now."

Suddenly, the air stilled. The remaining clouds parted in the sky. The cliff shifted in the silver light of the emerging moon, appearing suddenly as a chiaroscuro in gray and black, a picture of something, but she couldn't say just what. And then it began to move, to fold in on itself.

"That's impossible," she whispered, watching the

stone turn smooth and glossy and then fold like curtains.

"No. Just improbable," Kris answered. Then he said formally: "Open to us, brothers and sisters of the rainbow wherein the magic dwells. Let us enter into the realm of the Goddess who watches the world with eternal unshut eyes, and find shelter there."

And with that, Kris put the car in gear and drove into the mountain.

There were no lights inside, but this didn't seem to bother Kris. He didn't squint against the darkness and his hands barely rested on the wheel.

Almost immediately Adora began to feel pleasantly stoned, and wondered what was causing the buzz. The baby too had quieted, drooling contentedly on its fingers.

"Do you feel it?" Kris asked. His voice was melodious. "There are certain psychic locales where magic congregates—mystery spots, they're sometimes called. Few pureblood humans can sense them, but to the fey, even of mixed blood, they are as obvious as a landing strip lit up at night—only a lot more exciting."

"We're getting closer," Adora said, smiling a little. A part of her knew that this was something she would normally be concerned about, but the rest of her didn't care.

Kris nodded. "We're in the vein, and about to enter the heart of the country." He stopped the car. "I'm afraid we ride shank's mare from here. The car will age too much otherwise."

"We walk?" she asked.

"Yes—well, sort of. Give me the baby."

Adora happily handed the child over and let herself out of the Jag. Her body was relaxed, anesthetized, as Kris joined her.

"It's best not to watch this part," he said, taking her in his free arm and urging her head against his chest as they stepped forward. It meant she had to walk backward, but she didn't mind. It was sort of like dancing. "It has something to do with spatiotemporal divergence—or so Thomas says."

"You know, you say the funniest things."

Kris looked thoughtful. "Do I? Hm—I suppose I do. It's rather like having double vision, but a hundred times more confusing. You see things that aren't there now, but were there and will be there, layer upon layer of unreality. It can drive people mad."

"Let me guess, this is all part of the laws-of-eternity thing," she mumbled, not really caring. She was *soooo* mellow.

"Yes. Stay close now and walk slowly. Don't worry about the wind. It won't hurt us."

Kris held Adora and the baby close, enjoying the physical comfort of having bodies pressed against him. It had been a long, long time. The impulse to keep Adora closer than plaster on a wall almost made him smile. Almost. They were in the Goddess's realm of power now and she hadn't waited to administer her first gentle nudge. Kris knew that if the hint didn't do the trick, She would soon bring out bigger guns.

That would be interesting. He had never refused her anything, so they'd never had a battle of wills. But this time he would refuse—would *have* to refuse—unless Adora was completely willing and informed about what such a union would mean. Maybe the Goddess couldn't or wouldn't understand or accept his judgment, but it was his belief that there was already too much hurt in this woman from past emotional betrayals. He would not add himself to the list of people who had done her wrong. If she didn't understand and agree that there would probably be no rose-covered cottage and rocking chairs for their golden years, then this relationship was a nonstarter. He had no illusions. The fey were going to war with the lutins and mankind both. That the battle would not be waged with conventional weapons did not mean that there would not be fatalities. And he was the chosen general, the one who would be targeted by the enemies. Anyone standing near him would also be in the line of fire.

But he didn't want to think about that right now. The moment was so wonderful. He was in the tomh-nafurach again, closer to Gaia than he had been in nearly two centuries, and holding both Adora and a child he had saved.

Adora felt and smelled especially wonderful. He turned his face into her hair and inhaled deeply. Beautiful, perfect. What a gift, if she would truly be his.

As a rule, Kris was indifferent to human packaging. He hadn't had his ideal woman created for him by any particular culture, and therefore did not mind that Adora wasn't from America's heartland, corn-fed, wholesome and sweet—or dark and exotic and decorated in tattoos and lip plates. Some people—many, in fact—would find her appearance startling, her body and face strong and unconventional by human standards. That made her interesting to watch.

Her mind and nature were equally unconventional, and this was her real attraction for him. If she was *the one* promised by the Goddess, then she needed to be strong mentally, a survivor instead of a sleek and pampered darling, or an obedient drone. He needed a consort—someone with greatness in her. Like Cleopatra. The Queen of Egypt hadn't been conventional. Helen of Troy, Ninon de Lenclos— these were not merely physically beautiful women. What they had were charm, wit and guts. Adora had those too, and something more besides—she was fey. A very strong fey, if she could ever access her magic without hurting herself. Or him.

He hadn't been indulging in idle flattery when he told Adora that he loved her work. Her books were truly wonderful—subtle, compassionate master-pieces that showed the most intimate sides of her subjects. She had a knack for finding out who they were, right down to their deepest fears and fondest desires, and she treated both with the greatest care while she distilled the essence of their lives into something that anyone could understand.

And she had now turned her mind to him. She finally believed the truth about him being fey, but a difficult time was probably ahead for both of them now that the first battle was won. Adora had taken the first step, and she was going to find out who he really was—no matter how it challenged her long-held beliefs and perceptions. This discovery wasn't something he could do anymore with his damaged mind. The door to understanding was stuck fast. No matter how he pushed, it would open no farther. But Adora would be able to open the door and look deeper into his heart than he had ever seen. Then she would tell him about the view from inside. What would she say? Probably not to come on in 'cause the water's fine.

Kris snorted. He at once knew too little and too much about his past. In many ways, in spite of his lifetimes of fragmented memories, he was a stranger to himself, and his past lives—which he should not be able to remember—were made up of a lot of dark, unexplored territory. And to make it all the more challenging, his mind was littered with funhouse mirrors that distorted what memories and understanding he had. Flawed mirror images refracted off other flawed glasses almost endlessly. The longer he looked, the more warped the picture became. Meaning had disconnected from purpose, and actions that had had meaning at one time no longer made any sense.

He truly wanted to know himself again so that he could understand why he had done and continued to do everything he did—why he was still filled with conviction that his course of action was correct when it flew in the face of all history and logic. He just had to hope that he and Adora were both ready for the portrait she would paint once all her deliberations were done. She had thought him a madman. Was he one? That he was fey did not prove anything one way or the other.

Kris exhaled slowly. Frankly, he would not have sought out this analysis at this moment had the situation been less urgent. He was not filled with hubris that needed to share his glorious past with the human world, and he did not revel in nostalgia for its own sake—that was for the young and sentimental. His cumulative losses through the millennia rendered the past too painful a place to visit casually.

But needs must when the Goddess drives and all that. He had also begun to question small things, to feel things, and he needed some answers. He needed to know why he had done all the things he had, whether they were worth the lifetimes of sacrifice and loss that now horrified him. Because from where he stood, his life—his many lives—seemed as crazy as Adora thought. Perhaps, given that nothing fundamental had changed in the human world, they were even futile.

He'd always been a good foot soldier and done what was asked of him, however impossible the odds. But he had neglected to leave space for a life of his own—for personal reward or joy while he fulfilled his duty. He had loved everyone generally and no one in particular. Why? Why had he done this? It made no sense to him now. Why had he never found a wife, a great love with whom he could share his dreams—or even a bed—for any length of time? Why were there no children? He who loved all children as he loved his own life—in fact, far more than he loved his own life—had none of his own. Why? It couldn't be because Gaia was jealous and had kept him from it.

Could it be because he was somehow flawed, incapable of feeling this kind of love? Could it be because he had needed to wait for Adora? Kris inhaled again, drawing in her scent, wondering if what he was feeling in that instant was love.

The baby wiggled and began to chew on his coat. Her teeth were very sharp and she was grinding through the fabric, but he let her gnaw. He could sense her hunger and the irritation in her gums. She was still teething. She would need a dentist soon. Her human-sized jaw would not be able to accommodate a full set of goblin teeth.

Kris looked away from the baby and back down at Adora's shining hair. On top of concerns about himself, he was deeply troubled by the fact that he had hurt her back in L.A.—that he'd frightened Adora to the point of blacking out, had been forced to invade her mind to shut down the submerged rage that had come bubbling out of her subconscious at the goblins that day at the farmers' market. Her resistance to his suggestion to calm herself and leave the scene had been abnormally strong—death feys were usually able to march right into whatever mind or body they wished to examine and have their way. But she'd fought—and was still fighting, still hiding. Since he didn't want to hurt her more, he'd had to remain on the outside ever since, eavesdropping on her stray thoughts whenever he could. This brain block she had in place—the thing she called Joy and a muse—felt like it was something separate from her waking conscience, and it was serious about its role as guardian at the gate. He'd had to overwhelm both Adora and Joy to cut off her rage at the goblins, and it felt like something very close to rape for both of them.

He didn't know what to do with this . . . this fragment of her personality that was Joy. It was clearly part of Adora's fey nature, deeply suppressed, probably violent when cornered, and he sensed it was guarding some part of Adora that was terrified and hiding, a small and perhaps defenseless memory from when she was young, a memory that whimpered every time he drew near because—for some reason—it expected to be attacked. He couldn't see the specifics, but there had been moments, especially when she spoke of her parents, that she had looked inward with the same mute misery and bewilderment as an abandoned dog left in the wilderness to starve.

He wanted desperately to comfort her, to offer reassurance of his intentions, but he could find no way to get near that part of her without damaging—perhaps even destroying—Joy. He couldn't risk that, not without knowing a whole lot more about

Adora and her personal history. He didn't know her magic. Destroying Joy might destroy her too.

He sighed again. Sometimes, life was tricky.

"Okay. You can open your eyes. We'll stop here for some water. We all need it."

Adora opened her eyes, but it didn't help much since she was in darkness.

A familiar scent tickled her nose. It took a moment to place. It was the smell of a linen cupboard that had gone too long without cleaning. Kris said something in that musical language he had used with the dying girl, and a blue light slowly came up around them.

Adora stared. She wasn't frightened. Her capacity for alarm had been anesthetized when they entered the mound. But something about this space was not right, was not . . . *human*.

"What is this place?"

At first glance, she thought the room was filled with carousel horses from some dismantled merry-go-round, but a second glance told her the truth: These were brightly painted mummies of fantastical beasts—griffins, satyrs, a sort of winged Cyclops whose face was painted garish colors. Beyond, the room sparkled under its layer of dust. There was a mosaic on the wall made of jasper, agate, coral and . . . mica? Surely it couldn't be gold! Some of the design had crumbled away, leaving colorful heaps of stone on the floor, but enough remained to show a pastoral scene of the room's dead inhabitants cavorting in a tropical jungle that had probably never existed on the human part of earth.

Kris's arms fell away. Adora turned slowly. The ceiling above was domed and ornamented with bas-reliefs of extremely fat, sneering cupids with unusually long arrows and oversized bows. There was no reason to believe that these cherubs were anything other than gilt paint on plaster, but somehow Adora was sure that they were. The detail was too great. It was as though someone had bronzed actual beings and then welded them to the ceiling.

"This way," Kris said.

Adora stepped farther into the room and reached out with her inner sight, something she was barely aware of doing. There were deep shadows in the areas near the walls that should be cool but somehow weren't.

The feeling of this weird tomb was not hallowed, it was more haunted than sacred, perhaps even watched over by hostile ghosts. Obviously death had visited and left behind souvenirs that, had they been more recent or she less—

Drugged? Joy suggested.

—might have overset her nerves.

Real or not, it was all a bit too much. The show of treasure should have aroused some avarice in her bosom, but all it did was make her vaguely homesick for a tiny house with its cheerful yard and sunny windows.

So, why not go home?

Why not, indeed?

Am I nuts? she asked Joy. *I'm in a tomb—a tomb! Why didn't I just pack my bags—*

You did!

—*and leave L.A. at the first sign of trouble? Was it really the hundred k?*

Joy snorted. *I wish it was because of the money, but we both know better.*

Adora looked over at Kris. Even now, her attraction for him overrode all else. "It's like Aladdin's cave," she said.

"Without the jinn," Kris pointed out. "And there's no forty thieves about either."

"Such color," she finally said. "I've never seen anything like it. It's . . ."

Not normal.

He nodded. "The wine red comes from juice squeezed from rose madder. Strange, glowing roses used to bloom wildly down here. They're almost all gone now, surviving only in the garden at the heart of Cadalach. A bit of the perfume still remains, though," he said, inhaling slowly. "The gleam in the sky comes from pixie dust gathered from fire imps. They mixed it with the blue chalk of ground mollusk shells. Those sea snails are now extinct too."

Adora pondered. Maybe those were the ghosts she felt. It seemed not so frightening to be haunted by flowers and snails. Certainly it was better than being surrounded by the spirits of Cyclops and satyrs tied up in those painted bandages of eternal slumber—or so she sincerely hoped.

"Is it a mausoleum?" she asked.

"Not really. It's a sort of storage room for lost things that are the last of their kinds," Kris said, suddenly matter-of-fact. "The Nephalim—the giants—collected them."

"So, these creatures are all extinct?"

"In this place and time."

"Does it bother you? Being with the dead?" she asked.

"No. The dead do not bother me—it's the dying. I have to stay away from active war zones where hate and anger thrive. The killing fields affect me, and in a terrible way," he admitted. "I used to have more control, but now I'm . . . I'm easily affected. It's why Mugshottz is nearly always with me."

Adora started to ask him what he meant, but he interrupted.

"Go to the back wall. There's a small stream there," he instructed. "You need to drink deeply."

She was used to him leaping about from the sublime to the mundane—though it was sometimes difficult to know at first which subjects were which. But this time she agreed about the urgency of drinking something. She was parched.

"I don't see . . ." But even as she spoke, water blossomed in the floor and wended its way along the wall Kris indicated. Light rose from it, showing the wall to be made of some kind of slag glass. She had seen samples before when lightning hit and melted sandstone. She couldn't imagine what force—short of a volcano—could have created this place. It also possessed a sort of eerie resonance that was almost like a living voice.

"Come. You and the baby must drink. In fact, bathing might be a good idea. I must see if she has any wounds."

Adora nodded reluctantly. The baby certainly needed washing, and she herself was feeling more than a little slimy. That didn't mean that she was ready for a strip-down in front of Kris and assorted dead creatures. Eventually taking her clothes off with him sounded keen, but this was not the place.

So, you can wait? Joy asked sarcastically.

While Adora knelt down to drink, Kris dipped his hands in the water and poured a trickle into the baby's mouth.

"Ah-abah," the child said, swallowing happily. Kris smiled back as he cradled it and scooped up more water, which he poured over the child's head in a protective gesture that looked something like a baptism. Watching them together reminded Adora of Sundays when she was a child and used to watch "Wild Kingdom" alone in the living room. She had actually envied the beavers and bears and other mammals who got to cuddle with their parents in a family den.

Envy is an ugly thing, Joy pointed out. *Don't go there.*

I know. I'm not jealous. And she wasn't. She was just sad that she couldn't join Kris and the baby, that they were not her family.

"Ah-haaa," the child said again.

Water tickled Adora's feet, urging her to wade in. It felt delightful even as it soaked her shoes, probably finishing the destruction started by the rain.

Adora put her hands in the eerie blue liquid and sighed. She agreed with the baby's happy evaluation, though she didn't coo out loud. The water, when she finally tasted it, was wonderful, and she could feel strength and energy pouring back into her body, easing away the cold stiffness that had affected her. She rubbed handfuls of it over her face and into her tired eyes, which suddenly cleared and showed things she hadn't noticed before.

"Let's get you changed," Kris said to the baby, either unaware or uncaring that Adora was staring into space, lost in bemusement at the new colors all around her.

She moved her head slowly, enthralled at the radiant auras but also watching from the corner of her eye as Kris worked, more fascinated than appalled, as he laid the baby on the floor and peeled off its filthy sleeper. He quickly freed the child's strapped lower arms from their dirty bandage and then tickled her pink tummy. Adora could see now that the rest of the baby's skin was actually a pale, glowing green—how had she not noticed this before?

The baby laughed and waved its arms and legs. Adora was oddly charmed in spite of the wrongness of the extra limbs protruding from the body. Feeling braver, she turned, looking openly.

"That diaper's probably filthy, but I don't know what—" she began then stopped as Kris pulled the disposable diaper away and tutted at how red the baby's legs and lower belly were.

Is that diaper rash? Adora thought, staring at the red skin covered in small blisters.

How the hell should I know? Joy answered. *It isn't like I've had kids either.*

"Don't worry," Kris said. "We'll borrow some linen and make a new one. That will do for now."

Adora glanced once at the animal mummies Kris was staring at, and then looked hurriedly back at the baby.

So, there's something scarier than a baby, Joy said, amused.

Those are mummies—bandaged dead monsters, Adora replied. She said to Kris, "I'll wash her. You get the . . . the diaper."

"Okay."

"Just . . . just don't get it from the Cyclops, okay? He looks mean. I don't want to piss him off."

"Okay," Kris said again. She could hear the amusement in his voice. Obviously, he didn't share her feeling of being watched. Or else he didn't care what the ghosts might think.

Adora kept her eyes firmly fixed on the baby and the dancing water while she soaked the only clean edge of the baby's sleeper, using it as a washcloth to scrub the baby's muddy face and head, and then to trickle water over the angry red rash. She tried not to listen to the tearing sounds behind her, and she also avoided touching the baby's skin, fearful that she might somehow hurt the child even though the red welts and spots were fading quickly under the stream of soothing, dribbled water.

Kris returned to her side. He blotted the baby with a small shred of linen.

"Okay, little lady, time to wrap you back up," he said, lifting up the baby and positioning her on an uneven rectangle of gauze. He tied her with a calm efficiency that said he had done this before.

"I think her sleeper's a lost cause," Adora remarked. "But we can wrap her in my coat. The inside is still dry."

"We won't need to wrap her," Kris said. "It's warm enough here. And the others will be coming soon."

"Others?" Adora asked.

"Yes. My nephew, Jack, and his wife, Io—and a doctor. His name is Zayn. Maybe others too." Kris cocked his head as if listening. "Hm—it sounds like a veritable parade out there. Maybe they're all coming."

"Zayn? He's the one you thought could help me."

"Yes." Kris got to his feet. He handled the baby easily, and Adora made no move to take the child back; she was okay with watching, and didn't really want to touch the child now that she knew it had a bad rash that might hurt.

You have noticed that Kris likes babies? Children of all types and sizes? Joy asked.

Yes.

And you don't, Joy reminded her.

No. At least, I don't know if I like them. They scare me. And that was the truth. A child's vulnerability terrified her.

Adora looked up to find Kris studying her with a slightly creased brow. "How . . ." he began, then shrugged. "Are you feeling better?"

"Yes. I feel good. I also feel . . ." How did she feel? Different—that was for sure. And it wasn't just physical. Something else had changed.

Adora turned slowly, surveying the room. It really was as though she were looking at a world through a special telescope that let her see with more than her eyes; and the room was filled with sentient things— things that shouldn't be alive but were. Rocks, water, even the mummies. From the corners of her eyes she could see something like movement where no one was. But no matter how quickly she turned, the flower or tree or stone had completed its transformation back into an inanimate object by the time she faced it. Surely it was some of that direct neural stimulation Kris talked about, but the effect was damned freaky.

"Kris . . . ?"

"Don't worry. It's just the others coming. They're almost here, and it's stirred the ghosts. Things will settle down after we're gone." He looked over her shoulder and his eyes widened. There was a sudden whoosh of sound and an explosion of voices. Adora turned quickly. . . .

And looked across the room at a dragon.

A dragon! Run! Joy screamed shrilly.

"Uhhhh—" But she couldn't; Adora froze under the red-eyed stare as the creature leapt toward her with claws extended. She was certain that death was imminent but was unable to move from its path. Her only reaction was to close her eyes against its fiery gaze, and to give a small, screechy exhalation that might have been Kris's name.

Surprisingly, the impact from their collision wasn't as hard as expected. Her body was grabbed around the waist and she was toppled onto a patch of sand that she could have sworn hadn't been there a moment before. She could feel a massive weight hovering above, but little was actually pressing down on her. Stranger still, there was the distinct sound of children's laughter coming from all around.

"You caught her! You caught her! Look, Mommy—he got her."

Children were laughing and clapping their hands. They sounded happy, playful. And "mommy" was there.

Okay, maybe she wasn't going to die. Maybe she'd had a hallucination. Or maybe she hadn't seen a dragon but just a very large dog that looked like a dragon.

Adora forced her eyes open and almost immediately regretted it, because all she could see was a long, reptilian snout filled with enormous yellowed fangs longer than her fingers. As she watched, the thin scaly lips rimming the giant teeth seemed to pull up into a grin. A long black tongue snaked out. Adora's eyes crossed as she watched it descend inch by inch. It stopped right above her face and then slowly, teasingly, flicked her nose.

"Tag!" the creature said in a deep voice after the tongue retracted. Its breath was scented with petroleum. "You're it."

There was more childish laughter, and then the sound of footsteps. Kris's voice interrupted the merriment. "Let her up. She's probably terrified. I haven't explained about you yet."

"Oh . . . Sorry about that, young lady. No harm intended. I would introduce myself—but then I'd have to kill you."

That's a joke, right?

The dragon backed away carefully, and Kris's

worried face swam into view, upside-down from
where she was sprawled. He still held the baby. And
even upside down, it wasn't cute. In fact, it had a
smile only a greedy orthodontist could love. However, a smile was a good thing.

Even on a dragon? Joy asked.

*Especially on a dragon. Holy shit! That's really a
dragon.*

Adora moved her head to get another look as the
living legend retreated toward the far wall. It was
huge, but apparently harmless. Glowing children
were crawling on it, though not near its twitching tail.

Hmph! Harmless like a heart attack. Joy was clearly
still shaken. *Kris should have warned you.*

No harm, no foul, Adora answered, though she
wasn't entirely certain what it meant. She thought it
had something to do with basketball.

"Are you ready to get up now and meet people?"
Kris asked kindly.

She rolled her head toward him. He was surrounded in a halo of light that glowed like the moon.

"Hello," Adora said, proud that her voice didn't
squeak.

"Hello," he answered, smiling down at her. "I can
give you a hand up, if you like."

"Yes, thanks. I seemed to have misplaced my
knees. And my spine. And all my muscles."

"Then let us offer all the help you need."

And then there were a dozen faces suddenly peering at her. Hands reached for her, setting her back
on her feet. It might have been frightening to be so
pressed in by strangers, but they all wore smiles of
welcome. There was something else too, something
she couldn't quite identify at first.

*What's wrong with them? Why are they staring at me
like that?*

I think . . . I think they're nervous. Joy sounded surprised. *Maybe even a little afraid.*

Of me? But why?

They may not be afraid of you, so much as for you.

What do you mean?

But Joy said nothing. This, like babies, was apparently new to her too.

Then the Goddess spoke. "Sit at my right hand. Let us feast together while you tell me of the state of the Sons of Man. The light has gone out in Rome, and I can no longer see them."

—*Niklas 10:12*

The moonlight spoke to him in a voice he knew well.

"Take her, Niklas. Accept what she offers." The shadows pulled back, revealing the offering. She was young, beautiful, eager to be given to a god. He knelt between her legs, cradling her face in his left hand. Power waited on his lips, hungry, excited, ready to devour.

Too much power. Too much hunger.

"No," he said in the old language, and drew back. "If I touch her, I'll kill her. This one wants to die."

CHAPTER TWELVE

Adora was given introductions to everyone before they ventured back into the tunnels and headed for Cadalach proper. All except the dark man called Abrial, who went to deal with the body in the trunk of the Jaguar. He was scary, but Adora liked his wife Nyssa.

Two of the other men also appealed to her, but for a different reason. The one called Thomas was very quiet and serious, and she suspected him inclined to deep thought. The other was Roman, a theatrical producer and . . . something odd. Thomas's wife, Cyra, was also a bit . . . well, fey. But none looked more otherworldly than Jack's wife. As strange as Io appeared, Adora felt an instant kinship with her.

Jack Frost himself was another matter. He sent trills of alarm—and maybe something else—down her nerves. There was a strong resemblance to Kris, but he wore his . . . his magic . . . much more openly. Adora wanted to like him, and perhaps eventually would, but he made her very uneasy. Was this what Kris was truly like?

Finally, there was Farrar. It was Adora's general—though admittedly not terribly thought-out—opinion that the dead should be neither seen nor heard. Not that she was prejudiced or anything, but natural laws—the ones that assured her of gravity and an eastern sunrise—said the dead were . . . well, dead. She'd never even believed in ghosts. And yet, here was Abrial's uncle, looking far more animated than many of her living friends. He was one of the noncorporeal feys Kris had mentioned, one so advanced psychically that he no longer needed to interact with the living to draw power to sustain himself—at least not inside this faerie mound.

Yeah, the freak show is in town.

Cadalach and its inhabitants were certainly challenging her many assumptions, but she felt too stoned to rally any counterarguments. Adora just nodded every time someone said they were a pooka or a siren or a selkie, and made a note to ask Kris what they were talking about.

Everyone made polite noises about feeding her and showing her around, but Kris overruled them, insisting that what she needed more than anything was sleep. Adora *was* exhausted. Her encounter with the dragon had used up the last of her energy in fear. But she wasn't so far gone that she didn't think to ask about the baby they had found. The child was gone, whisked away by someone called Chloe, who apparently was Zayn's wife, neither of whom she recalled meeting.

Most of Cadalach was a blur. They did pass through the underground city's amazing garden, filled with flowers of shapes and scents Adora had never known. She might have lingered there, listening to watery music, but Kris took her arm and gently propelled her down another long hall.

For some reason it didn't surprise Adora when she was informed that she would be using Kris's room. Perhaps she was beyond being surprised. Or maybe there was something about this place that made all things seem acceptable and possible.

It might be that. Though tired, she still felt a bit giddy.

And it might not. Joy wasn't giddy.

The last of their escort, Kris's nephew, said goodbye to them at a dark door carved in a pattern of roses and mystical beasts. Kris promised to be along to see Jack in a short while. The nephew cocked an eyebrow at this assurance, but Kris only shook his head and opened the door.

"I suppose it is a bit . . . untidy," Kris said finally, looking about the room with a creased brow. "I was trying to relearn everything all at once, and I went on a bit of a reading binge."

The smell of old books rolled out at Adora.

"I see that." She walked over to the edge of the room and ran a finger along the spine of an ancient folio inscribed with a phrase in Latin. "You speak a lot of foreign languages?" she asked.

"Yes—too many."

The room seemed at first glance to be built of books. There were no shelves, just stacks of old tomes piled from obsidian floor to glassy blue ceiling. The books weren't arranged in any pattern that she could see—no ABCs, no grouping by theme or color or size. This didn't dismay her. Adora's own library refused conventional organization. Figuring out the pattern would be one more step in understanding who Kris was.

It was telling that the room had none of the trappings of wealth she associated with Kris in his persona of Bishop S. Nicholas. She had the distinct feeling that Bishop Nicholas was another construct created purely for human edification. He was the new Santa Claus.

"Mugshottz will be here soon. He has your luggage with him." Kris seemed to be waiting for something from her.

"And your other employees?"

Kris shook his head. "They had to go on to San Francisco. We can't let a little thing like bloody revolution get in the way of our plan."

"I had almost forgotten that," she said slowly. "I mean, what happened in L.A. I think my brain is drugged with fatigue."

"It's been a long night," Kris agreed.

"Are they okay? They weren't hurt?"

"Yes, they're all okay. They've been in touch with Thomas."

"I'm relieved to hear it." Adora almost asked if they'd had any reports of the numbers killed, but she decided against it. Tomorrow would be soon enough to hear the grim details. "What happened to your plane, do you know yet? Did your friends get it?"

Kris nodded. "Yes, but not until someone had a go at it. The autopsy suggests death by bludgeoning," he answered sadly. "Fortunately, Jack has a knack for resurrecting old machines. She may fly again."

Adora didn't want to think about that. Instead, she continued her slow inspection of the chamber. She found the books she'd written at the top of a precarious pile, and felt a rush of warmth. He had read her after all!

"They say you can tell a lot about a person by what they read," she said.

"And what can you tell about me?" Kris asked.

Adora picked up a roll of parchment covered in writing she could not identify. She smiled a little. "It means that I don't understand you—and may not be bright enough to ever do so. This isn't Greek, is it?"

"No." Kris looked a bit stiff.

"Don't worry. It's good to be a bit of an enigma. Simplicity can be boring."

The next item to catch her eye was a painting. She stood in front of the old portrait that leaned against the wall, and marveled. It was undoubtedly Kris who had posed, but a Kris very different from the man she knew. The colors of the portrait were rich—too rich, given Kris's present preferred severity of dress. The man in the painting wore a green velvet ruffled coat, embroidered in gold thread and draped with an emerald-studded chain. That wasn't the only thing that was different, though. The Kris in the painting was happy and more than a little amused as he smiled down at her. Her Kris was more focused inward; whatever he saw or heard these days, it was a lot more serious than anything this Kris had known.

"You should hang this," she said, glancing back at him. "The likeness is . . . flattering."

Kris shrugged.

"It isn't really me. Not anymore. I don't need reminders of what I was."

There were pieces of furniture in the room, she discovered after a second look, but all were buried under books, only their general outlines showing. The bed was visible, but it was partly obscured with scatterings of files, which Kris was gathering with great care.

Though the scene was chaotic, Adora felt immediately at home. She was with one of her own kind, another bibliophile.

"I'm going to leave you to nap," Kris said, straightening. He moved around her, being conspicuously careful not to touch—which was thoughtful of him, since she might have been feeling somewhat awkward.

However, she wasn't feeling awkward at all. In fact, she was feeling . . . Well, she was feeling more awake by the minute, and more drawn to Kris than she ever had been. She wouldn't mind at all if he stayed.

Stop. I . . . I don't like this. We're . . . something is going on, Joy said.

What? What's wrong? Adora asked.

I . . . I don't know. There's something in here with us.

They weren't alone? That was important, but Adora couldn't seem to care.

She watched as Kris backed to the door. A part of her wanted to throw herself at him. She suddenly wanted to know what he would be like in bed. Even more, she wanted to know who she would be with him.

"Kris?" She swallowed, unsure what to say. She touched her cheeks. She was feeling very warm.

"We'll talk soon," he promised. If she hadn't known better, she would have said he was nervous at being alone with her. "Just . . . try to get some rest."

Rest. She certainly needed it. But . . .

Kris disappeared behind a heavy door, carved on the inside with serpentine bodies and blackened with age and perhaps actual fire.

She was alone. In Kris's room—and she knew it was his room. She could be blind and still know he lived there. Her senses recalled Kris clearly, even when he wasn't beside her. Her hands knew the feel of him. She knew his scent, his taste, though they had never kissed. They permeated this room, but she wanted more.

What the hell? she whispered, alarmed.

I don't know, Joy said. *I feel very strange.*

She hadn't known that Joy could feel strange.

"I can't quite take this in. To believe in this—all of this—you'd have to have a screw loose. Maybe more than one," Adora said aloud.

I think your screws are tight enough. You just have them in some odd places.

Adora started looking for a bathroom. That need, at least, hadn't changed.

Kris had to talk to Jack and Thomas about what had happened in L.A., but his first stop was to see his niece by marriage. It took him a while to explain everything that had happened with Adora, including her reaction to the baby. Afterward, instead of feeling relieved at unburdening himself, he found his body bracing for bad news.

"Of course she's resisting you. She's part siren, Kris. She isn't Welsh. I think maybe she's a grandchild of Bar and Ogir. She has the Norse look about her. I think she may be part fire-starter, too. And perhaps there's some demon blood," Io said. "Thomas would be the one to ask about this."

Kris grimaced. "I don't think I'll mention it just now. If Adora has anything to go on, she's likely to do some research, and I don't want her finding out who Granny was just yet."

"Fair enough. The thing is, with sirens, whatever our origin, we—*she*—has to be careful with men. We can get so easily ensnared. And with a death fey . . ." Io exhaled.

She went on; "It's not your fault, but it's like your breed implant in us a death wish, a need to be subsumed, obliterated even. You bring out something dark and fatalistic. And she does have darkness inside; Cyra and I both saw it. We don't know the details, but I'm betting that she was attacked as a child. I also strongly suspect a lot of parental neglect. She probably senses all of this even if she has no clear memories, and is terrified that she'll end up like her suicidal mother. I know that fear haunted me all of my adult life until I met Jack. My mother was a goblin-fruit addict and a sex addict as well." Io cleared her throat. "Someone has to talk to her about this. We can't let her walk about ignorant of the dangers around her."

"And?" Kris asked, his face tight. "There's more, isn't there?"

"Yes. You won't like it, but you need to know that you're vulnerable too. And not just to her anger. Little affects death feys except a siren's call. Death and sex—it's all so close. It makes relationships very tricky." Io's smile was wry. "They can be great beyond measure, but they can also lead to what has been called assured mutual self-destruction. You must be careful—for all our sakes."

Kris nodded again. He had sensed this. He also understood what Io wasn't saying. The danger wasn't just to Adora and Kris. If he ever lost control, gave himself over to the killing impulse, he could end up slaughtering both of them and anyone else who was nearby. Maybe everyone in Cadalach.

It was going to be tough resisting, though. He hadn't reckoned with the strength of the Goddess's call inside the shian. He had never in his life had a violent impulse toward a woman, but from the moment they'd arrived at the stronghold, his strongest desire had been to have sex with Adora whether she was willing or not. And it was a sexual impulse, not love, which moved him. He didn't care for the alien feeling, and he swore he would not touch her if he had no affection in his heart. As Io pointed out, it was just too damned dangerous. He would touch her with love or not at all.

Adora didn't sleep, but a look at her watch told her there had been a lapse of hours as she had sat unaware. She sighed. She had to make a decision—make it soon. Before Kris came back. And she had to make it right, since it would dictate the direction of the remainder of her life.

It was difficult, though, because she felt unsettled, torn in two directions. Kris left a certain exuberant turbulence in his wake. He was a tornado, picking up her safe assumptions and throwing them around until she was dizzy. This should have left her irritated, but somehow it didn't. Because . . . this was just Kris.

And maybe because she hadn't liked her previous assumptions all that much anyway.

She tried a last time to imagine Kris as Bishop Nicholas, or as a demi-god surrounded by worshippers, but for once, her imagination failed. This was Kris—Kris of the laughing eyes and ready grin and generous thoughts. Not a god, not a saint, not Santa. Whatever he was in the past, he was simply Kris now.

Heaven help her, that was problem enough. He was a sort of homme fatale for her, both terrifying and magnificent. She wasn't sure how it had happened—though he had first seduced her into giddy pleasure by asking her opinions and encouraging her to talk about herself without making any harsh judgments about how she lived. That sounded pretty silly when she thought about it, but for her that was a better gift than flowers and jewelry. She could live without gems and gold, but she was hungry for understanding and caring.

And he was living, breathing expiation— forgiveness for any sin or burden she carried.

That sounds like a demi-god to me, Joy sneered.

But the way he moves. . . .

Hyperdynamism—that's the scientific word for a rare but explainable human condition.

Why do you keep arguing? Adora asked

Because you want me to. You don't want him to be . . .

Fey, Adora finished for her. That was the word. But he *was* fey. How could she have not seen it before? The strength, the range of motion, even his skeletal structure! He moved like a cheetah or a . . . fey. That was the only answer. She had to accept it: Kris wasn't human. He was fey. She probably was too. Not human—at least, not completely.

Adora clutched Kris's pillow like it was a teddy bear that would comfort her, and in an odd way it did. Kris's scent clung to it. If she closed her eyes, she could almost believe he was there with her.

Old memories rose up suddenly, but they were just ghosts now, and though strong they had no physical form to harm her. Their only ploy was resurrected emotions, but given her new reality, they had no power unless she gave it to them. And she wouldn't. She'd acknowledge them; after all, she had been miserable—more miserable than . . . well, beyond a certain point it was meaningless to assign degrees. She had been wretched, frightened and alone most of her life, and that hurt. But that was a long time ago. And after Joy came, she'd never been that alone again. And now there was Kris and . . . this place.

She was seeing many things more clearly now. Her early lustful feelings for Kris were partly an act of defiance. In spite of Joy's warnings, Adora had secretly been encouraging her attraction to Kris the way a mother would urge a toddler into taking first steps. It was a roundabout way of demonstrating to the distrustful part of her that Kris could be one of the good guys and there was no need to fear him. Or, more to the point, no need to fear caring about him.

But will he care back?

Hell's bells, Joy. What am I, the psychic hotline? I just know that he's—

Overwhelmed you.

Maybe that was true. She was still limited by the filter of her five human senses—though she sometimes suspected that there might be more that she sometimes reached when she dreamed. But all her waking senses said that there was something about Kris that was unique—though it couldn't be that he actually looked better, smelled better, felt better than anyone else in the world. He *couldn't*. Yet that was her experience of him.

It's called pheromones.

No. Adora knew she sounded smitten. And gloomy. *That's too simple.*

Then it's love, you blighted idiot.

Nooooo.

No?

Well, okay, maybe. But Joy, it's more than that. He's . . .

Yes, he is. Joy sounded resigned. *And if you're determined to do this, then I think there are a few things we need to deal with first.*

You mean about . . . how I'm different.

Yes.

Adora took a slow, deep breath. She had spent most of her life trying to hide from the knowledge that inside her was Another, a not quite normal being who—above all else—she did not want to be. Because if she was this *other*, then she would never, ever be loved. Not by her parents. Not by anyone. The fact that her parents were now—and had been for a long time—beyond loving or disapproving or anything else, hadn't registered in her gut.

Not until now. Finally the internal truth was catching up with reality. Perhaps because of Kris. Perhaps because of being in this place. Whatever the cause, Adora didn't need to hide from herself anymore. She could look inward and see who and what she really was.

Are you certain you want to remember? That you're really ready to face this?

Adora started to answer, then paused to really think about Joy's question. *I think I need to know,* she decided at last. *I can't go to Kris as a cripple.*

Okay, maybe you're right. Maybe you can finally look at these things head-on and give them their eviction notice. Hang on, though, we're in for a rough ride.

Adora felt something shift in her brain, like a rusted door being forced open. A light was switched on, illuminating the dark, neglected corners of the attic of her memory. Though nervous, she forced herself to take a long look, to pull the first dust cover off the sinister shapes that had been shoved to the edges of her mind. It took all her will not to flinch from what lurked there. Only the thought of Kris and his endless capacity for acceptance gave her the power to go on.

Her first shroud was pulled away to reveal an old eight-millimeter projector and a yellowed screen with a still image on it. She focused on the frozen picture, a blurry snapshot of a spring day when she was five. It might have been her birthday. She was never certain back then just when it was, because no one ever remembered to get her a cake or presents, so she would just pick a day in the summer and pretend that was her birthday.

Ready? Joy asked.

Yes.

The film stuttered and then came to slow life, sprockets clicking loudly. Adora was standing outside a neighbor's house, eyes dazzled by the sun as she gazed through the bleached pickets of the leaning fence. Around her there rose the soft shushing of waves meeting up with land.

"It's Aptos," she murmured, almost able to feel the grit of sand trapped in her sandals and the crinoline of her starched slip scratching her legs.

Yes.

A breeze brushed by her, ocean chilled and unpleasant, and it banged shut the screen door of the bungalow in front of her.

That was Old Man Fletcher's house, she said.

Yes, Fletcher.

Adora shivered violently as she thought the name. There was nothing sinister about the house itself. It was a typical beach bungalow, white with blue shutters, a little salt-worn and rubbed around the edges. The succulents blooming in the yard were actually pretty. But she was suddenly afraid. Because she remembered a bit more now; a monster lived there. It had beer breath and watery blue eyes, and filthy fingernails that hurt when they pinched her.

That bastard. Adora's small hands wrapped around the weathered pickets and squeezed tightly. Fletcher wasn't the kind who lured children in with toys and candy. There was no seduction involved. None.

She recalled a rough voice calling her names that she didn't understand but instinctively feared. And she recalled those giant hands turning rough, slapping her when she cried and then tried to fight back.

Do you need to see more? Joy asked, making the film still.

No. I remember now. That really happened, didn't it?

Yes.

Unable to help herself, Adora looked at her younger self and began to cry.

I was alone.

Joy's voice was matter-of-fact. *It's sad, but all quite true. You were often alone back then. No loving parent was there to hide the toxic cleaners when you were a toddler. No one was there to tell you not to stick bobby-pins in electrical outlets. And no one warned you not to talk to strangers. . . . You avoided drinking bleach and the bobby-pins. Two out of three isn't bad for a five-year old. You should be proud.*

Proud? Adora stopped crying. Anger choked off her tears. She began to remember this too—all the dangerous things she had done as a preschooler, like riding her tricycle in the middle of the busy street, playing at the beach at high tide when the water was running fast. Or going into the neighbors' houses when they offered her cookies or a chance to play with their pets because she was allowed none of her own. She had even let a strange man take her for a ride on his motorcycle. They had spent the day playing games at the boardwalk.

You went home afterward. Joy paused. *Your mother asked what happened to your good dress, but you never told her the truth. You never told anyone.*

"Why?" Adora whispered. But she knew. She *knew.* Fresh rage began to blossom inside her. She tried to throttle it down.

You were afraid—afraid that if you were too much trouble, or if they were ashamed of you, that they would give you away, Joy answered. *Maybe to someone like Old Man Fletcher.*

And I was more afraid of being abandoned than I was of that monster down the street. Damn them! Her voice was miserable and angry. *How the hell could they not notice what happened? It got worse after that, you know. I was always weird, different, but after that day . . .*

I know.

Why? Why didn't they protect me? Were they ashamed of me—is that it? Because I was a firebug?

No. If it helps any, I don't think they ever suspected what happened. And you did burn his house down. You damn near got him too. He carried the scars forever. They were like a scarlet A that warned other children away from him.

I burned his house down? Adora asked.

Joy was silent, but the memory came back like the others, muted but complete. He had screamed when his clothes caught fire—screamed just like she had when he had hurt her. Adora digested this, wondering if the fact that she had fought back against the monster and won would help melt some of her anger and shame away. She decided it was too soon to tell.

And that's when you came, she thought. *That was the day.*

Yes, I awakened that day, Joy said. *You needed help—strength. And after . . . well, the fire frightened you badly, and you couldn't afford to go on remembering, having nightmares. But you couldn't really forget, either. So you made me, gave me a name, and I kept the memory of the scary thing for you.* Joy paused. *I know you don't like me—or the cause of my creation—but really it was the healthiest thing for you to do.*

Was it? To run away from what I'd done?

Of course. Do you really think it would have been better to taxidermy the moment, embalm it so your five-year-old brain could live with the torment forever? Even as an adult, you'll have trouble excising this hurt. It's branded into your memory, burned into your soul. I don't really think you'll ever forget or forgive what happened—and you shouldn't have to. But you do need to make peace with yourself and admit what you are. I can't keep you safe anymore, and your magic affects Kris.

Are you the . . . power? Are you the fire, Joy?

Partly. I am that part of you.

Am I schizophrenic?

No. I'm not sure what you are, really. But you aren't mentally ill.

Adora laughed bitterly. *You'd say that anyway, wouldn't you? To protect yourself.*

Probably, Joy admitted. *But that isn't such a big deal around here. Look at Kris—he's a death fey and Santa Claus. He has a pet dragon.*

Joy had a point. Adora decided that she would have to think about this for a while, to re-create a new hierarchy of weirdness with which she could measure things. She was too stunned to do it now, though.

The main thing, Joy said, *is that you understand that though your parents were flawed—fatally so—it doesn't mean you are. There is no law that says you have to repeat their mistakes.*

It doesn't mean I'm not flawed, though, Adora pointed out, feeling exhausted. *I could be just as twisted as they are. I might be just as bad a parent.*

True, but I'd say this is all up to you. How crippled do

you want to be? How much power will you give your parents or Old Man Fletcher? After all, they're dead and you're not. Doesn't that give you the edge?

That was a good question, but Adora collapsed on the bed and fell asleep before she answered.

And Gaia spoke to Niklas saying: "Thou art a wonder unto many, and thou mayest well be so, for I have wrought great marvels in thee and for thee that thou should go forth and in turn give comfort to the Sons of Man who wander lost in the lands of the North."

—Niklas 11:2

It was the feast of Mabon, the time of passing for the Great Son, Lord of Shadows, Keeper of Mysteries. It was the time when the Wise One returned to sleep. But first there came the Wild Hunt, where the Keeper would ride the great storm. Many feared this night, but the Keeper calmed them and said they should not go in fear, for the Goddess would spread her hand of protection over them while her Son returned home.

Then the Keeper of Mysteries went to the top of the hill and laid his golden robe aside. Naked, he opened his arms wide and laughed at the silvered moon. The sky threw down lightning and boiling clouds, but still he laughed, bathing in the divine fire as he prepared to return home. From out of the night there came a great stallion made all of shadows and fire, with hooves forged of steel. The Keeper of Mysteries snatched at the steed's fiery mane as he thundered by, and the Lord of Shadows was still laughing joyously when the sky split in twain and the stallion plunged into the void.

CHAPTER THIRTEEN

"I just don't see how there can be so many goblins in L.A. Hell's bells! We've killed off thousands since they first started interfering in Las Vegas," Roman complained.

"Not all the illegals coming over the border are humans. L.A. is the first hive the southern lutins come to, and most stay," Kris answered. "I know it's bloody inconvenient and hard to imagine, but try to understand that the goblins are mostly victims too. Their leaders are as tyrannical as any third-world potentate and you can't blame them for looking for a better life in 'the land of the free.' And the L.A. hive turns this hunger for freedom to their advantage. They're smart and they use word of mouth to get fresh recruits for the war. The people there—lutin and human—have had their brains waxed by fairy tales to a high gloss at an early age, their thoughts sealed off from the influence of outside logic and even basic information. All this varnish and propaganda will have to be stripped before we can make any headway there."

"You have a plan for brain-stripping?" Thomas asked.

"Of course."

"Are Cyra and I a part of it?" he asked evenly.

"I sincerely hope so."

Thomas sighed.

There came a tap on the door. It wasn't Kris; Adora knew that immediately. "Come in," she called. Her voice was thick with departing sleep and disappointment.

The door opened slowly, and Io stuck her head in. She smiled, but there was a complete absence of humor in the curve of her mouth. Her eyes were worried.

"Did I wake you?" she asked.

"No, I was coming up from the depths," Adora assured her.

"Good." Io came in and, after having a quick look around for something to sit on and finding nothing but stacks of books, she approached and perched on the side of the bed, being careful not to touch Adora.

First Kris and now Io. What? Have I got cooties?

"I thought maybe we should have a talk. There has to be a lot that's strange for you here." She paused and then got straight to the point. "And you are probably feeling some very . . . unusual things about Kris."

Adora blinked, coming fully awake. "About Kris?" she repeated, and felt herself blush.

"Well, aren't you?" Io asked. There was no judgment there, only a bit of curiosity. "You'd be the first if you did not."

"Yes, I guess I am," Adora admitted. "I don't seem to be myself today."

"No, you're you," Io assured her. "You are just seeing—sensing—things for the first time without the hindrance of human . . . expectations and limits."

Adora waited, but when Io said no more she responded: "Okay."

"First of all, Kris and I have talked a bit. About your situation. He senses many of the same things in you that I do, and is concerned about not doing anything to . . . burden you beyond that which cannot be avoided. Unfortunately, there's a lot we won't be able to avoid. You haven't a lot of time to . . . adjust." Io stared at Adora with her weird blue eyes. "May I be frank with you?"

"Please." Adora pulled her knees up to her chest. It was a defensive posture, but it comforted her.

"It's clear to both Kris and me that you are at war with yourself. The part of you that was attacked and abandoned as a child is shying away from any deep relationship, and understandably so." Adora knew that her eyes widened and that Io saw. Io also saw the abortive gesture of her raised palms, trying to ward the next words away. "I'm sorry, Adora, but you are part siren—and your fey nature is to seduce and be seduced. Your body is built for this, and it will work to fulfill its destiny. There are some things you can do to . . . avoid certain problems. You need to know that, just like with selkies, your tears can and do enslave men. Have you ever noticed how insane they act when you cry around them? Unfortunately, those same tears can bind you just as surely to other magical beings, so you need to be careful."

Great, another bodily fluid to avoid, Joy joked.

"You are especially vulnerable to death feys." There was compassion in Io's eyes, but she spoke with almost heartless, hopeless clarity. "So far, you have avoided a confrontation of these two emotional needs—to be safe and yet to seduce and be seduced—but only because you were not involved with a magical being. That has changed. New game, new rules. Nature will win over nurture. The feelings you have for Kris will not go away—not this side of the grave, anyway. Maybe not even after. You have to find some way to make peace with this or it will tear you apart."

Adora almost groaned. It seemed she had a lot of things she was going to have to make peace with. She was sorry she'd woken up.

"Kris and I haven't slept together. Our relationship is theoretical at this point. Hell—he hasn't even kissed me! And I haven't been crying. . . ." Adora stopped. But she had cried on him once. No, twice. She recalled how he had rubbed the tear between his fingers and said, "I'm so glad that this does not belong to me."

Io nodded, as though sharing the memory.

"You may not have made love yet, but you will. And soon. Kris will resist the call as long as he can, but even he will eventually have his will eroded. So close to the source, it is impossible to refuse the Goddess forever. And it would be good if you were . . . able to make things easier on him. And on yourself too. Those who fight their nature . . . well, they do damage. And Kris has some special circumstances that need to be considered."

Adora pulled her knees in tighter. She didn't say anything. She couldn't argue Io's point, because she didn't understand a lot of what was being said. But what she did get, she didn't like it. She wanted Kris, but she didn't want to *have* to want him.

Io smiled encouragingly. "I know this is all a bit much, but the good news about being fey—and there is some—is that you will age very slowly and not know much of the suffering that humans do. It's sort of like being tapped into a fountain of youth. You won't get sick once you have built up immunity to the sun. We don't suffer senility either."

Adora considered. Was this good news? Did she actually fear old age, outliving her physical usefulness and beauty? No, that wasn't her fear, losing herself to wrinkles and senility. What she feared was losing herself—her mind and soul—to blind, unrequited love. Not just passion, but love.

Which was a risk with Kris. She had felt it all along, and now Io confirmed it.

Still, there was something new that she thought she feared more than losing herself, and that was that she was so screwed up that she would never have the chance to know true love at all.

"I know you are . . ." Io trailed off, waving her left hand. Adora noticed the nails for the first time. They were beautiful, like the inside of an abalone shell, and she was willing to bet that it wasn't nail polish that made them that way.

Seeing what she was staring at, Io smiled a little grimly. "Yes, we're different. And sometimes after you taste something bitter, it takes a while to be able to recognize what is sweet. You are overwhelmed by all this, by what you are and what is going on around you. But . . . give Kris a chance."

"Would it be okay if I took a walk?" Adora asked, knowing she was disappointing Io with her lack of reaction but feeling unable to process any more information, or to hear any more bad news. She added, "I need to stretch my legs and clear my head a little. My brain is still clogged with sleep."

"Sure," Io said. She looked like she was going to say something else about Kris, but instead she added, "Just don't go far. And don't wander into goblin territory. There's a sort of dead zone—hard to miss—that marks the edges of the two domains. Don't go beyond that. Things can get . . . weird."

Io stood and looked down at Adora, compassion in her eyes.

"Feel free to come to me at any time if you have questions—go to anyone. We are all anxious to help you." She added almost carelessly, "You can see the baby if you want. She's out with Chloe in the garden. You'll recognize Chloe because she looks like a ghost—a ghost with scars even deeper than your own."

Adora nodded, but Io's words only increased her nervousness. She wasn't sure she wanted to meet the ghostly Chloe; and with everything she'd just learned, she knew she wasn't ready to see the baby she and Kris had rescued.

Jack, Thomas and Kris met for a second council of war—or, given Kris's nature, a council of strategic peace.

"There are scattered hives throughout Europe and Asia. There's only one in Africa, and one in Australia that we know of. That hive peacefully shares territory with the Aboriginals—so far. In fact, none of those hives are as . . ." Kris sought a word.

"Confrontational?" Jack suggested.

"Yes—nor are they as entrepreneurial as the ones here in America. And it is mainly in the U.S. that lutins have embraced technology for violent purposes. This is where we need to begin. The United States first, and then Central and South America and Europe. It's basic triage. This is where the most danger lies, so we put our resources here."

"And giving a small vial of Cadalach's water to

everyone will do . . . what?" Thomas asked. "Assuming we can arrange it logistically."

"If there is any magic in them, they will be drawn to the water's call. It will guide them to their spiritual home in their dreams, and awaken their dormant natures. Cyra can help with this. I've never met a stronger kloka. There may be a role for Farrar as well. It could be handy to enlist some people on the Otherside."

"And we want that—an unsupervised confederacy of uneducated, magically awakened half-breed humans, feys and even goblins?" Thomas sounded skeptical.

Kris made himself sound certain. "Yes, my doubting Thomas. I know it isn't the traditional way of dealing with this problem, but it's the only course I can see that will save us from annihilation. We have to shift the balance of power—win the masses' minds to our side before they are addicted by goblin fruit or succumb to lutin propaganda." Kris laid a hand on Thomas's arm. "My friend, this won't happen overnight. The awakening will take place over the space of months, even years. Some will come right away. Others will be slower to believe their dreams. But word will spread, and a sense of community will grow among those touched by magic. The Internet will help make this possible. And it isn't as though they'll overrun Cadalach—not at all. They have their human homes and jobs and families out there."

"But—"

"It is hard to remember, but there was a day when magic was everywhere in the world. It wasn't always confined to a few faerie strongholds. Nor were the races segregated as we are today. It's time we set our magic—and all people—free. Then we can begin to heal the earth and ourselves, and undo the thousands of years of damage we have wrought."

"They'll try and stop us," Thomas said. He sounded resigned, but made one last effort. "Kris, I know these hive masters, and many of the fanatical human groups. They won't want a confederacy of magical beings that might align themselves with us. And they will kill or die to prevent this from happening."

"I know." Kris's voice was wise but sad. "And we can't stop them from throwing their lives away if that's truly what they wish to do. But the tyrants and fanatics will fall one by one. Reason will prevail. All we have to do is keep the peace long enough for the tide to change in our favor."

"You have foreseen this?" Thomas asked.

"Yes." And he had. In a vision. Long, long ago.

"Okay, so let's talk about how we make this happen," Jack said.

In spite of what Adora had said about needing a walk, she didn't leave the room right away. Instead, she stood and stared at the life-sized portrait of Kris, as though it would eventually feel her attention and deign to speak to her. She was thinking hard about everything Io claimed, and liking none of it because it felt like the truth.

When pressed, Adora would admit to having had an almost Pavlovian aversion to men in the past. This hadn't been bad, because when she was younger it had kept her focused on her education and career when other girls were being led astray by hormones.

Didn't you give up on guys and the idea of marriage rather young, though?

She had. Adora had decided on her twelfth birthday, when she stood alone at the school dance, shunned by her classmates for being different. She had decided then that she would probably never marry. It wasn't that she didn't find boys attractive. But then—and now—it was apparent that most men were not going to share her odd obsessions, or even tolerate her having them. In fact, her first lover had told her flatly that her priority should be supporting her man—whenever he wanted—by: A) having sex whenever he felt like it (whether she was in the mood or not), B) feeding him whenever he wanted (again, whether it was convenient or not), and C) by babying his ego—constantly. The last item annoyed her most of all. Assuming she had any maternal instinct—and there was absolutely no proof that she possessed one—it wouldn't be wasted on a male who refused to grow up.

Fortunately, immaturity wasn't Kris's problem.

No, he's just insane and inhuman, Joy answered. *A crusader. You know I'm right. All he's missing is the tights, mask and cape.*

Adora shook her head.

He wasn't insane—not really. And if he was, was that so bad? After all, wasn't he touched by something . . . ? Something like Divine Madness?

You are so gone. Your only hope is that he doesn't know you're gaga for him and he lets you get away. Io could be wrong, you know. Maybe the cup can still pass you by. You don't have to be like your mother and lose yourself to this man and his crazy schemes.

Her mother? Anger raced through Adora's body. *You bitch! You cruel, heartless bitch. I am nothing like her—and Kris is not like my father. Take it back!* she hissed at her inner voice.

If you aren't, then you have nothing to worry about— have you? Joy asked coldly.

But Adora was worried, because Joy had it right. Under all the other logical reasons she'd enumerated for not marrying, Adora's chief reason for avoiding "good" men and a permanent relationship was the fear that she would become like her mother: blind, selfish, dependent—unable even to live without her other half nearby.

So, you're going to let the dead rule your life? Joy asked.

I don't know, Adora replied.

She sighed and pulled her dirty coat tighter, then thought again about going out to get some air. Love might warm the cockles of her heart, but it did nothing to keep chills out of her mind. What on earth was she going to do?

Joy, I want to get away—to have some fun. I want to not think for a while.

So, go already. I want to have some fun, too. Geez— don't blame me that you think too much. I told you to leave this be.

Adora was worried about getting lost without a guide, but the mound seemed anxious to help steer her to the gardens. There she had a charming few minutes wandering about, smelling dizzying flowers and listening to the peaceful whispers of the blue water that seemed to flow beside her wherever she walked, offering her strength and to quench her thirst.

The first person Adora saw in her wanderings was a slight female who seemed too frail to be carrying around a baby as well as dragging a reluctant child behind her. This had to be Chloe, Io's "almost ghost." Not certain why, since Chloe was so small and harmless, Adora backed away, stopping only when she reached Kris's Jaguar, which had somehow appeared at the far side of the garden.

"Hello," said a voice from below her. Jack? "I didn't think I'd see you again so soon. We've been a bit worried about you and Kris. He didn't stay with you very long."

In fact, he could hardly wait to get away from me, she thought.

"Why would you worry about me? I'm completely harmless," Adora said lightly as she continued to watch the frail Chloe from behind the car.

Jack snorted. "No beautiful woman is ever completely harmless—especially if she's a siren fey. I know. I married one."

Adora finally looked down and saw Jack's upside-down face emerge from under the car. He had a streak of grease on his right cheek, which should have marred his beauty, but it instead only underscored the perfection of his features.

"Thank you for the backward compliment. I think. Is that Chloe?" she asked softly, jerking her head.

Jack twisted, peering around the tires. "Yep," he said, then disappeared again.

"What's wrong with her?" Adora asked. She hoped he was still in the mood to talk. "She seems . . . distracted. Unhappy. Is it . . . the baby we brought? Is it sick?"

"No. She's worried about Clarissa. The child with her." Jack's grease-smeared hand appeared. "Could you pass me the blue-handled socket wrench? It's in the toolbox to your left."

Adora looked at the preschooler happily throwing rocks down the tunnel out of Cadalach and didn't know what to say. The child resembled a capybara, which would worry most mothers, but she sensed this wasn't the main problem. After all, these people had a friend who was a dragon and an uncle who was a ghost. A fuzzy-faced child shouldn't seem that weird. Not here.

"Why? What's wrong with Clarissa?" she asked at last, finally handing Jack the wrench. She folded her knees, sitting down on velvety moss. "Is she sick?"

"No, she's not sick either. Chloe's worried because Clarissa is half troll and half human. That makes her smart as well as strong-willed. And the terrible twos are apt to last until puberty—when her moods will get worse. Frankly, the terror can last even beyond that. Trust me, it's worse than the usual acne-driven teen angst human parents deal with."

Adora digested this, thinking about the child they had rescued and wondering uneasily if it would have similar problems. Four arms had to be worse than pimples.

"Mugshottz is part troll and he turned out fine," she mentioned hopefully. "He's actually rather wonderful."

"He is wonderful. But Mugshottz is an exception. I hate to think of his fate if Kris hadn't adopted him. Being part gargoyle makes him an abomination even in the goblin world." Jack's hand appeared long enough to pick up another socket wrench, then disappeared back under the car. "The thing with most trolls is that they don't really have what you could call a conscience. If they were human, we'd call them sociopaths. But trolls are bred that way. They are born violent and raised by goblins as attack dogs—which is okay as long as they're kept on a leash. But their handlers have to make sure they stay leashed, and be eternally vigilant about demonstrating who the boss is."

Jack picked up the other wrench and continued, "But Chloe doesn't want to raise her daughter like a vicious animal that needs to be whipped and caged. She wants Clarissa to be *normal*. It's a fine line to walk. You have to be firm and school them while they're young, because once they're adults you can't teach them to grow morals and discipline. You can't force them to feel empathy."

"You can't do that with people either," Adora said, and then flinched at her gaffe. Her views had broadened in the last few hours, her definition of "people" expanded to fit more of Kris's worldview. "Humans, I mean. I still think of *'people'* as human," she said by way of explanation and apology.

"I understand. It takes a while to adapt to a new vocabulary. Speaking of adapting, how are you dealing with the whole Goddess thing? It can be a bit frightening when you feel the full weight of . . . Her. And Kris is . . . well, Kris. I know we death feys can be a bit overpowering."

Eat my heart. Drink my soul. Love me to death.

Adora shivered. It was that other voice whispering in her brain again—the one that wasn't Joy.

No, it isn't me, and it's getting really crowded in here. I'm not sure how long I can keep it from taking up permanent residence.

Please try. Two's company and all that.

"I don't know how things are. It's . . ." Adora paused to really consider her answer. It was damned confusing, that was for sure. And her desire for Kris was still clouding her reason. Her attraction seemed thick in the air, a sort of perfume cloud that enveloped her and that she feared must be apparent to everyone else. In fact, she wasn't entirely sure what Jack meant and was reluctant to ask. She chose to think he was talking about religion rather than their overwhelming sexual attraction.

Not that the religious question was an easy one to

answer, either. She had very mixed feelings about religion. Her only experience was with whom Kris would call Worshippers, and she had never been at home in their churches. So many of those buildings felt like mausoleums, large coffins that contained faiths that no one wanted to admit were deceased. She thought again about what Kris said—people putting God in a box.

They sometimes did that to their souls as well, chaining them in one place forever. She had never liked the theory that said after death her soul would go to Heaven, where it would be weighed, examined for hard mileage and then kept unused in some celestial storeroom for eternity—if it wasn't found defective and sent someplace warmer to sweat out her sins. In spite of her initial rejection of the notion of Kris reincarnating, she was actually much more comfortable with that, of getting more than one chance to live a good life.

But that didn't mean that she didn't sense there was something beyond that. Her theological sense was underdeveloped, but she had always experienced a strong pull to the ocean. She felt peace there. Still, she was a long way from being one of Kris's Gaia-as-constant-companion-Celebrants— and speaking of Kris as a Celebrant . . . well, being near him was challenging in that respect too. He was like a walking television, tuned in to a twenty-four-hour channel that was All Gaia, All the Time. She wasn't sure how she felt about that. It certainly bothered—even shamed—her that their faith was so unequal. That he believed so utterly, and she barely at all. How could this ever work?

"Yeah, that's Kris," Jack said. "He's always in communion with something the rest of us barely sense. Really, I think that he's the mortal repository for the Goddess's master plan for this planet. We're *all* humbled by his faith. Or perhaps I mean 'certainty.' Faith implies that there is room for doubt."

Adora blinked and tried to focus. She realized that she must have been speaking aloud. That, or Jack could hear her thoughts too.

"It's odd for all of us to be near him," Jack went on. "He's so driven, so plugged in. It isn't what we're used to. That isn't surprising, I guess. Most people have no real faith, and they value only what animals value—a meal, bodily comfort, their short physical lives. Perhaps they value the lives of their children or lovers or parents. A few love abstract ideals like patriotism, or dreams of fame that will provide them with better meals, bodily comfort, etc. But only a handful have ever been able to love all people—all *peoples*—more than themselves. Kris is one of those, the rare one or two born every century." Jack looked at her.

"Go on." This was very important. Adora sensed that Jack was leading up to something—something she needed to understand.

"But something inside Kris has been broken, or knocked askew. The others don't know it, but something is breaking up the reception between him and Gaia. He can talk to the Goddess, but he isn't receiving any new instructions from Her. He must find some other way to reconnect." Jack paused. "The traditional way to Divine Love is through earthly love. I hope to the Goddess that he finds it with you. Because I'm afraid that we're in trouble if it doesn't."

"But no pressure, right?" Adora grimaced. So Jack thought Kris was broken, just like she was.

"I don't envy you," Jack admitted, then banged on something under the car. A piece of manzanita flew out. "But if you give us a chance, we will all love you—whatever happens. We'll be your family, if that's what you want. There's no need to ever be alone again."

Adora ducked her head. "I want," she whispered.

"Good." Jack threw out some more broken shrubbery. "You know, even the first time I saw Kris—badly wounded, his mind shattered—a part of me looked at him and felt . . . right. Something inside went, Ah-ha, there he is! He's the one we've been waiting for."

"Here he is, the one I've been waiting for," she murmured. "Yeah, I guess it was kind of like that—finding something important to me that I didn't even know was lost. . . . I guess I just need to figure out what to do now that I've got him."

Jack's head reappeared and his teeth flashed white as he grinned at her. Again, she caught a flash of energy that was a distant echo of what Kris made her feel. If Io was right, it was because Jack was a death fey. The thought chilled her. She didn't like the idea of not being in control.

"Such an expression of dismay and distrust!" Jack chided. "You know, Chloe shared with me once that her husband told her he'd walk through Hell barefoot to bring her a drink of water. She came to Io and me for advice. This devotion of Zayn's worried her because—well, she has never felt entirely worthy of him. Not since the rape and her addiction to goblin fruit. And Zayn has always been concerned about her feelings for him being a mixture of gratitude and being fey-struck. That's a kind of addiction too. But I don't have to tell you about it, do I? Your parents were probably affected."

"They certainly were." Even as she said it, something twisted inside of Adora. It was compassion for this unknown woman who didn't feel valuable. She herself was entirely too familiar with this shadow of unworthiness, which was capable of obscuring even the brightest rays of happiness. A part of her again wanted to weep for Chloe's damage, and for her own. She was glad that Jack was under the car again and couldn't see her face, since she seemed unable to hide her expressions today.

"So, what did you say to her?" Adora asked, controlling her voice.

"Io was kinder, but I finally told Chloe to just say thanks and drink the damn water if he bothered to fetch it. Women! There's no need to make a federal case out of everything a guy says."

Adora laughed. "Okay, your opinion is duly noted. So, how far would I have to walk to actually see some sunshine and breathe fresh air?"

"I take it you don't want a guide interfering?"

"Not really," she admitted, liking that she could be frank. "I brood best alone."

"If you can ask nicely, you may take the tunnel behind me until you reach the fork, and then go left. About a hundred yards in, you'll hit a dead end. The wall will be sealed, but if you explain your wish for air—*politely*—it will open for you. I think Zayn may be down there as well, and he can help you if you get stuck." Jack again emerged, his face more serious. "Just don't go far, okay? The terrain can get treacherous if you stray, and there are lots of poisonous critters about."

"Okay." Adora unfolded herself. "Um . . . you wouldn't happen to know what time it is?"

"Outside? It's about eleven in the morning. The sun is up and it's hot. Don't stay out too long. You aren't fully healed yet."

"I won't."

"Have a ball, then."

Adora nodded, though Jack couldn't see her, and headed in the direction he'd pointed.

And the people watched the fiery sky that remained red throughout the night. Some cried out that there was blood on the moon because their god was slain. Others trembled and wept at the gates of the temple. When the skies were crimson for three days and three nights and the tremors shook the ground, it was decided that a sacrifice would be made. A great bull was chosen and also a maiden. One was to be given as a burnt offering, the other thrown into the sea. But Niklas, now called Poseidon, appeared before them and said to the king that no such sacrifice should be made. Instead, the people should flee, for the end of Thera was nigh. But the king did not pay heed and instead delayed to gather up his worldly treasure, and thus was the island and all her people buried in fire and brimstone.

—Niklas 22:18

Scathach nUanaind, undead queen of Scythia, approached. She was naked except for a belt of rubies, was pale as snow, and her eyes were pools of green darkness. Shadow, they called her.

"I seek the one they call Niklas," she said, studying in turn each man in the glen until she found the one she sought. "My daughter is dead in battle and I must have a father for another. Come lie with me on yonder hill."

But Niklas, who did not believe in war, said, "Begone, warrior goddess. You shall have no children of me."

CHAPTER FOURTEEN

"Raxin." General Anaximander continued to stare out his window into the night. "I have a very special job for you. It seems that Niklas has finally found a mate. I simply can't have that."

Raxin said nothing. Nor did he look at Miffith, the general's shadowy secretary, who stood in the room's darkest corner. Miffith probably knew that Anaximander had killed his own father and all his male siblings. That made some employees nervous at job evaluation time. A bad performance review tended to mean death by strangulation.

"As you know, I can't kill Niklas and risk him coming back with his mind intact," Anaximander went on. "But we can get rid of *her* before she breeds. Go to Cadalach. Take the old roads and don't be seen by the fey. Adora Navarra likes to wander in the dead zone. Make sure she gets good and lost. And then dead." The general turned and looked into his enforcer's eyes. "It would be good if she suffered. Be as creative as you like."

Raxin nodded. A shivering Miffith pulled deeper into the shadows.

As Jack had predicted, the sun was well up outside and, though slightly overcast, the day was almost unbearably hot. Even thermometers had to be sweating.

Adora sat on a rock—a flat rock with a narrow band of hazy shade that jutted over a canyon that was a long, long way down—and stared at the man-sized stone beside her. She waited for Kris. She waited because she knew—somehow—that he was coming. He had probably felt the emotional earth-quake of her returning memory. There would be af-tershocks, too. She wasn't done remembering yet.

Unwanted, Adora saw another sudden snippet of herself as a child. It was July in Aptos. There was one street in the neighborhood where the sidewalks were smooth and long, and where, in the summer, children gathered for roller skating. Adora would sometimes join the other girls, for most mornings were nice and cloudy. She had to be a bit careful, though; by afternoon the fog would sometimes thin enough for the sun to shine through. This particular day was a special one. There was another new girl who had come to skate. She was shy, with bright red hair and freckles so vivid they looked painful. The others were uncertain about welcoming her, and Adora sensed that here at last was someone differ-ent whom she might obtain as a friend. The girl had agreed to be Adora's skating partner—a first for Adora, who never got to be part of the human span when they played London Bridges. But just when things were looking perfect, the fog had failed her, and the day, which had begun so gloriously, became yet another afternoon of rejection. Though she wanted desperately to continue skating with her new friend who sailed through the sunlit salty air with red ringlets flying, the sun had started to burn her, and Adora had been forced to crawl under the oleander bushes until the shadows grew long enough for her to find a protected path back home. The redhead had eventually found someone else to skate with, and Adora was again left alone.

Stop it, Joy. I've had enough.

It isn't me.

Adora stared fixedly at the rock before her, trying to slip into a meditative trance where she could calm her mind. Peace refused to come, though, and the longer she stared at the granite protrusion, the more the disquieting impression grew that the stone was wrapped around something sentient, and that it was aware of her, maybe even eavesdropping on her thoughts. The rock had no eyes, of course, but there were two hollows that were suggestive of sockets, a protrusion that could be a nose, and a deep horizontal fracture that looked rather like a mouth—one full of teeth. Unlike the mound behind her, it loomed over her with unsympathetic intention.

So stick your fingers in and see if it bites, Joy said suddenly, making the nervous Adora shriek and jump.

Unfortunately, it also made her land on top of an ill-tempered scorpion who—understandably—took exception to the sudden intimacy.

At her cry, Kris came flying over the chest-high stones like Baryshnikov—only leaping much higher than any human she had ever seen. Also, most dancers—at least in the ballet—had clothes on. Kris had somehow mislaid most of his.

He was beautiful, like Michelangelo's David, without flaw of face. She could only stare with wonder and longing as he landed beside her on bended knee. It was enough to keep her from noticing the pain of the scorpion sting for a full thirty seconds.

At thirty-one seconds, though, she began to swear. "This is all your fault," she accused. "You've made me crazy and careless."

"There's a lot of that going around." Lightning arced in his eyes. Kris laughed once and then pulled her to him with hands so strong they almost hurt. Though she had never liked a rough touch, her body instantly transmitted a message of joy. This was Kris's touch, which she craved. Air left her lungs like she was giving up the last breath in the world. Lips to lips, heart to heart, heat to heat. This was as close as she would ever come to sharing her soul with another, she thought dizzily.

He kissed her as if she were his only hope of salvation, but even through her desire she sensed a form of anger under the longing. She thought that she understood. She wanted him as well but didn't *want* to want him because it was part of some plan.

Eat my heart. Drink my soul. Love me to death. Say it.

No, she thought, but it was a weak protest because her body longed to do just that. She wanted to give herself over and stop fighting.

By the time the embrace was broken, her hair was a mess and her mouth slightly bruised. Adora ran her tongue along her lip and tasted blood—most of it hers. Not that she was complaining. She was too stunned by the sudden intimacy to use her voice or brain. She was light-headed, too. Whenever Kris touched her, there was insufficient oxygen in the air. He also gave her fever, made her skin burn.

Okay, this is suggestive clue number sixty-one that I'm not embarking on some average love affair, Adora thought giddily. *This is—well—epic.*

Kris had pulled back from her, at least mentally. His hands continued to hold her while she fell to her knees. Oddly enough, though the rest of her felt buffeted, her hand had stopped hurting. Looking down, she could see the wound was healed.

I've heard of kissing away boo-boos. . . Joy began.

Don't, Adora replied. *No jokes. Not now.*

"I'm sorry," Kris said, looking at her lips. But he didn't look sorry. In fact, if he felt some emotion other than hunger, she couldn't see it.

"I'm not." The words came out without thinking.

Kris's eyes widened, and then he looked away from her, studying the sky with great attention. Away from his gaze, her heart slowed by degrees and the dizziness receded. Maybe she wasn't going to have a heart attack after all.

"But, Kris, much as I enjoyed it, I think I should tell you that I've never been good at passing my body around to near strangers—no matter how attractive the man," she warned him gently when she could finally speak. "My last misadventure with Two-face was an aberration. With me, the mind goes first, the heart follows. The body comes last. It isn't fashionable behavior these days, I hear, but as with most things, I prefer vintage: clothes, cars and courting rituals. I think it's because I've always suspected on some level what I really am and don't trust people to accept me."

Kris smiled and asked with equal calm, "Do you really imagine that I would want it any other way? It's not as though I'm a hormone-driven teen."

No, but he is Goddess-driven, Joy said.

"Were you ever a horny teenager?" Adora asked, unable to picture it. "I can't quite imagine. In fact, I can't see you as a child at all."

His lips quirked. "I think that goes beyond the

288

scope of the biography I plan—but, yes. At least, I had moments when I felt the fey equivalent of teen lust. However, I soon learned that, in my world, a man who can't control himself will end up being controlled. And being part of the Dark Court was never an idea that appealed to me. I don't think it appeals to you, either. That's why you're resisting the pull."

She shook her head. "This is so weird, Kris. You don't—can't—understand," she complained. "And I don't just mean the dragon and stuff. I can feel your desire battering me. I can hear your thoughts—feel them touching my skin. This isn't normal, and I don't know how to evaluate anything I'm feeling. I'm afraid that my senses have turned into liars."

Evaluate? Did you really say that? I mean, I wasn't expecting you to quote sonnets, but—

Shut up!

"I know it's odd. But all you must understand—*believe*—for now, is that in spite of this . . . this moment of craziness, I am not a caveman who would take you against your will. Nor do I use magic to manipulate people. No matter what the Goddess wants, Adora, I will accept only willing gifts from you."

"But you do need me . . . to reconnect to Gaia?"

"Maybe. Probably. I'd like to tell you a soothing lie about this but will not insult you that way. I need you. I also know that you must come to me because it's what you want to do: Otherwise, it won't work." Kris's voice was slightly harsh and he was breathing harder than usual, but she would stake her life that he was in control of himself. "And nothing will happen until I see some sign that it is you and not the magic that moves you toward me. I know what's authentic and won't settle for anything less than the real deal."

Which was more than she could say. Lust was still crawling through her body and fogging her brain. Was she fey-struck? The ever-shrinking rational part of her mind wondered if she gave in to the desire, would their infatuation eventually be as bad as her parents' had been? Would Kris become her meat and drink? Her oxygen? It seemed like it could happen, because in that moment when their lips had met, she had wanted him more than she wanted her next breath.

Fight it, Joy said uneasily. *There's no taking it back if you make a mistake.*

Damn it, I'm trying to resist, but it's like I'm crawling with ants.

She noticed then that Kris was damp with sweat and there were faint scars on his body, long claw marks that disappeared under the towel he had hitched at his waist. The sight chilled some of her ardor. The marks, though pale, were wide and deep, and they would never have healed had he been human—he'd have died first. Jack had said that when he found Kris, Kris was badly wounded, but she hadn't expected anything like this.

"Oh, Kris . . ." Adora reached out tentatively, wanting to smooth away the evidence of suffering, but Kris dropped his hands from her shoulders and stepped away. The sunlight glinted off his body, almost blinding her, but she was sure that she had seen him stir under that inadequate towel. A part of her was terribly pleased. The rest of her felt very nervous. She sensed that desire still circled them, ready to resume the attack if they gave any sign of relaxing their vigilance.

"I'm pretty sure that I meant everything I just said, but let's not test my resolve," Kris suggested.

She swallowed, trying to think clearly. It was like

fighting through dense smoke. "I want to say yes. I just . . . I don't understand who you are. You're . . . too many people. I'm confused," she almost wailed. *And I don't know who I am, either.*

Kris sighed and scrubbed the side of his face. "What makes you *you?*" he asked. "Your body? The color of your hair or eyes?"

Adora blinked. The question helped her focus. "I don't know. The matter of identity is complex—," she began.

"Of course you know. What makes up an identity may be complex, but what alters it is not. Are you *you* because you're blonde?" he persisted. "If you colored your hair, would you change inside?"

The question was annoying, banal. Being with Kris was like watching a foreign film without subtitles. General actions were clear, but the subtleties of conversation were often beyond her.

"Of course not," she answered when he didn't go on.

"Is it your nationality? Your job?" he pursued. "If you changed either, would you cease to be you?"

"Well . . . no. But, Kris—"

"And neither do I. I don't change, either— whatever my age or body or occupation." He exhaled slowly. "Adora, you liked me before you believed in my past. Before we were here and exposed to the magical attraction. Have some faith that what you're feeling, though enhanced by proximity to magic, is real. Ask any questions you have, think it through. Take all the time you need. But I'm asking you not to reject me out of hand—however odd this seems— because you're frightened."

Faith. But that was her problem, wasn't it? She had very little, except faith that things would go wrong.

"Anyway, you don't think that you might be considered a little—uh—different, yourself?" Kris asked. "That maybe your once-imagined ideal man or life isn't out there?"

"I'm only weird when compared to normal people," she answered. But Adora found herself smiling. He had a point. She had always been peculiar, and being in the most glass of houses, she really had no right to be throwing stones.

She leaned against the large rock that had frightened her, took a few long breaths and relaxed. As she slumped, she could see some of the tension ease from Kris. Still, the air seemed thin and too hot for comfort though she wasn't in the direct sun.

"What's it like here during the summer?" she asked.

"Hell at high noon. This particular stretch of valley is like a blast furnace. It wasn't fire that did this. It's the slow, torturous heat from the sun that burned away all life."

They stood side by side with arms almost touching, Kris looking into the day and Adora looking at him.

Do you really think you guys have a chance? Joy asked.

I don't know, Adora replied.

And she didn't. Kris had never married, and she thought she knew why. He had deep passions—she could even see, at least in part, the vision that moved him. And it was on this goal that his focus lay. What was a woman—even all women—next to that?

"Everything," Kris said, turning his head to look down at her. "If she's the right one."

The answer left her shaken.

"Did you know that every soul has a résumé of wants and expectations?" Kris asked suddenly, again looking out over the baked valley. "A wish list of what it feels it needs and deserves."

"How does yours read?" Adora said. She was able to think again, now that he was a few steps away and his gaze turned elsewhere, but her body still pulsed dully, still wanted to just lie down on the ground and invite Kris in.

"Hm. *'Eternal optimist seeks same to make peaceful planet. Must play well with others—dictators and liars not wanted. Life insurance recommended'.*"

Adora smiled a little, but did not ask Kris to read her. She wasn't ready to know what he saw; she was too vulnerable and unsure. She might accept his evaluation of her character because she was so lost, and though she trusted him, she didn't want anyone making her over in some image that wasn't truly natural.

"The trick in life is aiming oneself in the right direction so their needs are met. It amazes me how people will go haring off after fame or fortune or family—even security—when they don't really want it. They simply accept the notion that they should pursue these goals, and do so blindly." He tilted his head and watched a buzzard riding the thermals overhead. "Of course, there are pitfalls the other way. The fearful and uncommitted rarely find joy, either. It takes balance."

He means you.

"I know," Adora said to both Joy and Kris. "I think maybe I just need some time to adjust. You probably can't imagine how weird this last week has been. My universe has been upended."

Kris nodded. "Maybe you should come inside, though, while you're thinking things through. The sun will make you sick if you stay out any longer."

"Okay." But she was reluctant. Inside Cadalach, the pull toward Kris was stronger, and she found it difficult to think when her body was constantly tingling.

"There are plenty of places to take walks, to sit on cliffs and look at Nature inside," Kris assured her. "You needn't stay with me. The mound is . . . huge."

"Because it isn't just one space, it's many spaces and many times?" she guessed.

"More or less," he agreed.

She tried to comprehend this, but was already lost. She sensed that to truly understand she would have to make a leap of faith—of acceptance. But she didn't much care for jumping blind. Even if she were willing, she hadn't a clue in which direction to jump.

Adora had always known that she could run away from life. But not from death. That was the rule she knew: Everyone died and stayed dead. And time only flowed one way. But Kris seemed to be saying this wasn't the case.

Except . . . he didn't really avoid death, did he? Joy asked suddenly.

No, not if she understood what the fey holy texts were saying. He had been . . . Her brain shied away from the awful word *sacrificed.*

He did mention life insurance. Maybe he knows it will happen again. Maybe he knows he's putting you in danger.

He wouldn't, Adora insisted.

Hey, things got pretty rough in L.A. And Jack said he needed you to get back in touch with his God. That would be one hell of a motivator.

Looking past Kris at the now open tunnels of Cadalach—tunnels that could take them hundreds, even thousands, of miles in minutes if what she'd been told was true—Adora could feel the outside world shrinking. It was so small that any place could be reached. Nowhere was safe. There was no place that Kris and this magic couldn't find her. Not even in death. Hadn't Io said that? There was no escaping her feelings for him, not this side of the grave and perhaps not even after death.

"Don't let it get to you," Kris said, touching her shoulder lightly, his words and presence dispelling the gathering claustrophobia. "Eventually, this will all feel normal. You will understand."

"That's partly what I'm afraid of. I can never go back to blissful ignorance, can I? I'll never see things the same way again."

Kris looked sad. "You'd be the first," he said. "I tried, but . . . Come to me when you're ready, when you can say what I need to hear and mean it. Until then . . . I think maybe I'll keep my distance. There are plenty of other rooms in the shian to stay in until. . ."

Eat my heart. Drink my soul. Love me to death. This time the voice was clear. If Kris could read her thoughts, she had to accept that she was now reading his. She could feel his longing as if it were her own—could feel it but couldn't respond.

With a long last look at her, Kris turned and disappeared back inside the mound.

The door remained open, but Adora didn't follow him immediately. Shade was shrinking, but she clung to the narrow band that remained, and there she perched on her rock halfway between the devil of desire and the deep blue sea of loneliness and tried again to think.

If she walked away from Kris and Cadalach—assuming she still could—it would probably mean some sort of emotional death. Or at least an amputation. But if she stayed . . . Well, that might mean death too. She could end up emotionally enslaved, fey-struck. What a choice.

But she would have to decide, and soon. There was a war going on for her . . . heart? Soul? Something. She could tell that the Goddess needed some element of her, either emotional or physical, and not just for Kris. A part of Adora wanted to keep whatever it was back, to remain whole and safe, if lonely. Another part was so tired of being alone—so horribly empty—and it wanted her to give herself to Kris and whatever else was moving them. Whatever the final cost.

The irony was, she might not actually have any choice.

There's always some choice, Joy argued.

Well, that's true. There's always suicide. Mom liked that one.

There are others. . . .

Yes, they just weren't easy. Would she embrace enlightenment and pursue knowledge of her fey nature, or would she cling to the comfort of what remained of her ignorance? Would she be brave and go with dignity to her Fate—

Eat me heart. Drink my soul. Love me to death.

—or would she resist to the end, no matter how much it hurt her or Kris?

The one thing that seemed certain was that she would have to choose. If she stayed here on the fence, the war would escalate and someone or something would end up firebombing her while she chose sides.

Adora summed it up: *Look, you want a guarantee. Unfortunately, with love you get no warranties.*

Kris laughed unhappily at himself. What an animalistic display. He'd done everything but beat on his chest and howl. He was lucky she hadn't screamed and jumped off the cliff when he'd come leaping at her.

Still, the experience wasn't a total loss. As a consolation prize for the failure of his control and dignity, he'd had an emotional epiphany—an erection too; the first in a century—so perhaps they were related. Certainly both were amazing. But at what cost was this insight? Adora had to have some real misgivings about trusting her safety to him now that he had admitted needing her.

But she hadn't fled, had she? She had just kissed him back with all the passion of a dying woman fighting for air.

Kris rubbed his face.

No, she hadn't fled. And as he held her, he had wanted to tell Adora what he realized—that he knew she *really was the one*, the other half of his soul he had never known was missing, his salvation.

But though she pressed herself against him in surrender, her beautiful eyes had been only half-filled with sensual entreaty. The rest had been something akin to panic, and he had realized that it was at least partly the Goddess's magic driving her, which she was both aware and frightened of. Then she had asked about his need to find Gaia. That hadn't seemed the moment to announce he thought he loved her and wanted her to be with him forever—with him in Cadalach, trying to save an ungrateful world. It would be challenge enough to make her understand what it meant to have sex with a death fey—after all, losing herself was what she feared most. His imagination faltered at trying to make her understand his greater mission.

But if she said yes . . .

At the thought of finally making love to her, blood swam back into his loins.

"This is ridiculous," he muttered to the air. "I understand what you want, O Goddess. But you'll just have to wait. She needs time, and I'm going to give it to her."

Propelled by restless limbs, Adora wandered the mound, ruminating fruitlessly.

That other voice she sometimes heard, coming from either Kris or the Goddess—"*Eat my heart. Drink my soul. Love me to death.*"—was the embodiment, or maybe she meant *dis*embodiment, of her deepest fear; losing herself, being overwhelmed by someone or something until even her mind was eclipsed. But much of that fear was gone now that she was back inside—or pushed down so far that she couldn't find it—and her thoughts kept returning to Kris and how much she needed to be with him, to see his plans through. Whatever those plans might be, above and beyond having her write this biography. If he still wanted her to write it.

If you still want to write it.

Yeah. That might be a problem. She wasn't feeling real focused or creative. Once in a while she'd had a story that laid down by the side of the road and refused to move on when she wanted. She knew from experience that whipping the literary beast did no good. All she could do was wait patiently until it agreed that it was time to move again.

That may be true. But aren't you dodging the real issue here?

Yes, she was. The book was nothing. She wanted Kris desperately. What she needed to know was if she was being coerced by some outside force—the Goddess—into hungering for him. Or did she want

Kris because . . . well, simply because she wanted him. Once she had this figured out, she could begin to address the matter of *how* she felt about *what* she felt.

"Can't you give me some sign?" she muttered, uncertain to whom she was speaking. "Some little hint that I'm not just a convenient pawn in some cosmic chess game?"

"Oh—I'd be real careful what I asked for around here," a voice said behind her. When she turned, he added, "I'm Zayn. You might not remember me. There were rather a lot of us when you arrived."

They sure do grow them handsome around here, Joy mentioned.

"Hello." Adora looked at the outstretched hand, feeling wary of touching him. He looked normal, but she hadn't forgotten what Io had said about being vulnerable to other magical beings. She needed another male attraction like she needed measles.

"Oh, are you having flashover?" Zayn asked, dropping his hand. "It's okay. I know it can be overwhelming until you learn to control it."

Flashover? That can't be good.

"It is all a bit much," Adora admitted, also wondering what flashover was and if she could ask Zayn to go away. Assuming she wanted him to.

You don't know anything today, do you?

Isn't that what I've been saying?

And saying and saying. Yes.

"So, what are you thinking so hard about?" Zayn asked, falling in beside her.

Resigned to the company and probably some highly personal questions, Adora sighed and resumed walking.

"What am I thinking about? That I'm on the verge of embarking on an affair with a man who was worshipped as a god—many times—especially by women. A god who, though adored by millions, never got around to marrying any of them." That wasn't exactly the truth, the whole truth and nothing but the truth, but it would do for an explanation for now.

Zayn laughed. "Yeah, as I heard it, women always fell for Kris like rain out of the clouds. It's all that pent-up power in him. Sometimes he almost sparks." Seeing Adora's frown, he went on quickly, "And he appreciated them too, like a shower of rain: needy, life-sustaining, beautiful. But just like drops of rain, every woman he met was pretty much like every other. There was no one important until you. If that's all that's worrying you, don't give it another thought. You're the one. The Goddess thinks so, too."

Bully for the Goddess. I feel so much better.

They walked through an archway and into a tunnel of black glass. Adora looked furtively at her reflection strolling beside her. The woman in the mirror seemed a little wild-eyed, flushed and disheveled.

Suffering from love or flu—those two things are hard to hide, Joy said.

I'm not in love. It's just . . . very strong attraction.

"Was he really so hot, even back then?" she asked. "I suppose he was. I mean, he was a god. Kris even said that with enough money or power, a cannibal with a hunchback and tentacles would be thought attractive by some women."

"Kris isn't a cannibal. And I'm his doctor, so I know he doesn't have tentacles," Zayn said seriously, this time not noticing Adora's stare of disbelief. "Are you worried about species compatibility? He isn't a shape-shifter or anything. Didn't Io explain that sirens and death feys are a great match,

300

even if one is Seelie and the other Unseelie? Physically, you'll be a good fit."

"She said they were a strong match, yes," Adora admitted.

"The strongest," Zayn agreed. "Most magical matings are like Superglue, but sirens and death feys go together like two-part epoxy. I envy you that."

Two-part epoxy? Joy queried.

I'm not going to ask.

"Did you know that the red corpuscles in human blood replace themselves every one hundred and twenty days?" Zayn asked. He went on earnestly: "But in feys, it's just six—and in Kris, less than four. Human skin cells replace themselves every five days; in feys it takes only three hours. And Kris . . . his tissue regeneration is almost instantaneous. Even the scars of his disembowelment will be gone in another few days. More importantly, we make exact copies—unlike human cells that can alter if exposed to strong environmental influences. We don't have cancer or birth defects. The only thing that can hurt us is the high doses of radiation the solar flares sometimes throw off. They can shoot right through our thinning ozone and zap us if we're aboveground. That may have killed your dad. Of course, you're going to be fine. Already you're healing, and your children would be perfectly normal and healthy. In fact, they'll be amazing. I can't wait to see them."

Adora felt the words like a blow to the stomach.

I guess we finally know what the Goddess is after— and it isn't just to "get Kris back in touch with Gaia," Joy remarked.

"What? *Children?*" Adora repeated the word like

she had never heard it before. Her tone was odd enough to give Zayn pause and make him really look at her.

"Yeah. Children," he said impatiently. "Didn't you know? It's what the Goddess wants. Especially Kris's children. It's the plan."

"Whose plan? Hers? Or Kris's?"

"Well, Hers especially. But probably Kris's too. Though with Kris, you never can tell."

No, you never can tell, can you?

Adora laughed harshly. The ugly sound echoed around them, and it clearly startled Zayn. "Well, wantin' ain't gettin'. Children! That is just not happening. Hell, I can barely bring myself to face the idea of loving Kris. I can't . . ." Adora swallowed the rest of her words, not wanting to let the dam of her fear burst on this near-stranger.

"Well, whatever. Just know that Kris is important to the plan. Our fates are all intertwined, and if the Goddess so much as sneezes we all catch a cold," Zayn answered, not trying to conceal his skepticism with her protests of independence. "Listen, if you're going to wander around down here you need to know some things. The goblins have an arsenal of new psychotropic drugs they've been experimenting with. They leave us little care packages sometimes, so be careful if you go into the dead zone. Don't touch anything, especially if it glows," he warned.

"Also, some of the walls have been plastered with a methamphetamine amalgam that sticks like dog shit on a new shoe. It gets above a certain temperature and it starts out-gassing. It gets into the lungs. Re-breathers help, but it can also pass through the skin. This stuff is like crack and it heads right for the central nervous system. It's a blast if you're human—until your heart explodes, of course—but it also revs up fey metabolism and makes it easier to access our magic."

"And that's bad, right?" Adora asked.

"For someone like Kris, yeah. Real bad. Especially with all the bad karma and ghosts down in some of those tunnels. They were killing-grounds during the last uprising. Well, the uprising before the last."

"What about me?" she asked patiently. "Is it bad for me?"

"You may be all right—as long as you don't act as a focus for Kris for a while, or end up catching his spillover magic and doing something rash. You don't have any problems with causing earthquakes, do you?"

Not earthquakes, just a fire or two.

"What do you mean? Why would I be okay when Kris isn't?"

"Well, it's like I was saying before. Feys are loaded with cytokines—healing proteins," Zayn explained. "Our brains—in the thymus—manufacture them at thousands of times the levels found in most humans. They boost our ability to heal and avoid infection, and resist certain goblin drugs. They're what prolong our physical lives. But something got screwed up in Kris's brain."

"But . . . what about the Goddess?" Adora asked. "Isn't She responsible for—well, everything? Even finding you proper mates. Why doesn't She just heal him?"

Mates. I hate that word, Joy complained. *It's so Tarzan and Jane.*

"Sure she's responsible. She made the cytokines. And she'll heal Kris when it's time. I think she won't do it now because she'd probably have to kill and then reincarnate him. Which she could, I guess." Zayn looked thoughtful.

Adora stared at him, utterly appalled. She could feel her outrage at this suggestion rising. He looked at her and shook his head.

"Look, I don't mean to be short and rude, but you need to stop thinking like a brainwashed human if you really want to understand what's going on. And I think you'll feel better when you do know and accept your part. We, the fey, don't have the problem of using both science and religion to understand the world. Divinity and medicine can exist side by side, neither diminishing the other in importance. Once you believe—once you know that both are real— you no longer fear that science will shake your faith. Nor will your faith interfere with study and the practical applications of science. And, frankly, you're going to have to learn to mix practicality with faith if you're going to stay with Kris, because the man is driven by both."

"I know." And she did. Adora deflated as her anger went south. Joy had made the point earlier; if she chose to stay she would be living in a battle zone, the second tallest target on the battlefield next to the commanding general. Adora stopped and turned to face Zayn. "Look, I'll see you later. Right now, I want to be alone."

"Okay, but don't go anywhere that has bad air— and don't touch anything."

"You said that already." Adora turned away. "Bye."

"Merry we meet, merry we part, merry we meet again," Zayn answered.

Annoying bastard, isn't he? Joy sniffed. *It's probably all bullshit. He's just trying to get you to do what he wants—what a manipulator.*

304

Takes one to know one, Adora answered. Actually, she wasn't all that annoyed with Zayn. It was good that everyone was being so blunt and truthful. She needed factual information to make an informed decision.

I suppose. But nothing they say seems to be changing your mind about Kris.

There's nothing to change. Yet. I'm still thinking.

Liar, liar, pants on fire. You're just looking for some way to make this seem okay.

Pants on fire? No, it wasn't her pants, but something down there was feeling the heat.

And the Goddess said unto him, "Creature of the Air thou art. To air thou shalt return. So it is with all your kind. Earth to earth, air to air, fire to fire. Each to his beginning shall go in the fullness of time."

—*Niklas 11:8*

They bathed before the ceremony, cleansing both their bodies and souls before they called upon Great Odin. They came in pairs to the place of solitude, bringing torches, drinking horns and mead. They had no weapons because he had forbidden it. He had come to stop a war, to end madness before it began.

The priest stepped forward, frightened because for the first time their god was with them, made flesh.

"O Great One, we gather to mark and witness the great change you have said is upon us. Allfather Odin, aid us that our hearts be strong on this the day of greatest challenge."

The fey, called Odin in this lifetime, rose from his throne and spoke to his followers.

CHAPTER FIFTEEN

Adora began to understand what Kris meant about time lying up on itself in multiple visible layers. She saw Thomas Marrowbone in his computer lab, fingers moving so fast on his keyboard that she could barely see them, and it would be the twenty-first century in some programmer's office. But then she would look about the rest of the mound and remember that there were no electric lights—and eerier still, no windows, though there was plenty of light. In those moments she would feel the weight of the earth above her and know that she was in a cave. Or rather, she was in a vast system of underground caverns that had once made up a metropolis of now dead—or at least *physically* dead—people. And though she did not know how to open the sealed doors around her, she sensed that behind what appeared to be stone walls there were many more chambers, locked away by will or magic when their inhabitants died.

Worst of all, though she saw and heard nothing, it

seemed sometimes that the walls actually slithered behind her, perhaps rearranging themselves so she would be forced to travel a predetermined path.

Are you lost? Joy asked, coming out of a dark pre-occupation.

I . . . maybe. Though I don't see how I can be. We haven't gone that far, and the path hasn't branched.

Are you sure? This looks weird—not like the mound.

It did look weird. Nothing was glowing, but there was a green pall to the air and the walls were now colored the filthy gray of wet newspaper. The shapes around her were odd too. Not random; they were actually quite regular, almost enough to be called architectural, but designed by someone who had no sense of the vertical or horizontal. Looking gave her a headache, as what she saw caught the eyes like barbed wire, and it took great effort to shut her lids against the view.

Adora noticed that she was very thirsty and a bit dizzy and short of breath, and that was when it dawned on her that the blue waters that were with her for the first part of her walk had disappeared. Goose bumps crawled down her arms.

Maybe she *was* lost. Lost in time as well as space.

It's like that wasps nest, Joy said suddenly.

Adora looked again and understood. When she'd been eight, a garden wasp had attacked her mother. Enraged, her father had followed it back to its nest and knocked the construction down out of the tree where it hung. He had thrown the nest in a trash can and doused it with gasoline before setting it on fire. Though it was probably only her imagination, Adora had thought she heard the tiny creatures screaming. She had sneaked close when the flames finally died down and stolen a look inside. The ash at the bottom of the can retained the pattern of the prisms housing the wasps' burnt young.

That son of a bitch! Joy's voice vibrated with anger.

Who? Kris? Don't be paranoid. Adora didn't want to hurt Joy's feelings, but she suspected that part of the reason she was drawn to Kris was that he was even more eccentric than she. That would help her as she began to deal with the implications of who and what she was; but her new dependence on him would likely make Joy somewhat jealous.

No—Zayn. He pointed you this way. I bet that bitch Goddess told him to.

No, Adora argued, startled by the idea. *Why would he want me lost? They all think I'm the next great breeder.*

Why would any of them do anything? They seem to be brainless zombies doing whatever the Goddess tells them. And she may have changed her plan now that she knows you don't want kids.

I don't think so. Don't get so upset, Joy. This is just nerves. I'll just turn around and head back. Something will look familiar soon.

Good. Do it now. I'm . . . I'm scared of monsters, Joy confessed.

Why? I mean, why now? Then Adora recalled her panicked reaction to the dragon.

Because now I know they're real. Ghosts, dragons— what else might be down here?

Okay, but don't panic. Monsters don't come out until after dark.

Hmph. Joy sounded unconvinced. *Even if that's true, we don't know what time it is. And, frankly, it's pretty damn dark down here even if it's light outside.*

Point taken. We're getting out of here.

But this plan turned out strangely difficult, because when she turned and started to retrace her steps, though she had taken no branchings, suddenly there was no tunnel behind her. It was simply gone.

We're lost, damn him! Damn him!

Hush, let me think. Adora didn't let herself panic like Joy, but her anxious breaths were making a small patch of fog around her that followed sluggishly everywhere she moved. *We have to go on.*

It's getting cold, Joy complained. *And that wind is creepy.*

What do you care about the cold? You don't have a body. I'm just going to keep moving—that'll warm me up. And something is bound to look familiar. Just listen for the water.

They heard nothing of the stream, but the creeping breeze that frightened Joy continued to moan in one almost endless exhalation. Never pleasant, something began to change as they neared a new cavern. A shiver shook her, and Adora felt as though she had stepped into a patch of deep, dank shade. It also seemed as if the unhappy wind was casting a psychic shadow over her.

She looked about uneasily but nothing was there. Nothing she could see or smell.

A place beyond time. A space between worlds. It was that voice again: the one that wasn't Joy and wasn't Kris. Adora did her best to push it away. Joy was freaking out enough.

A short while on, she began to notice that her shoes were getting heavy and found that the cracked earth was caking itself to her soles. Looking around, she noted evidence of earthquakes or some other natural disaster.

This isn't safe. That's Zayn's goblin dogshit. And I hate that damned wind.

Adora agreed with Joy, though she didn't want to admit it. Caves, tunnels—they should be quiet, shut away as they were from the surface noise. But this part of the labyrinth wasn't quiet. It seemed to breathe, inhaling and exhaling a hundred unpleasant sounds. The color had changed again too. The walls had taken on a sickly green glow and seemed to be coated in a phosphorescent mold.

Adora had to face facts: In her distraction, she had taken a wrong turn somewhere, gone down a side path without noticing, and gotten very lost. She didn't know for sure, but she thought maybe she had somehow wandered into a part of the tunnels that belonged to the goblins. That was the only explanation.

Her path ended abruptly after a sharp turning. The ground at her feet fractured and tumbled away into a vast void.

Go back—now, Joy urged. But when Adora turned around, she couldn't see the tunnel. Behind her was a pile of loose stones where the opening should have been.

How the hell . . . ?

I hear something, Joy whispered. *Someone's coming.*

Adora heard it too. Something large was moving behind her, down in the dark abyss at her feet. Reluctantly, she turned around and crawled close to the broken edge of the floor, peering down into the darkness.

She smelled the creature before she saw it. She had never smelled baking bones, but that was the first thought to enter her head: This was the smell of damp bones being shoveled into a fire.

Her eyes adjusted to the darkness, slowly revealing what stalked her.

She saw its back first. She didn't know what the creature down below was but thought he seemed unhealthy. He turned swiftly, and she could see that moths had been at him, chewing away his eyebrows and beard. His furred skin was also failing, tearing off in little shreds. She realized that he had been singed, and it was necrotic tissue that was flaking away.

Though she knew that she should run—now, while the beast was occupied—Adora crouched and watched, horrified and disbelieving. The monster slowly pulled off his pale skin, unzipping his entire torso with a terrible ripping sound, and then stepped out of it. He turned the skin, flapping it lightly while bits of pinkish fluid splashed on the floor. He redressed then, this time with the gray muscles facing out. He shrugged a few times and then did a few deep knee bends—also horrifying because the knees jointed in the wrong direction. Slowly spikes extruded along the limbs and spine.

The creature was some kind of insect. But it also had the face of Old Man Fletcher. The sight made her cold somewhere deeper than her bones, and she felt her muscles spasm.

Oh Goddess, protect us.

As though hearing her thought, the creature turned suddenly and looked at her. Then smiled. It was the nastiest thing she had ever seen.

She didn't know what she was facing, but she knew that she was in danger—immediate, life-threatening peril. Adora's brain began to recalibrate, overcoming her horror and flooding her body with adrenaline. All those mortal fears rushed in and tried to disable her—fear of the dark, of being eaten, of being crushed under a ton of heartless rock and never found. But she controlled it, and this extra bit of panic gave her the strength she needed to resist the creature's strong mental call.

Adooorrraaaaa. It was Fletcher's voice, and the call was like being dragged over broken glass.

No! It can't be.

But it isss! Why don't you sssave uss ssome time and jussst come down here like a good girl.

She put a hand to her head, as if that might ward off the fear and pain the voice inflicted. She felt dizzy, her brain becoming some sort of accordion, wheezing in and out as it tried to find balance with this thing's malevolence pushing in on her. It was difficult, because her thoughts were becoming sluggish, sodden with its slime. She shuddered and tried again to retreat mentally behind her usual barriers, but the slime slowed her.

Ssso you're Niklasss's little writer now, the fey'sss great new hope. Well, we can't have thisss. The horrible, chiding voice was following her even as she retreated on hands and knees until she was well back from the edge. *We can't have you making Niklasss happy, maybe making more little Niklasssesss. No, I'm just going to have to chew your head off and then have sssome fun with the rest of you. You owe me, you little firebug.* The voice laughed then, and it was the worst sound she had ever heard. *But don't take it persssonally, little writer. This isn't anything important—like literary criticisssm.* Then: *Come here, you little bitch!*

The shockwave of his voice hammered her mind, then pounded every vertebrae in her spine, leaving her rigid, fused upright by terror and revulsion.

Joy, where are you? Adora whispered. *Can I . . . can I burn him this time? I want to. I want to burn him up until there's nothing.*

No, you can't. You're still connected to Kris.

I don't feel him! she said, panicked. *I can't feel him at all.*

I feel him. He's coming. This is a trap. They're using you as bait. If you open yourself to the fire it will affect him, too. It might even let this thing into Kris's mind. Just hang on. Kris knows what's happened and help will be coming.

Adora tried to believe this, but she couldn't feel anything except the monster prying at her skull, trying to get in.

I hear you, little writer, talking in your head. I hear them too—the fey. They're looking for you high and low, but I know they won't get here in time — because we're in the placcce between timess. You're all mine now. I'm ssso hungry for you. Let'sss eat!

Claws gripped her brain and tried to rip her mind open.

Shit! Joy—some help, please!

Adora gave a last shove at the creature in her mind, pushing at the voice with all her might. The monster, perhaps surprised at the strength of her defense, slipped back a short ways, and she was able to slam a door on it as Joy dropped some sort of mental brace. It was a flimsy door, though, and wouldn't keep the thing out for long.

What now?

Are you kidding? That's not just a voice. It has teeth! Run! Joy answered.

Still dizzy, Adora turned and bounded forward— the only possible path that wouldn't put her in the creature's reach. As she scrambled upward, the scree beneath her feet shifted, and she felt herself over-balance. Her body wanted to obey gravity. But as a fall from that height would get her killed—if not from a broken neck, then because the beast would get her as she lay stunned—she insisted that her limbs obey her mind, and amazingly, they did. In fact, she felt more in control of her body than she ever had in her life.

All that yoga and meditation is paying off, she thought hysterically.

Just keep climbing.

The urging was superfluous; Adora clawed her way over the top of the ramp. Instead of a second ramp down, she was faced with a broken wall. Ahead of her was a crevice tight and dark with a rim of fractured teeth. Aside from the hole, the only place to go was up, and up was so far away that she couldn't make out the top.

Oh, no.

Just climb.

I am not the Scarlet Pimpernel, she thought with asperity. *I don't scramble over turrets and swashbuckle on castle heights.*

You do now. It's that or the hole.

Adora stared up at the ceiling and then into the crack, trying not to breathe. The crack looked like a mouth, a gullet, waiting to swallow her. It was not an attractive hole but it had one thing going for it—it was too tight to let the larger beast in.

Why don't I ever get an easy choice, like the lady and the tiger? she complained.

Behind her, the beast howled and started digging into the mountain of shale. Blocked by stone, its words were unintelligible. Its anger was clear, though. Joy began to whimper.

Stop it! Adora almost shouted, and Joy froze midsniffle. *You have to help me.*

Admittedly, I would rather a tiger than either of our two choices, Joy answered. *But since that isn't one of our options . . .*

It looks slimy in there—glowing.

It's slimy in the monster's mouth too.

You have a point . . . and I really don't like heights.

Just go.

Adora used a string of words that she had only uttered twice in her life, and then she bent down. She took a last breath and forced her head between the stony teeth. She kept her mouth and eyes shut against the tentacles of dripping slime that left stinging trails on her skin.

Dark, dark, Joy whispered.

Adora hit her head once when the tunnel narrowed into a tight jackknife turn, and she bit her lip hard enough to draw blood. But the sound of giant claws ripping through the loose stone of the ramp helped her convulse her protesting body into the turn. A few more feet . . . just a few more and she'd be safe. Surely it couldn't follow her into the tunnel. Its body was too big and the tunnel too narrow.

Joy? Joy! But there was no answer. Her friend had eventually curled up in a fetal position and would be no help.

The monster wasn't in her brain yet, but she felt him surrounding her, trying to cut her off before she could reach Kris. His presence was like maggots crawling on her skin, trying to chew their way inside. Within her mind, she screamed for the only person who cared enough to help her. She cried out for Kris. She cried forever as the slime ate at her skin.

Adora? She finally heard him. Relief made her weak

Kris? Help me! What is that thing?

Another assassin. I'm close, love—keep moving. You're almost out.

But it was hard. There was no air and she felt so sick and dizzy, and the tunnel seemed to be getting tighter, strangling her like a python. Just when it got unbearable in the cruel dark, warm hands grabbed her, pulling her from her strangling hole and banishing the monster from her head. Adora blinked rapidly, unable to believe that she was in Kris's arms, safe from the fiend.

And looking over Kris's shoulder was a concerned Mugshottz. His hard face had never looked so good.

And someone else was there: Abrial Nightdemon, the Executioner. . . .

She knew the title somehow, had plucked it from Kris's head. The fact that she could do this almost without effort underlined the fact that they were now mentally connected.

The Executioner will take care of that thing. Joy's voice was back and more vindictive than Adora had ever heard. *Look at the claws on him!*

Good, and I hope he guts him like a . . . Adora began to answer, but then felt Kris's hands tighten, and a thread of ozone streaked through the air where it curled around them. Joy immediately retreated, taking her anger with her. Something about Kris frightened her even more than the monster.

Though a part of Adora wanted to follow the transforming Abrial as his winged and clawed body slithered back down the hole she had just escaped, and to watch as he did something awful to the creature who had tormented her, she did not allow herself to do anything more than wish the worst upon the evil thing.

"Adora." Kris's voice was low and rough. "Don't. You have every right, but . . . just don't. Please. I can feel your rage and it's making me crazy."

"But—"

She watched, fascinated and horrified, as black ink spilled over into the whites of Kris's eyes and small bolts of lighting appeared in that darkness. As disturbing, she could smell ozone rising rapidly around them: It was about to storm again. That seemed highly dangerous, confined as they were to a small cavern.

"Boss! Let go!" Mugshottz reached for her, but Adora waved him away though Kris's touch was now fire on her skin. The bodyguard added urgently, "Kris, hit me if you need to. I'm half gargoyle. I like lightning. Just don't hurt her."

"Hurt her?" He said the words like they held no meaning. "I don't want to *hurt* her."

Eat my heart. Drink my soul. Love me to death.

She knew what was happening—that there was a growing danger. It was happening to her too. Kris was feeling Abrial's rage, perhaps even experiencing the creature's death at the nightdemon's hands. Adora could feel it as well, and it was calling up her own dark magic, the part that wanted to burn everything that frightened her before she could be hurt again.

"Kris," she said gently, pushing down her emotions. It took several seconds to corral the fear Joy had let loose in her psyche. When she was calmer, she called to him again, this time with her mind. His black eyes, shards of night, flicked over her.

"Don't go there. Don't feel it. Be with me here," she said. She paused; then, putting her lips to his throat, she added, "I have my answer now, and I think it will make you happy."

And she did. She wanted Kris. Being near him now made her shiver with delight. Something inside her had ripened and was ready for harvest. She could almost picture him laying hands on her and calling this sweet fruit of desire up through her skin.

"Are you in pain?" she asked softly, laying a hand against his cheek. Small electric shocks danced over her skin. She and Kris were both too hot, too charged with energy. "Does the goblin lair make you feel ill?"

Kris cleared his throat. "Ill? Not exactly. Being near the goblin assassin and his plans of murder only makes me stronger. Don't forget what I am. The energy feeds me and is redoubled."

"But . . . is that good?" she asked, remembering what Zayn had told her.

"It depends entirely on what I do with it."

"You could kill?" she asked tentatively.

He laughed. "Oh, yes—on a massive scale. All I have to think is *die* and every living thing will. Even you would obey. But, Adora, I don't kill. Ever."

Mugshotts shifted his weight, clearly as nervous as ever.

"It's tempting, though," Kris admitted. "And why I stay away from war zones. It isn't cowardice, as some have thought. Such death is like a drug in my system." He rolled his head slowly, like a sprinter loosening up before a run. Adora hoped it was her imagination that made his eyes take on an eerie silver glow and made his hair appear to flutter in some breeze she couldn't feel. The smell of ozone remained strong.

Mugshotts continued to look anxious, and Adora understood why. She was catching some of Kris's confused subconscious thoughts: He must not falter, could not give in to the urge to just let fly, to dump all his stored-up rage on the goblins.

Kris also sensed the other feys had doubts about his plan, but he didn't know how to address them. Logic could only carry a person so far, and then they had to rely on emotional intuition or faith, neither of which were as strong in him as before the goblins' poison had weakened his links to Gaia.

Pain shot through him at this thought, reminding

him of his promise. Gaia. His task was left undone, his work dangerously delayed by goblin poison and by the death of all the pureblood feys in the Great Drought. The difficulties had multiplied in his absence, making his task seem almost impossible. Usually it was enough that he appear for awhile, a bulwark of hope and faith against Nature or a changing social tide, protecting humans as Nature or politicians altered their world. But that would not suffice now. There was nearly two centuries' worth of damage to undo—and he could barely keep control of himself when exposed to a single creature of evil.

The other problem was that his memory was at once too full and too fractured to be of much help, especially in light of the long catalogue of losses he and his brethren had endured. Though he resisted, Kris had begun to look at these losses collectively rather than as individual events, and the big picture was depressing. Eventually they would erode his confidence and make him and the others too weak to be effective. He needed help, a spiritual bandage to bind up his ailing heart while his mind finished healing. He needed Adora—but she needed time. Perhaps lots of it. He had to give that to her.

"You *have* given it to me," she whispered.

"I know that my path sounds indirect and painfully slow," Kris said abruptly, his voice low. "But it's the only one I can take that won't bring destruction on all of us. O Goddess! My gift is my curse. And how I long to use it." He shook his head and swayed. Though nervous, Adora reached for him with her body and mind, pressing as close as he would allow. "Kris! Stay with me. Use me as an anchor."

"War and death are odd things." His voice was

low and rough, his eyes still focused somewhere else. "They have no memory and therefore learn nothing. They just consume. It wouldn't be so bad if they grew old and eventually died, but they don't. Hate and avarice are eternal—and supplied with ever-deadlier weapons, they just get stronger, more determined. And what have my poor children had to defend themselves with while I was gone? They have been forced to use the devil's weapons."

"Kris," Adora said again, trying to bring his focus back to the present. His eyes were now like lasers and his hair writhed like ribbons in a current of spiraling wind.

"We need to leave here," he whispered. "I've tried to stop it, but something inside me is calling to Death. And if He hears the summons, He will come. And once called, He will not stop his harvest until ten thousand years of deaths are collected."

"This . . . this thing is retroactive?" she asked, appalled. Lightning was beginning to dance over her skin in painful arcs, but she didn't pull away. She sensed that she was a lightning rod, the only thing drawing the rage away from Kris.

"Yes. It's like I told you: Everything—*every*thing—comes at a price. Except love," he added to himself. "That is always there. Always. Even when we can't seem to find it."

Gaia again. Adora still didn't feel any of that great cosmic love that Kris believed in, but something had to be done. It was time to take the leap of faith and trust that she had been avoiding.

"Yes, there is love," Adora agreed, and then, though it frightened her, she stood up on her tiptoes and pressed her mouth against Kris's.

As quickly as that, he was back with her, focused. His eyes stopped their strange display, and the scent of ozone began to subside. The small electric tingles diminished on her skin. But that didn't mean that their connection lessened. Not at all. Inside, that feeling of sweet emotion was coming to a boil.

"You bleed." His lashes were black fans against his pale cheeks when he turned his gaze downward. She could feel that her blood both excited and appalled him. The hands that gripped her felt larger than before, and her clothing less substantial.

"Only a little."

He ran his tongue over the wound on her lip. The sting of this strange kiss was quick and shocking, and it tightened her entire body and sped her heart to dangerous rhythms. The kiss said he wanted to devour her.

"Adora?" he asked.

"Yes." She looked into his eyes, which remained wild, stripped of all humanity. It took effort to say, "I'm ready. I have faith. The answer is yes."

Kris made a noise at the back of his throat and scooped her up in his arms. His hair made a silver curtain around them.

They moved quickly through the slowly brightening tunnels and, gradually, his eyes began to dim. The worst of the murderous tension drained away, leaving behind what Adora recognized as a kind of lust, though she had never encountered anything like it before. Kris wanted so much more than her body.

They stopped suddenly. When she looked up, she found that they were in Kris's bedchamber, alone with just his portrait and the many piles of books that stood as testimony to his avid desire to learn about her age.

"You're here," he said softly. His voice was a caress. She realized that a part of her had been close to

Kris for a while—perhaps from the beginning. It had been love at first hearing, she thought, though she also found pleasure in the way Kris moved: confident, graceful, as if he had dominion over everything. Really, he was all that she was not and yet longed to be.

He kissed her roughly, interrupting her thoughts. She kissed him back—harder—and knew when he again tasted the blood from her bitten lips. Her hands tightened on his face in case he thought of pulling back.

No, he said inside her head, his words a balm. *Not now. It's far too late for retreat.*

And she believed him, because she could feel his sex growing between their tightly pressed bodies, growing ridiculously. And then he deepened their kiss, maybe excited by the blood from a wound she could no longer feel, and she forgot to think about anything else except that her flesh began to cry out for more of his touch.

She broke away to pull his shirt over his head, wanting to feel him closer, to lay his skin against her own, perhaps to use some arcane magic to make them one. As she looked again into his eyes, a new primal urge flickered and then flamed into life. For an instant, her resolution wavered. But this was Kris and she was certain—fairly certain—that he would never hurt her.

Still, danger floated in the air around them—and heat. Too much heat. They should be cautious, but neither of them pulled back, though their breaths and touch almost seared the skin everywhere their flesh met.

Faith. She had faith. Didn't she?

Kris grunted once and then tossed her on the bed. He jumped up himself, straddling her like a mother bear protecting her cub. Except it wasn't maternal protection she saw in his eyes or read in his body. His torso was a long column of icy white, every muscle tensed as he looked down at her with unblinking eyes.

"Adora, I need the words. Now."

Adora stared up at him. She knew the words he wanted her to say—*Eat my heart. Drink my soul. Love me to death*. But she couldn't say them. Not yet. It would be an act of final surrender, and her faith wasn't that strong. Instead, the words that came from her in a whisper were, "Kiss me. Help me. Love me." And when Kris hesitated, she added passionately, "Kiss me—because my heart has hurt forever and only that will heal me. Help me—my soul is chained and I can't get free to know this love you speak of. Love me, or it's death in every way that matters. . . ."

Something moved through his eyes. The urge for bloodshed had been restricted, confined, but the heat of those emotions was still there. And the hunger.

Adora spoke gently, as she would to a wild animal. "Kris, I don't know how else to be with you when I'm still afraid. Please—kiss me so that I can remember what love should be. And kiss me so I can forget what has been."

Kris made a low noise in his throat and dropped down on her. He moved so quickly that he was little more than a silver blur. He pulled her close for a third time, looking deep into her eyes as his groin pressed into hers.

"So shall it be," he said in a low voice that was almost a growl. It sent vibrations deep into her body and made her shudder. And then they kissed. This time it was different. Pouring into her mouth and down her throat came a stream of emotions Adora could not identify. They filled her up and left her pliant and stunned.

Kris removed her clothes with ungentle hands, and her skin as well, or so it seemed, leaving her nerves and emotions naked. His touch was delicate but still devastating, and he explored, proving desire of a degree she had never even imagined existed. Even now, a part of her wanted to hide from him, but she didn't flinch or shut her eyes.

Was this love?

Who could say? Certainly not she. But whatever strange emotion she was feeling, it was accompanied by a longing that reached to her very bones. More than breath, more than life, she wanted Kris inside her.

Not sure how she got there, Adora found herself pressed against his belly, her cheek pillowed against his groin, the thick ridge of his sex on her cheek. The slight gap in memory gave her a moment's pause. She lifted up slowly and studied Kris with interest, wondering if he varied from other men in ways other than size.

He was beautiful, alabaster and pure spun silver. But not cold, she thought, kissing him lightly. Nothing about him was cold.

Her gaze traveled upward over his muscled torso, still lightly scarred but its beauty in no way compromised. His shoulders were wider than she remembered, his arms more muscled, and his silver hair glowed as if bathed in moonlight. She knew every strand was waiting for her touch.

"It's been a day of revelations," she said at last, turning her head the rest of the way and facing him. His gaze was direct, heated, but now controlled. She knew hers was too. She let him see the hunger in her, the need to be touched—touched in a way that she had been deprived of all her life.

"It has indeed." Kris rolled over suddenly, contracting his long muscles as he sat up and reversed their positions. He let his head slide down her body, his hair leaving a fiery trail as he kissed his way back to her mouth. "And I'm pleased with you too."

"I can still feel it in you—the wildness. But I'm not afraid now," she whispered. And she did feel his lack of complete control. It was roaming her as well, flames licking at her body from the inside where no hands could reach. Yes, that beast was banished but not defeated.

"Yes." His gaze met hers and scorched. "Does it bother you that I've transformed bloodlust into desire?"

"No," she whispered. "Not at all." But she did mind what was going on inside her. It was hot, so hot—she was burning up.

He reached for her, his fingertips sliding over her thigh, moving along the sweat-moistened skin. She was very wet, but still she could feel herself catch fire every place he touched. His hand cupped, and he slid a finger inside her. His other hand wrote a fiery blessing on her skin, and he gave her the gift of knowing she was beautiful in his eyes.

Emotion swelled in her heart, pressed hard against her breastbone. Her lips parted but no sound came out. Her feelings for Kris were so large that they could never be poured out through her small throat. There just weren't enough words to carry her inner love to the outside world.

Yes, there are. You know them, she realized.

"Eat my heart. Drink my soul. Love me to death," she finally murmured—because now it was safe to say it.

Darkness again moved through Kris's eyes, and Adora felt something powerful roll over her. Kris shifted above, lying between her legs, his weight supported on his arms that were lean and wiry but that could probably bench-press a truck. He pressed his mouth to hers, and this time she felt him drink her in, stopping her heart, drinking her soul, loving her almost to death.

Around them the air roiled and grew smoky. She had little warning except the movement of his hips before he was inside her, the power of his thrust driving the breath from her body and thought from her mind. In the black-glass ceiling she could watch him as he drove into her and slammed her into the bed. She saw her own back arch as she writhed against him, just as violent, just as lustful as he. It was a pleasure that was almost brutal. Almost pain. Yet it was neither.

And then, overwhelmed by both sensation and imagery, her eyes closed so that she would see no more of the wanton, animalistic creatures that coupled on the bed, so she would not see the expression of hunger on her own face. It was difficult enough, knowing that she hungered so desperately to actually place her life in someone else's hands.

Brightness poured through her eyelids, and she knew it came from Kris, that somehow he had transformed his shadow into pure light. Inside her body, something opened and flew outward like the universe after the Big Bang, and something else rushed back inside. It was the approach of fiery creation. It was soul called home from the cold wilderness of Hell, though whether hers or his, she could not say. And for an instant, Adora understood what Kris had meant about the laws of eternity not being the laws of time. Whatever this thing—this feeling—

was, it could not be confined to, or explained by, any experience she had ever had.

He put his lips firmly against hers, muffling her voice, and she screamed into his mouth. All the power was trapped between them. She was barely aware when he pulled out of her body and emptied himself on her belly.

Not yet, Kris said, even as the last echoes of pleasure shook him, and she knew that he was speaking to the Goddess, denying her the new life she had hoped would be created when they made love. And in that moment, Adora knew that it was possible that she could love Kris and do so without fear. Even if he didn't understand why, he knew her dread of parenthood, and he was protecting her even against the Goddess he served.

She might have said something then, foreign emotional words, but Kris reared back suddenly and jerked her from the bed. He held her only until he was sure she would not fall, and then he turned and ripped off the fur coverlet and dropped it on the floor.

Adora stared, openmouthed, as the hide slowly blackened and smoke circled the room. She leaned against a stack of books, feeling them shift behind her. She clapped a hand over her stomach as Kris's seed began to slide down her body. It burned slightly in the palm of her hand, and her stomach was marked with a long red blaze.

"Holy cow!" she said inadequately. "We actually set the bed on fire."

"I guess we both have some control issues," he said—and then Kris started to laugh.

And Niklas worshipped thusly: "Love and light Thou offer. Life and hope Thou offer. And I shall offer too." And then Niklas lay himself on the barren earth and spilled his power into the ground and all around him wheat did grow.

—*Niklas 19:36*

Nicholas's face twisted. He knelt before the cowering woman and gently freed her face from the cruel cage, carefully removing the sharpened bit from her bloodied mouth. He stared at the object in his hands with an emotion somewhere between distaste and horror. A scold's bridle—he hadn't seen such a device used in years.

He kissed the woman, Sarah, on the forehead, and then on the mouth, stopping the bleeding. When her tears had ceased, Nicholas rose and turned toward the man who had so harshly used his wife. He felt old anger stir in him, a black ice that rose from the guts and reached for the heart. That one touch of cold was warning enough to deter his anger. Just as he had feared, the monster, the bringer of death, was still inside him.

"Black Peter," Nicholas said to his goblin friend, his voice harsh enough to strike fear in the human husband's

heart. He knew his eyes had turned. "Take this woman to her family. See that she is given enough gold that she need never return to this house. Then return here. This sinner and I shall have words while you're gone."

"Nicholasss . . ." Black Peter said nervously, for he too could feel the creature inside of Nicholas and knew to fear it as he would Armageddon.

"Go," Nicholas added in another tongue. "Don't be afraid. The only thing that will kill this man is kindness, and that I shan't be sharing. I am sure such a pleasant, selfless emotion would be poison to him."

Black Peter backed out of the room as Nicholas weighed the cage in his hand, his eyes fixed on the cruel human who now cowered on the floor and called out for Saint Nicholas to save him. The irony of the man's choice of saviors had the goblin smiling.

"Asssk and ye ssshall reccceive," he muttered as he wrapped the stunned woman in a cloak and led her from the small cottage. "And reccceive more than you wish."

CHAPTER SIXTEEN

Kris was higher than a kite in a hurricane, and mostly due to Adora. *She has a lovely laugh,* he thought. *Soft and contagious, and precious for being so rare.* And her voice—*Kiss me so I can remember. Kiss me so I can forget.* Her words still reverberated within him, leaving him shaken.

He had also loved the shock in her eyes when pleasure overcame her. He loved that this woman of words, who could describe in detail every nuance of human emotion, was rendered speechless by their lovemaking. Above all else, he relished the feeling that flowed through him from her heart, a stream of emotion that rolled through his body and restored hope and faith and even memory. For he too had needed to remember, while also needing to forget.

The Goddess wasn't pleased with half a loaf, but Kris was content for now. Adora wasn't ready to think about children, but she had given herself over to him, and in a different way than he had anticipated—and he had held her life safe for that long instant before he suppressed the death fey impulse to send her soul onward, returned her life to her. And as the current between them sent her life back into her body, that soul surely told her that her faith in him was not misplaced. She could trust him. It was a sign. The pattern of destruction was broken. She could love. Perhaps. Eventually.

And he knew that he could trust himself. The deathbringer had not harmed her when it had the chance, even though he was flooded with killing rage. Gaia had not forsaken him, the promise was kept. With Adora's help, he could now go on. He could go into the goblin lands and not fear that the urge to kill would overwhelm him.

The race was not to the swift but to the sure, and now he had certainty. They would not lose.

Adora toweled herself dry, staring pensively into the dark glass walls of the bathroom. Low down, her abused body still throbbed, as though she had a second heart in her loins. This velvet bruise wasn't painful exactly, and it was subsiding, so she decided that she could—would—ignore its physical reminder of the madness for now.

It was somewhat difficult to ignore in the quiet, though, because her own thoughts were restless, noisy companions now that Kris was gone and they had again found their tongues. Why the hell was she alone, anyway? Kris, the ever-energetic, had put out the fire and then dashed off to do something with Jack.

That was a rhetorical question, right? Joy asked, speaking for the first time in awhile.

Yes, Adora replied.

He had taken the time to push a ring onto her finger and bestow a last, knee-weakening kiss on his way out the door. "Is this like an engagement ring or something?" she had asked as she stared at her hand in bemusement.

"Yes, I suppose it is. I'll explain later," he said happily and then disappeared.

I still say it's a twelve-carat bribe, Joy grumbled. *But twelve really nice carats.*

Bribe or not, Adora liked having it—a gift from Kris. His first one, if she didn't count the coat he'd sent Pennywyse to buy.

"I'm pathetic," she told her reflection.

Of course you are. But why bring it up now? Is it the ring? Are you actually getting sentimental?

Maybe.

But it wasn't her sudden sappiness that distressed her. Her unease was because she finally understood why it was that hurricane victims would choose to move right back onto their soggy beachfront property the minute the deadly water and wind receded, or why people rebuilt in the same place after a forest fire or earthquake took their homes. It wasn't that they were stupid—just possessed by the illogical conviction that such a thing couldn't possibly happen again. Sure, tsunamis happened now and again—but not to them. They had paid the price already. Earthquakes, volcanic eruptions, those were for other people. Sure, maybe God had blown down the trailer park three times, or wiped out Pompeii or Krakatau—but never again. A just God would never let it happen in the same place a half dozen times.

Are you saying that sex with Kris is a natural disaster? Joy asked. *Because from where I was sitting—*

Shut up.

Well, are you saying that?

N-no. Of course I'm not saying it was a disaster. But

he is something of a force of nature. And dangerous. I felt it, you know, that moment while he wrestled with whether to give my soul back or to send it onward. What if sex is always like that? What happens if some day he isn't paying close enough attention, he starts thinking about baseball or something and I end up dead?

Good questions, but I notice that you aren't packing up and leaving him. He stopped your heart and you set the bed afire, but you're still here and so is he. At least, I assume he's still here.

I know. And it's crazy, but . . .

Let me guess—you're sure that it'll never happen again. Your trailer park is safe.

Adora didn't answer as she tossed the towel aside. She wasn't sure of anything just then, except that once again she wanted to go for a walk.

Oh, geez. Have you forgotten your last walk already?

A short walk. In the mound, Adora promised. She had to get out. The room was too full of Kris and she was feeling overwhelmed. Speaking of love—even to herself—had opened something inside of her. And every scary memory she had held at bay for the last two decades was catching up, overshadowing her, and she needed space to wrestle with them.

What's that? Joy asked, distracting her.

Adora walked to the bed and reached for the dress laid out there. It was arranged like a fainting lady, its skirts draped over the edge of the mattress in a long, graceful fall. She held up the bright green garment with the rolled velvet, and tried to find a bit of glassy wall that wasn't obscured by books. The shade was as subtle as neon and the style a bit grand for daywear. But it was very pretty, she admitted, even if it wasn't exactly what she was used to. And it went with her ring.

You're hopeless, Joy said.

"So, what will you do to the goblins? Will you let us kill the goblin king who poisoned you? And what of this attack on Adora?" Thomas asked. "Something must be done. This was too bold."

"Anaximander already took care of my poisoner when he wiped out all the males in his family, and his assassin Raxin is as dead as Abrial can make him. Instead I shall let you do something far worse than kill them," Kris answered happily, making Thomas look suddenly uneasy. "We shall make the goblin children love me—or rather, Santa Claus. I will begin the campaign by bringing them presents this Christmas Eve when I visit the humans. We start making plans at once. I know Pennywyse will probably give birth to imps when he hears about it, but he'll rally. And this year, it will only be in the United States."

Jack gave a low whistle.

"You don't believe in starting small, do you?" Abrial asked. He once again looked normal, and no trace of his former deadly incarnation could be seen. He was, however, careful to keep his distance from Kris. "I've got to admire you, though. It's the last thing the goblins will ever expect."

"It will make an excellent diversion too." Kris leaned back and steepled his fingers.

"Diversion?" Abrial asked. Now he looked uneasy.

"Yes. I plan on getting Molybdenum's people out of prison. It's partially my fault that they're imprisoned."

This time, Abrial whistled. "A jailbreak? From the heart of the L.A. hive? I'd pay cash money to see that."

"You wish to help, Abrial? Then mark your calendar and prepare to travel. I am going to need help this year—from all of you, since you know the Unseelie roads here better than I. And I will let you guess where your delivery duty will take you first." Kris smiled at Abrial's look of dismay. "I know, Abrial. But L.A. goblins have children too. And you wouldn't have any luck controlling the reindeer. Besides, you'd scare any human children who might be peeking out their windows. We have to shift their perception of Santa Claus by slow degrees. No offense, but the black bat wings might be a bit too much."

The nightdemon shook his head. A moment later he said, "Not to change the subject, but does Adora realize how much time has passed in the outside world? She was joyriding on those fairy roads for quite a while. Even for us . . ."

"No. I doubt she does. I'll put it on the list of things I still need to explain."

"I'd pay to see that list too," Abrial replied. "I guess it will be easier now that you two have joined. She should be more accepting."

Kris looked surprised. "You know we've joined?"

"Of course. We had half a dozen fires blaze up in the mound."

"Oh. Sorry. We'll work on that."

Abrial grinned. "That's okay, the sudden rainstorms put them out."

"*Enough*," Jack spoke up. "And don't be teasing Adora about the fires, either. She's still very skittish."

"Okay. But you'll have to do something about Roman. He never has been able to resist a good joke."

"What can one do about Roman?" Thomas asked.

Kris caused sudden silence to fall by asking, "You all know why we must do this, right? We are agreed? You all know that even if we retreat inside the mound and let the humans and goblins have at it, we can't survive. This much death will poison the earth and then us." Kris looked at each fey in turn. They weren't grinning now. "We are the last of our kind, the last of the checks that balance the human and lutin worlds. As such, we have a moral obligation to survive—and to keep the peace."

"Amen, brother," Jack said, getting to his feet.

Joy, what's wrong? I can feel you ruminating, and it's getting in the way of my own. And that was saying something for Adora, because all around her the garden was whispering urgently. To her or about her, Adora wasn't sure which, but it was damned distracting. She even wondered if, should she turn about quickly, she would catch the vines behind her bent toward each other like old ladies gossiping behind their fanlike blossoms.

"Hush!" she finally said to the plants. "Look, I'm not trying to abridge your right to free speech, but what about my right to freedom of thought? You're stuffing my ears with noise until I can't think. Just hold it down until I'm gone, okay?" There was sudden silence.

Joy? Talk to me.

Sorry to bother you. It's just . . .

What? Spit it out. You've never been mealy-mouthed, so don't start now.

Look, you've always thought of me as a shadow, something always close by but still separate from you. But really I'm not separate. I've always been a part of you, and without you, I don't exist. The confession was made in a small voice. *And I'm not sure that Kris likes me. The whole fire-sex thing is dangerous, and he probably thinks it's my fault. He may want you to get rid of me.*

Adora thought about this. *You know, Joy, it would probably be healthier if I were an integrated personal-*

ity . . . but that's not happening anytime soon that I can see. Anyway, you're what helps me control the fire thing—which I'm sure he has guessed. But if not, I'll explain. Adora grimaced. She was going to have a lot to explain. *So, let's not worry about it too much. The future will just have to look after itself for a bit. Let's concentrate on getting through today.*

Joy in turn thought for a moment. *Okay. So, what are you ruminating about? I haven't been listening.*

Before Adora could answer, she came upon a strange animal out in the garden, perched atop a giant flowering vine. It was an odd mix of scales and fur, and looked vaguely like a rodent that had been grafted onto a lizard. She found the long drooping mustache that reached its waist especially appealing. The creature looked like the Frito Bandito.

"Oooh. Hello, handsome," she said softly. "Will you let me pet you? I'll be very gentle if you let me."

The creature drew itself up, either insulted or preparing for flight.

"Here. Try this." A boy who looked a bit like Huck Finn rolled out from under a bush and reached into his pocket. He pulled out a lint-covered dog bone and offered it to her. The creature was suddenly interested. "But he isn't handsome, he's an imp. He likes dog cookies. And electrical wiring. That's why he isn't allowed in Thomas's computer lab. No, greedy guts! The *lady* wants to feed you."

The imp's teeth chattered excitedly.

Adora stared at the chatty boy who stood in a place where no one had been only moments before. A line from *The Wizard of Oz* popped into Adora's head— *People come and go so quickly around here.* There was something very will-o'-the-wisplike about his arrival, but there was nothing phantomlike about the boy himself. In fact, he looked exceptionally sturdy for a fey.

"Thanks." Adora took the cookie with only mild trepidation.

He's just a boy. They're very common—not like a person with a second head or a third eye. She forced a smile for the waiting child and then slowly knelt. She offered her treat tentatively to the vibrating imp.

"His name's Wessley," the boy informed her. "But don't call him that either. He doesn't like it."

"I see." She kept her eyes on the imp. Not sure what to say, she went with the first thing that popped into her head: "I wouldn't want to be a Wessley either."

"Well, you're a girl." That was said sympathetically.

"I never had a pet, either," Adora confided. "My parents thought that—eek!"

The imp's nose twitched once more and then it jumped forward with teeth bared. Adora fell back on her butt and squeaked again, but she managed to keep her arm extended long enough for the imp to get his cookie. He didn't bite as he snatched the bone from her fingers, but he scampered away with great haste, the dog biscuit clutched to his chest, sharp teeth chattering.

Adora exhaled nervously and got back to her feet, dusting off her skirt. She needed to be careful; she didn't want to ruin another expensive piece of clothing.

That little beast has enormous teeth. I thought he'd take my fingers off, she thought.

Joy chuckled. *Of course it didn't bite you. It knows what side its dog cookie is buttered on.*

The imp gave Adora a long look from its regained floral perch, and shoved the dog biscuit between his jaws and crunched noisily until it was gone. He waited a full fifteen seconds for her to do something more, but not seeing any other cookies in the offing, he turned and scampered away, leaving a small trail of shredded blossoms behind him.

"Oh," she said sadly. "I wanted to pet him. Maybe he doesn't like me after all."

"He doesn't really like anyone," the boy said. "It's why I wanted to eat him. But my sister said no."

"Um . . ."

"You're pretty funny when you squeak," the boy went on. "And your dress is crooked."

Adora felt Kris move up behind her, and was relieved at the interruption. Boys didn't make her as nervous as babies, but children were still not her favorite beings. She pulled her bodice back in place, then turned quickly and smiled. She hoped Kris didn't notice the color blooming in her cheeks as her body sang with awareness of him.

"You could pet me instead. I promise to sit very still and not bite." Kris did his best to look limp and harmless, but she wasn't buying it. She'd petted him before and it had only led to trouble.

"Uncle Kris!" Huck Finn cried. "We're back now. Did you bring me a present? Does it have gingerbread in it?"

"Hello, Hansel," Kris said, kneeling down to hug the boy. "Yes, Mugshottz has something for you and Gretel. Ask him to look through my luggage."

"Mugshottz is here too?" Hansel galloped away with a whoop of joy.

Hansel and Gretel? Joy asked.

Sure. Why not? We have Santa Claus, Jack Frost, the

Pied Piper and a dragon too. Why not some Brothers Grimm?

"I'm sorry I had to leave you so abruptly," Kris said. "It's just that we have so many plans to make, and the others have all been waiting for me. I . . . I was kind of lost for a while."

Lost? He looks manic, Joy said. *I think your boyfriend is still amped up on the sex.*

"That's okay. I needed a few minutes to recover my breath," Adora admitted. She ducked her head so that he wouldn't see her creeping blush or the pulse that hammered away in her throat. "So, what have you been working on while I fed ungrateful imps?"

"A plan," Kris said immediately. "The world simply must stop wasting its resources on this cold war. Then and only then will it be time for a renaissance—a new world that will encourage Michelangelos and Shakespeares, Beethovens and Xatrids—"

"Xatrids?" Adora asked. "I'm not familiar with that name."

"A famous lutin architect," Kris explained quickly. "He introduced ninety-degree angles into their hexagonal world."

"Interesting concept. More human, certainly. . . ."

"Humans." Kris blinked. "They're a problem too. So many men these days have lost their respect for Nature and her blessings. '*O, Babylon the Great is fallen! Fallen!*' Man—especially here—has forgotten that there is a delicate balance to be upheld. Man has sturdy houses, central heating, instant light whenever darkness threatens, and all his food is tidily packaged. His hands are rarely bloodied or blistered. He neither sows, nor does he gather, nor

343

does he hunt. Death is all around him, cold and darkness too—just as it always has been—but he is blinded by the new magic of electricity and feels safe behind his technology. He has forgotten that everything comes with a price. He doesn't understand that the bill always comes due. They sell themselves and their souls to multi-national companies, their children and their country into debt so they can go on consuming cheap imports and amusing drugs, human and lutin alike."

"Uh . . ." Adora felt a bit stunned by the tirade, though she didn't actually disagree.

Kris began to pace. "Understand, I am not wishing hardship or suffering on Mankind—far from it. Man has suffered much already from being divorced from Nature and the Divine Love that created him," he asserted with renewed enthusiasm. His gaze was distant, and she knew he was seeing something she could not. "But it would be good if Man occasionally recalled that he is just Man, and that he did not actually create the Earth. We are all servants to the Great Good. Man's job is temporary guardian of this planet, which he should hold in sacred trust for those who will come after. And he has to quit placing himself in lutin power. This most of all, or America, the greatest experiment in democracy and freedom, will fall!"

"Do you ever work for Greenpeace?" Adora asked when the moment had stretched out long enough to be uncomfortable. "Or maybe the U.N.?"

Kris blinked and returned to himself. "Not yet, but my foundation has given heavily to the World Wildlife Fund and the Nature Conservancy. I'll consider the U.N. on the day the goblin cities are recognized as sovereign states and asked to join with the other nations."

"Well, good—about the World Wildlife Fund and the Nature Conservancy," Adora said inadequately. "I support both charities. I haven't had much to do with the U.N., though."

Kris looked down and saw her weary bemusement with the swift turn their conversation had taken. He said: "Sorry, I'm babbling. And I can sense there is something you want to tell me." He took her hand, his grasp warm and comforting. "And I have things to say to you as well—later."

"Want to tell you things?" she repeated. Did she want to bother him with all her tiny, selfish thoughts when he was out to save not just one but three species? "Not really, but—"

"Kris!" Mugshottz's voice floated up the tunnel. The bodyguard sounded as wired as Kris, and Adora began to wonder if the two were somehow connected, like the troll-cross was an overflow duct where Kris's excess emotions went when they got too dangerous. At least, all the emotions that weren't sexual. He seemed to reserve those for her. "Can you come to the lab? Thomas has something for you. I think he's found Molybdenum."

"Adora—" Kris said.

"Go," she interrupted, meeting his eyes. The garden had stopped whispering. "I need a little longer to get over the . . . smoke inhalation, anyway. I'll be just fine out here. And I promise not to wander off."

"Are you sure?" he asked. Then: "Gorgeous dress, by the way. It almost does you justice. And I'm glad you're wearing the ring. It will make Roman very happy. He loves marrying people."

"Thank you, kind sir. I am flattered." She felt lightheaded enough to curtsey. "But as for Roman and his marrying us, I'm not—"

"Kris!" Mugshottz bellowed.

"Coming!" Kris called back. He leaned toward her. "I have to go, but first . . ."

"No kisses," she warned, putting out her hand and resting it against his chest. Her skin tingled where they touched. "You're bad for my blood pressure. Go at once, then hasten ye back. We do need to talk."

"I fly on winged feet," he promised, grinning, and then he bounded away.

"And watch the caffeine!" she called. "You don't need any more stimulants."

Ha! I think he's part reindeer, Joy grumbled.

Adora didn't answer. She was suddenly feeling oddly deflated, as though Kris had taken the light from the room when he left.

This is going to get real old, real fast. I don't want my happiness to depend on someone else, she found herelf thinking. Of course, until very recently, she hadn't had any happiness at all.

You just need some food, Joy suggested. *Let's go find the kitchen. Then we'll go bury the dead. It's time you let your past rest.*

Beware, and be ever vigilant. For our enemy, Hate, stalks the land like a ravening beast, looking for faithless to devour.

—*Niklas 17:2*

"Sweet Jesus Lord, he's done for!" cried the cowboy from atop a high rock.

The man in black heard the cry but did not respond. Instead, he faced the monster that rushed at him, four thousand hooves strong, and held out his hands as though welcoming a child. Then the beast was upon him.

For a long moment no one could see through the thick dust swirling in the air. But the bellowing herd of panicked cattle finally passed, and the others could see that they had parted evenly around the blond man in black, the living river divided as if by a giant stone.

The cattle passed on and then slowed abruptly, finally coming to a complete stop.

"Damn, Padre—excuse my French," the first cowboy added conscientiously, since the stranger was clearly some sort of man of the cloth. He slid to the ground.

"The good Lord must be looking out for you," the sec-

347

ond cowboy added, with something that might have been religious dread as he joined his older friend.

"The good Lord, and Lady Luck," the stranger agreed.

The first cowboy blinked. "I gotta tell ya, Padre, I ain't much for goin' to church. Most religion fits me kinda tight, you see. But if there's somethin' you'd like to say to me now, well, I am surely willin' to listen—maybe even make a donation of somethin'."

The man in black began to smile. "Now that you mention it, there is something you can do for me. I am looking for a guide."

"Well, me and Bob know this territory pretty well. What are ya after?"

"I am searching for the Tomb of the Nephalim."

"I beg yer pardon?" the one called Bob asked.

"The giants. I'm looking for their tomb."

The two cowboys exchanged a long look.

"Oh. Well, Padre, you should really be talkin' to the Injuns about that. Only, I don't reckon that anyone is talkin' to them much right now, things being somethin' less than peaceful in these parts."

"Nevertheless, I must find the Nephalim," the man in black said firmly. "And I would appreciate your help. Please don't be concerned about the natives offering us a violence."

The two cowboys turned and looked at the stampeding herd that had stopped their wild rush and were standing about docilely in the hot sun. They both swallowed hard. It wasn't strictly Old Testament, but they both knew a miracle when they saw one.

"Okay, Padre. We'll do what we can."

"Thank you. And please, won't you call me Nicholas?"

CHAPTER SEVENTEEN

Adora wasn't ready for a face-to-face with the shian's resident ghost, but apparently Chloe was. She was waiting for Adora right outside the garden, hovering nervously in the shadows. Adora wasn't thrilled to see her, but was grateful that she hadn't brought either Clarissa or the goblin baby along.

"I thought we might take a walk together and get acquainted," Chloe said. "The mound can be very confusing at first. I was always getting lost."

"Sure. I'd like that," Adora said, though she knew the lie wasn't very convincing. "Did they send you to make sure that I didn't get lost in the goblin tunnels again?"

"No," Chloe denied. "I . . . I just wanted to talk to you. I think I know how you must be feeling about . . . well, things. But sometimes we just have to do the hard thing no matter what we feel."

Adora felt her smile freeze on her face. *Please, please, don't let this be about the baby.*

Chloe said, "I'm probably a fool to ask this, given

your obvious misgivings about . . . well, everything. But, why are you with Kris?" Adora raised a brow, so Chloe went on: "I mean, why did you sign on to the book project to begin with? The whole thing sounded kind of . . . well, insane."

"Oh." The book. She could talk about that. Adora thought about it; then, as was getting to be a habit, she answered truthfully: "It was probably because I had nothing to lose. My family is dead, my career as good as, and my life was a sort of sick parody of what a life should be. Still, I wasn't sure I would take the job until I arrived in L.A. Then I met Kris in person and . . ." She shrugged. "The rest, as they say, is history."

A long, long history, with lots of missing footnotes.

"I understand," Chloe said. She added wistfully, "It must be wonderful to be so very sure that he's the one. It will make everything else so much easier."

Adora opened her mouth and then closed it without speaking. *Was* she sure?

Of course you are. You think that Fate has handed you a winning lottery ticket. Take it, Joy said.

Gee, thanks, Joy. You have only to add that you think I'm delusional.

No, just unprepared. But I guess everyone goes into new relationships blinded by one thing or another.

Adora felt the weight of Chloe's nervous stare, an oppression of her already faltering mood, and couldn't stand it anymore. "I really need to get some air. I thought I'd step out here. There's a ledge."

"Oh." Chloe shrank back. "I'm . . . I'm not real big on going outside."

Good.

"I guess I'll see you later then," Adora said, knowing she was being rude, but wanting away from Chloe and any possible discussion about her taking care of the goblin baby.

All in good time, my pretty. All in good time. Joy cackled like a witch.

"Can you be ready in time?" Jack asked Kris when they were alone.

Silvered eyes met silvered eyes. Neither fey was afraid.

"Yes," Kris said definitely. "Pennywyse has been very busy. Haven't you been watching the news? There is virtually no unemployment in the human urban centers of California. And there are also a lot of new jobs in the Third World."

"I know your resources are vast, but how long can you sustain this . . . plan?"

"I don't know," Kris admitted. "That involves calculating economic variables that are not yet seen. A lot will depend on how my various film projects do at the box office. Fortunately, most of Hollywood is onboard and willing to volunteer their time and talents for the Bishop S. Nicholas Foundation."

"What about Washington?" Jack asked.

"We have friends even there. Not as many, but their number grows. In time we'll win them over."

As soon as Chloe left, Adora switched directions. She really wanted something to eat. But instead of the kitchen, she came upon the men of Cadalach at a round table in one of the many rooms she had yet to explore. She felt a quick and almost enjoyable chill. These were Kris's family. The Chosen. They could be her family too, if she wanted.

"Hey, Adora!" Roman called to her. His grin was easy. "Come tell us about your encounter with the beastie. Abrial is being stubborn and won't give up the details."

"Well . . . what sort of details?" she asked, having no desire to relive her time in the tunnels. "I didn't see what Abrial did."

"Oh." The pookah sounded disappointed. "But what about before? Even before he shape-shifted, was his gaze so hot that it could spot-weld anything his breath failed at?"

"Yes." Adora hesitated to mention that the creature had looked like the monster who'd haunted her childhood dreams. She wasn't ready to tell anyone but Kris about Old Man Fletcher.

Roman whistled. "I told you, Thomas. That would likely make him a barghest or a boggart—that's a really nasty shape-shifting goblin who can look in your mind and see what scares you most. What did you do when you saw him?"

She snorted. "I ran."

"Popular choice."

"A *wise* choice," Thomas added.

"How would you deal with a boggart?" Adora asked, genuinely curious.

"Four-speed chainsaw," Roman said promptly.

"Do they make one?" Thomas asked with interest.

"Oh, yeah. I want one for my birthday."

"Well . . . I didn't have a chainsaw," Adora said. "I didn't have anything, except maybe some harsh language."

"That can be good—if they're words to spells," Roman answered.

She shivered. No, she wasn't in Kansas anymore.

"I couldn't do anything that might affect Kris." She shuddered again, thinking of the wildness she had seen in him. Then she admitted, "I can still feel that thing's slimy fingerprints in my head. Sometimes I look at shadows and think I see him there. He was so gross. He turned his body inside out!"

"Kinesthetic perseveration," Thomas explained sympathetically. "Bad memory sticks around for a bit. It will fade, though. And you're being avenged—that should help. I'm bankrupting that hive even as we speak." He pointed at the portable computer on the table and grinned. The screen was flashing, numbers scrolling by at an incredible rate.

Adora dared to tease him a bit. "Internet fraud? You look very cheerful. I'm beginning to suspect that you have a natural aptitude for thievery."

"What gave me away?" Thomas asked with an even wider smile. His eyes were gold and very kind.

"Was it the shifty eyes? The sneaky smirk?" Roman suggested helpfully. He ducked as a computer manual sailed at his head. "It's kind of like porn, isn't it—hard to define, but you just know it when you see it."

"Don't mind him," Thomas said. "Roman is something of a hound, and he has no manners."

"Actually, I'm a horse," Roman corrected. "A river horse."

"Hound, horse—I don't mind so long as you don't drink out of my toilet," Adora replied calmly.

Thomas began laughing. "You've seen him at parties, huh?"

The computer manual sailed back.

"Will you join us for lunch?" Thomas asked, snagging the book out of the air. Adora didn't think she would ever get used to how quickly feys moved. "I don't know when Kris and Jack will get free, but you're welcome to eat with us."

Kris. Her momentary lightheartedness fell away, as did her appetite. She was going to have to talk to him, tell him about what she was and why she was.

They couldn't move forward until he knew the truth.

"Come on. I won't drink out of the toilet," Roman promised. "You look pale. You should eat. Cyra will be there, too. She and Thomas are expecting a baby any day now—did you know? Maybe you and she could compare notes."

A baby? Another one? Adora's stomach rolled over in warning.

He thinks you're pregnant, Joy whispered. *They all know that's the Goddess's plan, and they just assume that you are.*

I got that.

"Congratulations—that's wonderful news," she managed to say. "But I'll pass on lunch. I just need some air."

Thomas looked at her closely, his gaze suddenly probing. She knew that he was about to suggest she see Zayn.

"I'll probably see you later, though," Adora offered. She pasted on a smile.

"Bank on it," Roman said. "I want to take you girls riding."

That distracted Thomas. "No way!" he said, throwing the book again. This time he threw a little harder. Roman laughed and caught it, then sent it back like a Frisbee, spinning through the air. They weren't watching as Adora backed out of the room on shaky legs.

She was back on her ledge in time to see the dawn—though this time without a scorpion; Adora checked. At first the sunlight seemed cruel, cutting open the night at the edge of the eastern sky, tearing the new wound wide. But the birth of the morning proved to be beautiful, and the early light so healthful that she soon forgot the sky's imagined pain.

Her own overly empathetic imagination wasn't the only thing strange about the morning; the morning air was touched with an autumnal chill.

Because of what had happened with Kris—the sharing of their thoughts and perhaps even some of his goodness—a part of her childhood had been rewritten, this time in more understood terms that could be viewed safely from a new and welcome distance. It was like she had taken a long vacation—though no one would choose to spend what had felt like that eternity down in that goblin hell-hole.

Yeah, that part is good. You needed a buffer, Joy said.

Yes. But even with it, anyone mentions babies and I still run away.

So, you have a few hang-ups.

A few?

She had been like the captive Gulliver, tied in place by the strings of a thousand assumptions about why her parents had done what they did. And most of them were wrong. It was strange to think, but she could probably let go of many of those unstated and unhappy beliefs that she had been carrying around as a personal ball and chain. She could—when she was ready—finally accept that she was in another world that had its own rules and logic and social culture. But she would have to accept all the way.

In other words, Miss Manners's etiquette guide can no longer be relied upon. You can probably throw out Freud and Jung too, Joy added.

Probably.

So, go ahead. Throw out the misconceptions and look again.

I am.

Adora shook her head sadly at what she saw. Her parents had been fey—but ignorant of it. How could that be, unless they were also raised by ignorant parents? And what if her mother had been as unprepared as Adora herself was to become a mother? She had never spoken of her childhood. Perhaps her mother had never been raised to feel a sense of responsibility for another being. A baby must have terrified her.

And then, to be overwhelmed with the kinds of blinding emotion that happened between feys when they had sex . . . Well, it explained a lot.

Enough to forgive them? Enough to let the guilt go? Maybe.

Kris and everyone at Cadalach had given her a priceless gift: understanding of her parents. Though it was still painful to think about, she felt that she could finally forgive them for their neglect, because at last she understood that they had been unwitting victims of a power of which they were not even aware. There had been no malice in what they'd done. They were not heartless. They were two people trapped in their genetic destiny without the knowledge of how to fight free—or even that they *needed* to fight free—and having now felt the blinding attraction of mated magicks that call to one another, Adora knew precisely how strong that draw was.

If her parents had felt as she herself had when she'd made love to Kris—been as afflicted with blind obsession—then she had to pity them. And also, to forgive. If they were still alive, she would call or maybe write them a note of apology for all the awful things she'd thought about them lately.

In fact . . . Adora frowned and began looking around for something to write on. She was much better at organizing her thoughts on paper, and until she wrote them down she'd continue the fruitless rumination. That was the one thing her time with the shrink had taught her.

As though something had anticipated her need, she found her notebook and a pen on the rock at her feet. A stone rested there, holding them in place.

How the hell . . . ?

It must have fallen out of my purse last time I was here, Adora answered.

You didn't have a purse.

My pocket, then.

Joy snorted but didn't argue any more.

Adora sat down and crossed her legs as though preparing for meditation. She wrote for a long while, then she set the pen aside and closed her eyes. Though she had rarely done it before, Adora prayed to Kris's higher power that wherever her parents were, they were together and at peace, and that they would somehow know—if ever they had been aware—that she wasn't angry anymore.

A shadow passed overhead. Adora opened her eyes and looked up quickly from the letter clenched in her hand. She stared into the sky. It was an empty, painful blue. Not a single cloud marred its brilliance.

Which was how she felt inside. All her resentment was gone and she was empty, waiting for something else to fill her.

"Are you there?" she whispered, and then felt foolish. First a letter to her dead parents, and now she was talking to them.

There was a soft rumbling behind her, and then Kris appeared. She wasn't surprised. They were connected now, and he would have known some of what she was feeling.

Adora turned to smile at him, then blinked in consternation. Kris often did strange things, but she had never seen anything quite so incongruous as a man in an Armani suit carrying what he was carrying.

"I thought maybe you'd want to send that letter," he said, offering the small flotilla of daffodil-yellow helium balloons. "I think it needs to be set free so it can do its work."

"You think they'll get it this way?" she asked, touched by the gesture but still feeling foolish.

"Yes," Kris said gravely. He promised, "They'll get your message if that's what you want."

Adora nodded, believing him because she needed to believe him, and then she reached for the balloons. Kris helped her tie the strings around her letter, forming a sort of crooked net for the loose pages.

"The sky is too empty anyway. It needs some color," she said.

Kris nodded, then released the balloons into the air. He and Adora watched until they were just a speck of gold headed eastward over the desert. It was probably psychosomatic, but Adora had to admit that she felt lighter with every minute, as though her sad memories were truly being carried away by the wind.

"I have some time now," Kris said. "If you want to talk."

Adora decided it really was time, and began telling Kris the details about her past. She held nothing back, as embarrassing and painful as it was to admit all that she had done and felt: Fletcher, the scorching shame, the blinding rage, the soul-destroying loneliness that only Joy had broken.

Kris was silent for a long moment after she finished speaking.

"My first impulse was to preserve my dignity,"

she said, when the silence grew uncomfortable. "You know, hope that you would never find out what a coward I was—and maybe still am."

"You're speaking of that first fire? Aren't you being a little hard on yourself?" Kris asked. "You were only five, and had absolutely no example set for you. It was only natural that you would defend yourself with your magic. I would hope that given those circumstances you would do it again."

"Really?"

"Really. You needn't worry about me. I have it under control now—thanks to you." Kris shook his head. "I'll make you a deal. You forgive yourself for your various trespasses, and I'll stop feeling that I was weak for losing my way. We both did the best we could, given the circumstances we were in. The best anyone can do is the best they can do—we can't ask for more from ourselves or from others."

There it was: absolution. And from the one whose understanding mattered.

You *matter*, Joy said.

Yes, but if he can see me and not condemn, then I can do that for myself.

"Yeah, I'm figuring that out," she said to Kris. "It's just hard to tear down the childhood beliefs that wallpaper the brain."

"Well, you're talking to me now. Some of the wallpaper must have come down. The rest will follow when it's ready."

"Joy thought you already knew all this," Adora admitted. "That's one reason I decided to come clean. After all, you might be thinking things are worse than they are."

"I knew a lot," Kris agreed with a small smile. He put an arm around her and urged her close. Though there was nothing sexual in his intent, she could still feel the pull rising between them. He added, "It was really loud wallpaper. Even Mugshottz could hear some of it."

Adora leaned into his arm and started telling him the rest. Kris remained silent, offering comfort with his arms while the last of her tears fell.

"It's autumn, isn't it?" she asked sometime later. Her voice was raspy from overuse and crying. "It seems that I have somehow managed to sleep the summer away."

"Nearly so. The autumnal equinox is but a week away—but you weren't sleeping. This happened while you were lost on the faerie roads. Some of them are . . . feral. They belong to the goblins now, and are hostile to those of our blood. They couldn't age you, but they could slow you down enough that the outside time changed."

"So, lots of bad things happen down there."

"Often," he agreed.

"Is that why Chloe can't go outside? Because she'd be old?"

"Perhaps. Chloe has many reasons for staying inside."

Adora nodded. "Did that mess up your plans—spending all that time looking for me?" she asked.

"No, but it brought them forward a bit."

Adora bolted upright. "It's been weeks! Ben must be worried sick—and my house and the bills!"

"All taken care of. You needn't worry." He pulled her back. "The Internet is an amazing thing."

Adora decided she would take Kris's advice. She was too tired to worry anymore. "But . . . I just don't understand how it all works," she complained. "I just don't get it. How is something like this even possible?"

"There are probably scientific or mathematical

formulas to explain it," Kris said, "but I think of it this way: Every memory we have is tied to a certain time and place. Out here, the rock you touched a minute ago is not the rock you see now. There have been microscopic changes. The wind that touches you is not the same wind of a moment before. It couldn't be, because it would be bumping into itself, constantly crossing its own temporal path."

"Er, okay."

"And just as this rock and the wind are different, so too are you. You are not the you that you were an hour ago. And that is as it should be in the human world. But inside the mound, the time-place—or time-space—is different. The mound is a crossroads between this world and another. You can run into things that were, things that are and sometimes things that are yet to be. Usually these things happen just with the mind. Like with Farrar. Or like how Nyssa and Abrial have learned to travel into the Yesterdays. Their minds leave but their bodies remain."

"And using the faerie roads to travel the length of the Sierra Nevada Mountains in just minutes . . . ?"

"Well, that is something that happens with the body as well," Kris said.

"It sounds like science fiction, you know."

"But it's really a faerie tale," Kris joked. "Well, as they say, truth is stranger than fiction."

Adora nodded. Then she changed the subject before Kris could go on. "I saw Chloe this morning. I forgot to ask her—what did she and Zayn decide to call the baby?" she asked.

"Shulamite."

Kris's voice was so expressionless that, in spite of her unattractively reddened eyes, Adora looked up at him. "As in King Solomon and the Shulamite

Woman?" she asked, startled by the idea. "The woman who married Solomon but then fled him to return to her one true love, a shepherd?"

"Yes."

"I guess Chloe isn't up on her Bible reading."

"Perhaps not. Though it has been said that she lived happily ever after—at least, after fleeing." Kris was smiling a little.

"That's true. And I suppose I like Shulamite better than Clarissa."

Kris chuckled. "As do I. I can't imagine calling a child Clarissa. Not even a human one."

A child. His child. Their child. That's what he meant. The one they would have.

"What now?" Adora asked, looking away.

"I have some plans to set in motion, and you have a book to write."

"That's still on?" she asked, surprised and a bit relieved. "You still want that biography?"

"Oh, yes. And you need to be quick about it. We've lost a lot of time."

"But if I tell the truth, everyone will think Bishop S. Nicholas is a kooky wackjob. Or else a total fake."

"Perhaps. But it amuses me to tell the truth. And it will accomplish other goals by distraction. The book is excellent sleight of hand. It will keep my enemies busy while I get on with my real agenda— which I will share with you soon." She loved his utter confidence.

"Sleight of hand?" Adora suddenly realized that she should be insulted. She laughed instead. "Is that what this is?"

"Definitely. While also the truth."

"Okay, I'll get down to work. After all, being a writer is about seeing the possibilities in people and situations. I believe that most of us are—or at least begin—as optimists. I'll probably come up with something semicoherent."

"That's the spirit. You still look a bit frazzled, though," Kris said, smoothing back her hair and urging her to look at him again. "You know, it isn't right to be an Indian giver. You gave your dark truths to me. It wouldn't be right to try and take their burden back."

"You can have them," she assured him. But she thought to herself: *Frazzled?* That didn't begin to cover it. But Adora didn't complain out loud. After all, Kris was calm and unruffled, and he was the one whose reputation was on the line.

But how was she to write a summation of Kris's life and do him justice? A mere statement of outward facts—crazy as they were—wasn't enough. Yet his interior thoughts and spiritual motivation wouldn't be readily accessible to the average reader. Hell! She was connected to his brain, and *she* didn't understand him completely. In fact, the longer she was with him, the more she realized that she was a footnote to his long existence.

"Not a footnote—a new chapter," he corrected. "You'll find the way, I promise. We fey are adept at balancing acts of all kinds," he said confidently. Then: "But that isn't all that's bothering you, is it?"

"No. This plan of yours—it's going to be dangerous, isn't it? There could be more attempts on your life. On mine too."

"Yes," he admitted. "But they won't succeed."

"You picked a lousy time to fall in love," Adora said. Then, hearing herself, she blushed. Kris had never said anything about love—not specific, romantic love.

He seemed unperturbed. "I know. I'm sorry, Adora. I should have said this straight off—I love you. I love you too much for peace of mind, actually. But I can't love you any less, so . . ." He shrugged. The gesture went oddly with his suit. "Things are as they are. I plan to lie in the bed I made and enjoy it."

Adora settled back into his arms. It was easier to deal with hard truths there. "I love you too. I think. I'm just having a harder time embracing everything else," she confessed. "People keep talking about babies, and I'm just not ready to think about those. I may not ever be ready."

He nodded, rubbing his cheek against her hair. "I know. A child would be a first for me too, you know."

Adora blinked. She hadn't thought of that. She had just assumed that Kris would be keen to have children right away.

Maybe when you have all the world's children to care for, you don't need your own, Joy suggested.

"What would you like to do when this is over?" Kris asked suddenly. "The world is ours to explore. I know people, as they say. Want to see the columned halls of the selkies' sunken castle in Scotland? Or see the lost city in the Ecuadorian rainforest where the dark pixies lived?" She looked up, and he smiled a little. "This is a hard job we have, but there are perks. Choose something—anything—and we'll plan a vacation."

A vacation.

"I'm not sure where I'd like to go. I'll have to think about it," Adora said. She felt a bit cheered that Kris was making plans for an *afterwards.* Plans that didn't involve children. Or saving the world.

Ask him why, Joy urged, curiosity getting the better of her. *Why is he doing whatever he's doing?*

Do I want to know? Adora asked, and found that she did.

364

"Kris, can you explain why? I mean, why it is that *you* have to do this—whatever it is you're doing?" He raised a brow. "Why you're giving me time to adjust when I know the others, and the Goddess, expect us to . . ." She stopped, embarrassed.

"I can explain, but understanding is up to you."

Adora sighed. "I know. And I'm dense. But try anyway."

"The children part is easy. You aren't ready, and given your childhood, I'd have to be a monster to ask you to have a baby when your heart isn't sure. The Goddess can just wait. As for the other . . . That's tougher. Goblins . . ." He sighed.

"I know I don't like what I've seen of them. They're violent and cruel."

"Some are," Kris agreed. "The leaders, often. You don't know much about the goblins because lutins have chosen to keep to their lives, unseen, much like the fey. We few have walked among humans for millennia, but cautiously, and with our identities unknown. I was an exception, and eventually even I was forced to present myself as human."

"Because you were in danger?"

"Yes—and still am. The species xenophobia isn't something of the long past, you know. Look at the hate-crime lists of Amnesty International. Many humans kill each other almost without hesitation. What might feys and goblins expect if they walked openly among them, proclaiming their differences and asking for a share of ever-diminishing resources?"

"But surely in this day and age—"

"No. Nothing's changed. There were always humans who welcomed us, and always those who hated and feared anyone different. And consider this: There is no law on the books anywhere in the

United States that says killing a fey or a goblin is illegal. Technically, it isn't even murder."

"But the Americans With Disabilities Act—"

"We aren't considered Americans. Even if we were, it only says that you can't discriminate against those of mixed-blood. It says nothing about killing them. And pureblood faeries, trolls, pixies or elves—dogs and cats have better protection under the law. In thirty-two states, it's illegal for a pureblood fey to have sex with a human. In two of them, it's a hanging offense—a terrible punishment, as hanging won't kill a pureblood sidhe."

" 'She?' "

"*Sidhe*—a fey."

"But Kris, lots of states have stupid old laws on the books. They just haven't changed them because they think the fey are dead."

"Is that why?" He shook his head. "I'll wager anything you like that, once they know I'm alive, they won't rush out to clean up their archaic laws. The only reason they haven't passed any recent repressive measures is that the mixed human-fey and the goblins have been at pains to present themselves to the public—on those occasions when they can't avoid interaction—as being essentially human. Humans don't know who we are, but since we look like them—walk like them, talk like them—the average man has offered us shelter under their umbrella of goodwill and given the politicians no reason to act against us. Supplied with an excuse, the politicians would be happy to play Us and Them."

Adora stared at Kris, stricken.

"What the hell are you doing, then—making yourself a target this way?" she asked. "You have goblins and humans after you, and you have me write this stupid book and expose you further?"

"I'm doing this because I—*we*—have no choice. We either succeed in ending this species hatred and uniting as one new nation or we all perish. Which means we have to stand up and admit what we are and talk about our differences until people stop being afraid of them. We have to all meet at the same table as equals."

"Kris . . ." Adora shook her head slowly.

"It can be done. An opportunity has presented itself. Remorse is not usually a human political failing, and it's all but unheard of in goblin hives. Molybdenum is a true rarity. It's why I worked with him, and why I must rescue him and his people now, in spite of the risk. He's media savvy, and one of the few leaders who aren't aggressive and blinded by race-hate—and I believe there is a chance he can regain control in L.A. Usually I wouldn't interfere in lutin internal power struggles, but this is too critical to pass up." He sighed. "I don't know if you can truly understand. So many goblin leaders are angry beyond any hope of reasoning with—beyond even bribery—and I fear they won't be content until they have ripped the belly out of human civilization. And this will happen before Nick and Zee's kid can resurrect the hobgoblins and turn them loose on the world."

"Hobgoblins?" Adora asked blankly. She didn't know what those were, but they sounded nasty.

"Yeah. Hobgoblins. They're the jokers in the deck who can skew the balance of power for good. The world was made by Gaia, but these days it's being run by some truly evil caretakers." Kris sighed. "But leave unto the day the troubles therein. We must do what we can when we can. We fey know that our war hasn't worked. The recent cross-breeding and cultural exchanges haven't helped either. We have to try something else. Something more direct and radical. Closer to my original plan."

"But what? What could possibly work?"

"A different kind of intervention. You know what the three species have in common?" Kris asked. "The children of humans and lutins and feys all have the capacity to love without judgment. We must teach them to embrace unconditional love while they are still young and uncorrupted by the hate and societal bigotry.

"Almost two hundred years ago, a goblin king decided to make himself master of the human world. He didn't hate me or my kind, but he feared what I was doing with the humans, that I would make a human-fey alliance—and steal his power over his people. Thus, he arranged for me to disappear. But that's okay, because I am fey and I have time. That king is dead and I'm still here. And I will remain until my work is done."

"So . . . all these terrible things happen to you, you're threatened on all sides—by unaccepting humans and goblin leaders who terrify the others into submission—and you want to fight back with love and understanding?" Adora was amazed.

"Yes. Trust me. It's the way of the Goddess. It couldn't be held off for long. You'll see. Even now, the world has begun to change for the better. I can sense it. Molybdenum will be set free and my other plans will be set in motion."

Adora shook her head. "So . . . Santa Claus rides again." She smiled a little to picture it, this time Santa's uniform being a designer suit.

"Yes. And we're going to get it right this time. I

can't belong to any one country or any religion—or even any species. There will be no race distinctions or preferences, no religious ties. The lutin leaders won't like it, but they'll adapt when they see it isn't harming the hives. It may take until this generation has died out, but we can win the fight for good."

And, gee, it sound like twice as much fun as a root canal, Joy said.

Adora digested his words as best she could. Partly they just sat there, a lump of dread in her stomach.

Kris went on: "As you yourself know all too well, children learn what they live. The next generation of lutins will know love as well as hate. Not all will allow themselves to choose love, but many—perhaps enough—will. And if not, we will persist with the next generation. If the sins of the fathers can be visited on the children, so can the blessings." His hand cupped her jaw, and his eyes probed at her.

"This is a little daunting," Adora said at last. "I don't have even one deadly enemy, you know, never mind a whole colony. And no god—however large or small—has ever asked me to do anything."

"I know. But look at it this way: It isn't every day that you have a chance to save the world. Isn't that kind of exciting?"

"Oh, yeah. It's exciting all right," she said.

Kris laughed. "You're gloomier than Abrial when I told him he was going to have to deliver toys to the goblin children on Christmas Eve."

"Abrial's going to be delivering toys?"

"Yeah, we all are."

"Will he wear your old Santa suit?" she asked.

Kris's eyes crinkled. "I'll have to offer it to him. I'm sure the thought never crossed his mind."

The fey Executioner in a Santa suit. The mind

369

boggled. Still, if she was with Kris . . . anything was possible. Adora might even consider raising that goblin child, doing a better job than her own parents had done with her, since she knew what she was. Maybe the world was changing. Everything was looking up.

"Let's do it," she said.

Miffith stared at the bloody knife in his lower left hand, unable to believe that he'd actually cut General Anaximander's throat.

Anaximander stared too, just as disbelieving. The goblin general gurgled out a question as blood poured through the fingers he had wrapped around his neck.

"Why?" Miffith repeated. "Because you're wrong. Niklas will win, and so will Molybdenum." He added: "And I did it for my father. You remember him? Mabbit? He worked for you until you strangled him. He always said our family owed its existence to Niklas. That Niklas saved my grandfather from being burned at the stake in France. Today, I'm paying off that debt. My daughter isn't going to grow up in a world full of mindless hate."

His half-breed daughter, the one he hadn't known about until yesterday, but whom Niklas and Adora had saved when her fruit-junkie mother died. The one who was in Cadalach with the feys whom Anaximander wanted to destroy. The one this goblin regime would exterminate for not being of pure lutin blood.

The dying Anaximander gurgled some more, but Miffith didn't bother to say anything else. He went to the sink and washed his hands.

Epilogue

Abrial looked quite dashing in Kris's old red suit, though Roman tended to snicker every time he looked at him.

It was Xmas Eve, and the fey had their teams positioned all over the United States, ready to deliver presents above- and belowground. Things would be tricky in the goblin lands, since the world had been put on notice that Santa Claus was back and ready to resume operations. The documentary that aired Thanksgiving weekend on PBS had attracted a lot of attention, as had the mass mailing of vials of water from the shian. Those had come with a tag—*Think you might be magical? Drink this, if you dare*. Government and the media had warned against anyone actually opening the vials from the anonymous sender, and were investigating how the water had ever gotten into the postal system—so far without any luck. But people being who and what they were, the feys were betting many had taken a swig. And many others would have tucked theirs away instead of turning them in as the government suggested.

Ben had guessed the truth and e-mailed Adora, asking her to pass on his congratulations to Bishop's publicist. Ben was now in AA, and doing a lot better. Not that it was as crucial to Adora—he was no longer tied to her understanding of her parents. No, she had found that here in Cadalach.

There hadn't been any overnight uprisings of magical beings across the country, but many Internet discussion sites had sprung up and the number of hits at the fey and goblins' corporate websites had gone way up. People of all species and races suddenly wanted to know who and what the lutins and feys really were.

Opinion on the messageboards seemed to be that whether this person claiming to be Santa Claus was real or not, America was headed for a global shipwreck if Greed was left as the pilot and Corporations as the captain, and it was high time that something changed. There was talk of finally forming a true third party. There was also talk of giving lutins and feys the right to vote. California, with their voter initiative process, was collecting signatures to get voting rights on the ballot for the next election, though many government workers were moaning about the cost of redistricting to include the lutin hives.

Adora stood beside Kris. Behind them were Mugshottz, Hansel and Gretel, who were dressed as elves in costumes Chloe had made—Kris had flinched when he saw the green coats and candy striped pants, but had hidden his dismay from Chloe—and the dragon, who was going to pull the sled for the A-Team. Adora still had some misgivings about using the dragon instead of reindeer, because they were bound to be caught on film when they landed in Reno, and that would create an uproar in the human world. But the dragon was very excited to have a chance to fly under Kris's power, and Adora had to admit that she was also thrilled at the chance to see this old magic at work. And, as Kris said, if they were going to come out of the closet, then they should come all the way out and show the world who they really were.

That said, the other teams were opting for discretion and stealth. They also had a lot more territory to cover, so they would be using faery roads and time manipulation to aid them. Cyra—who had just given birth the week before—Nyssa and Farrar were working together inside Cadalach to influence as many minds as they could, attempting to fill the world with a calm desire for peace—and to not shoot any odd-looking strangers bearing bags of gifts. Delivering presents to every home was impossible even with magical aid, so they had opted for leaving gifts in town squares, city halls, libraries and other public institutions. These were really symbolic presents. Most of the gifts were monetary and headed for charities. The logistics of the operation had been horrendous, and had made Pennywyse's hair go gray, but everyone agreed that they were ready.

Adora still had moments of fear when she thought about how easily Kris might be taken from her. Word was out that the goblin leaders had united and put a bounty on his head—ten million dollars, dead or alive—and there were weapons that could kill the fey for good, she'd learned.

But not in L.A.

No, not in L.A., where Molybdenum had been restored to power after one of General Anaximander's aides had slit the general's throat and said it was to thank Kris for some undisclosed good deed. In this goblin leader, Kris had a fast friend. Kris was happy and filled with certainty that they were going to turn the tide of race relations, so Adora did her best not to worry and be grateful that they had today and would have tomorrow. If Gaia smiled on them, they would have many more days as well. And that was all that anyone could ask.

"Ready?" Kris called.

"Yes!" shouted the children.

The dragon nodded. He looked odd in his harness, even though it was a tasteful brown and had no sleigh bells.

Kris looked deeply into Adora's eyes and smiled blindingly.

"Kiss me for luck?" he asked.

"And for any other reason," she answered, standing on tiptoe and putting her mouth against his. "Merry Xmas," she whispered a moment later.

"Merry Xmas, love." And then Kris launched them into the sky. Around them, the heavens answered with a blaze of silver stars.

AUTHOR'S NOTE

Yes, America, there is a Santa Claus. I know because he appeared to me one night in a dream and interviewed me for the position of his official biographer. Of course I protested—I'm a novelist, I don't write biography, and I was busy. I tried to evade him, this Kris Kringle with a K, but never could. He visited my dreams until I simply gave in.

While Kris was the driving force behind the story, I have to give thanks to a few human people, including Lydia in the public relations department at the Beverly Wilshire. She listened with a straight face when I explained that Santa—being a traditionalist—wanted to stay at that hotel while he was in L.A. (in my book, though he may stay there in fact as well). Likewise, the folks at The Museum of Automobiles were wonderful about giving me the history of Kris's 1937 Packard (see http://www.museumofautos.com/cars_on_exhibit.htm). My husband went right from listening to me babble about the amazing Lord Byron to hearing me talk about an even more amazing Santa Claus, and he never once suggested medication or a long stay in a quiet psychiatric facility. And finally my editor, who was enthusiastic from the get-go. I have long suspected Santa enlisted him. My editor denies it, as does Kris, but I am still suspicious.

On a separate note, many of the concepts Kris talks about—laws of eternity instead of laws of time, etc.—can be explained by quantum physics. However, his understanding of this science surpasses my own, so I had to rent *What The Bleep Do We Know?* to get a grasp of the discipline.

Sadly, this is the last of the planned goblin books. Of course, it's exciting to move on to new projects, but it's still hard to say good-bye to old friends. Thomas Marrowbone has arranged it so that if you get lonely, you can write to any of the fey at @lutinempire.com. For example, just type Kris@lutinempire.com and eventually your mail will get through the goblins' sneaky mail filters.

Merry we meet. Merry we part. Merry we meet again.

Melanie Jackson
P.O. Box 574, Sonora CA 95370-0574
www.melaniejackson.com

ATTENTION
BOOK LOVERS!

Can't get enough of your favorite **ROMANCE**?

Call **1-800-481-9191** to:

✳ order books,

✳ receive a **FREE** catalog,

✳ join our book clubs to **SAVE 30%!**

Open Mon.-Fri. 10 AM-9 PM EST

Visit **www.dorchesterpub.com**
for special offers and inside
information on the authors you love.

We accept Visa, MasterCard or Discover®.
LEISURE BOOKS ♥ LOVE SPELL